EDGE OF
HONOR

EDGE OF HONOR

A THRILLER

Brad Thor

EMILY BESTLER BOOKS

ATRIA

New York   Amsterdam/Antwerp   London
Toronto   Sydney/Melbourne   New Delhi

**EMILY
BESTLER
BOOKS**

ATRIA

An Imprint of Simon & Schuster, LLC
1230 Avenue of the Americas
New York, NY 10020

For more than 100 years, Simon & Schuster has championed authors and the stories they create. By respecting the copyright of an author's intellectual property, you enable Simon & Schuster and the author to continue publishing exceptional books for years to come. We thank you for supporting the author's copyright by purchasing an authorized edition of this book.

This book is a work of fiction. Any references to historical events, real people, or real places are used fictitiously. Other names, characters, places, and events are products of the author's imagination, and any resemblance to actual events or places or persons, living or dead, is entirely coincidental.

First Emily Bestler Books/Atria Books hardcover edition July 2025

EMILY BESTLER BOOKS/ATRIA BOOKS and colophon
are trademarks of Simon & Schuster, LLC

Simon & Schuster strongly believes in freedom of expression and stands against censorship in all its forms. For more information, visit BooksBelong.com.

For information about special discounts for bulk purchases, please contact Simon & Schuster Special Sales at 1-866-506-1949 or business@simonandschuster.com.

The Simon & Schuster Speakers Bureau can bring authors to your live event. For more information or to book an event, contact the Simon & Schuster Speakers Bureau at 1-866-248-3049 or visit our website at www.simonspeakers.com.

Manufactured in the United States of America

1   3   5   7   9   10   8   6   4   2

Library of Congress Cataloging-in-Publication Data has been applied for.

ISBN 978-1-9821-8227-4
ISBN 978-1-9821-8231-1 (ebook)

For Gary Urda
A truly remarkable man who helped shape my career.
I remain forever grateful for his wisdom and friendship.

The alternate domination of one faction over another, sharpened by the spirit of revenge . . . is itself a frightful despotism.

—GEORGE WASHINGTON, FAREWELL ADDRESS, SEPTEMBER 17, 1796

CHAPTER 1

S cot Harvath's six-month honeymoon had been fantastic. He and Sølvi had traveled the world and had spared no expense.

Upon landing back in the U.S., he'd introduced her to his favorite ritual. Once they had cleared passport control and Customs, he'd sought out the best cheeseburger and coldest beer he could find. *It was good to be home.*

Despite the length of their trip, it now all felt like a blur. After getting married in Oslo, they'd spent a week on the fjord; a "mini-moon" as Sølvi had called it, before buttoning up her apartment and requesting an open-ended leave of absence from the Norwegian Intelligence Service.

With those boxes ticked, they celebrated an early Christmas with her family and then hopped a flight back to the States. There they attended the christening of their goddaughter, celebrated Christmas with friends, and passed a few days as Scot tied up some of his own loose ends.

He had wanted to make a clean break with his past, which meant officially resigning from the Carlton Group—the private intelligence agency he had worked for. Once that was complete, they were free.

After visiting his aging mother on the west coast, they booked a flight to New Zealand and spent their new year chasing the sun and warm temperatures across the Southern Hemisphere.

In the spring, they headed north to Singapore, Malaysia, and Thailand before dropping in on Scot's friends in India.

From there they traveled to Greece, where they rented a beautiful villa with an uninterrupted view of the sea and swam in the clearest, bluest water either of them had ever seen. On many nights, after multiple glasses of wine, there was talk of never leaving; of making this their new permanent home.

But despite how much they enjoyed the island lifestyle, they eventually grew restless and wanted to get back on the road.

They sailed to Italy next and, after exploring it thoroughly, traveled through Austria, Switzerland, and France before surrendering Europe to the throngs of summer tourists and flying back to D.C.

The crowds notwithstanding, their goal had always been to return by the Fourth of July. Sølvi was married to an American now, and outside of attending a couple of celebrations at the U.S. Embassy in Oslo, she had never properly experienced the holiday. Harvath intended to change that and to give her an Independence Day she'd never forget.

Washington, D.C., was renowned for putting on the ultimate July Fourth fireworks show. Next to the Inaugural Ball and the White House Correspondents' Association Dinner, the only thing harder to score prime seats for was the annual fireworks display.

You could drag a blanket or a couple of folding chairs down to the National Mall but it would be beyond packed. And if the Park Police caught you with any alcohol whatsoever, you'd be in front of a firing squad by morning. Not exactly Harvath's idea of a good time.

Better would be to score one of the coveted VIP invitations to watch the display from the South Lawn of the White House or the Speaker's Balcony at the U.S. Capitol.

The Canadian Embassy was also known for throwing a nice, invitation-only event on their rooftop, but Harvath was hoping not to have to "leave" the United States in order to celebrate America's birthday.

He had put a few feelers out, but with a brand-new administration having just been sworn in, he didn't have the kind of White House connections he once had. He had even less pull in Congress and the new Speaker's office.

The Fourth of July was a week from Friday. All of the swanky hotel rooftops and bars had already been sold out. Anyone who owned a boat and planned to watch the show from the water was at capacity. Short of chartering a helicopter and hovering just outside the restricted airspace, he was running out of options.

Making matters worse, Sølvi had received a pair of invites to the Norwegian ambassador's Midsummer party within days of their D.C. arrival. Apparently, being a deputy director for the NIS, even one on an openended leave, had its perks.

The fact that she had scored such a coveted D.C. invitation only amplified his desire to create the perfect Fourth of July experience. He was nothing if not competitive. So, too, was Sølvi.

She also had a fantastic sense of humor. If she ended up delivering the better summer celebration, he'd have to hear about it for the rest of the year. That wasn't something he was going to let happen. It was red, white, and blue—or bust.

Getting ready for the embassy Midsummer party, Sølvi had been blasting ABBA. When Scot brought up the fact that the group was from the country next-door to hers and that she was appropriating Swedish culture, she smiled and gave him the finger. Closing the door to their bedroom, she turned it up even louder.

Twenty minutes later, the music stopped, and he heard her coming down the stairs. When she stepped into the kitchen, he was blown away.

She wasn't wearing the traditional Norwegian folk dress known as a *bunad*. Instead she wore a very sexy, white sheer dress that showed off her long legs and toned, tanned arms.

Her blond hair was pulled back and up in a high ponytail, just the way Scot liked it, allowing you to see a thin blue line of script that ran from the base of her neck to the midpoint of her spine. The words were from French philosopher Jean-Paul Sartre. *Il est impossible d'apprécier la lumière sans connaître les ténèbres.* It is impossible to appreciate the light without knowing the darkness.

The quote summed up Sølvi perfectly. She had known hardship and heartbreak—both in her professional and her personal lives. Instead of allowing those things to beat her down, she had used them to make herself stronger. It was one of the many things Scot loved about her. The fact that she was off-the-charts smart *and* drop-dead gorgeous didn't hurt either.

"Come here," he said, wrapping his arm around her waist and pulling her close so he could kiss her. "You look gorgeous."

"And you look very chic," she replied, kissing him back.

He pulled her in tighter. "We could just skip the party."

Sølvi laughed and gave him one last kiss before pushing him away. "Not a chance. I haven't seen you in a suit since the christening, much less a linen one. We're going to this party, and I'm going to show you off to everyone. Now grab your shoes so we can get going. I don't want us to be late."

"Vikings," he replied, rolling his eyes. "*So* strict."

"You have no idea what strict is." She smiled. "Believe me."

Surprising her with one last kiss, he went off in search of his shoes. Ten minutes later, they were on the George Washington Memorial Parkway, headed for D.C.

Because he was driving, he got to choose the music. His Norwegian playlist made her cringe, especially a song titled "Popular" by the Albino Superstars—a duo from a tiny village outside Oslo. The song, which was in English, had been extremely *popular* twenty years ago, back when she was in high school. She knew better than to complain, however, because whenever she did, he only turned it up louder and further exaggerated his lip-syncing. It was why, as a playful payback, she was threatening to have his windows tinted. They were both cut from the same cloth.

After torturing her for a little bit longer, he handed over his phone and told her she could play what she liked—as long as it wasn't more ABBA. Sølvi laughed, pulled up her favorite Dinah Washington album, and hit shuffle. The first song up, "My Man's an Undertaker," made them both chuckle. Gallows humor had been a psychological survival mechanism in both their respective military and espionage careers.

And while Scot didn't relish the taking of human life, he had never hesitated when it had been necessary. As his colleagues, who were also practitioners of gallows humor, were fond of saying, Scot Harvath had killed more people than cancer.

Though it was an obvious exaggeration, Sølvi knew enough about his past to know they weren't off by much. She had also seen him in action. When his friends asserted that guys like Scot didn't get PTSD—they gave it, she nodded knowingly because she understood completely what they meant.

He took few people into his confidence, and unless you knew him well, you'd have no clue as to his background, nor his fluency in violence. For all intents and purposes, he was an extremely charming and handsome man, who made more than his share of jokes and didn't seem to take anything too seriously.

A bit of that nonchalance was on display as they approached what Harvath liked to refer to as one of the most politically interesting intersections in the nation's capital—the point at which Thirty-Fourth Street T-bones Massachusetts Avenue.

The residence of the Norwegian ambassador sat on one corner, the Apostolic Nunciature of the Holy See—also known as the Vatican Embassy—sat on the other, and directly across from them both, on an almost perfectly round, heavily fortified, seventy-two-acre wooded parcel, was the United States Naval Observatory.

In addition to its many horological and astronomical functions, the observatory campus was best known for housing the official residence of the Vice President of the United States.

As Scot and Sølvi Harvath sat idling in traffic, waiting for the light to change, they observed a large protest taking place outside the gates.

"What's going on over there?" Sølvi asked, reading some of the placards and banners aloud. "*Stick to the plan! The voters have spoken! Keep your promises!*"

Glancing across the street, Scot replied, "Democracy in action."

"Obviously. But what are they actually protesting?"

"No clue."

She looked at him. "You sound like you don't care."

He didn't. Their honeymoon had been a wonderful break from politics. He hadn't picked up a paper, turned on a TV, or logged onto a website the entire time. He couldn't remember the last time that he'd been that relaxed.

"Welcome to D.C.," he replied. "We get protests here every day."

"Sure, but this is a relatively big one. Why aren't there more police?"

It was a fair question.

After scanning the immediate area, he pointed to an unmarked white van with smoked windows and government plates. "The cops have backup. They're just keeping it quiet. Believe me, they're not going to let things get out of hand, especially not this close to the Vice President's Residence."

"In Norway," Sølvi chided him, "we wouldn't *let* them get this close to the Vice President's Residence."

She loved to play this game. Everything—it didn't matter what— was always better back in Scandinavia.

Scot laughed. "A," he stated: "Norway doesn't have a vice president. And B, even if it did, why would anyone in the world's most perfect country ever protest anything?"

It was an excellent response. "See?" she replied with a smile. "My friends didn't believe me, but I told them, *he's teachable.*"

He was about to add "And great in bed" when he noticed two men in hooded sweatshirts, carrying black backpacks and wearing face masks and sunglasses, step away from the crowd.

Even before they had tossed their backpacks under the van, his instincts had kicked in and he knew what was about to happen. There was no way that he'd be able to punch through the traffic in time.

Instead, he yelled at Sølvi to "Get down!" and, unbuckling his seat belt, threw himself on top of her, covering her body with his.

Less than a second later, the bombs exploded, lifting his nearly six-thousand-pound Tahoe clean off the ground.

CHAPTER 2

The synchronized blasts shattered the vehicle's windows, showering the interior with broken glass. Scot prayed to God that Sølvi hadn't been injured.

"Are you okay?" he yelled over the ringing in his ears, fumbling with her seat belt.

She was dazed and it took a moment for her to respond. "I'm all right," she finally answered, flashing him the thumbs-up.

The unmistakable odor of lit gasoline and burning rubber filled the air. They needed to move. There could be another explosion coming.

"We're going to exit out your door," he instructed, as he unbuckled her and reached for the handle. "In three, two—"

He stopped just as he got to the number one and was about to open the door. The sharp cracks of gunfire, even with the ringing in his ears, were unmistakable.

"Stay down!" he shouted.

With bullets flying, they were sitting ducks inside a thin-skinned vehicle. Movement was life. They needed to get off the X.

Rolling off his armrest, he popped the center console lid, handed the SIG Sauer pistol and two extra mags beneath it to Sølvi, and then opened the console vault underneath that and pulled out his most readily accessible "truck gun."

It was a compact, highly maneuverable personal defense weapon, or PDW for short, known as a Raider 365.

"When I say *go*, I want you to get out and position yourself behind the engine block," he said, springing the stock and making sure a round was chambered. "Understand?"

Sølvi nodded.

As she prepared to open her door and bail out, Harvath popped up in the driver's seat and identified three more men in hooded sweatshirts, wearing face masks and sunglasses. They were armed with short-barreled, automatic weapons. But it wasn't their rifles that sent a chill down his spine. It was their tactics.

While one of them fired into the crowd, the other two covered his flanks, engaging the surviving police officers. They fired in tight, controlled pairs—two shots in rapid succession—delivering their hits quickly and precisely. Whoever these men were, they were professionals.

Harvath seated the Raider's stock against his shoulder and shouted "Go!" as he brought the weapon up and began firing.

With bodies dropping left and right, there was no time to develop a formal plan. As soon as he had a sight picture, he engaged the first target, pumping two rounds into his back, before moving quickly to the next shooter and repeating the process.

There was just one problem. Neither man went down.

Body armor, Harvath thought to himself. As soon as the thought entered his mind, he began adjusting his aim.

Center mass was the biggest and easiest part of the body to hit. The moment you panned down for shots in the leg or panned up for head-shots, the degree of difficulty skyrocketed.

Not only were the shots he needed to make much harder, but he had also blown his element of surprise.

As the two men he had shot spun and began putting rounds on his Tahoe, he knew he was in big trouble.

"They're wearing body armor!" he yelled to Sølvi. "I'm coming to you. Give me some cover fire."

As she peeked above the hood of the SUV and began shooting at the attackers, Harvath scrambled out of the vehicle and joined her.

While their situation had improved by putting the heavy Chevy engine between them and their opponents, it hadn't improved by much.

"Reloading!" Sølvi shouted as she crouched back down and inserted a fresh magazine into her pistol.

The Tahoe rocked back and forth as it was riddled with a withering barrage of bullets. From the sound of the gunfire, Harvath could tell the shooters were getting closer. They were crossing the street, walking their rounds in, determined to eliminate the threat. He signaled to Sølvi what he wanted her to do.

The two flankers may have been bold enough to traverse the street, but that didn't cancel out any of the other facts on the ground. They still needed to keep their heads on swivels and deal with anyone else who popped up and began shooting at them.

That was why Harvath had decided not to pop up—at least not immediately. Removing his left hand from his weapon, he squeezed Sølvi's shoulder.

As he did, she dropped to her left side, pointed her pistol beneath the SUV, and began shooting at the boots of the approaching attackers. That was when Harvath leapt up and, leaning across the hood, began putting his own rounds on the men.

He was aiming for anything he could get—from the upper torso, above where the body armor stopped, all the way up the throat, into the facial area, including the forehead.

He nailed the first shooter with a shot to the suprasternal notch right between his clavicles and a second round through his lower jaw.

The second man had already been dropped to his knees by Sølvi. While she continued to pump rounds into his lower extremities, Harvath double-tapped him in the back of the head.

With the third shooter still firing at the protesters, there was no time to waste.

Coming out from behind the SUV, Harvath moved past the two shooters, giving them each a final headshot, just to be sure.

As he did, the third shooter spun, catching Harvath out in the open. But before he could fire, Sølvi, having once again swapped in a fresh mag, began painting a racing stripe of 9mm rounds right up his torso from her new position at the back of the Tahoe.

With the bullets bouncing off his body armor, the man jerked his rifle to the right and was just about to fire when Harvath let loose with his own volley of controlled pairs.

The first two rounds ripped open the side of the shooter's neck, while the next bullet tore through the base of his skull, followed by a final shot through his left ear. He was dead before his body even hit the ground.

Nevertheless, Harvath gave him an additional shot to the head and kicked his weapon away. Changing his own magazine, he was about to yell for Sølvi to grab the medical bag out of the back of his SUV so they could render aid to the injured protesters when he heard her begin to fire her pistol again. Spinning to his right, he saw two more shooters. They were the same men he had seen place the bomb-laden backpacks under the van.

Sølvi drilled one man in the lower abdomen beneath his body armor and then put a round through the other man's hip, shattering his pelvis. As they staggered forward, Harvath shot each of them in the head.

Quickly, he scanned for more threats. Then he saw it.

A sixth, hooded man had his head down and was walking, not running like the rest of the civilians, away from the chaos. He wasn't carrying a weapon that Harvath could see, but both of his hands were hidden in the pouch of his sweatshirt.

In the distance, police sirens could be heard approaching from all directions. He had no intention of letting this guy get away.

"You!" he shouted, raising his PDW. "Black sweatshirt. Stop where you are. Let me see your hands."

The man ignored him and kept walking.

"Black sweatshirt!" Harvath repeated, picking up his pace. "Show me your hands! Do it now!"

The man began to move faster as well.

"Black sweatshirt! Last chance! Freeze!"

For a moment it looked like the man was about to break into a sprint, but instead he pulled a Glock from his sweatshirt pouch, turned, and fired three rounds in rapid succession.

Harvath dove for the pavement.

As he did, the man took off.

Getting up on one knee, Harvath reshouldered his weapon and took aim. Pressing his trigger, he let loose with two rounds low and two rounds high.

One caught the man in the back of his left leg. Another hit him in the back of his left shoulder. The moment the bullets found their targets, everything changed.

Harvath leapt to his feet as the man stumbled and almost went down. But instead of continuing along the street, the man cut across the pavement and jumped the waist-high, wrought-iron fence of the Norwegian ambassador's residence. Landing in the grass on the other side, he quickly disappeared from view.

Seconds later, there was the sound of more gunfire, as well as glass being shattered. It only took Harvath a moment to figure out what was going on.

Unable to escape on foot, this guy was either looking for a vehicle he could steal, or he had breached the residence and was looking to take hostages.

Arriving at the fence, Harvath could see across the empty driveway and right up to the shattered glass and iron front door.

Inside the residence, two of the Ambassador's security detail were down. There was only one thing Harvath could do.

CHAPTER 3

L eaping the fence, Harvath ran across the driveway and, gun at the ready, stepped over the bodies and into the residence.

He didn't need anyone to tell him which way to go. The man he was after had left a bright red trail of blood for him to follow.

It stretched across the polished marble floor of the entry foyer and up a sweeping staircase.

The security agents wore earpieces, which would have connected to radios beneath their suitcoats. Had they had enough time to radio colleagues for help? The embassy was only just behind the residence. Or had it gone into a full lockdown?

There was no way of knowing. And waiting wasn't an option. The shooter couldn't be allowed to get away. He also couldn't be allowed to hurt anyone else.

It was at that moment that Harvath heard another gunshot, followed by a scream from somewhere on the floor above.

Mounting the stairs, he took them two at a time as he kept his back to the curved wall and his gun pointed up.

When he hit the second-floor landing, he followed the blood spatter straight ahead into a large, empty reception space. It wasn't a surprise to find it empty. According to Sølvi, the Midsummer party, which would already have been in full swing, was taking place outside, in the embassy's grass courtyard.

His own head on a swivel, he quickly passed through the reception space into an elegantly appointed, formal dining room.

The blood trailed off to the far corner and what appeared to be a service door of some sort, likely leading to a kitchen.

Harvath quickly crossed the room and paused at the door, listening. A woman's voice could be heard from the other side. She spoke with the same accented English as Sølvi and, for a moment, his heart stopped cold in his chest. But there was no way she could have beaten him here and gotten all the way upstairs. It was either a member of the staff or . . .

Harvath didn't want to go where his mind was leading, and he pushed the thought from his head.

Admittedly, however, there was one big thing in the plus column right now. Whoever the woman was, she was alive. It was his job to make sure that she stayed that way.

Taking a step back, he rapidly scanned the door. It had double-action hinges, allowing it to swing open and closed in both directions. Gently, he leaned against it with his shoulder, opening it just enough to peer into the next room.

It was a commercial-grade kitchen, lined with stainless-steel appliances. On the floor, just past the center island, a man in a white chef's coat was bleeding out. Crouched next to him was the one person, after Sølvi, he had hoped not to see—the Norwegian ambassador.

As she applied pressure to the chef's wound and tried to stop the bleeding, she was attempting to negotiate with the shooter to let them go.

Why she and the chef were in the residence while the Midsummer party was happening next door was beyond him. An event of this size would have been catered and staged out of the embassy. None of that, however, mattered now. What mattered was eliminating the threat just inside the kitchen—a threat Harvath couldn't yet see.

The crack in the door offered a limited field of view. If he was going to get a bead on the shooter, he was going to have to open it farther. But as soon as he did that, he would be running an even greater risk of exposure. He didn't need to dwell on it. There was no other option.

Using the Ambassador as his guide, he tracked where she looked when she spoke to the shooter and edged the door, millimeter by millimeter until he could see the edge of the killer's sweatshirt. The man was partially obscured by a set of metal shelving.

Blessed with the element of surprise, Harvath would easily be able to get a shot off, but it would have to avoid both the shelving and the man's body armor, and even then, might not do any good.

Without a flash-bang or some other means to create a distraction, surprise was all he had going for him.

That said, the shooter knew Harvath had been on his tail. He had to be expecting someone to burst through the kitchen door at any moment. By bleeding all over the place, he had drawn Harvath right to him. Hopefully, the man had lost enough blood to slow down his reaction time. Any advantage would help. And as Harvath knew, action beat reaction every time. Taking a deep breath, he prayed that would be true right now.

Adjusting his weapon, he applied pressure to his trigger and exhaled as he pushed open the door the rest of the way and rushed into the kitchen.

He got off four shots, unsure of where they'd struck, before the man raised his own weapon and returned fire. Harvath dove for the floor and used the island for concealment.

As soon as he hit the tiles, he began moving. Crawling forward, he made his way toward the Ambassador and the chef. He could see the latter's leather clogs only a couple of feet ahead. That was when he heard the Ambassador scream again.

"I'm going to shoot her!" the killer bellowed. By the sound of his voice, he was in a lot of pain and was having trouble breathing. "Toss your gun where I can see it. Then stand up. Slowly. If you don't, I swear I'll kill her."

He had no doubt the man was telling him the truth.

With no time to come up with a better plan, he transitioned his weapon to his left hand and snatched a Norwegian cooking device he had seen Sølvi's family use, called a *krumkake* iron, from the bottom shelf of the island. Cocking his right arm back, he threw the cast-iron device as far as he could toward the other side of the kitchen.

The moment he let go of it, he shoved himself forward on the floor and, with his weapon gripped in both hands, snapped around the corner of the island.

Though it seemed like everything was happening in slow motion, it all took place in a matter of seconds.

The killer had grabbed the Ambassador by her hair, yanked her to her feet, and had his gun to her temple, using her as a human shield.

When the *krumkake* iron hit a shelf loaded with pots and pans, the man took his pistol off the Ambassador and fired multiple rounds toward the back of the kitchen. It wasn't a flash-bang, but it had done a good enough job.

There was only one shot available to Harvath, and as dangerous as it was, he took it.

Pressing his trigger, there was a *crack* when the round sizzling out of his weapon broke the sound barrier and caught the killer right between the eyes as he began to turn back around.

His head snapped backward as blood, bone, and pieces of brain matter covered the kitchen wall behind him.

Getting to his feet, Harvath peeled off his jacket, folded it into a makeshift pressure bandage, and, kneeling, applied it to the chef's chest.

The Ambassador joined him and was about to say something when two new Norwegian security agents burst into the kitchen and, with their weapons pointed at him, yelled for Harvath to put his hands in the air.

CHAPTER 4

Brendan Rogers knew he was being followed. He had clocked the two men behind him earlier in the day while out running errands.

They both appeared to be in their late thirties to early forties, fit, and around six feet tall. Each had short, dark hair, and was clean-shaven. They could have been ex–service members who, just like him, were also training for D.C.'s popular Marine Corps Marathon, but that wasn't the vibe Rogers was getting. There was a menacing intensity to these two men— like a pair of wolves, stalking him.

Though he had long held to the maxim that *when in doubt, there is no doubt*, he needed to be sure. Up ahead, the paved trail he was on intersected with a dirt bridle path, which pushed deeper into the woods. That's where he would get his confirmation. Picking up the pace, Rogers headed for it.

When he reached the bridle path, he hooked a left and then broke into a sprint. If these guys really were after him, they were going to have to catch him.

The trail led uphill, cutting into his speed and causing his legs to burn. His only consolation was that if he was being chased, his pursuers were being slowed as well.

In fifty yards he came to a switchback and reduced his pace, but only enough to not lose control and wipe out. Racing forward, he shot a quick glance downhill to his right. Both of the men were sprinting after him and closing the distance. The situation was now confirmed.

Rogers didn't need to ask why they were after him. He already knew. He also knew what would happen if he stopped running. Those two men were going to kill him.

With his heart pounding so hard that it set off a warning on his smart watch, he heaved for breath and kept moving as fast as he could. He needed to figure out how to shake these two.

Racking his brain, he tried to recall the limited training he had been given. *Change your appearance. Lose yourself in a crowd. Enter a building through one door and quickly exit via another.*

That was all well and good in the middle of a large city or some crowded Middle Eastern souk, but this was a remote trail on a Monday evening in Rock Creek Park. The bottom line was that Rogers hadn't been trained for this kind of thing.

He was a hard-charging former officer in the Navy JAG (Judge Advocate General) Corps who had wound up as the Special Presidential Envoy for Hostage Affairs, or SPEHA for short—a position the press often referred to as the "Hostage Czar."

During his tenure, he had secured the release of a number of Americans who had been kidnapped or otherwise unjustly detained abroad. He was a highly intelligent, highly skilled negotiator who was as comfortable flattering his counterparts as he was threatening them—and had done whatever it took to win.

And when he had won, those wins had made big, international headlines. But Rogers had never felt comfortable in the media spotlight. He had preferred to remain in the background, allowing the President to receive all the credit. His satisfaction came from getting American hostages home and seeing them reunited with their families.

It was that humility and sense of duty that had caught the attention of the White House. With his knowledge of geopolitics and extensive experience dealing with some of the planet's nastiest actors, he became the President's choice to replace the outgoing National Security Advisor.

Rogers accepted and remained in the position just over a year, until the President's term came to a close.

On Inauguration Day, as was the custom, he was the last to leave the White House, handing over the keys to the new, incoming administration and its own National Security Advisor.

That was six months ago.

Since then, two of his colleagues—the former secretary of state and chairman of the Joint Chiefs—had turned up dead.

One had been ruled an accident. The other's death had been attributed to "natural" causes.

There was nothing natural or accidental about either. Both men had been murdered. Rogers was certain of it. Unfortunately, no one else had believed him.

Right now, it made no difference. The only thing that mattered was that he had no intention of becoming victim number three.

Bolting off the trail, he began to scramble up the hillside in a zigzag pattern, using as many of the thicker trees as he could for cover.

There was no way of knowing if the men behind him were armed and, if they were, if they planned to open fire. The more difficult he could make things for them, the better.

But by not scrambling in a straight line, he was lengthening the distance he needed to escape and was exhausting himself. His lungs were burning and he could feel his legs turning into lead. He wasn't going to make it. Meanwhile, his pursuers were getting ever closer.

Rogers didn't dare look back. He knew that any moment a bullet could be fired, severing his spine, or ripping right through the back of his head. Had he been a religious man, he might have used these final moments to beg for God's mercy; to ask for deliverance from his attackers. Perhaps he might have prayed for forgiveness and atoned for the moments in his life where he had fallen short.

The lizard part of his brain, however, that place that controlled his very instinct to survive, wouldn't allow it. He needed to push harder and his body responded to the call by pumping even more adrenaline into his system.

Ignoring the deadening of his legs, Rogers struggled up the hillside, putting every ounce of energy he could muster into each lunge forward.

He had spun up into such a frenzied pistoning that when he arrived at the top, his legs kept pumping and he was unable to stop.

Losing his balance, he launched face-first down an embankment and rolled into the paved two-way road at the bottom.

Car horns blared. Drivers shortcutting through the park to avoid D.C. traffic swerved to get out of the way. Others slammed on their brakes. One of those vehicles belonged to a National Park Service ranger.

Fighting his fatigue, Rogers forced himself to his feet and, waving his arms overhead, made his way as quickly as he could to her.

"Sir, what's happening?" the ranger asked, getting out of her truck. "Are you okay?"

The first thing Rogers checked was to see if she was an armed officer. She wasn't. "We need to get out of here."

"Sir, I need you to calm down and tell me what's going on."

"My name is Brendan Rogers. I'm the former U.S. National Security Advisor. I'm being pursued by two men. Possibly armed. We need to move. *Now.*"

"I know who you are, sir. I've seen you on TV," she replied, reaching into her pocket for her cell phone. "Let me call Park Police."

Rogers glanced over his shoulder, back toward the hill he had just tumbled down. And though his pursuers weren't immediately visible, he could feel them—the two wolves, somewhere in the trees, staring at him.

"Unless you have a weapon in your vehicle, you and I are both in harm's way," he stressed. "As is every single motorist out here. Please, I'm begging you."

The ranger's eyes followed the same path that Rogers's had just taken. She didn't see anything either, but the man was emphatic. He was also the former National Security Advisor.

"Get in the truck," she said, sliding her phone back into her pocket.

Once he had closed the passenger door, she walked backward to her vehicle, her eyes never coming off the hillside.

Instead of driving forward, the savvy ranger reversed her truck until she felt she was a safe enough distance away, and then pulled a U-turn.

Removing her phone and putting it on speaker, she called Park Police, had Rogers relay his story, and informed them that she was inbound.

Despite the fact that Rogers's description of the two men could apply to lots of park visitors, a BOLO went out via radio and text message to all employees. Neither of the men was located.

Two hours after entering the Park Police station, Rogers was driven back to where he had parked his car and wished well. Out of courtesy, the Park Police arranged for a marked D.C. Metro police officer to, within reason, accompany him wherever he wanted to go.

The one place he knew he couldn't go was home. He needed to drop off the grid, if only for a night, as he figured out his next move. So he quickly assembled the best plan he could think of. He asked the cops to escort him to Reagan National Airport.

At the long-term parking lot, he pulled into a spot, thanked them for their help, and sent them on their way. After looking up a couple of things on his cell phone, he grabbed his wallet from the glove compartment and walked around to the rear of his car. Popping the trunk, he opened his go-bag—a small carry-on with toiletries, a couple changes of clothes, and, most important, an envelope of cash in various currencies, tucked behind the lining.

It was an old habit from his past life when his phone could ring in the middle of the night and he would be expected to hop on a plane at a moment's notice. When those calls came, it was always easier to already be packed.

After cleaning himself with some disposable wipes, he changed into a new set of clothes, grabbed his go-bag, and locked his Audi. Placing his key fob behind the cover for the gas cap, he then walked to the nearest shuttle-bus stop.

Two other travelers were already there waiting. One was an older woman with a large, soft-sided suitcase on wheels. When the bus came, Rogers asked if he could help her. She gratefully accepted.

They made small talk on the way to the terminal. She was headed to see grandchildren in Colorado. Rogers lied and told her he was headed to Texas.

When the bus arrived at her stop, he helped remove her bag and placed it on the sidewalk for her. She thanked him and he watched her walk inside. The woman had no idea that he had slipped his cell phone into the outer pocket of her bag.

Entering through a different set of doors, Rogers headed down to the arrivals level, passed several baggage claim carousels, and made his way outside to where the complimentary hotel shuttles picked up guests. It only took about ten minutes for the one he wanted to arrive.

At the hotel, he thanked the driver, gave him a small tip, and de-bussed with the other passengers. He then walked two and a half blocks to a much cheaper, considerably run-down motel where he paid for two nights in advance, in cash. The idea was to leave no electronic trail— nothing that the people who were hunting him could follow.

After checking into his room, he grabbed a quick shower, changed, and then took the metro to Pentagon City, where he bought a prepaid cell phone at Target, along with a baseball cap and a handful of other items. Once he had everything he needed, he picked up some take-out food and returned to the motel.

Sitting at the desk, with its cracked Formica top, he tucked in to his beef and broccoli as he made a list of names. Whoever he decided to con-tact would not only have to be one hundred percent trustworthy, but they would also have to be someone who knew what they were doing.

Ranking the names based on their skill sets, experience, and network of contacts, one name kept rising to the top. Rogers circled it with his pen. This was who he needed to get in touch with.

His only question was *how*.

CHAPTER 5

FBI Headquarters
Tuesday morning

F BI special agent Jennifer Fields set a cardboard coffee carrier atop a stack of file boxes and, looking around the suite of
dingy basement offices, asked, "What's this? Are we the fucking
X Files now?"

As a rule, her boss, supervisory special agent Joe Carolan, didn't care
for profanity. But when it came to his number two, he had learned to let
it slide.

They were from different generations. He had been at the Bureau
longer than anyone could remember and was nearing the end of his
career. Fields, on the other hand, was less than eight years in and had
nothing but wide-open space in front of her.

"Welcome to anonymity," he replied, waving her over and clearing
some room for her to sit.

Pulling one of the large black coffees from the carrier, she handed it to
him saying, "Your Mocha Cookie Crumble Frappuccino."

Carolan stood six feet four, weighed two-fifty, and could swing from
a calm, highly skilled investigator to a bite-your-head-off-and-breathe-
fire-down-your-neck monster if you wasted his time. Colleagues had
long ago taken to calling him "Bear." Somedays that meant Gentle Ben.
Others it meant full-on, bloodthirsty grizzly.

From day one, however, Fields had made it clear that she wasn't going
to let his size or his demeanor intimidate her. Embarrassing Carolan, who
only took his coffee black, with ridiculous-sounding coffee orders, had

been one of her ways of keeping him in check. It had become their running joke and she did it whether they were alone, like now, or in a room full of people. That was the kind of relationship they had built.

Shaking his head, Carolan thanked her, peeled back the lid, and blew some of the steam off the surface. "When did you ever watch a single episode of *The X Files*?"

She shot him a surprised look. "Black people can't watch *X Files*?"

"Jesus, not again."

"Or," she continued, "are you saying that people from Harlem are just too poor to have TVs?"

"Yes, that's exactly what I'm saying," Carolan replied, rolling his eyes. "Give me a break. Your dad was a cop. Your mom was a nurse. You weren't that poor. You went to Penn, for crying out loud. And this isn't a Black-White thing. It's an age thing. *X Files* was before your time."

Fields smiled. She loved needling him. "My grandma, actually, was a fan. A pretty big one. She had all the episodes on VHS. Whenever she took care of me, we'd watch together."

"That's great. Now I feel old. Thank you for that. I'm sorry I asked."

"Technically," Fields said, correcting him, "I asked. What is all this? What are we doing down here?"

"Hiding."

"No shit. From who?"

"The new administration," Carolan replied.

"Does the director know?"

"Nope."

Fields smiled again, even broader this time. "Look at you. Big, bad Joe Carolan breaking the rules."

"A, this wasn't my idea. And B, don't think for a second that I like it. In fact, it turns my stomach."

"Then whose idea was it?"

"Gallo's."

Alan Gallo was head of the FBI's Counterintelligence Division, under which the Russia Operations Section, known in Bureau shorthand as CROS, was housed.

The mandate of CROS was to hunt down and disrupt all Russian cyber and intelligence activities that threatened the United States. It was the department that Carolan and Fields called home.

Back in November, the pair had torpedoed a sophisticated Russian influence operation and in the process had rolled up a valuable, deep-cover Russian intelligence officer. The man had wisely been willing to negotiate a new, free life in the West rather than go to prison. He turned out to be a treasure trove of information, and both Carolan and Fields had received commendations for their work. Then came the inauguration.

At forty-four years old, James Alexander Mitchell was the youngest U.S. president since John F. Kennedy. The youthful, charismatic candidate had won the popular vote as well as the Electoral College and his margin of victory had been unassailable. The campaign, however, had been brutal, especially near the end.

As a Russian studies major, Mitchell had spent his junior year of college abroad, living and studying in Moscow, St. Petersburg, and Novosibirsk. Though his political opponents had tried to use it against him, his fearless embrace of his time overseas had only endeared him further to voters. But one particular smear had come close to toppling his campaign and had angered him beyond measure.

While studying in Russia, he had fallen in love with a beautiful young Russian woman. He wasn't the first American to fall in love while living abroad and he certainly wouldn't be the last. This woman, however, was noteworthy.

She was from a prominent Russian military family. Her father had close ties to the Kremlin and Russian military intelligence. She herself would go on to work for Russia's Foreign Intelligence Service, also known as the SVR.

It didn't matter that the affair had happened over two decades ago, nor that Mitchell had ended up marrying his high school sweetheart and that they had two wonderful young children. His opponents had tried to paint him as a ticking Russian time bomb; a deep-cover "Manchurian candidate" who couldn't be trusted to place America's interests above Russia's.

President Mitchell had never told anyone about Anna. Social media hadn't even become a thing yet back when they were together. The only pictures of them were those they, themselves, had taken. Or so they had believed.

Right before the election, photos of the pair, in various romantic scenarios, had broken around the world. It was the kind of "October surprise" every political candidate feared.

Mitchell's campaign had been blindsided. His top people thought for sure it would sink them, but the public had responded with a different reaction. They loved the photos and couldn't get enough.

The college version of Jim Mitchell showed him to be every bit the heartthrob he was now—tall and devilishly handsome, as well as something the public hadn't seen before, surprisingly bohemian.

No matter what you thought of him as a political candidate, there was no denying that his younger self could rock jeans, T-shirts, and a pair of work boots better than any sports or Hollywood superstar.

Nevertheless, hostile members of the opposing press tried to denigrate him and use the "Affaire Russe," as it became known, against him.

They had a field day with all sorts of tabloid-style headlines like "Sleepless in St. Petersburg," "The Bridges of Moscow County," and the lamest and most obvious of all, "From Russia with Love."

When interest in the love story only grew, they switched to attacking the lovers personally. They called him "Comrade Crush" and Anna the "Kremlin Cutie."

Eventually, as the attempts to tar him with scandal failed and Mitchell kept surging in the polls, bitter partisan journalists resorted to calling him the "Populist Pinup." It was all they had. He was running away with the election and everyone knew he was going to win.

The revelation of his relationship with Anna, however, had struck a nerve with him. Mitchell was an unknown in his college days. There was only one explanation for him and Anna to have been followed by someone with a long lens camera back then. It had to have been an intelligence organization. But whose?

It seemed pretty obvious to Mitchell and his team. The Russians had nothing to gain by embarrassing him. He was a post–Cold War candidate who hadn't grown up with duck-and-cover drills and the specter of Soviet communism. By his own admission, he was the forward-looking candidate, eager to turn the page and move on from the "outdated" and "unnecessary" antagonisms of the previous century.

That left only one intelligence organization that would have wanted to use his time in Russia and his relationship with Anna and her family to hurt his candidacy—the CIA. And where the Central Intelligence Agency was involved, the FBI was always close at hand.

As a candidate who had stirred up so much popular passion and support by promising to reform government and make it answerable to the people, Mitchell was well aware of the threat he posed to the entrenched bureaucracies of Washington, D.C. And while he couldn't do away with America's preeminent intelligence agencies, he could place people in charge who would be answerable and completely loyal to him, which was what he had done. He wanted the CIA and the FBI on a short leash, especially when it came to anything having to do with Russia. He didn't trust either organization further than he could throw them.

That was why Agents Carolan and Fields had been given a new assignment and were now setting up shop in the basement of the FBI.

"Okay," said Fields, taking the lid off her own coffee and leaning back in her chair. "So this was Gallo's idea. My next two questions should be pretty obvious. What's our assignment and why are we hiding it from the White House?"

"Remember when you called me last night and we were wondering who might be behind the attack on the protest outside the Vice President's Residence?"

The younger agent nodded and took a sip of her coffee.

Picking up the topmost folder on his desk, he slid it over to her. "We may have an answer."

Fields opened it and began reading the contents. When her eyes widened, Carolan knew she had gotten to the bombshell.

"This came from *our* Russian intelligence officer?" she asked. "The motherfucker who shot me when we tried to take him in? Josef Vissarionvich. Aka Joe Nistal?"

"The one and only."

"The FBI has had him for seven months. How did this not surface until now?"

"Because that's what the Russians do. They give you some decent stuff up front to establish their bona fides. You get some so-so stuff in the middle. And then the really good intel comes at the end. That's what they use to hammer out the best possible deal."

"Has any of it been verified?"

Carolan shook his head. "Not yet. That's what you and I have been assigned to do."

"I understand why you're sick to your stomach. This is going to be radioactive."

"Now you know why we're hiding it from the White House."

"Is that even legal?"

"For the moment," Carolan replied. "But we're in a pretty gray area."

"I didn't join the FBI for the gray areas," said Fields.

"Me neither, but here we are."

"Why us?"

Carolan took a sip of his coffee before responding. "Gallo says that we hit such a home run collaring Nistal, he couldn't think of anybody better to give it to."

"Bullshit. I can think of lots of people."

Carolan shrugged. "And yet, like I said, here we are."

They sat in silence for several moments until, finally, Fields asked, "So where do you want to start?"

"Seeing as how it's day one of a new assignment, let's keep it easy," he said. "We're going to get our hazmat suits on and jump right into the blast zone."

CHAPTER 6

FAIRFAX COUNTY, VIRGINIA

Just as the Norwegian security agents rushed into the kitchen, the Ambassador had ordered them to stand down. Harvath wasn't the threat. Harvath had taken out the threat.

Hot on the security team's heels was Sølvi, who made sure to loudly announce herself so as not to be accidentally fired upon. It took her a fraction of a second to assess the situation and she fell right in with Harvath administering lifesaving aid to the chef.

They were able to keep him alive until an ambulance arrived, stabilized him, and transported him to the Center for Trauma and Critical Care at George Washington University Hospital.

As the EMTs carried off the chef, Scot quickly brought Sølvi up to speed on what he needed her to do. "Don't speak with D.C. police, the FBI, the U.S. Diplomatic Security Service, none of them," he had said. "Speak only with the Ambassador. This is for your protection. Do you understand?"

Sølvi had nodded.

"Do you still have my pistol?"

"Of course I do," she had replied, handing it over to him.

Scot had checked to make sure a round was chambered and then began opening refrigerator doors until he found what he was looking for.

Pulling out a gallon jug of milk, Scot had asked her to bring one of the security agents back into the kitchen.

As soon as she was gone, he had unscrewed the cap, picked the safest direction to aim, and had fired one round through it.

The bullet lodged in a wall adjacent to the dead attacker. It's location, however, hadn't been the point. Firing through the jug had suppressed the crack of the round breaking the sound barrier and had prevented setting off a panic inside the residence as well as out. The last thing he needed was for people to think that more gunmen were afoot.

Ejecting the magazine, Harvath had then cleared the chamber, left the slide locked back, and placed everything on the island. His pistol and his PDW were now both pieces of evidence in a criminal investigation on the sovereign soil of Norway.

Harvath had unending respect for D.C. Metro Police. The people he couldn't stand were D.C. politicians. Regardless of the untold lives he and Sølvi had saved today, the D.C. City Council would demand that they be prosecuted for "illegal" firearm possession. He had no intention of serving himself, much less his wife, up on a silver platter like that.

When Sølvi entered with the security agent, he gave a quick explanation and pointed the man to the SIG Sauer pistol and the Flux Defense Raider that he had rendered safe and placed right next to each other.

An active Norwegian law enforcement officer, the man had instantly understood what was going on. With a nod toward Harvath, he had said, "Don't worry. I'll take care of it."

Harvath spent the next several hours firmly planted at the Ambassador's residence. During that time, he learned that the Ambassador had been planning a smaller reception for later in the evening and had popped back over to check in with the chef. That was why the two of them had been in the kitchen.

With that mystery solved, he then sat for a series of interviews and gave a flurry of statements—DSS, USSS, FBI, it seemed that all of the alphabets in the soup had descended upon the residence. No matter how many questions he was asked, he answered all of them to the best of his ability.

The only people he had refused to speak with were the D.C. cops, which didn't seem to matter as they had quickly been booted from the scene once the feds showed up and asserted jurisdiction.

By the time he and Sølvi had made it home, it was almost midnight. And, because his Tahoe had been totaled, they had needed one of the Norwegian Embassy personnel to give them a lift.

The next morning, despite how late they had both gone to bed, they were up early and had gone for a run. After, while Sølvi showered, Scot cooked breakfast. The TV in his kitchen updated him on all the latest news surrounding the shooting.

So far, authorities had no idea as to motive, nor if a larger organization of some sort had been behind the attack. Seven protesters had been killed and eighteen wounded. Twelve police officers had also been killed and seven wounded, three of whom were in critical condition. It was an incredible tragedy.

Scot had lost his appetite.

Carrying a mug of coffee to the kitchen table, he muted the TV and tried to put last night out of his mind. That wasn't his world anymore. He had fifty million reasons not to look back. Fifty million and one if you counted Sølvi.

His years of kicking in doors and shooting bad guys in the face were over. And, as much as he loved his country, America was on its own.

He had more than earned his release. Whatever the United States had asked of him, no matter how dangerous, no matter how deadly, he had always answered the call.

But when the CIA had attempted to blackmail him into spying against Sølvi, that had been the end of the line.

Of course, they didn't like taking no for an answer and had attempted to bring him to heel by freezing his assets. Chief among those assets was an account with $50 million. It was half of a $100 million bounty he had agreed to split with the wife of a nutcase Russian oligarch who had tried to kill him.

Threading the needle, and almost losing his life in the process, Harvath had found a way to get the CIA what they wanted without betraying Sølvi. The bridge between him and Langley, however, had been completely burned. He was never going to work with them again.

As they were the source of over 80 percent of the Carlton Group's business, it made no sense for him to remain. Besides, with all that money *and* a beautiful new wife, what idiot suits up in the morning and heads into an office? He had hit the jackpot. And in so doing, he planned to live it up and bounce his final check to the funeral home.

That said, if he was being completely honest, there were times when he missed it; missed the action, the intensity. There was nothing else in the world that provided that kind of rush.

And while loathe to admit it, last night had felt like returning to who he really was. He had both loved it and hated it all at the same time.

He hadn't minded the danger for himself. He had been in the zone. What he couldn't stand was Sølvi having been in harm's way. After all the people he had lost in his life, he couldn't bear the thought of losing her as well. It would be too much.

Before he could get any darker, his phone chimed. There was motion down the road from the house.

Picking it up, he checked the camera feed. A silver Chevy Bolt was approaching. Zooming in on the red and blue State Department license plates, he saw the letters *PK* and wondered why a vehicle from the Norwegian Embassy was paying them a visit. He doubted it was because someone was already bringing his guns back.

As the vehicle approached the call box, he switched to a different camera. There were two people inside—a driver and the Norwegian ambassador herself, Kari Hansen.

He was about to alert Sølvi when he looked up and there she was. She had entered the kitchen so quietly, he hadn't even heard her. It was this crazy gift she had and it was why he jokingly referred to her as the *Norwegian ninja*.

"Ambassador Hansen is here," she said, checking out the same camera feed on her phone.

"Maybe she found my sunglasses."

In addition to his weapons and his Tahoe being held for evidence, he had lost a new pair of Ray-Bans last night.

Sølvi rolled her eyes. "Nobody cares about your sunglasses."

He shook his head in response. "That's not what the FBI told me. They're going to keep a lookout for them."

Before she could reply, the front gate chime sounded. Answering in Norwegian, she buzzed the Ambassador in and told her driver to proceed up to the house.

Scot and Sølvi went outside to greet them.

CHAPTER 7

mbassador Hansen was dressed professionally in a navy pantsuit with her brown hair pulled back and very little makeup.

After all the federal law enforcement agents had departed her residence, she had probably spent a good chunk of the night next door at the embassy relaying everything that had happened back to her government in Oslo. With the residence having been breached, two Norwegian security agents dead, and her Norwegian chef in the hospital, the powers that be would want to know everything. There would also be concern over the upcoming NATO Summit, scheduled to be held in only a few days, right in downtown D.C.

It was one of the first big international meetings to be hosted by President Mitchell and his new administration. Not only was the NATO partnership on the agenda, but so too was a proposed European-wide missile defense system known as Sky Shield. The Norwegian Prime Minister would be flying in to represent Norway and was hoping to sway the handful of members not yet signed on. The safety and security of the summit would be of more pressing interest than it had been just twenty-four hours ago.

Despite the tragic circumstances of the night before and the very little sleep she had likely been operating under, the Ambassador was the picture of professionalism and composure.

With a leather briefcase slung over her shoulder, she exited the car, strode confidently forward, and greeted them warmly.

Out of respect for Scot, both the Ambassador and Sølvi spoke English.

After a few pleasantries, Sølvi asked, "How is Chef Markus?"

The Ambassador's expression grew grim. "As you know, he lost a lot of blood. They had him in surgery for seven hours. I'm headed back to the hospital after this."

"Please know that we are thinking of him."

"Of course. That is very kind of you."

"Would you both like to come inside?" Harvath asked, speaking to the Ambassador and then nodding at her driver, who, judging by his build, probably also doubled as her security. "We have coffee."

"Ah," the Ambassador replied, "a Norwegian's three favorite words." Looking at her driver, she raised an eyebrow and asked if he would like some coffee. He politely declined and stated that he would wait for her outside.

Smiling, she said, "Looks like it's just me."

Sølvi led Ambassador Hansen inside and, as Harvath poured three fresh cups of coffee, gave her a quick tour.

She explained the history of the property, known as Bishop's Gate, and how the small stone church, rectory, and various support buildings had been constructed by the Anglicans before the Revolutionary War, how the estate had gone on to become a site for Naval Intelligence, and how it eventually had been deeded to Harvath by a grateful former U.S. president—provided Harvath continue to pay his one-dollar-a-year rent and maintain, if not improve, the property.

"And Mount Vernon is the adjacent property?" the Ambassador asked.

Sølvi smiled yes. "We have fun telling friends that George Washington is our next-door neighbor."

"Mine is the pope, so we're both in excellent company."

Sølvi smiled again. "We are."

"What's this?" Hansen asked, pointing to a very old, hand-carved sign that had been mounted to the wall.

"Scot found that up in the attic. *Transiens Adiuva Nos,*" Sølvi said, reading the Latin phrase. "It's the motto of the Anglican missionaries. Roughly, it means I go overseas to help."

"Quite appropriate considering your husband's background. It's almost as if this house was meant for him. And for you as well, considering your service to Norway."

She couldn't tell if it was a casual remark, meant to be flattering, or if the Ambassador was hinting at something else entirely.

As an exceptional spy, Sølvi was comfortable with silence and let the Ambassador's observation hang in the air without a response.

Keeping the smile on her face, she continued the tour and walked Hansen into the kitchen, where Scot was placing the coffee and a few other things on a tray to take out to them.

"Perfect timing," he said. "How about we sit in the living room? Or, if you're up for it, we can walk down to the dock. There's a great breeze on the Potomac this morning."

"How about we just sit in here?" the Ambassador responded, pointing at the kitchen table.

"Are you hungry?" Sølvi asked.

"No, thank you. Coffee is all I need."

Harvath carried the tray over to the table and they all took a seat.

Centering her mug in front of her, Hansen said to him, "On behalf of the Norwegian government and especially me and Chef Markus, I want to thank you for what you did. For what you both did."

"We're very sorry for what happened," Harvath replied. "For all of it."

"It would have been much worse had you not been there."

"Is there anything we can do for you? Your staff?"

"Actually," said the Ambassador, "that's one of my questions for you. I not only wanted to thank you, but I also wanted to make sure that you're doing okay. Is there anything that either of you need? Anything that we can do for you?"

Scot looked at Sølvi and they both shook their heads in unison.

"I think we're good," he stated.

Hansen held up her index finger and said, "Wait," as she bent down and removed a small manila envelope from her briefcase. Sliding it across the table, she continued, "I think these belong to you."

Opening it, he looked inside and pulled out his Ray-Bans.

"The FBI found them outside, by the fence."

"The *FBI*," he repeated, glancing at Sølvi. "They're amazing."

"Indeed," Hansen agreed. "Although we still don't know much more this morning than we did last night. They're still trying to identify the attackers and come up with a motive."

"Well, if anyone can do it, they can. They're the absolute best when it comes to this kind of thing. I'm sure they'll have something soon."

The Ambassador nodded, took a sip of her coffee, and then said, "That brings me to my other question."

"What's that?" Harvath asked.

"Technically, it's a question for Sølvi."

"Okay," he responded, leaning back in his chair.

Hansen looked uncomfortably at her and then at him before saying, "Would it be okay if Sølvi and I spoke in private?"

Leaning forward, he picked up his mug and stood up from his chair. "Of course."

"Thank you. I just have a couple of things I have been asked to speak with her about."

"I totally understand."

Topping off his coffee, he poured one in a to-go cup for the driver, just in case the man had changed his mind, and headed outside.

He had no idea what business the Ambassador might have with Sølvi. Technically, she was still a deputy director with the NIS, even if she was on an open-ended leave of absence. And while her position had been primarily focused on Russia, there was no end to what topics the Ambassador might want to discuss with her.

But there was something about Hansen's visit, so soon after the attacks, that bothered him. She wasn't here to drop off a pair of sunglasses and she hadn't come for a simple chat.

There was something more, and already Harvath didn't like it.

CHAPTER 8

The Ambassador's driver was also, in fact, a security agent. His name was Christoffer. Or, as he had instructed Harvath to refer to him, "Just Chris."

As it turned out, Just Chris was only being polite earlier and appreciated that Harvath had brought a coffee out to him.

The two men stood in the driveway, leaning against the car and chatting as they enjoyed their coffee.

A consummate spy, Harvath probed in an attempt to learn more about the young man, as well as his role back at the embassy.

He came from a village of less than eight hundred people called Isebakke, along Norway's southeastern border with Sweden. He had briefly served as an infantryman in the Norwegian Army before beginning a career in the Norwegian Police Service, when the opportunity to sign on with the Foreign Service had presented itself.

Until last night, it had been an amazing experience with nothing but upside. Having two colleagues gunned down inside the residence, however, had changed all that. Everyone back at the embassy was understandably in shock.

When the younger man shared how grateful the team was that Harvath had responded so quickly, Harvath brushed it aside. Leaning in, the young man pressed on, confiding that every single embassy employee was grateful that he had not only saved the Ambassador, but had also ended the gunman's life.

Harvath thanked him and expressed sympathy for the loss of his colleagues.

Just Chris nodded and changed the subject as he took another sip of coffee. "It's very peaceful here. You have all of these beautiful trees. The water. It reminds me of Isebakke."

Harvath nodded back and was about to ask him another question when the front door opened and Sølvi and Ambassador Hansen stepped out of the house.

"Everything good?" he asked as they approached.

"Everything is excellent," Hansen replied as she shook hands with Sølvi. "We'll talk soon I hope."

Sølvi nodded and said something in Norwegian. Harvath noticed that it didn't have her normal, playful spark. It was serious. Official.

After the Ambassador said goodbye to Harvath, the young man thanked him for the coffee, and the pair got back in their car and disappeared down the drive.

Once they were out of sight, he turned to Sølvi and said, "That was a little bit of a strange goodbye. What was it all about?"

"I don't want to talk about it standing here," she replied.

"No problem. Where should we talk?"

"Let's go down to the dock."

Harvath nodded and let her lead the way.

Passing through the house, she grabbed a bottle of cold water from the fridge while he topped off his coffee. They then headed out through the French doors off the living room.

Walking in silence, they made their way down the gravel path to their long white pier. At the end was a storage box that doubled as a bench, along with a small teak table and four teak chairs.

Harvath retrieved his American flag from the storage box, ran it up the flagpole, and then sat down at the table with Sølvi.

Looking out over the water, she said, "They want me to come back."

If there was one thing Harvath had learned in his life, it was that some conversations are ones in which your partner just wants you to listen to their troubles. In others, they want you to help them find solutions.

He wasn't yet sure what kind of conversation this one was, so he erred on the side of caution. "Interesting," he responded, acknowledging that he had heard her. "How do you feel about that?"

"I'm not sure. What's that famous line from *The Godfather*?"

"Ambassador Hansen 'made you an offer you couldn't refuse'?"

Sølvi turned her gaze from the Potomac back to her husband. "That's the one. Except it wasn't Hansen who made me the offer. She's just the messenger."

Harvath took a sip of his coffee as he waited for her to continue.

"The good news is that it's only a temporary assignment," she finally stated.

"And the bad news?"

"I have to start right away."

None of this was doing anything to tamp down his concern. "What's the assignment?"

She took a deep breath and said, "The Norwegian Prime Minister wants me on her security detail for the NATO Summit."

Harvath's hand tightened around his mug. He used to do this exact same job and knew exactly what it entailed. Not only could it be extremely dangerous, but this request was completely unnecessary. Norway would be sending a full detail of its own protection agents with the Prime Minister.

What's more, the moment they touched down on U.S. soil, they would be augmented by a full complement of Secret Service agents. Adding Sølvi made no sense at all.

"I don't get it," he said. "Your special forces background more than qualifies you, but dignitary protection isn't your field of expertise. Why do they want you working halls and walls?"

"Do you want the short answer or the long?"

Almost out of coffee, he answered, "Short."

"Prime Minister Stang doesn't trust the U.S. Secret Service."

That didn't exactly come as a surprise to him. The Secret Service had experienced some highly publicized failures recently, not the least of which were assassination attempts in the run-up to the general election. While no one, thankfully, had been killed, dramatic, inexcusable mistakes had been made.

Though he had only worked with the Secret Service for a short time, he felt compelled to mount some sort of a defense on their behalf.

"I am not going to argue that there haven't been some screwups recently. But presidential elections open up a whole Pandora's box of threats. I highly doubt anyone is going to be gunning for the Prime Minister of Norway. And even if someone was, the United States Secret Service remains the best protection agency in the world."

"Really?" Sølvi asked. "What about what happened in Dublin two years ago?"

"*Dublin?*" Harvath replied, trying to jog his memory.

"As the presidential motorcade was leaving the U.S. Embassy?"

He had almost forgotten about the incident and winced thinking about it.

The president's backup limo, which always traveled with him, was identical to the bullet- and bomb-proof Cadillac known as "The Beast." It was in the motorcade, ahead of the actual limo carrying the President and First Lady. When it reached the top of the concrete ramp leading out to the street, it scraped its belly, high-centered, and became stuck. The rest of the vehicles behind it, including the limo with the President and First Lady, were forced to reverse into the parking garage and leave via an alternate exit.

Normally, the Secret Service agent responsible for the Beast is supposed to drive every inch of every possible route before the President arrives. Whether or not the agent practiced exiting the embassy properly was never publicly revealed.

It was extremely embarrassing for America and the previous president. It became a metaphor for the United States being bloated, overweight, and unable to maneuver. It was also catastrophically embarrassing for the Secret Service.

Video and still photographs of the teetering limo, with its American and Irish flags above the fenders and presidential seals on the doors, made headlines around the world. And in so doing, they made America and the Secret Service a laughingstock.

"Dublin wasn't good," he agreed. "But like I said, the Secret Service is still the best at what they do, bar none."

"Do you want me to cite the other examples the Prime Minister is concerned about?"

He shook his head. "No organization is perfect. Not even the Norwegian Intelligence Service. Let's not forget that your people had a Russian mole in the center of everything who almost got you killed."

It wasn't a card he was eager to play, yet it felt necessary to inject a modicum of perspective into the conversation.

Sølvi, however, wasn't happy being reminded. The experience was still too raw; too painful.

While debriefing a Russian defector at a top-secret NIS safe house in Oslo, she and her team had come under attack. Every protective agent on-site was killed. Sølvi and her defector were the only two to make it out alive. And even then, just barely. She had been betrayed from within her own organization.

"I haven't forgotten," she replied. "How could I?"

Harvath knew he was going to strike a nerve, and now that he had, he regretted it.

"I'm sorry," he said.

"You're not wrong about what happened."

"All I care about is you. Which is why I'm trying to understand this. What does the PM not trusting the Secret Service have to do with you?"

"She wants me on her detail to protect her *from* the Secret Service."

Harvath's eyes widened. "She thinks the Secret Service is going to try to harm her?"

Sølvi shook her head. "No, not intentionally."

"Then what are we talking about?"

"After the assassination attempts, your government launched a sweeping investigation; top to bottom. They found a lot of things that were wrong in the organization. Inadequate training, too much time on, not enough time off. It was a pretty damning report. A report, which my government read in earnest, looking for any takeaways that could make our agents better at their jobs."

"As they should."

"One of the key findings was that the Secret Service needed a significant boost in its budget in order to revamp training and hire new agents.

The problem, however, is that none of that money has been appropriated, much less released."

"So in other words," said Harvath, "nothing has changed."

With a solemn expression, she nodded. "That's the PM's fear. She wants me on her detail not as another gun, but as another set of eyes. She wants to make sure there are no mistakes."

"She can't add another person from Oslo to do that?"

"I asked Ambassador Hansen the same question."

"And?"

"The PM thinks that my involvement in countering the attack last night will give me some celebrity status with the Secret Service. They may decide to assign better, more experienced agents to the Norwegian delegation."

"Norway is one of our most important allies. They're going to put exceptional agents on the PM's detail."

"The Prime Minister also believes that with me on board, the Secret Service will work twice as hard. And if anything is amiss, will get it fixed immediately."

"That explains why the PM wants you," he said, not fully buying the argument. "What was her offer? The one you couldn't refuse."

Opening her water bottle, Sølvi took a deep drink before responding.

"A long time ago, when I was in a very dark place, I made a promise to someone. That promise created a debt. Prime Minister Stang has now come to collect."

CHAPTER 9

S tarting at the British Embassy, all the way to Thirty-Fifth Street, Massachusetts Avenue had been completely closed off to through traffic.

After Carolan and Fields flashed their FBI credentials, a D.C. Metro cop pulled back a police barricade and allowed them to proceed.

Two blocks before the crime scene, a staging area had been established. Parking their car, they got out and headed for the cluster of blue tents and FBI Evidence Response Team vans.

Until this morning, Carolan hadn't planned on visiting the scene. It had nothing to do with him. That had all changed when Assistant Director Gallo had called him at home and had instructed him to get down to headquarters as soon as possible.

They met in Gallo's secure conference room, where the assistant director played an eleven-minute video of Russian intelligence officer Josef Vissarionvich being debriefed. It was in this debrief that the man had dropped his bombshell. Within the last twelve months, Russia had launched a new covert spy unit, the Department of Special Tasks, or SSD for short.

Composed of veterans of Russia's most dangerous clandestine operations, its goal was to destabilize the West via a series of shadowy attacks, including sabotage, assassinations, cyberattacks, and bomb plots, as well as political influence operations involving blackmail, disinformation, and cultural subversion.

It was housed under the auspices of Russia's military intelligence agency known as the GRU, and had absorbed key elements of the FSB, Russia's largest intelligence agency, as well as completely consuming Unit 29155, a deadly black ops group.

One of the SSD's first and most audacious plans had been named *Chernaya Liniya*. Operation Black Line.

It was a plan to tip America into chaos; to rupture the social fabric, pitting citizen against citizen, and collapsing the country from within.

According to Vissarionvich, a tidal wave of violence and terror was to be unleashed, making every American feel unsafe. Then the media outlets sympathetic to the party in power would be used to turn members against each other, creating factions that would further do battle among themselves.

The concept was akin to the Reign of Terror during the French Revolution. Russian intelligence was convinced that America was already so partisan and so divided, that with a push here and a little nudge there, it would—much like the ancient symbol of the ouroboros, the snake eating its own tail—devour itself.

What had prompted Gallo to summon Carolan, however, was a very specific tactic outlined in the plot—high-impact, mass-casualty attacks on highly visible political protests. Exactly like what had happened last night.

Wondering if perhaps Vissarionvich had seen news of the attacks on TV and fabricated the Russian plot to leverage a better deal, Carolan put the question directly to his boss.

Gallo's response had chilled him to the bone—the interview was eight days old.

"Eight days?" Carolan had responded angrily. "Why the hell weren't we read in?"

No sooner had the words left his lips than he knew what the answer was going to be. First and foremost, they had to tread lightly. It could have all been bullshit.

There was always the possibility that Vissarionvich had allowed himself to be captured just so he could spin falsehoods and get the FBI and CIA chasing their own tails.

Without any corroborating evidence, anything the Russian gave up had to be treated as highly suspect. There had been no reason to disseminate any of it until now.

The attack on the protesters outside the Vice President's Residence might have been an amazingly unfortunate coincidence. Any intelligence operative worth their salt, however, was taught to never believe in coincidence. That was why Gallo had put Carolan and Fields on the case.

Because there could be a Russian link, the assignment was a political hot potato, which was why the assistant director wanted them hidden in the basement and reporting only to him.

Their job was to find out if the Russians were behind the attack and, if there really was an Operation Black Line, to smash it. Gallo would make sure they had anything they needed to get the job done.

Carolan had lingered in his boss's office, watching the rest of the debrief, gathering as much information as he could. One of the most disturbing revelations, if it could be believed, was that the Russians had unnamed American politicians under their control in both political parties. Had President Mitchell lost the election, the SSD had another plan, Operation Red Line, ready to target a new administration under his opponent.

If this was true, it was a massive breach of the United States government. What's more, given the current political climate, Carolan had no idea how the hell the FBI would ever be able to smoke these people out. Under President Mitchell's orders, the Department of Justice had already shut down its FBI-run election integrity unit, which focused on keeping America's enemies, especially Russia, from tampering with U.S. elections. If a single word leaked that the FBI was looking into the potential Russian subversion of any American politicians, much less from Mitchell's own party, heads would be on pikes outside the White House by lunch.

Making matters worse was the fact that Vissarionvich's knowledge of the Black and Red Line operations wasn't firsthand. As a deep-cover operative in the United States, his assignments had been adjacent to the SSD, but he'd never had direct access to the new organization.

Unless the Russian spy was holding out a name or something else really big to trade, these broad brushstrokes were likely all that Carolan was going to get. If there was any "there" there, he was going to have to make it work. Hence his dragging Fields to the literal scene of the crime.

As they signed in, a voice from behind them said, "Would you look at this. The office overachievers have arrived."

Carolan didn't need to turn around to know who it was. He recognized the man from his voice.

Agent Matthew Kennedy had been in the FBI almost as long as Carolan. He was a South Boston guy, born and raised. And despite having spent decades living in the D.C. area, he had never fully lost his Southie accent nor his caustic sense of humor.

He looked like a Hollywood version of a G-man straight out of central casting. He was tall, trim, and had a jaw like an anvil. The only thing shorter than his nails was his hair, which bordered on a crew cut.

His dark blue suit was perfectly pressed, and despite the rising heat and humidity, there wasn't a bead of perspiration on him. His shoes were so highly polished that you could shave in them. Capping it all off was a tie bar—a piece of personal flair and a relic from a bygone age. Carolan, who was certain the man carried stainless-steel toothpicks and wore a pinky ring off duty, hated the guy's guts.

"Hello, Matt," he said, clicking into diplomacy mode. "It's good to see you."

"What the hell is CROS doing here?" Agent Kennedy asked. "I don't see any Russians around here."

"Well, part of the crime scene includes the Norwegian ambassador's residence and Norway shares a border with Russia so—"

"You need to work on your geography," the man said, interrupting him. "Norway shares a border with Sweden."

Fields, who had absolutely no time for this guy, rolled her eyes and walked away. She didn't want to say something she'd regret.

"We do a lot of intelligence sharing with the Norwegians," Carolan explained. "We're just here as a courtesy to our contacts back in Oslo."

It was the cover story he and Fields had developed on the drive over from headquarters. It seemed to satisfy Agent Kennedy.

"If you need anything, we've got an admin team on-site. They've been logging all the evidence," the man said.

Looking around, Carolan asked, "What about the bodies?"

"Those have already been transported."

"Have you ID'd any of them?"

"The victims? Yes. Although the cops in the van were burned beyond recognition. The fire was so hot, it even melted their badges. We're going to need to do DNA testing on the remains, but in general," said Kennedy, "we know who they are."

"What about the attackers?"

"Nothing yet. None of them were carrying ID. We'll run their prints and photos through all the databases and see if we get any hits. We'll also be tracing their weapons, and BATF already has samples from the explosives and is running tests."

As much as Carolan didn't care for the man personally, professionally he was a solid, by-the-book agent. Based on everything he had said, he was doing everything right.

"Is there anything that doesn't fit? Anything you're trying to make sense of?"

Kennedy shook his head. "Beyond the motive—the *why* of something like this? No. We've got the guns, the shell casings, all of it. The shooters were White, American-looking males in their thirties. It doesn't appear to be Islamic terrorism, but we don't know that for sure yet. Prima facie, it looks like a homegrown scenario."

"So that's the working hypothesis? Extremism?"

"I don't know what else you'd call it," the agent replied. "Who shoots up a bunch of unarmed people exercising their First Amendment right?"

Carolan didn't disagree. "What were the victims protesting?"

"They're unhappy with the new administration."

"So, opponents of President Mitchell."

Kennedy shook his head again. "We interviewed all of them. Every single one voted for Mitchell."

"Then why were they protesting?"

"They're angry. They think Mitchell has gone soft; that he's moderated and is backpedaling on a lot of his promises."

"He's definitely not the same guy he was on the campaign trail, that's for sure," Carolan replied.

"What was that old comedy bit about a president's first day on the job? They take you out to Area 51, let you give the alien they have locked up there a purple nurple, and then they drag you back to the Oval, sit you down behind the Resolute Desk, and plop this huge binder in front of you with all that world's problems, which have now become *your* problems."

"I'm guessing that would be enough to change a person."

"The alien or the binder?"

Carolan chuckled. "Both."

"You're probably right," Kennedy said with a smile before continuing. "Listen, I've been here most of the night and am about to head home. There's a new lead site agent taking over. I'll let him know you're here. If you need anything, he'll take care of you and you can always get me on my cell."

"Thank you," Carolan said, extending his hand. It was easily the most civil exchange he'd had with the man in years. Perhaps the asshole in him was petering out.

The pair shook hands and went in different directions.

Carolan had only made it a few yards when Kennedy called out to him and said, "Hey, Joe! I was only kidding about Sweden. I know Norway also has a border with Russia, up top in the north. A little over a hundred miles."

"No points for looking it up on your phone as I walk away, Matt! Better luck next time."

Kennedy grinned and very subtly, not to mention very unprofessionally, gave him the finger.

Shaking his head, Carolan turned around and kept walking. Maybe the asshole in him wasn't receding. Maybe it had just been taking a nap.

Kennedy took his time logging out from the crime scene. He kept his eyes on Carolan and Fields until they disappeared into the Norwegian ambassador's residence.

Once they had, he returned to his car and removed a second cell phone—his burner—from beneath the passenger seat.

There were only a handful of numbers in the list of contacts. As he pulled out of his parking spot, he found the one he wanted and he pressed the call button.

When a voice answered on the other end, Kennedy said, "I think we may have a problem."

CHAPTER 10

B rendan Rogers exercised great caution to make sure he wasn't followed. An hour and a half after leaving his motel, he arrived at a small café and bakery where he ordered a large black coffee and a breakfast sandwich, then took a seat at one of the tables outside.

The temperature was already in the low eighties and it was only going to get hotter. He had purposefully picked a spot that would remain shaded for at least the next couple of hours. There was no telling how long he would have to wait.

Another large coffee and a bottle of water later, he had his answer.

The blacked-out Mercedes Sprinter van came around the corner and headed toward the underground parking garage across the street. As it approached, the security bollards dropped and the heavy metal doors opened wide, like the mouth of an enormous whale about to gorge on a cloud of krill.

Rogers watched as the van was swallowed up and disappeared inside. Making himself comfortable, he waited fifteen minutes and then placed a call.

Somewhere high inside the glass and steel office tower across the street, a phone rang. When a receptionist answered and asked to whom he wished to be directed, Rogers only had a first name to provide her. He had no idea if the man he was calling even had a last name.

When asked for his own name, Rogers gave an alias—a name that he knew wouldn't be appreciated, but which would instantly be recognized.

It was the shortest hold time in history.

"The only Colonel Josef Kozak I know," a voice said, taking his call, "is dead. So you've got three seconds to tell me who this is before I hang up."

"I'm the man who first identified Kozak to you. I need your help."

Ten minutes later, the service entrance at the southwest corner of the building opened and two ex–special forces operatives in suits waved him inside.

They made sure that Rogers was alone and unarmed before walking him into a private elevator and accompanying him upstairs.

Avoiding the reception area, they escorted him down a back hall to a secure conference room where a very small man with two very large white dogs was waiting.

In his past life, the man, with primordial dwarfism, was known as "The Troll." His friends and coworkers at the Carlton Group knew him as Nicholas.

"Ambassador Rogers," Nicholas said, using the honorific that had been assigned to him as the Hostage Czar. "This is an honor."

"Sorry to show up on your doorstep announced," Rogers replied, pausing as he took in the enormous Caucasian Ovcharkas on either side of Nicholas. "Argos and Draco, right?"

"You have a good memory."

"May I?" he asked, indicating that he wanted to approach the dogs.

"Of course. Just do it slowly."

Nicholas then gave a quiet command and allowed the dogs to sniff the visitor's hand.

Ovcharkas had an amazing ability to catalog and recall scent. They immediately remembered Rogers from the time they had spent at the Hostage Recovery Fusion Cell. Nicholas remembered it as well. It was one of the most dangerous and stressful cases of his life. Even the former president had felt the need to make a personal appearance at the cell to reinforce to every single employee how important it was to rescue Scot Harvath and bring him home.

From start to finish, Rogers had done an amazing job. It was why, once Nicholas had confirmed that Rogers was indeed Rogers, he had swept the man into the building and up to the Carlton Group's heavily secured offices.

Thanking the security officers, Nicholas waited until they had closed the conference room door and then, shaking Rogers's hand, offered him a seat and said, "Of all the names you could have used. *Colonel Josef Kozak?*"

Kozak was the Russian GRU colonel who had been in charge of the Spetsnaz team that had killed the Carlton Group's founder, its acting director Lydia Ryan, a Navy Corpsman who had been taking care of Carlton, and Harvath's then wife, Lara, before putting a bag over his head and dragging him off to Russia. Without Rogers and his amazing team at the Hostage Recovery Fusion Cell, there was no telling how things might have ended up for Harvath.

"I'm sorry for the cloak-and-dagger," Rogers replied. "I didn't know where else to turn. And I'm way out of my depth. If nothing else, I figured the less people who know I am here, the better."

"Why don't you tell me what's going on?"

Rogers eyed the carafe of coffee on the table and Nicholas motioned for him to help himself.

Pouring a cup of coffee, he said, "Three weeks before the inauguration, we received intelligence that Qasem Soleimani, the head of the Iranian Quds Force, was going to be traveling from Damascus to Baghdad. Both the United States and the European Parliament had designated the Quds Force a terrorist organization. Soleimani and his soldiers were behind the deaths of hundreds of American and coalition service members.

"Soleimani was responsible for advancing Iran's goals of religious fascism by supporting militias such as the Houthis in Yemin, Hezbollah in Lebanon, and a whole host of Iraqi terrorist groups. He helped orchestrate proxy wars in Syria and Iraq, was responsible for the mass killings of civilians in multiple Middle Eastern countries, and helped the mullahs in Tehran brutally crack down on uprisings across Iran. The man was both a terrorist and a straight-up war criminal."

"In other words," Nicholas clarified, "a legitimate tier-one target."

"As far as the National Security Council was concerned, absolutely. He landed in Baghdad shortly after midnight and we had an Air Force MQ-9

Reaper drone on station, loitering above the city. He and his entourage, which included several pro-Iranian paramilitary personalities, split themselves between a Toyota sedan and a Hyundai van. As they were exiting the airport via an access road, the President gave the order to engage.

"Cleared hot, the Reaper then fired multiple Hellfire missiles, obliterating the convoy. We later identified Soleimani's remains via DNA testing on a severed finger found in the rubble, which still had the gaudy silver and red ring he was known to wear."

"It was a bold move, especially at the end of an administration," Nicholas offered.

"It was unquestionably bold. And if we had to do it all over again, I would still recommend it to the President wholeheartedly and without reservation."

"Our new president is a bit of an isolationist, so that might be a tough sell, but I'd like to think that when push comes to shove, he's willing to do the right thing."

His comment caused Rogers to grimace. It was a quick, involuntary reaction and it immediately vanished, but Nicholas had noticed it nonetheless.

Looking at him, he asked, "You don't agree?"

"That's part of why I'm here," said Rogers. "In the aftermath of taking out Soleimani, a press photo from that night was released by the White House. It shows all the key National Security Council members gathered in the Situation Room. Two of the people in that photo are now dead. I believe the Iranians had them killed. I think I'm next."

"Wait a second," said Nicholas, somewhat shocked. "You're talking about the former secretary of state and the chairman of the Joint Chiefs, right?"

Rogers nodded.

"One of whom fell down a set of stairs at home and broke his neck, while the other died from a massive coronary. You think these were assassinations? Hits by the Iranians?"

Rogers nodded again.

"I don't have to tell you that the SecState was a well-known, heavy drinker. Port was his poison, if memory serves. And the chairman of the

Joint Chiefs wasn't exactly in fighting shape. He was a somewhat portly man *and* a smoker. What's more, they were both getting up there in age. Neither of them was in any condition to outkick the actuarial tables. In fact, it's a wonder neither of them died while in office. With all due respect, if you were running a dead pool, you'd be crazy not to have had squares on both of them."

"All I know," said Rogers, "is that the Iranian Republic swore to get revenge against every person in that photo."

"Undoubtedly, nothing would make them happier. Soleimani was like a cult figure in Iran and the cult has only grown bigger since his death. But a bad fall and a heart attack don't necessarily add up to a murder spree. Do you have any evidence? Any intel that they were assassinated?"

The man shook his head. "Not until yesterday."

"What happened yesterday?"

"Two men, who had been following me earlier in the day, ended up chasing me through Rock Creek Park last night while I was on a run."

Nicholas's expression changed. "*Chasing* you?"

"If I hadn't been able to flag down a park ranger, I don't know what would have happened."

"What did they look like?"

Rogers gave him the same report he had given the Park Police and then laid out everything he had done afterward—right up until he had arrived at the Carlton Group this morning.

When Nicholas asked why he hadn't taken any of this to the Secret Service, the former National Security Advisor's answer stunned him.

Pulling out his phone, Nicholas knew what he had to do next. He composed a quick text and hit send.

When he was finished, he looked up at Rogers, who asked, "Who'd you send that to?"

"The one person who can help you."

CHAPTER 11

S cot was familiar with Sølvi's past. She had been brutally honest with him and had shared everything—her drug addiction as a model in Paris, her recovery and entry into the Norwegian military, and her relapse when her previous husband left her because of her inability to have children.

It was an incredibly painful story, but only by owning and acknowledging it could she move beyond it.

One thing that Scot didn't know, though it didn't surprise him, was the number of strings that needed to be pulled to get her reinstated at the Norwegian Intelligence Service after her relapse.

Her mentor, an NIS legend named Carl Pedersen, had moved heaven and earth. He had not only vouched for her, but he had also called in every single debt owed to him.

In the end, one person had stood between Sølvi and getting her career back—the head of the Norwegian Parliamentary Intelligence Oversight Committee, Anita Stang, who now, years later, had become Prime Minister of Norway.

Without a debt Carl could call in from her, he was required to make her a promise. If the day came that she needed something, all she would have to do is ask. But before she had been able to cash in her chit, Pedersen had been killed. As the Prime Minister saw it, however, the debt was binding and transferable. Sølvi agreed.

And so when Ambassador Hansen had left the house, she had already secured Sølvi's cooperation. Sølvi would join the Prime Minister's protective detail and be with her for the duration of the NATO Summit. All Sølvi had requested was to be the person her husband heard it from. Hence the cryptic goodbye from the Ambassador and the shift in Sølvi's demeanor when seeing her off.

One of the things Scot loved about his wife was her integrity. She was doing the right thing. He respected her for that.

What's more, she knew how to handle herself. If anything went down, the Norwegians would be thanking their lucky stars that they had brought her onto the team. He had seen her in action enough times, including last night, to know what a badass he'd married.

With the added comfort of knowing that the NATO Summit was going to be one of the most secure events of the year, he said the very thing to her that she would have said to him had their situations been reversed: "What can I do to help?"

Sølvi kissed him. It was the perfect answer on every level as far as she was concerned. Like nobody else before in her life, he "got" her.

He understood that what she was doing was not only out of loyalty to her mentor, but also out of allegiance to her country.

She hadn't yet decided if she was going to return to the NIS, but agreeing to work the Prime Minister's detail could only help to keep a seat warm for her.

After checking the husband box, Scot immediately went into tactical mode. "You're going to have a gun and body armor, right?" he asked.

Sølvi nodded. "They're bringing my full kit from my weapons locker in Oslo."

With that, there was nothing else he could do, except to figure out how, without a car of their own, she was going to get back and forth from "work."

Hopping on a car-sharing site, he was able to find a whole bunch of vehicles, available immediately in their area. He screened out the EVs as Sølvi couldn't stand them and he didn't have a charging station anyway. Choosing vehicles that could be delivered next door to Mount Vernon, he winnowed the list even further.

"Volkswagen Jetta, Mercedes-Benz C-Class, or Ford Mustang?" he asked, picking out the top three listings with the best ratings.

She looked at him like he was nuts. "Duh," she replied. "Mustang."

"That's my girl," he smiled, selecting the vehicle.

"Hold on. It's not a four-cylinder, is it?"

Harvath checked the description. "Nope. Dark Horse Premium Package. Comes with a five-liter V-8."

"Good. I wouldn't be caught dead in a four-banger Mustang."

He smiled again. "They can drop it off at Mount Vernon around lunchtime."

"Book it," she stated, and he did.

He was indulging himself, scrolling through the super high-end cars, the McLarens, Lamborghinis, and Aston Martins—all vehicles that now, thanks to his windfall, were within his reach to own—when he received a text from Nicholas.

He and Sølvi had just been over at Nicholas's place to see Nina and the new baby. It was amazing how much she had grown since the christening.

Opening the text, he read Nicholas's message.

"You're never going to believe this," he said, looking at Sølvi. "I've got to go back to the office."

"Did you forget something? Can't they mail it to you?"

He shook his head. "No, it's not that. Brendan Rogers is there."

"The former National Security Advisor?"

"Correct."

"Wasn't he part of the team that helped get you out of Russia?" she asked.

"Yeah, he was the Hostage Czar at the time."

"What's he doing at the Carlton Group? Is something going on?"

Scot shrugged. "I don't know. Nicholas just asked if I could come in. He says it's important."

"Then you should go. I would offer to give you a ride, but."

"I'll tell you what," he replied. "How about you come pick me up in your hot-shit American muscle car in a few hours and we'll grab a late lunch together?"

"Burgers?"

"Whatever you want. As long as it's not lutefisk, I'm in."

Scot hated the traditional dried cod cured in lye that the Norwegians served at Christmas. He'd had one bite with Sølvi's family back in December and had thought he was going to hurl. He couldn't even get their dog to eat it under the table. It was that bad.

He decided it must have been some kind of torturous communal penance dreamed up by the Vikings to appease their angry and vengeful gods.

That night, before going to bed, he'd made it clear to Sølvi that if she ever tried to make him eat it again, he'd have her dragged to The Hague and brought up on war crimes.

"Still *so* angry about the lutefisk," she said with an impish grin. "My brothers warned me that you were weak."

"If your brothers had to eat half of the terrible stuff I've eaten over my career, they'd be curled up in a corner crying and sucking their thumbs."

The image of her two very large brothers crying over bad goat, fried scorpions, or whatever other foul things Scot had been forced to ingest in the field made her laugh.

"Okay, I promise. No lutefisk. For now."

"Not *ever*," Harvath reinforced, giving her a kiss. He needed to get back up to the house and get changed. Board shorts and a Parliament-Funkadelic T-shirt weren't exactly office attire—though he was tempted to keep his flip-flops on, just as an f-you to the system.

Twenty minutes later, he came downstairs to the kitchen in a light gray houndstooth suit that had been hanging at the back of his closet for over a year. Underneath the jacket he wore a crisp, white, oxford slim-fit shirt, but no tie. Now that he was retired, he didn't intend to ever wear a tie again. Caving on footwear, he opted for a pair of black, cap-toe shoes. In his outer breast pocket, a half-inch block of a perfectly folded linen handkerchief was visible. On his left wrist was the Seaholm Offshore dive watch Sølvi had given him as a wedding gift to replace the one he'd been forced to part with in Afghanistan.

"Doesn't that suit fit just right in all the right places," she said approvingly, as he gave her a slow 360 to take it all in. "I think I like corporate Scot. A *lot*."

Harvath laughed. "I'll let my tailor know you give him five stars."

"And then some. I could get used to seeing you like this."

"Please do us both a favor and don't. This is the last thing I want to be putting on every day."

"I'm just saying, this is a really good look on you."

Glancing at his phone, he saw that his Uber was getting closer.

"Gotta go," he said, giving her a kiss. "I'll text you later about lunch."

It was a short walk from the house to the pickup point he had entered into the app. For security purposes, he preferred to share his true address as seldom as possible.

The driver was right on time, had the car perfectly air-conditioned, and wasn't much of a talker. It made for the perfect ride as far as Harvath was concerned. They made the thirty-five-mile trip in just under forty minutes, which was practically a world record considering the ubiquitous D.C. traffic.

Arriving at the Carlton Group offices, Scot found it a little strange not to be entering through the garage and taking the private elevator up. But without a key card and parking pass, he had to enter via the main lobby like everyone else.

After being announced and granted access, he was directed to the appropriate elevator where the floor for the Carlton Group had already been entered. He stepped into the carriage and rode up by himself, humming the Albino Superstars song he had teased Sølvi with just the day before.

When the chime sounded and the doors opened, he entered the office for the first time since having cleared out his desk. He had wondered how it would feel and it actually felt pretty damn good. He traded pleasantries with the two security agents standing near the desk, inquired after the receptionist's children, and then thanked her as she told him which conference room to head toward and buzzed him in.

Taking the back hall, he only saw a handful of people. As usual, the Carlton Group was in the thick of a hundred different things and no one really had the time to stop and make small talk. He waved, traded a few fist bumps, and kept moving. At the conference room door, he knocked and then let himself in.

The dogs perked up the moment they saw him, but with a quiet command, Nicholas directed them to stay put.

Scot walked to the table and greeted the Ambassador, before shaking hands with Nicholas and then bending down to give Argos and Draco a little attention. When he was done, he took a seat across from Rogers.

"Thank you for coming," said Nicholas. "I hope Sølvi doesn't mind that we called you in."

"Don't worry. She thinks I'm playing golf."

"In a suit?"

Scot smiled. "Of course not. Come on. She knows exactly where I am and why I'm here. If it wasn't for you two, I wouldn't have made it out of Russia alive. I'm at your service. What do you need?"

"The Ambassador may have an issue that needs handling," said Nicholas.

"What kind of issue?"

"I think the Iranians are trying to kill me," Rogers replied.

"Because of the Soleimani hit?"

The Ambassador nodded.

"If that's true, you don't need to hire the Carlton Group. If you drew the Iranians' ire while working for the U.S. government and carrying out the policies of the previous administration, that is a cut-and-dried Secret Service issue."

"Which is what I told him," Nicholas replied. Then turning to Rogers, he said, "Now tell Scot what you told me."

The Ambassador cleared his throat and stated, "The Secret Service said no."

"Excuse me?" Harvath responded, certain that he must have heard the man wrong. "They said what?"

"According to the Secret Service, I'm on my own."

CHAPTER 12

Apologizing for making him do it a second time, Harvath had the Ambassador go all the way back to the beginning of his story and tell him everything he had relayed to Nicholas. No detail was too small or too trivial. And when he was done, Harvath made him repeat it all again and battered him with questions at every turn.

Seeing the two goons earlier in the day, only to see them again on a running trail in Rock Creek Park that evening might have been the world's most incredible coincidence—something Harvath didn't believe in—but when they had chased Rogers up and over a hill into traffic, that's where all mystery surrounding their intent should have evaporated.

Rogers was right to be concerned, and Harvath believed the man's instincts were spot-on. He wasn't overreacting and had no reason to make any of this up.

Wisely, the Ambassador had asked the Park Police to forward a copy of their report to the Secret Service. There would be a paper trail putting them on notice.

What made no sense, however, was that as Rogers had been driven toward Reagan National, he had called the Secret Service again, only to be told that once they received the report, someone would look into it.

Exposing a U.S. government official, active or retired, to the predations of a hostile foreign actor was unethical, unconscionable, and absolutely un-American. And it pissed Harvath off. *Big-time.*

He still had a few contacts at the Secret Service and, taking a break from the meeting, excused himself from the room. Grabbing an unoccupied office nearby, he closed the door and made a call.

Russ Gaines had been a member of the Secret Service's Counter Assault Team back when Harvath had been a protective agent stationed at the White House. They had trained off and on together and had seen more than their fair share of action.

Like a professional athlete, eventually Gaines was unable to outrun the physical demands of the job. But instead of cashing in and going the private sector route, as many of his colleagues had, he chose to remain with the Service and had worked his way up to a big position in the Special Operations Division. If anyone could clear a roadblock for Ambassador Rogers, it was him.

"If it isn't the Norseman himself," said Gaines, referring to Harvath's call sign as he picked up the phone. "How the hell are you?"

"I'm good, Russ. How 'bout you?"

"I'm not shooting-up-bad-guys-along-embassy-row-with-my-new-blond-wife-good, but I'm getting by."

Harvath laughed. Of course Gaines knew. Part of his purview at the Special Operations Division was overseeing the Secret Service's Emergency Response Teams, which provided exterior tactical security at the White House and the Vice President's Residence. He would have been informed immediately of the attack and kept constantly apprised of the investigation.

"Anything new on last night?" Scot asked.

"Not yet. The FBI is leading the investigation and they're still working on identifying the attackers."

"Have any groups claimed credit?"

"Plenty of domestic crackpots," said Gaines, "and a few bad actors overseas. Nothing credible so far. The press, as you can imagine, are extremely eager to get their hands on your name, as well as Mrs. Harvath's. Speaking of which, congratulations on your nuptials."

"Thanks. Sorry you didn't get an invite. It was a pretty small ceremony."

This time it was Gaines who laughed. "Don't worry about it. If I ever get married again, I'm doing the Elvis Chapel in Vegas and will have to pay someone off the street to be a witness. I'll be so far under the radar, any pings will be in Chinese."

Harvath didn't relish the idea of his and Sølvi's names being released to the press and circled back. "I assume the Bureau is running point with the media?"

"They are."

"Any clue as to what their thoughts are regarding the release of our names?"

"From what I hear, they don't want to put targets on your backs if they can help it."

"That's nice of them."

"You're lucky," said Gaines. "You've got more than a few friends left in this town. On the intel and law enforcement sides, everyone sees you as one of them. They're not going to throw you under the bus."

"But the press isn't going to give up. Sooner or later, it's going to leak. This is Washington after all."

"Which is why the Bureau is thinking about getting out in front of it and releasing an attribution."

"An *attribution*?" Harvath replied.

"You've been secretly moved around so much, that you're still on the books at some of your old agencies. Technically, we've still got you and so does DHS. The idea is to 'deconflict' the press by telling them that a plainclothes federal agent accompanied by a Norwegian protective services agent were in the area and responded to the attack and ended up saving countless lives. Out of respect for the agents' privacy and the sensitive nature of their jobs, both governments are withholding their identities."

"Do they think that'll work?"

"I suppose, but what do I know? I'm an ex–trigger puller. Media strategy isn't exactly my forte."

"Fair enough," Harvath admitted. "I guess it could be worse."

"Now I get to drop the other shoe. Unlike the Bureau, the Vice President's people think this is an excellent media opportunity. They want to throw a reception, at the residence, where the Vice President will thank you in person for your bravery. You and Sølvi both."

"*Fuck.*"

"I take it you're not a fan?" Gaines asked.

"Of the Vice President? I don't care either way. This isn't about politics. It's about privacy. We'd be happy to go and meet with him. I just don't want it splashed all over the press."

"Well, he's a splash kind of guy. The bigger the better. It's an attention economy out there. And he who commands the most attention wins."

"*Fuck,*" Harvath repeated.

"Maybe I can make your day a little brighter," Gaines continued. "Sølvi's packet came through from the Norwegian Foreign Service office. I didn't know she did close protection work."

"She and the Prime Minister have a history together."

"I made sure it went to the top of the stack and got approved right away."

"Thank you," said Scot.

"You're welcome. Just understand that if you two get in a squabble and she reaches for her sidearm instead of a rolling pin, she's covered by diplomatic immunity for as long as the Prime Minister is on U.S. soil."

"I'll do my best not to piss her off."

Gaines laughed again. "Good luck. Knowing you, my money's on two to your chest and one between your eyebrows before the summit even starts."

"Speaking of the summit," Harvath said, transitioning from a chuckle to a more serious tone, "whatever you can do to put your best people on her team, I'd really appreciate it."

"In light of what happened at the Norwegian ambassador's residence, the State Department has made the same request, so I'm already ahead of you. But I have to be honest, with all the cutbacks, we're stretched pretty thin, especially with so many dignitaries coming to town. We're working on it, though. We're not going to let anything happen to Sølvi or the Norwegian PM."

"Thanks, Russ. I appreciate it."

"Any time," Gaines replied. "If there's nothing else you need, I've got to get ready for the hourly update call with the FBI."

Harvath looked at his watch. There was fifteen minutes until the top of the hour. Gaines had been terrific, but they had not yet discussed the primary reason for his call.

"I do have one thing to ask you," said Scot. "Completely off the record."

"Go ahead."

"I just met with Ambassador Brendan Rogers. He thinks the Iranians want to kill him."

"They probably do," Gaines agreed.

"He thinks it's more than that. He thinks he's an active target."

"I know he does. The Ambassador has even more friends in Washington than you do."

"Are you aware that two men chased him through Rock Creek Park last night?"

"No," Gaines responded. "I was not. Is he okay?"

"He managed to find a park ranger and get away. He says the pair had been following him earlier in the day. He filed a report with U.S. Park Police and asked that it be forwarded to the Secret Service."

"So they didn't catch the guys."

"No," said Harvath. "They didn't."

"Were either of the men captured on video?"

"No idea."

"Do you have a vehicle description or license plate number?"

"Negative."

"Did you happen to hit the jackpot and one of them dropped an Iranian passport while pursuing Ambassador Rogers?"

"If that were the case," Harvath replied, "you'd already have it in your inbox."

"Listen, I'm not trying to be a wiseass. Please understand that our hands are tied."

"What about the deaths of the secretaries of state and defense?"

"We looked into those, along with the FBI and local law enforcement. One was an accident and the other was natural causes. It wasn't the Iranians."

"So what I'm hearing is that you need airtight, actionable intelligence before you can do anything."

There was a long pause on the other end of the line. It was so pronounced that Harvath wondered if maybe the call had dropped.

"Hello?" he said.

"Since we're off the record," Gaines replied, having finally found his voice, "I am going to let you know something. And if it ever comes back to me, I'm going to deny I ever said it. Even if you brought me airtight, actionable intelligence, my hands would still be tied."

Harvath couldn't believe what he was hearing. "What? That's insane. You'd let the Iranians assassinate him?"

"I wouldn't be letting anyone do anything. This comes from much higher up the chain than me."

"The Secret Service director?"

"Yes, but he got it from even higher up."

"The White House?" Harvath asked.

"Bingo."

"I don't understand. Why would we serve up a former U.S. government official to one of America's enemies?"

"I'll give you two reasons. One, the type of protection the Ambassador would need costs around two million dollars a month. President Mitchell ran on dramatically shrinking the size of government and slashing what it spends."

"Lots of politicians run on that," Harvath interrupted. "It's eye-watering, I get it, but it's a drop in the bucket budget-wise. More important, this is a serious national security issue. How is an administration ever going to recruit top-tier talent, much less get personnel who'll be tough with America's enemies and carry out the President's policies, if they know that one day they might very well be thrown to the wolves?"

"Off the record, I don't disagree. And if you asked me on the record, my position would be to refer you to the White House, which is the official position of the Secret Service on this."

"I really can't believe I'm hearing this."

"It gets worse, so hold on to your hat. When you asked why the United States might serve up a former government official, I told you that, off the record, there were two reasons why that might be happening. First was the cost. The second is the amount of time Ambassador Rogers has spent on TV criticizing the new administration."

Harvath was beyond stunned. "They're that thin-skinned? You've got to be kidding me."

"I wish I was."

"So, no matter what kind of intel Ambassador Rogers might bring you, this White House, and by extension the Secret Service, will not protect him."

"I don't like it any more than you do, but yes, that's what I'm telling you."

After that, there really wasn't much more to discuss. Harvath thanked Gaines for looking out for Sølvi and asked to be kept in the loop on anything the Secret Service man learned about the attack. They said goodbye, then Harvath disconnected the call and returned to the conference room. He was still pissed-off.

"How'd it go?" Nicholas asked.

"I've had better calls," Harvath replied.

The Ambassador wasn't hopeful. "Are they going to help?"

"No, they're not."

"So what are we going to do?"

Harvath looked at them both and said, "We're going to help ourselves."

CHAPTER 13

B y using me as bait?" Rogers asked once Harvath had sketched
out the broad strokes of his plan.

"It's the only way," he replied. "We can't go after them, because we don't know who they are. Our only option is to bring them to us."

"Can't we go after some local Iranian diplomat and use them for leverage?"

"That's not how Tehran works," Nicholas interjected. "They wouldn't run something like this through their embassy. It's too risky. Everything would be self-contained, compartmentalized."

"Meaning what?"

Harvath envisioned how he would put something like this together if he were in the Iranian's shoes. "Depending upon the number of targets, they'd probably send two to four men. If it was four, they'd split them into two teams and house them in two separate locations. One team would conduct all pre-attack surveillance and the other team would actually carry out the deed.

"They'd also require a local contact, a fixer of sorts—someone established who could help get them anything they needed and sort out any problems. In addition to English, this person very likely speaks Farsi and is of Iranian descent. The fixer would be the conduit back to Tehran, handling all the message traffic, lowering the risk that the operatives would be discovered."

"There's only one problem with this," said Rogers.

"What's that?"

"The men last night in Rock Creek Park didn't look Iranian. I've been to Iran, I've dealt with those people. These guys were not that."

"I wouldn't put it past the mullahs or the Quds Force to have agents who were more physically suited for operations in the West," Nicholas stated. "Considering the high profile of the targets they appear to be after, they'd want to leave nothing to chance."

"What if we're wrong?" the Ambassador asked.

"About what?" Harvath replied.

"What if it's not the Iranians?"

"Do you have someone else it could be?"

"We killed a lot of bad guys and we weren't quiet about it. This could be coming from any of their organizations."

"And it wouldn't make a bit of difference," said Harvath. "We'd still be in the same position with the same limited options and I'd still be recommending the same approach."

"You're sure there's absolutely no Plan B we can kick around?"

"I'm sure."

For several moments, the Ambassador sat in silence as he pondered the situation. This was not at all what he'd had in mind when he first set foot in the Carlton Group's offices this morning.

Harvath attempted to put the man at ease. "You can always say no. I don't know what our next steps would then be, but I'm sure we'd come up with something. This, however, is a good plan. The sooner we put it into action, the better off you're going to be."

Rogers looked at him, still thinking, still silent.

"You saved me once," said Harvath. "All I'm asking for is the opportunity to return the favor. I'm not going to let anything bad happen to you."

Whether it was the words or Harvath's tone, something clicked. The Ambassador relented.

"Okay," he said. "Let's do it."

With the decision made and the green light given, Rogers excused himself to use the men's room, leaving Scot and Nicholas to discuss next steps.

"I'll want to run three shifts," said Harvath. "How many guys from my team can I get?"

Nicholas held up his right hand and made the international signal for "zero."

"What do you mean, none?"

"They're all downrange on assignments."

"*All* of them?" Harvath asked.

"We're still running a business here. That didn't stop just because you did."

He knew Nicholas was simply telling him the truth, but the remark still stung. Even though he'd made the best decision for himself and Sølvi by turning in his resignation, there had been a part of him that felt like he was abandoning his colleagues. He was feeling that sensation again now.

"What about from any of the other teams? Hell, I'd even be glad to have Thing One and Thing Two from the lobby."

"With all the cutbacks in D.C., our business is booming. In fact, we've had to turn down work. We don't have a single body to spare."

"So the only thing standing between Ambassador Rogers and a possible Iranian hit team is me?"

"And me," said Nicholas. "I'm more than happy to provide whatever support I can."

"As long as it doesn't require you to physically be in the field."

The man nodded. "Correct. That has not changed. When I told you that in the South of France, I meant it."

Harvath hadn't doubted it then and he didn't doubt it now.

What he was trying to figure out was how the hell he was going to pull something like this off with no backup.

"What about Haney?"

"What about him?" Nicholas replied.

"He's not downrange."

"Because he's still in rehab after you got him shot for the second time."

"A, technically, the Russians shot him and B, how close is he to being done with rehab?"

"No."

"*No* what?" Harvath asked.

"No you can't pull Mike Haney into this."

"Don't you think that's a question for him to answer?"

"Not when we're paying for his rehab and a hazardous-duty bonus, all of which is because *you* got him shot."

"Fine, I'll leave Mike alone."

It was obvious by his expression that Nicholas didn't believe him. Harvath changed the subject.

"If I wanted you to kill the Ambassador's old phone, the one he slid into that woman's suitcase, could you do that?"

Nicholas didn't even need to think about it. "Sure. If it's attached to the cloud and he can give me his password, it's a piece of cake."

"What about cloning a new one for me?"

"Also a piece of cake, but do you think the Iranians are actually tracking his phone?"

"I have no idea," said Harvath. "I just want to make sure we put enough chum in the water. Which brings me to his car."

"What about it?"

"I don't want him to have to start it with a stick if you know what I mean."

Nicholas's dark sense of humor got the better of him and he chuckled at the image. "No, you don't want that."

"So how do we make sure it hasn't been rigged with a bomb?"

Rubbing his chin, Nicholas ran some options through his mind.

"He parked in the extended lot at Reagan National, correct?"

Harvath nodded. "Correct."

"I know somebody out there in airport operations. They've got a couple of trucks that are their own mini version of AAA. They help fix flats, jump batteries, that sort of thing. We might be able to get one of our tech people to ride along and make it look like Rogers is having trouble starting his car. The tech could pop the hood and give it a full, top-to-bottom, bumper-to-bumper sweep, just to make sure it's clean."

"Perfect. Let's get that in motion. In the meantime, I've got to recruit some more muscle."

"As long as it's not Haney, who are you thinking about?"

"I have an ex-federal employee that I've heard is very angry. I think he'd be great for this job."

Nicholas looked at him. "Because he's angry?"

"No, because even though he doesn't know it yet," said Harvath, "he's got his own skin in this game."

CHAPTER 14

D ead bodies give me the ick," said Fields as they pulled into the underground parking garage of the D.C. medical examiner's office.

"Since when?" replied Carolan as he searched for an empty spot.

"Since always."

"I've been at multiple crime scenes with you where we've had to deal with dead bodies. You've held tarps and sheets up for me, you've gone through their pockets, looked in their mouths and under their fingernails. I've never heard you complain. Not once."

"Because when they're at the scene, they're victims. But the minute they get to the morgue, they become corpses. And corpses freak me out."

"So moving them from the scene to here somehow transmogrifies them?"

"It amps up the ick factor. That's all I'm saying. It amps it way up."

"I'll bet you don't like hospitals either," replied Carolan as he found a vacant stall and pulled in.

"What the hell do hospitals have to do with anything?"

"It's called nosocomephobia and it's nothing to be ashamed about. At least ten percent of the population has it. A fear of doctors, lab coats, clinical settings, and hospitals. It stems from unresolved issues around illness, pain, and death."

"Listen, I don't like cherry ice cream. I don't like men with back hair. And I don't like corpses. Okay? It's that simple. None of it needs to be explained by me having a phobia."

"What is it they say?" Carolan asked as he turned off the ignition and opened his door. "The first step toward fixing a problem is admitting you have one?"

Fields gave him the finger.

"It would appear we're still in the denial phase," he stated. "We'll have to work on that."

Fields gave him her other finger and got out of the car.

"You want to explain to me what we're doing here?" she asked as they walked across the garage.

"Newton's first law of investigations," Carolan replied.

"Which is?"

"An investigation that's in motion tends to stay in motion."

"Well, let me tell you something about motion. If I see a single corpse so much as twitch in there, my Glock's coming out and they're getting a free ride on the nine-millimeter train to hollow-point station."

Carolan smiled. "Now we're getting somewhere," he said. "Kinemortophobia. Fear of zombies."

"Just keep your eyes open," Fields responded, squaring her shoulders and stepping through the large glass doors. "It's always the people who don't believe in zombies who are the first to go."

After presenting their credentials at the desk and signing in, they waited for a member of the ME's team to take them back. Out of curiosity, Carolan scanned the names for anyone he might recognize. None rang a bell.

A few minutes later, a young man in scrubs appeared. "The FBI was just here an hour ago," he stated.

"And now we're back," Carolan responded.

Exasperated, the young man checked his clipboard and said, "This way. Follow me."

The young man took them back to a large, rectangular room. The far wall was studded with stainless-steel icebox-style doors, behind which human bodies could be stored on pullout drawers and kept cold.

The rest of the room was painted a chalky, pale blue with large porcelain floor tiles to match. The ceiling was covered with white acoustic panels. Stainless-steel counters, shelving units, and deep sinks lined the remaining walls.

Amassed in the center of the room, perfectly spaced, were six metal gurneys with a black body bag atop each.

"These are the attackers from outside the Naval Observatory?" Carolan asked.

"John Does one through five," the young man replied, confirming the information on his clipboard. "John Doe number six was bagged inside the residence of the Norwegian ambassador. Where do you want to start?"

"That one," said Carolan, pointing at the nearest body bag.

"Lucky number six," the young man stated as he grabbed a pair of latex gloves from a box on the counter and put them on each of his hands with a snap.

Carolan and Fields followed suit, albeit with considerably less flourish, especially Fields, who quite visibly would have preferred to have been anywhere other than here.

"What are we looking for?" the ME staffer inquired as he unzipped the first bag.

"Pornography," Carolan replied.

"Excuse me?"

"Back in 1964, when Supreme Court Justice Potter Stewart was asked for his definition of pornography, his answer was 'I know it when I see it.' That's my answer too. What are we looking for? I'll know it when I see it."

Whether or not the answer made sense to the young man, it had the desired effect of getting him to stop asking questions. Carolan wasn't here for chitchat. He needed to think and to observe.

While he and Fields inspected the first body, he sent the young man to unzip the other bags.

"Hell of a shot," Carolan commented as he examined the hole in the corpse's head.

After reading the report, he had gotten down on the floor of the kitchen in the Norwegian ambassador's residence and had re-created what it had taken for Harvath to make that shot. Only someone who had gone through as much trigger time as a guy like that could have had both the ability and the balls to pull it off.

"Besides porn," said Fields, keeping her voice low as she forced herself to be professional and stand next to her boss, "what exactly *are* we looking for?"

"Anything that shouldn't be here. Anything unusual or out of the ordinary," he replied. "Their clothes have already been bagged for evidence, so we're looking for distinguishing features like scars, tattoos, unusual bone growth—anything that might help us identify who they are."

"Wouldn't the agents before us have done this?"

"Yep. And now we're doing it. Here," said Carolan, opening the bag wider, and lifting up the man's left arm, which was covered in a sleeve of tattoos from his shoulder to his wrist. "Hold this so I can get some photos."

Fields shook her head. "This is why Black people always die first in horror movies. They listen to the White people," she replied, pulling out her phone. "*You* hold the zombie's arm up. I'll take the photos."

As she began snapping pictures, the young ME staffer informed her, "The other FBI agents already did that. They had proper cameras and everything."

Without missing a beat, she responded, "Somebody must have screwed up because they sent us to retake them all."

"But they had proper cameras, lenses, all that. You've got what? An iPhone?"

She ignored his question and instead gave him another task. "As soon as you're done unzipping those bags, I need you to come back over here and help my colleague roll John Doe number six onto his side."

"Looking for more pornography?"

Fields smiled at him. "Sometimes it hides in interesting places."

The young man wasn't thrilled to be put to work, but the quickest way to get on with his day was to help the two FBI agents wrap up their examination and move along out his door.

They were on the second-to-last corpse when one tattoo in particular caught Carolan's attention.

"Make sure you get a good picture of this," he said.

Fields looked at it and snapped two photos, just to be sure. It was on this John Doe's upper right thigh and appeared to be a half sword, half tree.

"What is it?" she asked.

Her boss shook his head. "I don't know, but I think I've seen it before."

"Where?"

"I don't remember. And if you don't stop asking me questions, I'm not going to tell you which of the bodies I just saw move behind you."

Fields briefly glanced over her shoulder before raising her left hand, palm out, as if to say, "I get it. No more questions."

They finished with the final corpse, thanked the young staffer, and exited the morgue back into the garage.

"Hungry?" Carolan asked.

Fields looked at him like he had grown a second head. "You've got to be fucking kidding me."

"No, I'm serious. I ran out of the house without breakfast this morning. All I've had is coffee. The low blood sugar is killing me."

"You couldn't pay me to eat right now."

"Come on. We're a nine-iron from the Wharf. There's got to be over a dozen restaurants down there. Just pick one."

"Are you buying?"

"If I'm the only one eating. If not, we split like we always do," Carolan replied. "There's the Grill, Bistro du Jour . . . I don't care. I just need something."

She looked at her watch. "Okay, we'll go to Hank's."

"The oyster bar?"

"They have some of the best damn fries in the city."

"So now you're eating?"

"Listen, it's Hank's or nothing. Your call."

"Fine. Hank's."

Within eleven minutes, they were sitting at a table outside with a view of Recreation Pier, the Potomac, and the boats in the Wharf Marina.

It was hot and steamy, but Fields didn't care. After the trip to the morgue, she wanted as much fresh air as she could get. It was also nice to see the water.

Everywhere she looked there were American flags as people got ready to celebrate the Fourth of July.

By the time the waiter came to take their order, her appetite had returned. She asked for a crab cake sandwich with Old Bay french fries on the side. Carolan ordered a shrimp po'boy and subbed in hush puppies. The setting and the food beat the hell out of the Shake Shack or the Five Guys near the office. For a few moments, she could relax and almost forget that she was a law enforcement officer.

Across the table from her, Carolan scrolled through the photos she had AirDropped to his phone.

Zooming in on several of them, he stated, "Based on all the red, white, and blue ink, I think we can safely say our John Does were not foreign actors."

"So they were Americans attacking Americans? Why?"

"I haven't gotten that far yet. I've got a splitting headache. Where's that guy with my Coke?"

As if on cue, the waiter appeared carrying their beverages. Setting the glasses down, he told them their lunch would be ready soon and disappeared back inside.

Carolan pulled the paper off his straw and went after his soft drink like a man who had just stumbled out of the desert.

"God, you have no idea how much I needed that," he said, pausing as the sugar from the Coke began to work its magic.

She was about to admonish him that he needed to take better care of himself when their phones chimed in unison.

"It's a text to us from Gallo," she stated, looking down at her phone.

Sipping his Coke, with his eyes closed and his face turned up toward the sun, Carolan replied, "What does it say?"

"The Bureau has compiled all the CCTV footage from the cameras in the area, as well as from the cell phones of protesters who were recording at the time of the attack, and have produced a master video. It's encrypted in the cloud. He's given us a login and password."

"I'm not watching that before I eat. But feel free," Carolan replied.

"And you make fun of me for being grossed-out by the morgue."

"The purposeful taking of innocent life doesn't give me a queasy stomach, it pisses me off," her boss responded. "And when I get angry and try to put food on top of it, I get acid reflux, which pisses me off even more."

It pissed Fields off too, but not to the extent that she couldn't watch the video and try to learn from it, which is what she did until their lunch arrived.

Once they began eating, the conversation shifted to sports—primarily how the Washington Nationals were doing and what their hopes were for the Commanders in the upcoming season.

Fields then mentioned that friends of hers were planning simultaneous bachelor and bachelorette parties in Vegas and that the guys had picked the dates to coincide with a big MMA fight they wanted to attend. Suddenly a light bulb went off for Carolan and he waved the waiter over.

"What's going on?" Fields asked.

"That tattoo of the sword and the tree," he replied, fishing some cash out of his wallet. "I remember now where I saw it."

As the waiter approached, he handed the money to him and told him to keep the change.

Taking one last bite of his sandwich, he washed it down with what was left of his second Coke and said, "Let's go. We need to get back to the office."

CHAPTER 15

Harvath had a long list of things to do before putting his plan into action. Step number one was to let Sølvi know what was going on.

The moment he stepped out of the Carlton Group building, she began revving the Dark Horse Mustang's beefy V-8 engine.

"Good meeting?" she asked as he smiled and climbed into the passenger seat.

"*Good* is definitely not the right word, but we can talk about it over lunch. Where are we going?"

"Pisco y Nazca Ceviche Gastrobar," she said, giving him a kiss. "It's Peruvian. And don't worry, I called ahead. They don't do lutefisk."

He smiled again. "Must be fancy. You look terrific. What's with the suit?"

"I've got a briefing with the Secret Service later this afternoon. We're going to discuss the Prime Minister's detail. Then I'll head over to the Norwegian Embassy to go over everything with Ambassador Hansen and her team."

"They're keeping you busy."

Sølvi nodded. "The Prime Minister arrives tomorrow. There's lots of moving parts."

"Speaking of which," said Harvath. "An agent named Russ Gaines may sit in on your Secret Service meeting or just introduce himself while you're there. He's a former colleague of mine from my days at the White House. Don't believe anything he says about me."

Sølvi smiled back. "In that case, I'll make sure to fully interrogate him."

Putting on her blinker, she checked her mirrors and, pulling away from the curb, asked, "Why would he be sitting in or introducing himself to me?"

"I called him for a favor this morning."

"What kind of favor?"

"A favor for Ambassador Rogers. But before we even got to that subject, he wanted to talk about what happened last night. Your PM was right, you definitely have celebrity status at the Secret Service."

"You too, I would imagine," she replied.

"Unfortunately, not enough to get Ambassador Rogers the help he needs. But I did put in a good word for you. Russ assured me that the Norwegian delegation is a priority. The State Department had already reached out before I even called him."

"Every little bit helps. Thank you for speaking with him."

"Of course. You're my V-VIP. I'm always looking out for you. Now, can we talk about this restaurant we're going to? *Peruvian?*"

"You're going to love it. Trust me."

"If I don't," said Harvath, "I'm going to call Russ back with an anonymous tip that the Norwegians are transporting drugs and bomb-making materials."

"Not only will they not find drugs or bomb-making materials," she responded, "but they won't find your body either. Not that it would matter, because I have—"

"Diplomatic immunity. Yes, Russ warned me to be careful."

"I think I'm going to like your friend Russ," she responded.

"Colleague," Harvath corrected her. "*Former* colleague."

Laughing, Sølvi hit the accelerator and pinned Harvath back against his seat. Apparently, she was going to test whether diplomatic immunity could be used for traffic violations as well.

When they arrived at the restaurant, Harvath pretended to be so shook up from the ride that he needed assistance walking. Sølvi laughed yet again and told him she'd see him inside.

As soon as they were seated at the table and Harvath was handed a menu, he realized why Sølvi had chosen this spot. The selection was unbelievable. In fact, for a guy who was always incredibly decisive when it came to ordering, he didn't know what dish to pick. Everything looked fantastic.

He ended up with something called Tacu Seco de Cordero—braised lamb shank in cilantro sauce with Peruvian chili peppers and red onion salsa. It was, hands down, one of the best meals he'd ever had.

Sølvi being Sølvi, she went the full culinary adventure route and ordered a creamy Peruvian fish chowder complete with queso fresco and topped with a fried egg.

She claimed that it was delicious. Harvath told her that he would take her word for it.

They were seated at a quiet table in back and as they ate, he unpacked for her everything that had been discussed in his meeting that morning.

Sølvi listened intently. It was shocking, especially the admission of Russ Gaines as to why, regardless of the evidence, the Secret Service would not be providing protection for Ambassador Rogers. Sølvi was every bit as angry about it as Scot.

"So what are you going to do?" she had asked. That was when he had laid out his plan in its entirety.

While she wasn't crazy about the idea, she agreed with him. Rogers had no other option. This was the way it had to be done. "How can I help?"

Harvath reached out across the table and took her hand. "Remember what you said to me, right before we got married, when I had those back-to-back-to-back assignments? Afghanistan, India, and then dropping behind the Russian lines in Ukraine?"

"I told you that the only thing I cared about was for you to come back safely."

"Exactly. And now, that's what I want. Just focus on your assignment and come back safely."

"I will. As long as you promise to do the same."

"Absolutely," he replied. "And when we're done, we're going to have a wonderful Fourth of July."

Smiling, she leaned over the table and kissed him. He kissed her back.

But as they kissed, the dark clouds that used to follow them in their professional lives—the danger, the deceit, the constant fear of betrayal— seemed to mass again, a silent reminder that their return to the field might come at a cost that neither of them was willing to pay.

CHAPTER 16

Once they were in the car, it was a straight shot up Seventh Street. They made a left at the National Archives onto Pennsylvania Avenue and then a right onto Ninth, passing through security and pulling into the Bureau's underground parking garage only eight minutes after leaving the Wharf.

Considering D.C. traffic, they'd made excellent time, largely due to the fact that Carolan had rolled through more than one red light in order to get them back so quickly.

A bonus of the new basement office was that they were able to bypass the main lobby. Gallo had updated their electronic access cards so that they could enter directly from the garage. It not only saved time, but it also cut down on bumping into other agents and having to make small talk.

Back at his desk, Carolan removed a ruggedized laptop and plugged an Ethernet cable into it.

"Is that your personal computer?" Fields asked, knowing that the IT division went apeshit over personal devices being connected to the FBI's network.

"Negative," said Carolan, powering it up. "It's technically a loaner from Cyber Crimes."

"Why do you say *technically*?"

"A, because they don't know they loaned it to me. And B, because I've got no plans to give it back."

Fields smiled. "Look at all the rules you're breaking today. I'm really liking this one-foot-out-the-door Joe Carolan."

"Don't get too excited," he admonished her. "Gallo swung the notebook for me."

"Why not just requisition one from tech services? Why the subterfuge?"

"Because these are used for surfing the Dark Web. They're loaded up with a bunch of special software to prevent them from being tracked and they access the internet via a completely separate system than the Bureau uses for its day-to-day operations."

"So what's this have to do with an MMA fight in Vegas and the tattoo you saw in the morgue?"

"Almost everything the Russians have been doing to influence the United States has been online. Troll farms, bots, websites made to appear American, etc. Last summer, in a suburb of Dallas, they established an online content creation company and spent over ten million dollars in a scheme to create and distribute media to U.S. audiences with hidden Russian government messaging.

"They spent a good chunk of their cash on high-profile, online political influencers—running ads on their podcasts and paying them to amplify certain Russia-friendly messages. They also paid them to take stances on various political issues, as well as having them advocate for and against a range of political candidates. The more water they carried, the more they got paid. TikTok, Instagram, X, YouTube, you name the platform and it was awash with Russian propaganda cooked up by this group.

"Eventually, they got nailed and were shut down by the DOJ. The company's principals were arrested and brought up on federal charges— the bulk of which asserted that they had been running a covert Russian operation meant to illegally manipulate American public opinion by sowing discord and division.

"Ultimately this effort failed, but it was an evolution. Like the velociraptors in *Jurassic Park* learning how to operate the doorknobs. They had gone from trying to appear like Americans in order to spread their propaganda, to just paying Americans to do it for them.

"No matter how you look at it, it was a huge step forward. The Russians had hit upon a new strategy and were eager to capitalize on it. We, however, were on to them.

"They couldn't run the same scam again, at least not right away, because they knew we were going to be watching for it. So they needed to figure something else out. They needed to find another way to reach American 'influencers' who would not just embrace but unwittingly spread Russian propaganda.

"In this push, political influencers were out. They wanted culture-war influencers. But they didn't want typical social media influencers. They wanted culture warriors.

"And instead of casting a wide net, they decided to microtarget members of a specific, pissed-off cohort. Like the old Pentecostalist saying, their plan was to meet these people where they were and then take them to where they 'needed' to be."

"So who are these people?"

"According to the Behavioral Analysis Unit," Carolan replied, "the Russians are fishing in a pond made up largely of young men, eighteen to thirty-four, who feel completely left behind by the system. These young men see themselves not only as overlooked, but also abandoned by their government.

"The opportunities that their fathers and grandfathers enjoyed, whether it be career-wise, family-wise, you name it, no longer exist for them. They contend with drug abuse and suicide at unprecedented levels and are the first generation since World War II to not only not advance, but to be driven backward. They're angry and I can't say I blame them. In the rush to maximize shareholder value by shipping manufacturing jobs overseas, no one, least of all our politicians, stopped to wonder what would happen to all those people in all those towns when their factories were shuttered."

"I can understand," said Fields, "why the Russians would see them as fertile soil, but what's the mechanism? How are they going after them?"

"Fight clubs."

"What?"

"They're channeling their anger into underground, no-holds-barred fighting matches."

"In the United States?" Fields asked.

"They started in Russia, spread to Western Europe, and have begun to take hold here. Whatever country they've popped up in, they have a very isolationist undercurrent to them. These men train in gyms together, building their combat kills, with the belief that eventually they're going to fight in the streets to protect their way of life, which is being stolen from them. The fight-club-style matches are simply dress rehearsals for the ultimate showdown they believe is coming."

"How come I have never heard of this?"

"It's way out there on the fringe. And they purposefully keep it quiet. If you're not consuming extremist content, you'd never know."

"How'd you find out about it?" she asked.

"The face of the whole thing is a rabid Russian nationalist named Sergey Gryzlov. Internationally, he's connected with the absolute worst of the worst, particularly White supremacist mixed martial arts networks. Their tournaments and gyms serve as recruiting centers for disaffected young men who then enter in a pipeline preparing them to commit political violence. The fitness market and combat sports market help serve as on-ramps. Algorithms and old-fashioned word of mouth do the rest.

"As to how all of this ended up on my radar, the State Department flagged a visa application by a business associate of Gryzlov. It got kicked to Gallo, who kicked it to me. I'd never heard of the guy and had no clue about his international string of fascist fight clubs. I did some digging, wrote it up, and Gallo sent my report back to Foggy Bottom. They denied the visa and put Gryzlov and the associates in question, along with several others, on a no-entry list.

"In the meantime, I've been keeping an eye on the movement here. Almost all of their activity happens in the darkest corners of the Dark Web. Hence the laptop from the Cyber Crimes unit. And as far as their fights go, they're pretty brutal. I'm surprised nobody has been killed yet."

"And that's where you've seen the tattoo of the sword with a tree growing out of it?"

Carolan nodded. "Twice. Two months ago at a club in Riverside, California. Then about a month later at a club in Laredo, Texas. One guy had that tattoo on his arm, another on his chest. Once I remembered the context, it all came back."

"The Coke probably didn't hurt either."

"Probably not," her boss agreed as he pulled up video of both fights and then froze the pictures to show her.

"That's definitely the same tattoo," said Fields. "Now what?"

"We need to have a tech run all the fights through facial recognition. I want to see if any of our six dead shooters at the D.C. morgue were in attendance."

"And if they weren't, then what?"

"Then we track down any fighter with that tattoo and, if we can establish leverage, we sweat them for information. All that matters is that we keep moving."

"Because an investigation that's in motion tends to stay in motion."

Carolan nodded.

Privately, however, his gut told him they were headed straight for a brick wall. And with every hour that passed, whoever was responsible for last night's attack was drifting further and further from their grasp.

CHAPTER 17

Bill Blackwood was the epitome of aging gracefully. When his jet-black hair went white, he didn't fight it, he embraced it. He traded the vanity of contact lenses for glasses with heavy, accetate frames, which drew even more attention to the white of his hair.

Tall and distinguished, he was an impeccable dresser and had often been referred to as the Cary Grant of the United States Senate.

Like the Hollywood icon, Blackwood was not only possessed of humble origins and a deeply cleft chin, but the sixty-five-year-old senior senator from Missouri had been married and divorced four times and was currently on his fifth wife, Katherine, who spent most of her time back in St. Louis—something many D.C. insiders whispered might actually help this marriage work.

Having survived decades in Washington, Blackwood's greatest talent was his ability to sense which way the winds were blowing and to shift accordingly. His ability to function as a political weathervane was without equal. Which had made his treatment by President Mitchell so shocking.

Blackwood had picked up on the rising, pro-Mitchell tide before anyone else and had been the first United States senator to endorse him. He had campaigned tirelessly for Mitchell, warming up rally crowds from coast to coast and becoming a fierce pro-Mitchell surrogate on TV.

Every Sunday, he could be found doing a "Full Ginsburg" for Mitchell—an unofficial term named after Monica Lewinsky's lawyer for someone who makes the rounds on all five major Sunday talk shows in a single day.

Blackwood had pulled out all the stops for Mitchell, but he hadn't done it out of the goodness of his heart. He had done it because he wanted something in return—a seat at the table.

Having held senior positions on the Senate Foreign Relations Committee, the Senate Select Committee on Intelligence, and the Senate Appropriations Committee, Blackwood fully expected to be appointed secretary of state. That appointment, however, never came. Mitchell offered it to someone else—someone who had committed far less time, energy, and personal capital to getting him elected.

In the days after the general election, Blackwood worked the phones, sent emails, and dispatched emissaries to lobby on his behalf. Surely there had to be a position in the new administration worthy of his stature.

But as cabinet positions and plum ambassadorships continued to be doled out to others and his name faded in the press, the truth began to dawn. Mitchell had used him.

Soon enough, Blackwood's disbelief shifted to anger, but he kept it in check, because in addition to being a D.C. weathervane, there was another talent that had served the senior senator from Missouri well—knowing how, and when, to get even. Nobody was better at shivving a political opponent than Bill Blackwood.

The key was knowing when to take your shot. As the saying went, if you come for the king, you'd best not miss. Blackwood had no intention of missing.

Just behind the Supreme Court, at the corner of East Capitol Street and Third, Blackwood turned left and walked halfway up the leafy block.

At a gray town house he swung open a small wrought-iron gate and followed a flagstone path to a short set of steps leading down to a door for the garden apartment.

Taking out his AirPods and returning them to their case, he pressed the specially modified doorbell, which would trigger a light to come on at the front desk.

When the lock released with a distinct *click*, he pushed the door open and stepped inside. The rush of cool air-conditioning felt good against his skin.

The receptionist pointed to the ON AIR sign and placed her index finger against her pursed lips. Blackwood nodded and closed the door gently behind him.

Through the large panes of glass that surrounded the broadcast booth, the man he had come to meet was wrapping up his show.

With a blazing American flag of red, white, and blue neon lit up behind him, radio host and podcaster Chuck Coughlin leaned into his microphone. He was a sweaty, overweight, middle-aged man with highlights in his receding hair.

Via overhead speakers in the reception area, Blackwood could hear everything.

"Let me make this perfectly clear for you," Coughlin said as he stared directly into the camera and paused for dramatic effect. "We were told that James Mitchell would be the man to stand up to the system. We were promised that he'd give us the revolution we've all been waiting for. The only thing *we* had to do was vote for him. Once he won the election, things were going to change.

"Well, since he's been in the White House, something has definitely changed—and that something is James Mitchell. He's gone soft, folks. He campaigned on fighting corruption and standing up for the people. And what do we have now? An attack, on Mitchell's very own supporters, right outside the Vice President's Residence.

"And let me ask you something. Where was the Secret Service while all this was happening? Where was the Secret Service while decent, hardworking Americans were being gunned down right outside the gates?

"If you listen to Mitchell's secretary of propaganda—excuse me, I mean *press secretary*, the Secret Service was following its mission. It was protecting the Vice President's family and his residence.

"But let me ask you something. They couldn't spare a single agent? In the worst attack on American soil we've seen in God knows how long, they couldn't have rolled one of their armored vehicles onto the street and taken the attackers out?

"It makes you wonder. What was Mitchell doing while all of this was unfolding? I'll tell you what he was doing. He was cowering in the White House, worried that the attackers were coming for him next.

"All of us were told that Mitchell had steel in his spine. That when the moment came and America was tested, he would rise and meet that test. Well, I'm here to tell you, ladies and gentlemen, he failed. And because of that failure, Americans are dead. Our fellow countrymen and women, who were peacefully redressing their grievances and practicing their First Amendment rights, were slaughtered—all because President James Mitchell didn't have the courage to act when his supporters, when his fellow American citizens, needed him.

"I don't know what more I can say. It is a dark, dark day for our country. We're rudderless morally and we're leaderless politically. America needs a miracle, but miracles seem to be in short supply these days. It's going to take action. Action from all of us. I just hope we have the willpower, the patriotic fortitude, to do what needs to be done.

"And that's going to do it for us today, folks. Another three hours of Bunker Radio in the can. I'll see you right back here tomorrow. Until then, remember—when you're under attack, Chuck Coughlin has your back. And we are all, *definitely*, under attack. Stay safe, America."

He kept his gaze steady, focused right into the lens until his producer stated, "And we're clear. Great job, CC."

When the red light on the camera went off, Coughlin pointed at the small blender on his desk filled with green juice and growled, "Get that crap the hell out of here. Just the smell of it makes me want to puke."

The producer walked into the booth, stuck his nose over the top of the blender and took a whiff. "Doesn't smell too bad to me. In fact, you know what I think it smells like?"

"No matter how I answer that, you're still going to tell me, aren't you?" replied the host as he gathered up the papers on his desk.

"It smells like money."

"And it *tastes* like dog shit. I don't know how I let you talk me into actually drinking that stuff on camera."

"Because by drinking it on-air, the company agreed to pay us even more. It's good for our bottom line."

Coughlin was about to push back when he noticed Blackwood out in the lobby.

"How long has the senator been here?" he asked.

The producer glanced over his shoulder. "Just arrived. Should I send him in?"

"I've got to take a piss. You can put him in my office."

"You got it, CC."

The producer showed Blackwood to the rear of the basement space where Coughlin's office was.

Despite air fresheners plugged into almost every outlet, the place smelled dank and musty with a strong top layer of cigar smoke. Blackwood never could figure out what the appeal for Coughlin was other than being able to live right upstairs.

The producer offered to bring Blackwood a water, and told him to make himself comfortable.

Driven by his love of political scandals and conspiracy theories, Coughlin easily had one of the wildest and most unique offices in D.C. Grabbing a seat, Blackwood sat down and took it all in.

There were reel-to-reel Watergate-era tapes allegedly from Nixon's tape recorder, along with a vintage press pass from the time. Near a collection of rebel memorabilia from the Iran-Contra scandal was a framed copy of the 1964 Warren Commission Report. A shadow box showcased a 2000 voting ballot, complete with a "hanging chad." Personal items supposedly belonging to Marilyn Monroe sat side by side with intelligence reports from the failed 1961 Bay of Pigs invasion. Objects supposedly connected to the assassinations of Martin Luther King Jr. and Robert F. Kennedy Sr. were juxtaposed with pieces of "alien metal" allegedly taken from Area 51. Magazine covers and newspaper articles covered every inch of wall space, while political posters covered the ceiling.

Chuck Coughlin was an eccentric piece of work. He was also an incredibly skilled propagandist. Using him to foment Mitchell's base had been an inspired choice. He not only understood them, he was one of them himself. Or at least he had been. Until Mitchell "went soft."

"Senator Blackwood," said Coughlin as he entered the office and walked over to shake his guest's hand. "It's always good to see you."

"You too, Chuck. Congrats on a real barnburner of a show today. You hit Mitchell hard, dead center."

"That was the plan, right?"

"Correct," Blackwood replied. "It was also the plan to talk up the Vice President."

"Then Vice President Cates is going to have to do more than walk out of his house and leave flowers at the site. What kind of a split screen is that? Mitchell is at the hospital, visiting the survivors, and Cates is standing at a fence surrounded by crime-scene tape. Which one looks more like a leader to you?"

Blackwood couldn't argue. "You're probably right."

"I'm definitely right," replied Coughlin. "Mitchell's PR people are good. They know what they're doing. Cates and his team need to be better."

"What should he do?"

"He needs to get out ahead of Mitchell. He needs to show that he's not only a capable leader, but a better leader."

"Okay," said Blackwood, "but in what world does Mitchell allow his vice president to upstage and outshine him?"

"Politics," said Coughlin, "like anything else in life, is all about timing."

"Meaning?"

"*Meaning* the next time something breaks, make sure Vice President Cates just so happens to be standing in front of a mountain of microphones. That'll be his moment. Whether he pulls the sword from the stone or not is up to him. But if he does, we'll be able to send his polling through the roof."

Once again, Blackwood couldn't argue. He knew the man was right.

He also knew that the perfect opportunity, the next big breaking-news event, was just around the corner.

The only question was whether his coconspirators would agree.

CHAPTER 18

After lunch, Harvath rode back into D.C. with Sølvi and caught the Metro Yellow Line out to Alexandria, Virginia. She had offered to drive him all the way back to the house, but traffic was building and he didn't want her to be late for her meeting. It was easy enough for him to grab an Uber to Mount Vernon for the final leg and then hoof it through the woods from there.

Luckily, Nicholas was handling his transport going forward. All he would have to focus on once he got home was pulling his gear together.

When he arrived at the house, he headed straight for his study and powered up his computer. Nicholas had promised to have satellite imagery waiting for him.

Opening the encrypted email, Harvath studied the photos. None of them contained good news. If anything, his plan was going to be even more difficult to pull off.

He sent the imagery to his phone, logged out of his account, and shut down his computer. Now the real hard work was going to start. Changing clothes, he headed outside.

At the property's small stone church, he produced a set of keys, opened one of the heavy front doors, and stepped inside. With its thick walls and heavy slate roof, all the sounds from outside—the birds, a leaf blower on some neighbor's property, the boats out on the Potomac—disappeared and he was instantly enveloped by the quiet and the calm.

Beneath the baptismal font was a narrow stone staircase, which led to a large security door.

Taking his keys back out, he unlocked the door and flipped on the lights, illuminating a modest crypt.

The small stone chamber had once been used by the Office of Naval Intelligence to store documents. When they moved to a new facility, they had left behind rows of shelving and a large, center worktable. By upgrading its temperature and humidity systems, Harvath had turned the space into a pretty decent gun room.

As a SEAL, it had been drilled into him to take pristine care of his equipment. No matter how tired or how many things he had to do upon returning from an assignment, he always properly cleaned and oiled his gear before putting it away. Other than the cosmetic wear and tear things normally got in the field, every item was in as good a shape as the day he got them.

Looking around the room, his first question was, how was he going to transport everything for tonight? Could he get it all into a backpack? Or would he need a duffle bag? He decided to lay all of it out on the table and go from there.

The number one piece of gear he reached for was his night-vision goggles. Removing them from their case, he checked them for cracks, scratches, or any other sort of damage before inserting fresh batteries.

Killing the lights, he powered them up and made sure they were functioning properly. They were in great shape.

Next up, he needed to select his primary weapon. It had to be something maneuverable that he could use at close range with a suppressor. Most of all, it needed to pack a punch.

Before he had even powered his night-vision goggles down and had turned the lights back on, he knew the weapon he was going to reach for.

The SIG Rattler, chambered for the 300 Blackout round, was a fantastic, ultracompact, short-barreled rifle. Not only that, but it had terrific stopping power and could go neck and neck with, if not beat, the 5.56 round out to about 150 to 200 yards. Harvath, however, doubted he was going to have to engage anything at that range. What's more, he was going to be using a quieter, subsonic version of the round.

It was smaller and lighter than the H&K MP5A3 he'd used both in and out of the SEALs. He had outfitted his Rattler with a night-vision-compatible Aimpoint Micro T-2 optic and a CGS Hyperion K suppressor made from grade-5 titanium.

As with his night-vision goggles, he thoroughly checked his weapon and its optic, making sure everything was in tip-top shape.

A big believer in "you can never bring too much ammo," he next loaded six thirty-round Magpul magazines, popped them in the front pouches of his plate carrier, and then selected a sidearm.

The 9mm G19X was Glock's first "Crossover" pistol. It comprised a full-sized G17 frame and a compact G19 slide. He would be running five nineteen-round magazines—one in his gun, plus a round in the chamber, and four more mags on his belt.

In addition to a double-edged Benchmade SOCP dagger, he grabbed a handful of plastic restraints, a Streamlight PROTAC flashlight, a trauma kit, a short roll of duct tape, an additional tourniquet, and a multitool.

Once everything was laid out on the table, he added a tactical helmet, along with a few more items, and then stood back.

Looking over his gear, he tried to envision how things might go sideways and, if they did, what he would want to have in that case. Unfortunately, frag grenades and a Spooky gunship overhead were not options. He was limited to what he had in his personal armory.

Judging by what he had selected, he was confident he could handle pretty much anything that popped up. Beyond that, he would adapt and overcome. That was how he had been trained.

Taking out his phone, he opened his flight-tracker app and checked the status of the inbound aircraft he and Nicholas had decided to use as their Trojan horse. So far, it was right on time.

With his backpack being too small and the duffle bag looking like a sure way to scratch, dent, and bang up all his equipment, he opted for an old sticker-covered Yeti cooler and foam inserts from a couple of his long gun cases, which he trimmed with a box cutter. It wasn't the most elegant solution, but it would do the job.

Packing everything as tight as he could, he locked up the gun room and carried the cooler back to the house.

By the time he had pulled together the rest of his gear and had tossed a few things into an overnight bag, Nicholas's people had arrived to drop off a car for him.

The idea was to give him something that wasn't too flashy—an older vehicle that would blend in and not cause him to stand out.

Stepping outside, he saw a piece of junk—a dark blue 2010 Chevy Malibu with dented rims and a scratch down the right rear quarter panel.

Adding insult to injury, it wasn't even a V-6. It was a four-banger.

CHAPTER 19

Harvath's preference for something a little more robust, perhaps a Toyota Land Cruiser or even a Ford Explorer notwithstanding, the Malibu would get him from point A to point B, which was all that mattered right now.

Thanking Nicholas's guys, he accepted the keys and, after making sure the care package Nicholas had promised had been placed in the trunk, went back into the house to finish getting ready.

In the background, he had the TV tuned to a cable news station and shared a panelist's surprise that none of the attackers outside the Vice President's Residence had been identified. He found it hard to believe that anyone capable of that kind of violence didn't have a police rap sheet a mile along.

His second thought was even more unsettling. Based on the tactical proficiency the attackers had shown, how had none of them surfaced as having served in the military? He prayed that wouldn't end up being the case.

As volatile as things felt at the moment, the idea of ex-service members attacking American citizens turned his stomach. Political opinions might burn pretty hot, but the United States wasn't a nation where it was okay to settle differences with violence. And it most definitely wasn't a nation where those who had sworn to protect it should ever contemplate taking up arms against their fellow countrymen and women. The thought of any of that being possible chilled him to the core.

Shaking it off, he tried to focus on what was at hand. There were multiple, small details that needed to be top of mind. Screwing up just one of them could put the whole evening, along with Ambassador Rogers's life, in jeopardy.

After staging his gear near the front door, he checked his flight-tracker app one more time. The plane must have been getting pushed by a good tailwind. It was now set to arrive several minutes early.

Pouring a coffee to go, he also grabbed a cold bottle of water from the fridge and then carried everything out to the car.

Once the car was packed, he texted Nicholas that he was en route, fired up the Malibu, and got on the road.

The car had a navigation system, but he had no idea how reliable it was, nor did he want to stuff it with digital breadcrumbs. Instead he used the app on his phone that would help route him around any D.C. traffic and automatically delete his trip once he arrived. Based on current conditions, it looked like the George Washington Memorial Parkway was once again his fastest route, just like yesterday when he and Sølvi had driven up to the Norwegian Embassy.

It was hard to process how much had happened in just under twenty-four hours. Hopefully they had both already logged their quota of excitement. Nothing would make him happier than to find out Rogers was in no danger and to have Sølvi's assignment be mind-numbingly dull. Unfortunately, he had a bad feeling that neither of those things was going to turn out to be true.

Cranking up the AC, he was greeted with a blast of hot air. He waited for it to cool, but it didn't. Cranking it back down, he opened the windows and basked in the thick, D.C. humidity. It was a bit ironic that after Rogers had saved him from the frozen wastes of Russia, he was now coming to his aid amid the oppressive summer heat of the nation's capital. As he continued to drive, he regretted not having bombarded his coffee with ice.

By the time he reached Daingerfield Island, he was moving fast enough that the wind coming through the windows was able to cool him off, if only a little bit.

At the sign for Reagan National Airport, he exited the parkway and headed for the long-term economy lot.

He found Rogers's Audi right where the Ambassador had said he'd left it and then kept on driving. Two aisles over, with a good view of the man's car, he pulled into a space and texted Nicholas to let him know that he had arrived. He received two thumbs-up in response.

Eight minutes later, he saw the customer assistance truck pull up and Nicholas's technician, dressed in a mechanic's uniform, climb out.

Being careful to make sure no one was watching, the technician took out an under-vehicle inspection mirror and went to work.

After checking the entirety of the undercarriage, as well as the wheel wells, he removed the key fob from where Rogers had left it behind the gas-cap cover and checked the trunk, under the seats, and throughout the engine compartment.

Satisfied that there were no explosives, he closed the car back up, returned the key to its hiding place, got back in his truck, and left.

Less than a minute later, Harvath received a text from Nicholas giving him the all-clear. Rolling up his windows, he turned off his ignition and used his untucked shirt to dry the sweat off the butt of the Glock sitting in his inside-the-waistband holster. Getting out of the car, he walked back to the trunk and opened it up.

One of the items Nicholas had included in his care package was the clone he had asked for of Rogers's phone. Tucking it in his pocket, he grabbed his overnight bag, closed the trunk, and headed for the shuttle bus stop.

When the mercifully air-conditioned bus eventually arrived, he hopped on board and rode it to the terminal. But when he got there, instead of walking inside, he headed for the garage.

Nicholas's blacked-out van was in an accessible parking spot on the second floor. Harvath rapped on the side door and Nicholas hit a button, sliding it open. Inside, Nicholas was joined by Argos, Draco, and Ambassador Rogers. Harvath climbed in and Nicholas hit the button again, closing the door behind him.

"Ready to go to work?" he asked the Ambassador, as he sat down in one of the handsewn leather captain's chairs and gave the dogs a little attention. Like the shuttle bus, Nicholas had the AC blowing full blast and it felt terrific.

"Meaning, am I ready to be the bait?" Rogers answered, reprising his earlier concern over the operation. "I guess so."

"You're going to be fine," Harvath replied as he checked his flight-tracker app again. "I'll be with you the entire time."

Once they had decided to help Rogers, one of the first things Harvath had asked Nicholas to do was to kill the Ambassador's old phone. If he was being hunted, the last thing they wanted was a hit team to show up at some sweet family's home in Colorado—all because Rogers had slipped his phone into grandma's suitcase.

After deciding which return flight they would use as their Trojan horse, Nicholas waited until an hour before its departure and then activated a phantom signal at Denver International. The goal was to make it look like Rogers had popped back onto the grid and was on the move. When the D.C.-bound flight took off, Nicholas made it appear as if the phone had been switched into airplane mode and was using the in-flight Wi-Fi.

Whether the people who were after the Ambassador had the tools and were sophisticated enough to put it together didn't matter to Harvath. His job was merely to scent the trail.

"Do you actually think they'd send somebody after me here? To the airport?"

"That's what I want to find out," said Harvath, glancing up from his phone. "It looks like the flight from Denver just landed. We're going to walk over to Terminal One and turn on the clone we made of your phone. Do you like Dunkin' Donuts?"

"Sure," he replied.

"There's a Dunkin' before the security checkpoint. Get a coffee. Get a bear claw. Whatever you want. We just need to give your signal long enough to populate. Then you're going to walk outside and wait for the shuttle bus to the economy lot. When it comes, you get on. Just like we discussed. Understood?"

The Ambassador nodded.

"Good. Let's get going."

Nicholas opened the door and Harvath and the Ambassador got out.

Per Harvath's instructions, Rogers put on the baseball cap and sunglasses, and had a small backpack slung over one shoulder. It was

important that he look like a man who was trying to remain incognito as
he moved through the airport. If he looked like bait, their fishing expe-
dition would be over before it even started.

Carrying his overnight bag and putting on his own sunglasses, Harvath rode down in the elevator with Rogers and then let him walk ahead.
It wasn't exactly "close" protection, but it was the best Harvath could do
given their situation.

When Rogers entered Terminal One, he turned on the phone he
had been given and then headed for Dunkin'. There, having already had
plenty of coffee, he ordered an iced tea.

Harvath hung back, watching to see if the Ambassador was being followed. So far, he didn't notice anyone on his tail.

As soon as Rogers had his drink, they moved through the baggage
claim area and, using different doors, exited the terminal.

They walked to the shuttle bus pickup, where Harvath stood close,
but not too close, to the Ambassador. While Rogers pretended to scroll on
his phone, Harvath kept his head on a discreet swivel. Neither man ac-
knowledged the other.

By the time they boarded the bus to the economy lot, it was standing
room only. Crowds were great to get lost in, but that could be a two-way
street. A skilled assassin could quietly attack and disappear at the next stop
before anyone knew what had happened. Harvath made sure to stay close
to Rogers and he kept his eyes wide-open.

Arriving at the economy lot, they debussed together and walked separately to their vehicles. All the while, Harvath kept his eyes peeled for
threats. This part—moving through the parking lot, with its practically
limitless possibility for ambush—was one of the steps in the plan that had
concerned him the most.

He moved slowly, allowing the Ambassador to get to his car first. If he
needed to spring into action, he didn't want to have to leap out of his car
to do so. He much preferred to already be on his feet and able to get his
gun quickly into the fight.

Thankfully, however, that hadn't proved necessary. Rogers made it
back to his vehicle, retrieved his key fob, and fired up his Audi. As soon as
Harvath saw him backing out of his spot, he picked up his pace.

Unlocking the Malibu, he tossed his bag on the back seat and climbed behind the wheel. Rogers had been told to go slow, even stopping and pretending he was searching for his ticket, until he saw Harvath's vehicle closing in.

Exiting the economy lot, Harvath allowed Rogers to get a couple of car lengths ahead. He didn't need to be right on his bumper. All that mattered was that he be able to spot any potential tails. So far, so good.

And as an additional set of eyes, several car lengths farther behind, Nicholas followed in his blacked-out van.

The drive to McLean was clogged with afternoon traffic, and as much as it sucked for Harvath to do it without AC, he knew that the next leg was going to be even worse.

When they arrived at their destination—an indoor public parking garage for an office building adjacent to the Tysons Corner mall—Harvath followed Rogers inside while Nicholas pulled into the open-air lot across the street and kept an eye on the entrance.

Though not eager to screw around, Harvath had agreed to one request from Rogers. If they were going to use an enclosed garage to ditch Harvath's vehicle, it might as well be one attached to a good restaurant.

The Capital Grille's curbside pickup service had the Ambassador's order ready to go the minute they pulled in. All he'd had to do was notify them that he'd arrived. He was not only a regular, but also a good tipper. They had no problem bringing it to the garage versus handing it to him at the front door.

The Ambassador put the bags on the passenger seat as Harvath loaded his gear as efficiently as he could in the trunk.

He had already mapped the trip to the Ambassador's house and knew how long, even in lousy traffic, it should take.

Unscrewing his water bottle, he took a long swallow and climbed into the trunk. As Rogers came around to close the lid, Harvath reminded him, "Right home. No stops. I don't want to spend a second longer back here than I have to."

"Copy that," the Ambassador said, carefully lowering the lid and pressing down on it to make sure that it was closed.

Within seconds he had started the car, backed out of the space, and was heading for the exit. Harvath had no idea if they were being followed. In addition to not finding any explosives in the car, Nicholas's tech hadn't found any tracking devices either.

The thinking behind leaving the cloned cell phone where Rogers could retrieve it was that if anyone was locked on to his signal, they would know that he had "returned" to D.C. and was on the move. After a brief stop at one of his favorite restaurants, he was now on his way home.

And, if they were dumb enough to come after him at the house, Harvath was going to make sure it was one of the last things they ever did. All he had to do was survive the car ride.

CHAPTER 20

A mbassador Rogers's house was on a heavily wooded, two-and-a-half-acre parcel backing up to the Potomac River. It was an absolutely gorgeous property. There was a reason they called this part of McLean the Gold Coast. It was also going to be a nightmare to defend.

From the moment Harvath had seen Nicholas's satellite imagery, he knew he was going to have his work cut out for him.

The trees were enormous, with leafy branches almost to the ground. You could practically hide half a platoon behind each one. And they came all the way up to the house.

There were bushes, hedges, and grasses so thick and tall they could swallow up an entire elementary school.

The house itself was a modern two-story, painted white, with a metal roof and black accents. From its sophisticated exterior lighting to the perfectly manicured grass between the pavers, it was obvious that Rogers was a detail guy. Harvath had only wished that he'd had that same eye when it came to the role landscaping played in a home's security.

Harvath was actually surprised that back when he was the National Security Advisor and had an active Secret Service detail, they hadn't gotten him to trim all the foliage back. It was, in his opinion, the Ambassador's biggest Achilles' heel.

His thoughts were suddenly interrupted as he felt Rogers's Audi slow and then turn off the main road onto gravel.

They had arrived at the house and were now crunching down his drive-way. Harvath was baking inside the trunk and couldn't wait to get out.

Using his remote, the Ambassador opened the garage door and pulled into the first bay. Turning off his ignition, he gathered up the bags of to-go food from the Capital Grille, got out of his car, and walked over to the door that led into the house.

There, he pushed one of the three buttons mounted on the wall and closed the garage door. As soon as the overhead lift fell silent, he set down the food and returned to the Audi to help Harvath out of the trunk.

Popping the lid, he looked down and asked, "Still alive?"

"Barely," joked Harvath, who was slick with sweat. Accepting Rogers's hand, he climbed out.

As he did, the door from the house opened, revealing a large man with a short-barreled shotgun.

"You're out of chocolate ice cream," he said.

Harvath shook his head. "Ambassador Rogers, I'd like to introduce you to Mike Haney. Mike, meet the Ambassador."

The ex–Force Recon Marine from Marin County, California, stepped into the garage and shook the man's hand. "You're also out of San Pellegrino."

Rogers smiled. "I'll add it on the grocery list."

"No trouble finding the place?" Harvath asked, arching his back as he tried to get the kinks out of his muscles before unloading the trunk.

Haney shook his head. "This place is basically in the CIA's backyard. The hardest part was deciding where to park."

"You guys didn't leave your cars at Langley, did you?" Harvath asked, concerned.

"What are we, newbs? Of course not. Bob has a buddy, retired Agency guy like him, who lives out this way. We parked at his place and he dropped us about two miles downriver. We hiked the rest of the way in. But don't tell Nicholas that. I'm still 'recuperating,'" he said, using his fingers to make air quotes.

"Don't worry. I'm not going to tell him a thing. He made it quite clear that I wasn't allowed to involve you in this."

"Ever since the baby came, he's no fun anymore."

It was a funny remark and Harvath chuckled. Things had indeed changed for Nicholas, but that was exactly what was supposed to happen when you became a parent. Priorities shift and responsibilities are reexamined. Nicholas had all but stepped away from fieldwork. The risks, in light of now having a baby, simply weren't worth it.

Harvath understood the man's reasoning all too well. Marrying Sølvi had caused him to look at everything with a fresh set of eyes. He had never thought he'd come out of the field. Or more succinctly put, he didn't think he'd be coming out this soon. He thought he'd be knee-deep in hand-grenade pins for several years yet to come. But love had a way of making you reevaluate your life.

"Speaking of Bob," said Harvath, getting back to business. "Where is he?"

"In the den. On watch."

Nodding at Rogers, Harvath said, "Come on. He'll be glad to see you."

Inside the elegant house, all the window treatments had been drawn. They stopped in the sleek kitchen, where Rogers placed the food from Capital Grille into a warming drawer and turned it on. Then they headed to the study.

Bob McGee, the most recent director of the CIA, was sitting on a leather couch watching the property's security camera feeds. When he heard Harvath and Rogers enter the room, he rose to greet them, a big 1911 pistol on his hip.

"Mr. Ambassador," he said warmly, extending his hand.

"Mr. Director," Rogers replied, receiving it. "It's good to see you, Bob."

"You too, Brendan. And I hope you don't mind. As soon as we got here, we made ourselves at home."

"Not at all. I'm just very thankful for your help."

"So am I," said Harvath as he shook McGee's hand. "All quiet?"

The ex–CIA director nodded toward the large flat-screen TV mounted in the center of a wall of bookshelves. "There's one squirrel that keeps going for the bird feeder, but other than that, nothing."

"For the moment then, no news is good news."

McGee nodded as Rogers asked, "What have you been up to? Someone said you'd moved out to the Eastern Shore."

The man was tall like Haney, but was in his early sixties, had salt-and-pepper hair and a thick, Wyatt Earp–style mustache. Tugging on the corner of it, he winked at Rogers and said, "That's top secret."

The Ambassador smiled. "You didn't opt for a security detail either. The way I hear it, you came in on your last day, said your goodbyes, and rode off into the sunset. Is that right?"

"There may have been a sheet cake, a few bottles of very expensive bourbon, and some cigars that may have gone missing from the presidential palace in Havana, but I can neither confirm nor deny."

"I'm sorry I missed that party."

"That's not your fault," said McGee. "In true National Security Advisor tradition, you handed over the keys and were the last one to leave the White House on Inauguration Day. You're a good man, Brendan. A good American."

"It was my choice not to have a detail. I figure I can handle myself if it comes down to it. But the new crew at 1600 Penn not giving you one is bullshit. I'm sorry to say it."

Rogers put up his hands. "Obviously, I agree. It's not how we would have done things. It's just different."

"It's fucked-up is what it is," said McGee.

"That too."

Harvath was about to say something when Haney poked his head in and said, "Mr. Ambassador, you're also out of microwave popcorn."

"Top shelf, back of the pantry," Rogers responded. "There should be a whole other box in there."

Haney flashed him the thumbs-up and disappeared.

"If nobody minds," said Harvath. "I'd like to get cleaned up real quick. Is there a shower I can use?"

"Top of the stairs, second door on the left. That guest room is all yours," the Ambassador responded. "Help yourself to anything you need."

Harvath thanked him, and after unloading his gear from the car and bringing it inside, he grabbed a large bottle of water from the fridge and began slugging it down as he headed upstairs. The bottle was empty before he even got in the shower.

He made it a super quick one and threw the temperature selector all the way cold at the end, forcing himself to stand under the icy spray for as long as he could. Climbing out, he toweled off, got dressed in fresh clothes, and headed back downstairs.

There had been a changing of the guard since he'd gone. Haney, bowl of popcorn next to him on the couch, had taken over watching the security cameras while McGee and the Ambassador were in the kitchen catching up. With Rogers having served as the Hostage Czar and the National Security Advisor, they had quite a bit of history together. They had also both worked tirelessly to get Harvath back when he had been taken by the Russians.

"So what's the plan, boss?" McGee asked as Harvath entered the kitchen.

"First, I'd like to run to Home Depot and pick up a chain saw to prune back a few of the trees outside."

"No way," said the Ambassador, fully aware that Harvath was pulling his leg. "If we have to start cutting down trees, then the bad guys have already won."

"In all seriousness," Harvath replied, "you do realize that having all that growth right up against the house is a legit security concern."

Rogers nodded. "I had this conversation with the Secret Service and I'll tell you what I told them. Call me John Muir, but many of these trees were here before this country was even founded. Their history goes back further than ours. I'm not touching a single one of them."

"Understood," said Harvath, though if their situations were reversed, he would have clear-cut the entire lot and simply donated the trees to some local historical society that wanted them. In his book, there was nothing that trumped security.

Pulling a stack of plates out, the Ambassador set them on the counter and replied, "Thank you."

"If anything's going to happen, I don't think it'll happen until after dark," Harvath continued. "We've got the existing camera system, which we'll keep monitoring and I've brought along a few other items that Carlton Group was kind enough to provide, which I want to get prepped and set up. In the meantime, I meant to ask, do you ever leave your car outside overnight, or do you always put it away in the garage?"

"Depends on the weather. The Secret Service used to insist that it always be put away, but since then, I leave it outside about fifty percent of the time. Why?"

"More bait. If anyone comes sniffing around and they see that the lights are on and your car is parked outside, that only helps."

"Do you want me to move it?"

Harvath nodded. "Bob can position himself at the far corner of the garage and I'll be at the front door."

"I'll let Mike know."

As soon as McGee gave Haney the heads-up, they took their positions and covered Rogers as he repositioned his car.

Once he had reentered the garage and closed the door, they regrouped in the kitchen.

"Easy peasy," said the ex–CIA director, patting the Ambassador on the back. "I know that none of this is fun, but you're doing a great job."

"Are you worried?"

"About what?"

"The Iranians," said Rogers. "You helped develop the intelligence for the Soleimani hit. If they're out there, picking us off one by one, it's only a matter of time before they get to you."

"I'm probably on a lot of lists," McGee admitted. "But to answer your question, I take this very seriously. That's why Mike and I spent over two hours in the woods outside your house this afternoon making sure nobody was out there conducting surveillance or sitting in a hide site with a high-powered rifle. It's also why, once Harvath sent us the door and alarm codes you gave him, we searched every millimeter of your home—checking for intruders, explosives, and anything that could do you harm."

"Thank you for that."

"It's the right thing to do. You don't have to thank me. You represented this country with courage, with honor, and with dignity. This is the least any of us can do. And until we have a full picture of what's going on, we're treating this as a legitimate threat and will take every precaution we can to keep you safe."

Rogers went to say thank you again, but McGee held up his hand to stop him. It wasn't necessary. He had meant what he said.

Harvath didn't have anything to add. He owed the Ambassador his life. They would stay for as long as he needed them. It was, as McGee said, the right thing to do.

Grabbing another bottle of water, Harvath decided to check in on Haney.

The two hadn't talked, at least not face-to-face, in a while. It had been over six months since Mike had been shot and he still hadn't been cleared for field work. That weighed on Harvath. Even their teammate Kenneth Johnson, who had been shot in the same gunfight in Paris and had suffered what appeared a far more serious injury, had been returned to full service status.

Walking across the kitchen to the den, he knocked on the doorframe.

"Go away," said Haney, his eyes fixed on the security camera feeds. "I'm taking a nap."

Harvath grinned and walked into the den. "Any updates?"

"All quiet on the western front. And the southern, and the northern, and the eastern."

"Need anything?"

"Yeah. A suitcase full of nonsequential fifty- and hundred-dollar bills."

Harvath smiled again. "I'll have Ambassador Rogers add it to the list. How's the arm?"

"Only hurts when I laugh."

"So don't laugh."

"Easy for you to say," Haney replied. "You're married."

"So are you," he said, grinning as he steered the conversation back. "How's rehab going?"

"They tell me I need to adjust my expectations."

Harvath braced himself. "How so?"

"Apparently, my dreams of playing violin for the Berlin Philharmonic are 'unrealistic.'"

Harvath shook his head. "Are they aware that you don't even play the violin?"

"Yet," Haney admonished him. "I don't play the violin *yet*."

"Mike—"

"Can you believe those rehab people?" he continued. "Who signs up for a job where you come in every day just to crush other people's dreams? It's not right. I'm telling you."

Harvath was well-versed in using humor to derail unwanted conversations. He was just about to pin his friend down and have a serious conversation about his injury when the camera feeds flickered and the TV went blank.

As soon as they disappeared, the feeds all came back online.

"What just happened?" asked Harvath.

"I have no idea," said Haney as he picked up the tablet used to run the security system and cycled through each feed individually. "Power surge? Or some other kind of glitch?"

Harvath doubted it and, by the look on Haney's face, he doubted it as well. Someone was probing their defenses.

CHAPTER 21

What's this?" Carolan asked as he and Fields got in the car and she handed him an envelope.

"It's a request for hazardous duty pay. According to HR, it needs to be signed by an immediate supervisor."

"We're going to Baltimore, for crying out loud," he said, handing it back to her. "Not Baghdad."

"Have you been to Baltimore lately?"

"I try not to."

"Exactly my point," she replied, pulling the request out of the envelope and grabbing a pen from the glove box.

"Now what are you doing?"

"Not your problem."

Backing out of his space, Carolan paused and looked down. "You're forging my name. On a government document."

"If I'm going to die, I want to be properly compensated."

"First, you're not going to die. And second, if you're dead, 'you' can't be compensated."

"It's for my mom. She's my beneficiary. It'd be a little something extra to ease her pain."

"No," said Carolan, laying down the law. "End of discussion."

"Fine," Fields replied, tearing up the document. "You know it's terrible the way you hate on old people."

"*Old people?* Your mom had you at seventeen. She's younger than me."

"Whatever."

"Can we just focus please?"

"Sure," said Fields. "We've got nothing but bumper-to-bumper rush-hour traffic to do just that."

"Listen, we're lucky we got those videos processed through facial recognition as quickly as we did. Practically every Bureau resource has been tied up working on last night's attack."

She knew he was right. The FBI was under massive pressure to make a break in the case. One of the reasons it was so hard to get Dark Web fight-club videos processed right away was that the facial-recognition systems were being used to sort through all the recent protest footage the Bureau had secured. The thought being that the attackers might have attended prior protests to conduct pre-attack surveillance. And while it had taken some arm-twisting, Gallo had eventually gotten the Texas and California videos into the cue.

None of the men in the morgue had shown up in either. As for the fighters with the sword-and-tree tattoos, one was from Texas and the other was from California. Neither of the men had a criminal record nor any ties to the D.C. area.

There was, however, a face in the crowd that appeared in both videos. It belonged to Lucas Weber—a twice-convicted felon who managed a mixed martial arts gym in one of the seedier neighborhoods of southwest Baltimore.

Weber was a White supremacist who had done time for kidnapping, armed robbery, assault with a deadly weapon, and attempted murder. He was definitely no altar boy.

"Help me understand your rationale here," said Fields. "This guy Weber is going to want to help us out because what? He's secretly pro–law enforcement?"

Carolan smiled as he exited the FBI garage and headed south for Interstate 395. "He's not going to want to help us out at all. At least not at first."

"So how do you plan to change his mind?"

"That'll be a piece of cake. Guess who didn't get permission from his parole officer for the trip to Texas or the trip to California?"

Fields smiled right back. "He's going to hate your guts when you tell him that."

"He's going to hate it even more because it isn't going to come from me. You're going to tell him."

"Me? What the hell for? You're the one who spoke to his PO."

"Because I want to rattle him; really push him off-balance. He's a real piece of shit, this guy. On top of being into all that master-race garbage, I think it's safe to bet he doesn't think much of women—especially women in positions of authority."

"So I get to wind him up and see if he springs?"

"I've watched you fight. You can handle yourself. Besides, I'm too old to be mixing it up with a guy half my age."

Fields shook her head. "I think we can officially pronounce chivalry dead."

"Assaulting a federal officer is a felony. If he's dumb enough to do it, it'd be his third strike. You'd also get to whup a Nazi's ass, which would make you queen for more than just a day at headquarters. You wouldn't have to pay for another drink all summer."

"Says the immediate supervisor who wouldn't authorize my hazardous duty request."

"It's a knock and talk. You can do this in your sleep. I'll be right there with you."

Washington Village, also known as "Pigtown" because of its nineteenth-century slaughterhouses and the pigs that used to be driven through the open streets, was a poor, down-on-its-luck neighborhood of crumbling rowhouses, vacant lots, and boarded-up businesses adjacent to Camden Yards. It was also home to White Wolf Combat.

Parking across the street, Fields and Carolan got themselves ready to speak to the MMA gym's manager, Lucas Weber.

"Windbreakers?" Fields asked, referring to the dark blue jackets with "FBI" stenciled in big gold letters across the back, the shoulders, and just above the left breast.

"It's up to you," Carolan replied, looking out the windshield at the dilapidated two-story commercial building that housed White Wolf Combat. All of its upstairs windows were wide-open, several of them with box fans whirling away. "Still pretty warm outside and it doesn't look like those guys are wasting money on AC."

As usual, Carolan was right. "No windbreakers," said Fields.

"Good call."

"No tactical vests either."

"Also a good call. We're here to make conversation. Not to execute a warrant."

Fields checked the security of her weapon in its holster. It was locked in place, nice and tight.

There was no need to pull it out and rack the slide in order to seat a round in the chamber. Her Glock was already hot. They only did that nonsense in Hollywood.

If your life, or the life of another, came down to how quickly you could draw and fire your gun, only a fool would walk around without one in the pipe. It would be professional malpractice.

Carolan looked at her. "You ready?"

She nodded. "Let's go make some new friends."

Exiting the vehicle, they waited for a car to pass and then crossed the street. Neither of them was wearing a suit jacket. Their weapons and bright gold badges were on full display. Based on the caliber of its management, it shouldn't surprise any gym goers that law enforcement was dropping by.

The run-down building was made of chipped cinder block, painted gray. The ground-floor level had one window covered with iron bars, a very old, olive-green, roll-up-style door from the 1930s, and a main pedestrian door, also painted olive green, which had been plastered with fight leaflets. There were motion lights and at least three security cameras.

Fields tried the door, but it was locked. Holding her credentials up toward the nearest security camera, she rang the bell. Seconds later, a buzzer sounded and the door unlocked. Returning her credentials to her pocket, Fields pushed the door open and she and Carolan climbed a narrow staircase to the second floor.

As they ascended, they could hear all the sounds one would associ-ate with a gym that trained MMA fighters—gloves hitting pads, battle ropes pounding the floor, the clank of heavy weights, and bodies thud-ding onto mats.

There was also the very distinct odor of sweat and leather, with an undertone of industrial disinfectant. Fields instantly hated it. For Carolan, it reminded him of growing up and one of his uncles who had been an amateur boxer.

At the top of the stairs, the gym revealed itself. It was a large, open space, but where they had anticipated seeing cheap, mismatched work-out equipment scavenged from discount liquidators and low-rent garage sales, they saw expensive, brand-name pieces that would have rivaled most high-end clubs.

There were also two brand-new rings with taut ropes, bright corner pads, and spotless canvases. Affixed to the ceiling above each was a huge American flag.

Someone had dropped some money in this gym. Not enough to get the AC up to snuff, but enough to give the people training here top-notch gear.

Vinyl banners celebrating cage matches and no-holds-barred fights from years past adorned the walls along with dozens of framed photos of White Wolf Combat fighters. It didn't shock Fields that there wasn't a Black or Brown face among them.

As they walked onto the floor, about fifteen people, all White, stopped what they were doing and a very uncomfortable silence descended over the gym. All eyes were locked on the two FBI agents. And not in a friendly way.

Suddenly, someone shouted, "Who told any of you to take a break? Get back to fucking work!"

Looking across the gym, Fields saw Lucas Weber standing outside his office. He was bigger, uglier, and nastier than she had expected.

CHAPTER 22

I n his mug shot, Weber had looked like your typical skinhead
scumbag. He was heavily tattooed, with a thick, Hitler Youth slo-
gan, "Blood Honor," encircling his neck, as well as SS lightning
bolts, two Totenkopf skulls, a handful of Norse runes, and a triskelion
"three sevens" tattoo.

Since being inside, he had added an Odin's cross, as well as an eagle
holding a swastika with the words "White Power" and "War Skins,"
which was popular with the White Aryan Resistance and signified
prison time by someone who had committed crimes on behalf of the
movement.

And those were just the tattoos Fields could see at this distance as the
man stood there in a pair of black MMA shorts and a Punisher T-shirt.

He had grown his hair out on top but wore the back and sides in a
skintight fade reminiscent of the "undercut" style popular from the 1910s
to the 1940s, which had come around again.

Most noticeable of all was the weight he had put on. He was no longer the scrawny punk he had been when he first went away. Weber had
packed on a good twenty-five pounds of what appeared to be solid muscle. In addition to working out, Fields figured the guy had to be juicing.
Nobody got that big, this fast, just by getting off prison food and shopping at Whole Foods.

"Can I help you officers?"

"Agents," said Fields, correcting him as she walked toward him and took the initiative. "FBI. I'm Fields and this is my partner, Special Agent Carolan. Are you Lucas Weber?"

"Do you have a warrant?" he replied.

"Why would we need a warrant?"

"Because, *Mizz* Fields, I know my rights."

He drew the word out, purposefully being antagonistic, trying to get a rise out of her.

"Again, it's Agent Fields, and technically you buzzed us in, which—"

"And now I'm buzzing you out," he said, cutting her off. "So take the same stairs you came up here on and fuck off."

Somewhere in the back of the gym, someone laughed. Another anonymous voice yelled, "You tell her, Lucas!"

Fields wasn't in the mood. Standing in the middle of the gym not only provided him with an audience, but also encouraged him to be disagreeable. "Maybe we can talk privately in your office?" she suggested.

"What part of 'you don't have a warrant, so fuck off' do you not understand?"

"Listen, you and I have something in common."

"Oh, really. What's that, Mizz Fields?"

"Neither of us wants me to be here. So, let's just go into your office, we can have a little chat, and then we'll be gone."

Leaning, trying to intimidate her, he said, "Or else what?"

Not at all intimidated by him, she also leaned forward and, without missing a beat, lowered her voice and responded, "Or else I'm going to pull parade permits for the Black Baptist Alliance, the Black Chamber of Commerce, the Black Justice Coalition, Black Lives Matter, the Black fucking Panthers, and any other Black organization I can think of, and will have them marching up and down your street from now until Christmas, just to piss you off. And that's just for starters.

"Did you know that there's a national association of Black IRS agents?" she continued. "You don't need to answer that. It's already written on your face. How about this? Can you guess who they absolutely *love* to target with audits? If you guessed twice-convicted White supremacists, you win today's prize. They also love to target their employers, because where there's one of you racist assholes, there's always more. Are you getting the picture? If not, we can talk about how many Black building inspectors Baltimore has and the kinds of businesses they want to make sure are up to code."

"This is a fucking shakedown."

"Relax. Nobody's shaking you down, Lucas. I told you, we just want to talk. Ball's in your court. Are you going to find your manners and invite us into your office?" asked Fields. "Or am I going to have to start making some phone calls?"

Weber might not have been the brightest bulb, but he was smart enough to know when to cut his losses. Taking a step back, he gestured with his right arm toward his office.

As he did, she noticed the 14/88 tattoo on the inside of his forearm. It was shorthand for the "14 Words"—a White supremacist maxim, which declared, "We must secure the existence of our people and a future for White children." The 88 represented the eighth letter of the alphabet, *H*, and so stood for "Heil Hitler." The sooner she and Carolan could get out of here, the better.

Inside the office, she took a seat while Carolan stood—one eye on Weber, the other on the door.

"I want to get my lawyer to listen in on this," the man said as he sat down at his desk and reached for the phone.

"You probably should call your parole officer first."

He looked at her. "My PO? Why would I call that prick?"

"Because he's going to tell you what he told us, which is that you never requested permission to leave the state of Maryland and travel to Texas and California."

Weber stared at her before his eyes nervously flicked to Carolan. He was trying to figure out what they knew and how much trouble he was in.

"I don't know what you're talking about," he stated.

"Give me a fucking break," said Fields. "Do we look stupid to you? We've got witnesses that put you in Laredo and Riverside. We've also got you on video at both of those underground fights."

Fields held up her phone and showed him two separate freeze frames from the Dark Web footage.

"Fuck," Weber muttered.

"That's one way to phrase it," Fields replied.

"What do you want?"

"Just a little cooperation. You give us what we need and the video goes away. We'll call your PO and tell him it was all just a misunderstanding. We had the wrong guy. But if you don't cooperate, you're going to go back inside for a long, long time."

Weber didn't like having his balls busted, especially by some Black bitch FBI agent, but she wasn't giving him any room to breathe. "You people are like fucking jackals. You know that? I don't even recognize this country anymore."

"Is that a yes? Are you going to cooperate?"

He took a long pause before replying, "Fine. Fuck it. I'll cooperate."

When Fields glanced over at Carolan, he gave her a subtle nod. She'd done a good job, so far. Now it was time to see if Weber could help take their investigation to the next level.

Scrolling through her phone, she pulled up a photo of the sword-and-tree tattoo they had taken in the morgue that morning.

"Ever seen this before?" she asked, holding out the phone with her left hand.

Weber squinted at the image and then leaned over his desk to get a better look. Fields extended the phone even closer toward him and noticed him stiffen. *He recognizes it all right.*

"Take your time," she said, continuing to watch him, studying how he reacted.

Crossing his arms, he leaned back, slowly.

"Don't recognize it," he stated.

He was lying.

"That's funny," Fields replied. "I get the feeling you do recognize it. And I shouldn't have to tell you the shitstorm that'll happen if I figure out you're lying to me."

Weber's eyes bore into hers. Particle beams of pure, unadulterated hate. The tension in the office, which wasn't good to begin with, was now off the charts.

"Mind if I smoke?" he asked.

"I'd prefer if you didn't."

"It's just my vape," he replied, tilting to his right and sliding open one of the desk drawers.

As he did, the sleeve of his T-shirt rode up on his left arm and there, on the inside of his biceps, she saw it. Weber had the exact same tattoo.

Dropping her phone, Fields pulled her Glock and barely had time to yell, "Gun!"

Weber was leveling a stainless-steel .357 and about to fire when Fields shot him twice in the chest and once in the head.

The felon's head snapped back as the bullet entered and then splattered bone, blood, and pieces of brain on the wall behind him.

He was dead before Carolan could even have drawn his weapon.

CHAPTER 23

H arvath's plan had, admittedly, been ad hoc from the jump. Taking a protectee and squirreling them away somewhere and keeping them safe was one thing. Taking a protectee and keeping them safe while attempting to lure in unknown bad actors was something completely different.

Having Haney and McGee get to the Ambassador's house first was a key part of his plan. They had done their sweep of the grounds as well as the interior of the home flawlessly. Harvath's job had been more complicated.

He not only needed to pop Rogers back onto the radar, he also needed to get him all the way home without anything happening to him.

As Rogers had driven and Harvath had remained hidden in the trunk, Nicholas had followed at a distance. He had not seen anyone tailing them. By the time he had peeled off, they were only minutes from the Ambassador's driveway.

After being successfully smuggled into the house, Harvath started thinking through next steps. Everything up to that point had gone according to plan. Even if someone had been watching, it would have appeared that the Ambassador had arrived alone and was inside the home, albeit with the blinds and drapes drawn.

That was a key part of Harvath's plan. Whoever was after Rogers, they needed to believe that he would be easy to get to, that they had the upper hand, which led to Harvath's next issue.

If the Ambassador was right and the deaths of the secretary of state and the secretary of defense had not been caused by an accident or natural causes, then what did the killers have planned for him?

Rogers was a fit guy in his fifties, training to run the Marine Corps Marathon in the fall. While it wouldn't be out of the realm of possibilities that he too could have a heart attack, you could only have so many connected people die via the same means before people eventually got suspicious. And that was what had been nibbling at the edges of Harvath's mind.

Were the Iranians strategic enough to realize that while dramatic attacks like car bombs and snipers would make for incredible headlines, they would only drive the rest of their targets deep into hiding? *They had to know that.*

Unless they could hit their targets all at once, all at the same time, they would risk spooking everyone else on their list and sending them underground. It made much more sense to take them one at a time and in a way that wouldn't raise suspicion among the others.

That was how Harvath would have done it, and he had to believe that the Iranians were that thoughtful, as well as that clever.

So what did that mean for Rogers? If the men chasing him through Rock Creek Park were indeed assassins, what was their plan? How would they have killed him and how would they have done it in such a way that it didn't arouse the suspicions of anyone else on their hit list?

That was the ten-thousand-dollar question. If he knew that answer, it might help him anticipate what they might have planned next for the Ambassador. But as things now stood, he had nothing. He didn't even know if they'd show up.

Then the camera feeds had gone down. It was only a blip. They'd only gone dark for a fraction of a second, but Harvath didn't believe in coincidences. And while he wished he had more information, he was a big believer in the saying "You go to war with the army you have, not the army you wish you had."

The one saving grace in the entire plan, besides having Haney and McGee with him, was that even though the Secret Service hadn't been able to talk the Ambassador into paring back his trees, they had been able to talk him into upgrading his master bedroom closet into a safe room.

The walls and floors had been lined with ballistic fiberglass panels and the door swapped out for a high-security version with hardened locking bolts, a galvanized steel core, and a triple-reinforced metal frame. But as good as that was, it was by no means perfect.

The safe room didn't have its own air filtration, which made it vulnerable to smoke and fire. Without any panels on the ceiling, it was also exposed to attack from above. Nevertheless, it was a hell of a lot better than just two-by-fours and a couple of layers of Sheetrock. If they needed to stick Rogers in there while they took care of business, none of them would worry for his well-being.

That was the lay of the land and this was the army they were going to war with. Now all they had to do was to wait and see if enemy forces showed up.

Serving the bone-in, dry-aged New York strip steaks and sides the Ambassador had picked up from the Capital Grille, they plated their dinners and joined Haney in the den.

They made small talk as they ate and then joked about not being able to have dessert because Mike had finished off all the Ambassador's ice cream.

At 8:30 p.m. the alarm on McGee's watch went off. In seven minutes, the sun would set.

Like a scene out of the postapocalyptic movie *I Am Legend*, the team went about securing the house. There was no telling what was out in the woods, waiting for darkness to launch its attack.

Rogers set up two pots and began brewing some of the strongest coffee he had ever made. After scraping the plates into the garbage, he placed them in the dishwasher and leaned against the counter.

"You good?" Harvath asked from the kitchen table, where he was attaching his night-vision goggles to the mount on his tactical helmet.

"As good as I think I'm going to be."

"It's all going to be all right. Trust me."

Rogers looked at him. "What if nothing happens?"

"You mean tonight?"

"I mean ever. What if I was wrong? What if there is no threat and I put you guys through all of this for nothing?"

"First of all," Harvath replied, "after what you did, you've got a blank check with me, so don't even worry about it. Haney and McGee feel the same. You're one of us and we're going to keep you safe.

"Secondly, there's nothing that would make me happier than to come to the conclusion that there is no active threat against you. That would be the absolute best possible outcome.

"Either way, the train has already left the station, so you might as well sit back and relax. In fact, what's your favorite adult beverage?"

The Ambassador didn't even need to think about it. "Bourbon," he responded.

"You have some in the house?"

"Lots of it."

"A man after my own heart," said Harvath. "What's your best bottle?"

"That's easy. I've got a Pappy Van Winkle. Fifteen years old."

"Go pour yourself a couple fingers of that. It'll help take the edge off."

"You don't mind that I have a drink?" Rogers asked.

"As long as it's just one, you'll be fine."

"How about you?" the Ambassador offered. "Would you like one?"

Harvath smiled, but shook his head. "Unfortunately, I'm on duty. I will, though, absolutely take a rain check."

"You can count on it. It's the least I can do."

Harvath watched as Rogers walked away toward the bar in his stylish den. He then returned to working on his helmet.

Once the goggles were attached, he went over his short-barreled Rattler for the umpteenth time and then did the same with his Glock. After that, he shrugged into his plate carrier and poured two big mugs of coffee.

Walking into the living room, he handed one of them to McGee and asked, "Everything all right?"

"Look at you," the ex–CIA director said. "Should I have brought a vest?"

"I told you you could if you wanted to."

"To be honest, I have so many boxes in my garage, I wouldn't even know where to start looking for it."

"You cleared out pretty fast," said Harvath as he took a seat across from him. "I thought you'd stick around D.C. for a while, maybe do a stint on a board of directors or dip your toe into the consulting world."

McGee smiled. "I don't think the corporate world would be a good fit for me."

"What about a think tank? Or academia? With your history, some university could offer a Robert McGee master's degree in black ops, covert ass-kicking, and shooting bad guys in the face. Those precious little college students would be lined up around the block and camping out for something like that."

"More like taking over the building and trying to firebomb my office," the man said with a laugh. "I think I'm just going to enjoy retirement. What about you? You've been out about as long as I have. Do you miss anything?"

"Maybe a little," Harvath replied, "but to be honest, I haven't had the time. For the last six months, it feels like as soon as I was unpacked, it was time to pack again and Sølvi and I were on to the next spot."

"Good for you. You deserve a little happiness. Especially after everything you went through."

"Thank you," Harvath said, taking a sip of his coffee.

"And by the way, you know that if I'd still been in charge, I never would have allowed what the Agency did to you."

"I know."

"What Andy Conroy did was flat-out inexcusable. Deputy director of operations or not, that was beyond bad."

Harvath appreciated the man's support and told him so, but because he wasn't in the mood to rehash the whole thing, he changed the subject back to McGee and his retirement. "That's it then? You've moved to some little beach cottage where you paint all day? At least tell me you're working on your memoirs. That's something I could get behind. I'd pay good money to read a Bob McGee book. Just based on the body count alone, you'd have to publish it in multiple volumes."

McGee smiled once again. "Nope. I'm not banging away on a typewriter. I do paint. I run on the beach. Do a little fishing. Some crabbing from time to time. That's it. And I like it that way."

"It sounds lonely."

"It's *quiet*. There's a difference. After decades of living at eleven, it's nice to dial things down to a three. It's relaxing. At least it was until today."

Now it was Harvath's turn to smile. "Ambassador Rogers needed the best, that's why I called you."

"You called me because you're running out of friends in this town. That's what happens when you hang around too long."

"I don't know. I'm pretty sure I could have squeezed a couple more years out of it had I wanted to."

"Life is all about timing," McGee remarked, his voice tinged with quiet wisdom. "Especially in this line of work. Knowing when to step away . . . that's what separates the wise from the reckless."

"The quick and the dead," Harvath mused.

"And yet here we are. No paycheck. No backup to speak of. Just us and the Ambo."

"So what does that make us?"

The ex–CIA director didn't even bat an eye. "Men willing to fight for what's right, even when the system won't. That makes us men of honor. Last of the American breed."

McGee had always been a fascinating character and Harvath could have spent all night talking with him, but he needed to finish getting everything ready.

"Comms check in five," he said, standing up.

"Copy that," the man replied.

Picking up his mug and heading back toward the kitchen, it struck Harvath that McGee would be a great choice to run the Carlton Group. But for that to happen, to convince him to give up his painting, his fishing, and his quiet runs on the beach, something would have to befall the country, the seriousness of which America had never seen.

CHAPTER 24

The luxury four-bedroom penthouse at the Ritz-Carlton Residences belonged to one of Senator Bill Blackwood's biggest donors. The wealthy couple, who rarely made it to D.C. anymore, was happy to have him use it whenever he wanted.

Spanning almost ten thousand square feet, with floor-to-ceiling windows, the apartment boasted some of the best views in the city.

In addition to in-room dining, housekeeping, and private chef services, Blackwood was able to avail himself of private access to an on-site, members-only health club, as well as key-card access to pass directly through to the Ritz-Carlton hotel and the use of an underground parking facility completely removed from the view of the passing public.

The security and exclusivity of the property were superb. It was the perfect location for Blackwood to entertain his six clandestine guests.

They had gathered in the opulent dining room and had been seated around a long Christofle designer table under a $2 million Chihuly chandelier.

Despite the expensive wines and cognacs that had been poured for them, not a single one of them had been happy. The recriminations had come fast and furious.

They had all been struck by the visceral nature of last night's attack. War, he'd been forced to remind them, was a bloody business, and they were most definitely at war.

Drilling down, he finally got to what they were most upset about. All that time, all that planning, and most importantly, all that risk—only to have President Mitchell come out looking like the hero, a *leader*.

His visit to the victims in the hospital, his remarks to the press, everyone had lapped it up. They had actually made him stronger politically. It was the exact opposite of what they had intended and they were pissed. Blackwood, however, had his talking points ready and, thanks to his visit with Chuck Coughlin, knew exactly what to say.

It had taken a few minutes to sink in, but his guests had eventually come around to his way of thinking. To be successful—to "out media" Mitchell—the Vice President needed to get to the microphones first and come out with such force, that anything the President tried to follow up with would look like weak tea in comparison.

He reminded them to trust the plan. The wheels were in motion and what was coming could not be stopped. They needed to hang together or, as Ben Franklin was alleged to have said after signing the Declaration of Independence, they would assuredly all hang separately. After a final round to stiffen their spines, he had sent them on their way.

It had been risky bringing them all together in one place like that so soon after the attack.

Secrecy was the sine qua non of their operation. None of them wanted to be arrested for treason, but they were fighting for the future of the nation.

President Mitchell had been given a once-in-a-generation opportunity and he was squandering it. He had assembled an army of Americans, citizens wholly devoted to him, who would do anything he asked. All they had asked of him was that he put the nation first. He had promised that he would and in exchange for that promise, they had voted for him.

But as they watched his first one hundred days in office, as those days turned to weeks and the weeks turned to months, he had disappointed them at practically every turn.

He had not only abandoned his principles and the voters who had swept him into office, but he had also allowed himself to be co-opted by the establishment. He had become the thing he had campaigned against— a creature of D.C.

Plenty of voters, out of slavish devotion and an inability to believe that he had turned his back on them, had stayed faithful. No matter how many examples they were presented with his showing infidelity to the movement, they refused to give up on him. In their eyes, the young, charismatic president could do no wrong and his detractors were simply "jealous" or incapable of realizing his brilliance. They were convinced that Mitchell was playing a sophisticated long game, intent on driving his enemies mad, and which would, inevitably, deliver for all Americans—especially his most devoted supporters. Bill Blackwood and his junto knew better.

After the last of the guests had left the penthouse, Blackwood removed his coat and tie, poured himself a Double Eagle Very Rare twenty-year-old bourbon, and stepped out on the terrace.

The air was still humid, but with the sun having set, the temperature had fallen a few degrees and a slight breeze had picked up. It was almost agreeable.

Sitting down on one of the outdoor couches, he kicked off his shoes, put his feet up on the table in front of him, and closed his eyes.

Like Paris or New York, D.C. was a city that didn't sleep. It had a heartbeat, a thrum, that could be felt all night long.

He was taking it all in when he heard the unmistakable sound of a bottle being slid from a half-melted bucket of ice inside.

Without opening his eyes, he knew that she had joined him on the terrace. The breeze had shifted slightly and it carried with it the faint scent of her perfume—refined with just a touch of mystery. It was called *Black Orchid* and even its name suited her so perfectly, simple yet elegant, with a hint of something deeper beneath the surface. Claire Bennet was the most intoxicating woman he had ever met.

She was a partner at a successful D.C. lobbying firm, and her confidence was unmistakable. It was one of the things that had instantly intrigued him about her. Her looks were another.

All of his wives had been blondes. Claire, however, was different— her long, chestnut-colored hair a striking contrast. But it wasn't just her hair that set her apart. Her long, thin neck, sharp cheekbones, full lips, and doe-like eyes, which seemed to see right through him, added a level of allure he had never experienced. And then there was the fact that she was thirty-six, and on their second evening out, she'd casually admitted that she found him incredibly sexy—and to his delight, utterly irresistible.

She had been in the back bedroom, listening to, and recording, everything that had been said. It was their "insurance" in case any of Blackwood's guests had second thoughts and attempted to go rogue. Her commitment to the cause all but rivaled his own.

"You did well tonight," she said, sitting down next to him, a glass of Krug, Clos du Mesnil in her hand. "Very well."

Blackwood opened his eyes and looked at her. She had gotten rid of her jacket, as well as her heels, and was wearing just a tight black pencil skirt and a white blouse, unbuttoned far enough that he could see the tops of her breasts. She was well aware of the power she had over him and always seemed to enjoy wielding it. On the outdoor speakers, he could hear that she had queued up some Etta James.

As the slow, sultry notes of "I'd Rather Go Blind" began to play, she took a sip of her champagne and set the glass on the table. Hiking up her skirt, she crawled onto his lap and started moving her hips to the music.

"Tonight wasn't the hard part," he replied, enjoying her effort to seduce him. "It's what comes next that I'm concerned about."

Leaning in, she gave him an even better view of her breasts as she unbuttoned the third and fourth buttons of his shirt.

"Is the Vice President going to be where we need him to be tomorrow?"

Blackwood looked up at her—that swanlike neck, those beautiful lips, those eyes—and nodded.

"Good," she responded. "Then there's nothing else that you can do."

He opened his mouth to reply, but before he could, she leaned the rest of the way in and kissed him. And with the taste of champagne still fresh in her mouth, she took his hand and guided it to the zipper on her skirt.

CHAPTER 25

With a few minutes left on Haney's shift, Harvath had appeared in the den and they conducted a quick debrief. Other than the fact that the Ambassador's cameras were dirty and in need of an upgrade, there was nothing significant to report. Haney handed him the security tablet and went to close his eyes for a few hours.

Harvath set his latest mug of coffee on the end table to his left and, unslinging his Rattler, set it next to him on the couch.

Via the home's automation system, all of the main lights had been turned off at 10 p.m., while certain accent lights had been dimmed, providing just enough illumination to see by. Had anyone been watching from outside, it would have appeared that Rogers had turned in for the night.

"Now the fun starts," McGee had stated as the lights had gone out.

Harvath knew it was more gallows humor, but he didn't find any of this fun. He felt like they were all sitting ducks. If they'd only had more manpower, he would have gladly spent the night in the woods, heat and mosquitos be damned, waiting for his chance to come up behind anyone dumb enough to approach the house. Unfortunately, it was just the three of them and Ambassador Rogers. Posting men outside was a luxury they couldn't afford.

He took a few moments to get himself familiar with the tablet, which was connected to the home automation system. The lighting, audio, video, and security systems could all be controlled via a simple interface. The tablet also had full access to the web, which felt to Harvath like another Achilles' heel. He thought about shutting off the Wi-Fi but worried that might compromise his ability to access the features he needed, so he didn't mess with anything.

In addition to trimming the trees back and not allowing the security system to touch the web, had Harvath been in charge, he would have also covered all the windows with ballistic film. Though it would have been expensive to do the entire house, and it wouldn't stop higher-caliber rounds like .308 or .50 BMG, it would have provided an extra layer of protection, and it was the layers that often made the difference between life and death. Regardless of how long they were going to be with the Ambassador, he was going to recommend that Rogers do all of them.

Watching the camera feeds was mind-numbingly boring, and despite the strength of the coffee, Harvath had to stand up every fifteen or twenty minutes just to keep himself from falling asleep.

Each time he got up, he did a set of push-ups, air squats, or dips—anything that got his heart pumping and his blood flowing.

He was looking forward to handing over the watch to McGee, but that wasn't until 4 a.m., an hour and twenty minutes from now.

Even though the coffee wasn't technically doing the trick, it still fulfilled a psychological need and he decided to top off his mug.

Picking up the tablet, he swiped to the screen with all the feeds shown, just like on the TV. He then carried it into the kitchen, and propped it up on the counter between the two coffee machines.

There was only a little coffee left in both pots. He emptied the remains of each into his mug and started two fresh batches. As he worked, he kept one eye on the tablet.

Haney had been absolutely correct about the condition of the cameras. Not only were the acrylic domes that covered them filthy, but several of them were also partially obscured by spiderwebs, which bounced back a hot white glare in their infrared mode.

Harvath was certain, if Rogers was willing to make the investment, that Nicholas could get a team out same-day to install the latest in AI-boosted cameras that could not only detect motion, but also follow objects and determine whether or not they were a threat. But at the very least, he needed to get all of the existing cameras cleaned. There was no telling how long it had been. It was yet another recommendation he would make to Rogers.

With his mug in one hand, he reached for the tablet with the other, and that's when it glitched. *Again.*

Setting his mug down, he tried to swipe through the different feeds, but they were all dead.

Quickly, he headed for the den to see if the cameras were still showing on the TV. Each feed had gone dark. All the boxes were still there, but nothing was showing inside any of them. As far as the outside property was concerned, Harvath and his team were officially blind.

With each second that passed, his certainty grew that the feeds weren't coming back and that they'd been cut on purpose. Whatever had happened earlier had, in fact, been a test—someone probing.

Now that the cameras were down, they had to assume an attack was not only in the works, but in fact also imminent.

Activating his radio, Harvath said, "Break. Break. Break. Cameras down. Possible breach. Repeat. Cameras down. Possible breach. Prepare for contact. Repeat. Prepare for contact."

As soon as his call went out, Haney and McGee reported in, and they activated their prearranged plan.

The first order of business was to get the Ambassador up and into his safe room. As Haney was on the second floor, that became his job.

McGee backed away from the windows and out of the living room, maintaining a position in the kitchen where he could still see everything.

Out of the care package that Nicholas had prepared, Harvath removed a small, all-weather case, opened it up, and pulled out a pair of tiny drones that looked like Dragonflies.

Powering them up, he did his best to stay hidden behind the drapes in the den as he cracked one of the windows, used his knife to cut a gash in the screen, and let them fly.

Closing and locking the window, he then headed to the kitchen to join McGee.

"Did you reboot the cameras?" he asked.

"Haven't had time," said Harvath as he pulled out his phone, which

Nicholas had set up to act as a monitor for the tiny night-vision and thermal cameras mounted to each of the autonomous drones.

Unlike the Ambassador's somewhat out-of-date security system, the Dragonflies were state-of-the-art. They would not just sit in one place waiting for movement—they would actively seek it out. If anything had breached the perimeter, they would find it.

"Friendly!" Haney announced in a loud whisper as he came down the back stairs and into the kitchen.

"How's the Ambo?" Harvath asked.

"Locked up tight," he replied, pivoting to the same question McGee had asked. "What's with the cameras? Have we rebooted?"

Harvath nodded toward the tablet sitting on the counter and said, "Not yet. Be my guest."

Haney took it and got to work, while Harvath watched the split-screen feed from the Dragonflies. It didn't take long for them to detect and identify an intrusion.

The first thing the drones were programmed to do was to locate any other drones in their immediate vicinity and jam them. As soon as they were airborne, they found one and gave it a digital aneurysm, causing it to drop from the sky and crash to the ground below.

Next they scanned for human beings, and within seconds the first Dragonfly returned a hit.

"Jesus," said Harvath, reaching for his tactical helmet and powering up his night-vision goggles. "We've got six hostiles, all of them armed, moving toward the house from the southeast."

"Six?" McGee replied, his pistol out as he kept his eyes on the windows in the living and dining rooms. "That's an insane amount of manpower for the Iranians to be sending."

Harvath agreed and was about to say as much when the second Dragonfly picked up an additional threat. "Hold up. We've now got two more," he said, trying to zoom in to get a better picture. "West side of the house. Moving through the woods. It looks like they're carrying something. I can't tell what it is."

"Reboot complete," Haney interjected. "But I don't think it took. The cameras are still down."

"Kill all the lights in here," Harvath ordered.

Haney swiped over to the home-automation screen with the light controls and turned everything off.

As Harvath continued watching the feed from the Dragonflies, he put his helmet on and cinched up the strap. He was about to activate the optic on his weapon when he saw the two men to the west of the house step out of the woods and he finally recognized what they were carrying—*a ladder.*

"They're going to go for the roof," he stated as he turned to Haney. "Get the Ambassador out of the safe room. *Now.*"

Haney didn't need to be told twice. Dropping the tablet on the counter, he charged back upstairs.

"I think I should have brought a bigger gun," said McGee.

The man was an excellent shot. Harvath knew that about him. The size of his gun didn't matter. "How many magazines do you have?"

"On me? Three. I've got two more in my bag in the den."

"Go get them," Harvath replied.

As McGee headed for the den, Harvath kept his eyes glued to the Dragonfly feeds.

The six-man team was nearly at the house. They moved in a tight, tactical "stack" formation, meaning that they had probably had some sort of military training. The two men with the ladder were getting closer as well.

Harvath couldn't wrap his head around what he was seeing. *Eight men?* To take out a former government official, who, as far as anyone knew, didn't even have a protective detail? It didn't make sense. *And what's with the ladder?*

They had to be going for the roof.

And in his mind, if they were going for the roof, it had to be because they wanted to hit the safe room. But how did they know about the room, much less its greatest vulnerability? And if they knew that piece of critical information, what else did they know?

He had his answer soon enough.

Suddenly the tablet on the counter came to life and the screen was a large number pad.

Harvath watched as the buttons were remotely activated and someone entered the Ambassador's security code. The LED warning light went from red to green.

The alarm system was now off.

CHAPTER 26

arvath had to think fast. They were outgunned by more than two-to-one. And though the house offered plenty of concealment, it didn't provide a fortified-enough fighting position from which they could effectively repel this many shooters over a prolonged firefight. There was only one thing he could do and he explained his plan over their encrypted radios as quickly as he could.

Clicking his phone into the hands-free mount on the front of his plate carrier, he powered up the optic on his rifle and readied to slip outside. As he did, he remembered his wish from earlier—that he could have had enough manpower to allow him to spend the night in the woods, hunting bad guys. Now he was going to get his chance, but at the cost of leaving Haney and McGee by themselves to protect the Ambassador.

Because of that, he decided to help them first.

There was a window for each bay in Rogers's three-car garage. That was how Harvath was going to get out. Leaving the lights off, he flipped down his night-vision goggles and entered the garage. As soon as he had, McGee closed and locked the door behind him.

He headed for the farthest window, crossing the garage as quickly and as quietly as he could. Once he got there, he checked the feed from the Dragonflies. The two men, just outside, were already setting up their ladder.

The other team was holding in place, just behind the trees, off the southeast corner of the house. This was where the living room windows gave onto a flagstone patio behind which was a long stretch of manicured lawn that ran down to the river. It looked to Harvath as though they were waiting for their colleagues to get into place up on the roof so they could all enter the house simultaneously. He needed to move now.

Opening the window, he removed the screen and climbed out, closing the window behind him.

With his rifle up and at the ready, he crept to the corner of the garage. Even though the drones appeared to show that he was safe, he did a quick peek, just to make sure. Seeing that he was, he moved around the corner and headed for the edge of the structure.

Checking the feeds once more, he could see that one of the men was already at the top of the ladder, ready to step on the roof. The other man was at the base, covering his teammate. It was now or never.

Applying pressure to his trigger, Harvath leaned out from behind the garage and sighted in on the man at the top of the ladder. Looking through the optic, he immediately got bad news. The man and his colleague were both wearing helmets. *Fuck.*

That meant they were probably also wearing body armor, which would make his shots even more difficult, especially from this distance.

His idea had been to take the two men out quickly, without the other team of attackers knowing anything had happened. But if he failed, and one of them was able to raise the alarm, he would lose the element of surprise and Haney and McGee would instantaneously be under siege.

Fuck, he whispered again under his breath. He was going to have to get closer, which would mean crossing the gravel driveway without being seen *and* without being heard.

Complicating matters was the fact that the only thing smaller than the Dragonflies themselves were their batteries. Nicholas had been crystal clear that once they were airborne, Harvath would have to act fast. And the more onboard features he utilized, such as jamming, IR, and thermal cameras, the sooner the batteries would run down.

His plan to peek out from behind the garage, pop the two guys with the ladder, and then retreat back behind the garage and head for the southeast corner of the house was off the table. He needed to get across the driveway, and to do it successfully, he needed a diversion.

Activating his radio, he gave his teammates a quick SITREP and then told McGee what he wanted him to do.

As soon as McGee had the tablet in hand and had swiped to the screen he needed, he confirmed with Harvath that he was ready to go.

The moment he did, Harvath told him to "hit it" as he sprang from behind the garage.

When the two attackers had set up the ladder to climb onto the roof, they had positioned it adjacent to the room Harvath had been given. One of the things he had noticed when he had dropped his bag and gone to take his shower was that the window shades were on a motorized track.

He assumed that like almost everything else in Rogers's house, it was connected to the home automation system, and he'd been correct.

With just two taps, McGee had turned on the lights in the room and had started the slow roll-up of the shades.

Not knowing what the hell was going on, the man at the top of the ladder—whom Harvath could now see was also wearing a backpack—had frozen. Then, all of a sudden, he stepped down a couple of rungs and trained his rifle on the window. The other man on the ground beneath did the same thing.

With their focus on the light and activity in the window, Harvath was able to get across the driveway and take cover on the other side without being noticed.

Having lost their drone, the attackers were likely on edge. Whether they were aware that someone inside the house was responsible for knocking it out of the sky didn't matter. Everything Harvath had seen told him that they were professionals. They would not have chalked up their drone going down to an accident. Their assumption would be that they no longer possessed the element of surprise and needed to be doubly cautious.

It would make Harvath's job harder, but at least they wouldn't have their own eye in the sky warning them that he was coming. Which was exactly the case with the two men who had been preparing to assault the roof.

Weaving through the trees, well aware that snapping just one twig could give him away, Harvath moved as quickly and as quietly as he could.

When he saw the man at the top of the ladder begin to climb again, he knew the clock had run out. He needed to act.

Stepping out of the tree line and back toward the driveway, he shouldered the Rattler, took aim, and fired two suppressed shots.

The rounds punched through the flesh of the man's lower back, just beneath his vest, knocking him from the ladder.

Before he had even hit the ground, Harvath had taken aim at his partner. He pressed his trigger again and again, the muffled spits erupting from his rifle, until they had found flesh and the second man dropped to the ground.

Charging over to the men, who were dressed from head to toe in black tactical gear, Harvath placed the tip of his suppressor under each of their night-vision goggles and shot them in the forehead, just to make sure that they were dead.

"Tangos one and two down," he radioed his teammates.

Rolling over the man who had been at the top of the ladder, Harvath opened his backpack. Inside were breaching tools, including a portable circular saw, which would have been extremely helpful in cutting through the roof above the Ambassador's safe room.

The questions Harvath had only multiplied. But now wasn't the time for questions.

It was time to take out the rest of the attackers.

CHAPTER 27

Coming around the house from the north side, instead of back-tracking through the woods behind the garage, meant that Harvath could gain a little extra time with the Dragonflies. There was a trade-off, however.

Instead of being able to sneak up behind the team hiding in the trees at the southeast corner of the house, he would now be on the opposite side of the open expanse of lawn. It was an even worse position than he'd been in when having to cross the driveway. Without some kind of off-the-charts diversion, it would be next to impossible to cover that much ground without being shot at. There had to be another way.

As he looked at his phone and saw that the remaining attackers were lining up and getting ready to move from the cover of the trees, he realized there was only one thing he could do—flank them.

Radioing his team as he changed magazines, he told Haney to get downstairs and join McGee. It looked like the attackers were going to come in through the living room. And when Harvath gave the command, he wanted Haney and McGee to absolutely unload on them.

With their confirmations that they understood what he wanted them to do, Harvath got himself in place.

Because the house was on a slight hill that sloped down to the water, the flagstone terrace outside the living room was built several feet above the ground. It provided Harvath just enough cover as he came around the corner.

Double-checking the Dragonflies, he kept one overhead and sent the other on a sweep of the property. The last thing he wanted to be surprised by was that a fresh crop of reinforcements had arrived and that the attackers had swelled their ranks.

So far, there were only the six remaining. What was odd, however, was that they had stopped moving.

With two of their colleagues down and not responding, were they scrapping their attack and formulating a new plan? It didn't make any sense. What the hell were they waiting for?

As Harvath continued to watch the feed, he saw two of the attackers break off and move down along the south side of the house, taking up positions beneath a pair of large floor-to-ceiling windows.

Raising his team over the radio, he told them what he was seeing and the subtle change he wanted Haney to enact.

The men confirmed his instructions, but the moment they did, the feeds started getting snowy. The Dragonflies were losing power.

The last thing Harvath saw before the feeds completely cut out was the remaining four attackers beginning to make their way out of the trees.

"Get ready," he radioed, turning off his phone and flipping up the mount. "Here they come."

From the far end of the patio, he watched as the now group of four men stepped onto the grass in a V-formation, their own suppressed weapons up and ready, and headed quickly toward the flagstone steps.

Because all of the remaining blinds and shades were drawn, McGee and Haney couldn't see what was happening outside. So, as the attackers moved, Harvath quietly called out their distance over the radio.

When the black-clad figures hit the steps, Harvath gave his team a ten-second warning.

Then, once the attackers came to a stop in front of the sliding glass doors of the living room, he radioed exactly where they were standing.

As the two men in the center faced the house, the man on either end turned and faced outward to guard against being flanked.

It happened so quickly, Harvath almost didn't have time to drop down and get out of sight.

He had lost the ability to have direct eyes on, but it didn't matter.

Activating his radio, he was about to give the "Go" command when the attackers facing the house opened fire.

They raked their fully automatic rounds back and forth, shattering all the glass and filling the living room with lead.

Even though the shooting had already started, Harvath activated his radio and ordered Haney and McGee to "Hit it!" and return fire.

The plan to surprise the attackers by activating the outdoor floodlights while simultaneously shooting at them through the blinds and the glass from the darkened house was now moot.

Above the suppressed shots of the attackers, Harvath could hear both the booming of McGee's .45-caliber 1911 as well as Haney's shotgun as they fought back.

At the same time, Harvath popped up over the edge of the patio and let loose with a barrage of fully automatic fire.

He swept his weapon back and forth, hitting the attackers in their lower extremities.

The man closest to him he nailed right in the groin. And when that man fell to the ground, he finished him off with a burst through his night-vision goggles to the face.

One by one, Harvath and McGee took out the men on the patio as Haney's shotgun only fell quiet when he was reloading.

Finally, Haney stopped shooting and his voice came over the radio. He didn't know if the two attackers on his side of the house were dead, even though they were no longer returning fire.

Harvath instructed Haney to stay put and let McGee know that he would be traversing his line of fire. He didn't want to be mistaking him for one of the attackers.

Once they had both responded, Harvath began moving.

The patio was covered with blood, bodies, and broken glass. As he passed, he signaled McGee to cover him.

Turning the corner, he moved along the side of the house where Haney had not only blown out the windows, but had also blown massive holes through the walls. The two attackers on that side had been ripped apart by the blasts from his shotgun. Ballistic helmets and hard plates in their vests had not been enough to save them.

Their faces were obliterated. It would take fingerprinting or DNA to identify them. Harvath doubted dental records would even be of any use. The bodies on the patio, however, were another story.

As Harvath circled back around, McGee had already used the toe of his boot to raise all of their night-vision goggles. He wasn't bothering to check for vitals. It was obvious from the extent of their injuries that they were dead as well.

All of them, including the two dead men with the ladder, looked Caucasian to Harvath. American. Not a single one of them looked Iranian.

Pointing down at one of the attackers lying in a congealing pool of blood on the patio, McGee said, "I think I recognize this guy."

"From where?"

"I think he was Agency. Maybe a contractor."

"You've got to be kidding me," Harvath replied.

McGee shook his head and, taking out his phone, began taking pictures of all the corpses.

As he did, Harvath told him not to bother with the two around the corner and had Haney go get Rogers and bring him back downstairs.

When the Ambassador stepped through the broken glass of the living room and out onto the patio, Harvath asked him if he recognized any of the attackers.

He took his time, examining each one, but ended up shaking his head. "I haven't seen any of these men before," he responded. "Who the hell are they?"

"I've got no idea," said Harvath as he patted them down. Not a single one of them was carrying any ID or a phone. It was another professional job.

Returning from examining the rest of the bodies, McGee held up his cell phone and showed Rogers pictures of the two men who had been attempting to scale the roof.

Harvath and McGee watched as the color drained from the man's face.

"That's them," the Ambassador stated. "Those are the men who came after me yesterday in Rock Creek Park."

CHAPTER 28

C arolan and Fields had been at White Wolf Combat almost
the entire night. The amount of red tape and paperwork the
shooting had created was record-breaking—even by government standards.

Baltimore PD secured the scene while agents from headquarters
and the FBI's Baltimore Field Office were brought in to conduct the
investigation.

There were plenty of familiar faces. Even Agent Kennedy had shown
up in a sign of solidarity and support, tracking down coffees for them and
sitting for a while making small talk.

As far as Carolan was concerned, it was an absolutely justifiable use
of lethal force. The final decision, however, would come down to the
FBI's Shooting Incident Review Group. Unfortunately for Fields, they
wouldn't be meeting again until September. Carolan couldn't wait that
long. He needed her with him on the street, not behind a desk on admin-
istrative leave.

The key was their boss, Gallo. He could push her through, but not
without airtight, unassailable evidence that she had been in the right.

Carolan had a gut feeling that evidence was sitting right at the crime
scene, just waiting to be uncovered, and he had leaned on the Baltimore
Field Office to find it for him.

In order to preserve the integrity of the investigation, however, anything they were able to come up with couldn't go to him, the partner of

the shooter and a key witness to the event, it had to go to their supervisor. That was fine with Carolan.

After driving Fields home and making sure that she was stable and okay to be on her own, Carolan had returned to his house, crawled into bed with his wife, and fallen instantly asleep.

When his phone starting vibrating on the nightstand, he was positive he'd only been out for a few minutes. In reality, he'd been asleep for six solid hours.

He could tell by the caller ID that it was Gallo.

"Carolan," he said, activating the call.

"In my entire career at the Bureau, that's the cleanest shooting I've ever seen," his boss stated.

Carolan's hope that in addition to the security cameras on the outside of White Wolf Combat, the interior cameras—especially the one in Weber's office—had been running and recording had paid off.

"How's she doing?" Gallo continued.

"Good. It's not her first rodeo."

"Any psychological or emotional issues? Shock? PTSD?"

"With all due respect, I'm not a shrink," Carolan replied.

"But you are her supervisor, as well as her partner. If I okay her to return to the field, am I going to regret it?"

"I don't think so. No."

"Okay, just to cover my ass, I want one of the Bureau psychologists to sign off. My assistant has got her an appointment at ten o'clock this morning."

"Thank you, sir," said Carolan. "I'll make sure she's there."

"You should pick her up in a limo and buy her the best breakfast in town on your way," Gallo stated. "If not for her shooting skills, that piece of shit Weber might have killed you both."

Carolan didn't disagree. After thanking his boss again, he hung up, placed a call to Fields, and filled her in.

As her vehicle was still sitting in the garage back at headquarters, he drove to her place and picked her up.

"Here you go," he said, handing her a large coffee as she got into the car, plus a bag with her favorite bacon, egg, and Gouda sandwich.

"What's all this?" she asked. "I normally get us coffee."

"It was Gallo's idea. He said that since you saved my life, the least I could do was buy you breakfast."

"He's right," Fields said. "And by the way, you're welcome."

"By the way," Carolan responded, "look at your cup."

Fields looked down and read aloud what had been written in black Sharpie. "Thank you. Love, Boss."

"Awwww, I'm going to frame this and hang it in our beautiful new office."

"Over my dead body. That thing is *not* coming in the building. I didn't put in decades of hard work just so you could blow up my reputation with a to-go cup."

"You should have thought of that ahead of time," she replied, peeling off the lid and blowing on the coffee. "Besides, it'll be good for people to see a different side of the angry, old 'Bear.' Maybe they'll start calling you the *sugar* bear."

"Good God, no. I'm telling you right now. If that happens, I'm putting a bullet in you and then one in myself."

Fields grinned. "Whatever you say, Sugar Bear."

Carolan knew, that for at least the next twenty-four hours, he was going to have to be a good sport and take it. Gallo was right. She had very likely saved both of their lives.

"You sure you're okay with getting back in the saddle right away?" he asked, changing the subject.

"I've got to be honest. After you dropped me off at home, I opened a bottle of Merlot and polished it off by myself."

"Understandable."

"Then I opened a second."

Carolan winced at hearing that.

"But instead of drinking it," she continued, "I put the cork back in, stuck it in the fridge, and went to bed."

"How are you feeling today?"

"A little hungover, but grateful for my bacon, egg, and cheese breakfast."

Carolan smiled. "The hangover's a given. You drink some of the shittiest wine I've ever seen. What I'm talking about, though, is the shooting. How do you feel about that?"

"To be honest, I'm angry. I mean *really* pissed-off. That motherfucker was going to shoot us."

"Yes, he was."

"We were just asking him questions. It was a fucking knock-and-talk. That's it. He didn't have to pull a gun on us. That motherfucker."

Carolan knew her well enough to know that the depth of her anger was often measured in "motherfuckers." Like the rest of her swearing, he had given up trying to move her off that one a long time ago as well.

She was putting things together in her mind, processing, and so he remained quiet and let her keep going.

"I wouldn't have even seen his damn tattoo if he hadn't reached for that hand cannon out of his desk drawer. But by then, he'd already made up his mind. Rather than waiting for us to leave, rather than just playing stupid for a few minutes more, he made a choice. That motherfucker decided he was going to murder two federal agents in cold blood. For what?"

He waited for her to look at him, indicating that she wanted a response, but when she didn't, he didn't offer one.

"So he must have known our guy—the one in the morgue with the same tattoo, right? Weber must have figured that we knew a lot more than we were letting on; that we weren't going to let him walk out of there a free man. He felt cornered, right? Like there was no way out."

This time she did look at him and Carolan nodded. "Obviously, the tattoo triggered him. And I think you're probably correct. I think Weber believed we had something pretty serious on him and he was going back inside, maybe to never come out again."

"But all of that over a tattoo? He didn't even ask us why we were interested in it. That just doesn't make sense."

"Unless," said Carolan, "that tattoo is tied to something so big that the minute the law shows up asking about it, you know it's game over. You're going down."

"Something big like the attack outside the Vice President's Residence."

Once more, Carolan nodded.

"So what's the plan?" Fields asked.

"I'm working on a possible lead for us," he replied. "But first, I need you to answer my question. Are you okay, mentally?"

"One hundred percent," she answered without hesitation. "And I would do it again. If someone pulls a gun on me, or you, we're not going to sit in a sharing circle and talk about it. That person is going down."

"Which is all I needed to hear," said Carolan.

CHAPTER 29

Even though Ambassador Rogers's property was heavily wooded and Haney and McGee had been inside the house while shooting, tons of the windows had been blown out and the pair had been firing big, unsuppressed weapons. It was likely that one, if not more, of the neighbors had heard the gunfight and already called police.

That had left Harvath with a big decision and not a lot of time within which to make it. Did he stay and deal with local law enforcement, thereby providing Rogers with ironclad proof that he was indeed an active assassination target? Or did he use the narrow window before the cops arrived to move the Ambassador to someplace safer?

Harvath chose the latter.

After a quick security check of Rogers's Audi, they threw their gear in the trunk, and all piled in. With McGee driving, they headed to the house where he and Haney had parked their vehicles. As they drove, they planned their next move.

The first item of business was where to dump Rogers's Audi. With all of its onboard tech, a sophisticated enough person could turn it into a homing beacon, leading the bad guys right to them. There was no way they were going to take it to their next safe house. To the Ambassador's credit, he came up with the terrific spot to drop it.

As a member of the nearby Washington Golf Club, he could leave it in their lot, likely for several days, without anyone giving it a second thought.

Next on their list was where to stash Rogers himself, and this time it was McGee who came up with the perfect spot.

The predawn drive to Kent Island, just across the Chesapeake Bay from Annapolis, went by in a flash. Riding shotgun in McGee's car, with Rogers in the back seat and Haney following behind in his Bronco, Harvath spent the entirety of the trip texting back and forth with Nicholas.

Only once, in the very beginning, did he break away from what he was doing to ask the Ambassador a question.

"After you lost your Secret Service detail," said Harvath, "did you change your alarm code?"

The look on Rogers's face said it all. He was mortified at what Harvath was suggesting. "You don't think the Secret Service had something to do with the attack?"

"I don't want to," Harvath replied, "but I have to keep every possibility open."

They had a brief discussion about who else over the years had access to the code. The only additional person who used the alarm system was his housekeeper, but she had her own secondary code, not the master. The Ambassador had only shared the master with the Secret Service once they had begun protecting him.

The next thing they had discussed was the lack of ballistic shielding on the ceiling of his safe room. Once again, an uncomfortable finger pointed toward the Secret Service. They were the only ones, besides the company who had put the room together, who knew about that vulnerability.

When it came to the exterior security cameras, cursory surveillance would have revealed them to anyone who had been looking for them. What Harvath was still stuck on, however, was the web-connected home automation system and the possibility that it had been hacked.

That was one of the first things he wanted Nicholas looking into— before the local cops started poking around. With his exceptional IT skills, Harvath was hoping that he might be able to pick up the trail of whoever had been responsible for disabling the alarm and the cameras.

Then there were the corpses, all of which—including the two whose faces Haney had removed—McGee had photographed. Harvath had sent the images to Nicholas, while McGee sent them to a person he trusted back at the CIA. Between the two of them, hopefully they'd be able to identify some, if not all the attackers, including the man who had looked familiar to McGee and the duo who had been after Rogers in Rock Creek Park.

Harvath had multiple other issues he wanted to war-game out with McGee, but he preferred to do it in private, without Rogers sitting right behind them. The less the Ambassador knew about what Harvath was thinking, the better.

Crossing the Chesapeake Bay Bridge, they had headed south. Kent Island was the third oldest English settlement in the United States, just behind Jamestown, Virginia, and Plymouth, Massachusetts. Encompassing only about thirty-one and a half square miles, once you were on the island, it didn't take long to get anywhere.

Their destination was a large home in a gated waterfront community at the southern tip of the island called the Cove Creek Club.

Covering over three hundred acres, the secluded club had its own golf course, marina, and private security force. The estate McGee drove them onto had to be at least double the size of the Ambassador's. It's custom, Nantucket shingle–style home was enormous and came with a hot tub, a saltwater pool, a private pier, and a thirty-five-foot Chris-Craft. The most amazing feature, however, was the unobstructed views of the water.

As they got out of their cars, the first thing Harvath noticed was the temperature difference. "Much cooler than D.C.," he remarked.

"With water on three sides, it really makes a difference," McGee replied.

Haney stood for a moment, taking it all in before saying, "Whatever you were getting paid as CIA director, it was definitely too much."

"This isn't Bob's house," said Harvath.

"It belongs to a lady friend. She's in Italy for the summer and asked me to keep an eye on it."

"This has got to be what, five bedrooms?" asked Haney.

"Seven," McGee stated.

"Wow. What'd she do to earn a place like this?"

"She suffered through a marriage with a real son of a bitch and then divorced well."

"Very well," Haney commented. "Okay if I look around?"

"Be my guest," McGee replied as he gestured for Harvath and Rogers to follow him down to the dock.

While they walked, McGee read them in. "There's only one set of immediate neighbors, just to the west, but they're in California till Labor Day. Everyone is friendly, but with these price tags, as you can imagine, they respect each other's privacy. The clubhouse bar and the pickleball courts get kind of chummy, as does the pro shop, so you'll want to avoid those. The least amount of people who know you're here the better. That goes double for you, Mr. Ambassador."

"I think I can force myself to make it work," Rogers joked. "Thank you, Bob."

"You're welcome. Sharon is also very generous with her wine cellar, so remind me to show you what bottles are on the approved list."

"Will do."

"And as I know you're training for the Marine Corps Marathon, I'm happy to let you run with me in the morning, as long as you promise not to slow me down."

Rogers smiled. "Deal."

"What about supplies?" Harvath asked.

"The house is pretty well stocked, but if you and the Ambassador give me a list, I can go out later and get anything you need."

McGee seemed to have it all figured out and so they made small talk as they walked out onto the dock and took in the view.

He gave them a quick rundown on the boat, explained where the keys were hidden, and then led them back to the house, where Haney had taken it upon himself to whip up breakfast. They could smell the bacon cooking before even stepping inside.

Eager to get cleaned up, the Ambassador asked which bathroom he could use and McGee walked him upstairs.

By the time the ex–CIA director returned to the kitchen, Harvath and Haney were already drinking coffee and had poured a cup for him.

With Rogers upstairs taking a shower, it seemed the right time to discuss next steps. They had some pretty serious choices to make.

CHAPTER 30

O ne thing is for damn sure," said McGee, taking a sip of his coffee. "Those weren't fucking Iranians at Rogers's house."

Harvath nodded in agreement. "Which begs the question, *who* were they and *why* were they after the Ambassador?"

"And why so many of them?" added Haney. "Not to mention, who brings a ladder to something like that?"

"Someone with inside information," McGee replied.

"And now we're at the heart of this thing," stated Harvath. "The guy at the top of the ladder had a circular saw and other breaching tools in his pack. There's no question in my mind that they were going to cut through the roof and down into the ceiling of Rogers's safe room."

"Then what?" asked Haney. "Make it look like he slipped in his tub? While there's a gaping hole above his master bedroom closet?"

"Mike's right," said McGee. "If the deaths of the SecDef and the Sec-State are connected; if the Ambassador really *is* next on some sort of kill list, then style-wise, this a pretty major departure."

"And," Haney continued, "why assume Rogers is going to beat you to the safe room at all? You're hitting his house at three in the morning. Wouldn't you expect him to be asleep?"

"Probably," said Harvath.

"And if you're skilled enough to shut down his cameras and turn off his alarm, shouldn't you be able to open a door or a window without waking him up?"

"Absolutely."

"Then why go the roof route?"

It was a fair question and Harvath had only one answer: "Because Bob's right, these guys had insider information. It's exactly the op we would have run. If we knew our target had a safe room, we would have come equipped to rip through it and pull the guy out."

"But they didn't come to pull him out. They came to kill him. Would it have made any difference where they caught him?"

"Probably not."

"Then, if Rogers is right about the demise of his colleagues, how would the killers have made this death track?"

"High-end home invasion gone bad," said Harvath. "It's the only thing I can come up with that makes sense. Disabling cameras, disabling the alarm, knowing about the safe room—that kind of attention to detail is all par for that course. Burglars at that level normally have an inside source and my guess is that some sort of evidence would have ended up being planted to frame the housekeeper. An untraceable payment to an account in her name would have surfaced, or they would have found a bunch of unexplained cash hidden somewhere in her house."

"And the cops would have believed that?"

"You saw his house. Rogers was a very successful attorney before going to work for the government. He stepped away from a highly respected law firm, but he didn't stop being a partner and having equity. I think it's totally believable that he'd be a target for that kind of home invasion. Whether or not it would spook the other high-ranking officials involved with the Soleimani hit is another question. Personally, I think they might discount it and continue to whistle past the graveyard."

"I sure as hell wouldn't," McGee interjected.

"Except for Bob," Harvath clarified, picking up his coffee and taking a sip.

"But based on that stack of bodies back at the Ambo's house," said Haney, "the hitters aren't Iranians. So doesn't that torpedo the idea that this is retribution for Soleimani?"

McGee agreed. "The attack we saw would mark a huge evolution for Tehran. Way too sophisticated. The ability to recruit well-trained, ostensibly American operators is simply beyond their capabilities. They could throw all the money in the world at something like this and still not pull it off."

"Then what are we looking at?" Harvath asked, legitimately exasperated. "I've now been in two serious gunfights, in two days, with what looks like American citizens. What the hell is going on?"

Looking into his coffee as if he might find the answer, the former CIA director shook his head. "I don't know. I think, maybe, it's ideological."

"*Ideological?* The protesters outside the VP's residence were members of his own party. Ambassador Rogers is from the opposite party and no longer in government. How could any of this be ideological?"

"In my experience," said McGee, "when something bad goes down, you look at two groups—those who benefit from what happened, and those who were pissed-off leading up to what happened."

"Okay," Harvath replied, humoring him. "Someone very publicly kills a group of Mitchell supporters, along with a bunch of cops, and then goes after Rogers, but not before they ice the SecDef and SecState? Assuming, of course, that the Ambassador's correct about their deaths. So then, looking at all of that, cui bono?"

"I don't know who benefits," he replied, exasperated himself. "But if you can nail that down, you've got your hands on the key to this whole thing."

"So let's look at the second group," said Haney, trying to keep things moving. "In the run-up to the attack at the VP's Residence, who was pissed-off?"

"Only about half the country," Harvath responded, standing up to get some fresh coffee. "You've got everyone who didn't vote for Mitchell, plus anyone who's lost faith in him since he took office. But none of that explains why the attack happened or who's behind the hit on Rogers, much less any connection between the two."

"If I may," said McGee. "Let's pull the lens back and think like I did at CIA. If you were a foreign nation hostile to the United States, how might attacking angry Mitchell supporters, as well as officials from the previous administration, serve your ends?"

It was an unusual question, and one that Harvath definitely hadn't considered. If a hostile foreign intelligence service was trying to stir unrest in the United States, the last thing they'd want to do was make the plot easy to piece together.

In fact, the more complicated and disjointed they could make it, the more successful they'd likely be at avoiding detection. But at the same time, he reasoned, there would have to be a through line, some sort of unified objective to it all. Chaos simply for chaos's sake hardly seemed like much of a plan.

What's more, while gunning down protesters and blowing up cops had the potential to grab people's attention and possibly spur them to some sort of action, you wouldn't get a single person in the streets because a bunch of government employees from a previous administration had been killed. Right or wrong, not enough people would care about them.

That was where the whole foreign intelligence service plot fell apart for Harvath. Killing Rogers and his former colleagues produced a juice that just didn't seem worth the squeeze. No matter how many angles he came at it from, he couldn't come up with an answer.

"I don't know," he finally admitted.

"Okay," McGee offered. "Instead of zooming out, let's change our lens altogether. If you wanted to hobble the new administration, how would you do it? Think big."

After topping off Haney, Harvath filled his own mug and said, "I'd want to make Mitchell as unpopular as possible; absolutely crater his polling numbers. I'd want to put him in a hole so deep that no matter what he did or said, even his dog wouldn't support him."

The ex–CIA director smiled. "And to guarantee that, to make him a full-on dead man walking, politically speaking, what would you do?"

"That's easy," Harvath stated as he leaned against the counter. "I'd make people afraid. I'd use murder and mayhem to make them feel that their world was spinning out of control, that they weren't safe, and that it was all because of Mitchell."

McGee raised his mug to him. "Now you're thinking like a CIA director."

"What I can't figure out, though, is how it ties in with Rogers and the deaths of his colleagues."

"That's even easier to explain. In fact, Mitchell may have handed the idea to our enemies on a silver platter."

"What are you talking about?"

"The President hasn't been shy about cutting the size of government—including Secret Service details."

"And?"

"And if it comes to pass that any officials, especially those involved with national security, were murdered because Mitchell didn't protect them, can you imagine the chilling effect that would have? Who would want to work for Mitchell, or any future administration, if you knew that one day you could be hung out to dry? How hard would you push America's enemies if at some point in the future, when you needed your country the most, the United States might not have your back? We'd never get top-tier talent into national security positions ever again. It would be an enormous win for the enemies of the United States."

It was an excellent point. And while President Mitchell was within his rights to deny ex-officials like Rogers protection, which could run upwards of $2 million a month, the potential consequences of doing nothing seemed incalculable to Harvath.

In his opinion, if there was a bona fide, active threat against any government official—past or present—and that threat was a result of their official duties on behalf of the United States, America should protect them. It was the morally just thing to do.

One would think it was also smart politics, regardless of party affiliation, but politicians were an odd breed as far as Harvath was concerned. There were very few he had met over his career that he had liked and fewer still that he had respected.

What troubled him was that as the character of America's politicians declined, so too did the character of its people. They were inexorably linked.

"We still haven't answered one of Mike's first questions," he said, getting back on topic. "Whoever is behind this, they originally sent two people after Rogers. Then, all of a sudden, last night they sent eight? Why?"

"You said it yourself," McGee replied. "They had insider information.

Someone either knew, or had reason to suspect, that the Ambassador was now being protected."

"A leak? At the Carlton Group?" Harvath found that impossible to believe. Only Nicholas knew what they were up to.

"Did you speak with anyone else?"

Just one. And as soon as the revelation hit him, his blood went cold. He had to get to Sølvi.

CHAPTER 31

As Harvath had left the crappy Chevy Malibu that Nicholas had arranged for him back in the parking garage in McLean, Haney let him borrow his Bronco.

The morning traffic had been terrible, but at least he'd had air-conditioning. Most important of all, he'd texted with Sølvi and she had promised not to leave the house until he got there.

Pulling into his driveway, he parked next to her Mustang and headed inside.

He found her in the kitchen, dressed in a black pantsuit with her long blond hair wrapped in a tight bun, ready to head out the door to work.

In order to make sure nothing they discussed was overheard, he asked for her cell phone, which, along with his, he walked back to his office and dropped in a faraday bag. Returning to the kitchen, he spent the next ten minutes laying out everything that had happened.

In a word, Sølvi was stunned.

"If it's not the Iranians, who is it?" she asked.

"We don't know," he replied. "Maybe the Chinese. Maybe the Russians."

"This doesn't sound like Beijing to me. The Chinese use finesse. They aren't messy like this. Bloodshed and brutality are much more a Russian calling card."

"Agreed."

"And the assault team at Rogers's house," Sølvi continued, "you're sure they were Americans?"

"We took photographs of the bodies. McGee and Nicholas are trying to identify them."

"From two men to eight men," she mused. "They quadrupled their forces. You don't go to those lengths unless you're expecting trouble."

Harvath nodded. "That's what bothers me. They came loaded for bear."

"And other than Nicholas, McGee, and Haney, the only other person who knew you had met with Rogers was Russ Gaines?"

"Russ Gaines and you. That's it."

"I can understand why you didn't want to tell me any of this over the phone," said Sølvi. "What are you going to do?"

"I'm going to have to go see Russ in person, look him in the eye. It's the only way I'll know if he's telling me the truth."

"What if he *is* the leak?"

Harvath shook his head wearily. "I haven't gotten that far yet."

"Did you get any sleep at all?" she asked, taking his stubbled chin in her hand. "You look exhausted."

"I'm fine."

Kissing him, she let go of his chin. "What can I do for you?"

"Nothing. Just be careful and come home safe. That's all I ask."

Sølvi looked at her watch. "The Prime Minister and the Norwegian delegation arrive this afternoon. I'm going to meet up at the embassy with the Secret Service and we'll drive out together to pick them up. When are you going to pay Russ Gaines a visit?"

"Part of me wants to show up unannounced at his house and catch him off guard. The only problem is, I have no idea what time he'll be home. I may just reach out to him and see if he'll meet with me in his office."

Sølvi looked at him. "With the full expectation that if he is the leak and wants to get to Rogers, he's going to put a tail on you the minute you leave."

Harvath smiled. "Then we'll know for sure."

"Don't do anything stupid," she ordered, kissing him one last time. "And try to get some rest. Will I see you tonight?"

He shook his head. "I don't want to leave Haney and McGee a man down. Besides, we've got to figure out what we're going to do with Rogers."

"I understand. Call me later if you can."

Kissing her back, he then retrieved her phone from his office and brought it to her.

He stood at the front door and watched as she walked out to her car. She was such an amazing woman. Her confidence, her poise, her strength—he loved everything about her.

After pausing to admire Haney's Bronco, she turned and flashed him a thumbs-up. He smiled back.

Sliding into the Mustang, she fired it up, gunned the engine, and then squealed the tires as she peeled out. Harvath chuckled as he shut the front door and walked back to his office.

Picking up his phone, he called Russ Gaines. The Secret Service agent sounded genuinely surprised to hear from him.

With dignitaries starting to arrive in town for the NATO Summit, the man's schedule was packed, but as Harvath had said it was important and that he needed to see him in person, Gaines agreed to squeeze him in at 3:30.

The meeting set, Harvath could now focus on the rest of his list. And right at the top, just as Sølvi had suggested, was grabbing a few hours of sleep.

Though he'd been trained to go long stretches without, only a fool would pass up a chance to rest.

Sleep was a critical tool in his toolbox—as important as any knife or gun. The better rested he was, the stronger he became. And something told him that he was going to need every ounce of strength he had for what lay ahead.

CHAPTER 32

There were only three more days of business before both houses of Congress broke for the Fourth of July holiday and members returned home.

Despite his staff having planned constituent events for him in St. Louis, Kansas City, Springfield, Columbia, and Cape Girardeau, Senator Blackwood had no intention of returning to Missouri. There was going to be a full-scale governmental crisis before his flight ever took off.

In the meantime, he had to proceed as if everything was normal. One of the items that needed his attention was the NATO Summit—in particular, the European Sky Shield program. It was one of President Mitchell's chief initiatives.

Similar to Israel's Iron Dome, the idea was to provide Europe with a security umbrella that could fend off incoming missile and drone attacks. And though these attacks could come from any state or nonstate actor, it was widely accepted that Sky Shield was intended to defend against Russian attacks.

Mitchell had thrown his support behind Sky Shield as a way to lessen NATO's reliance on the United States and bring more American troops home from Europe.

While that position resonated with many voters, there were also those in Mitchell's base who didn't like that the program would use American missiles and American technology. Russia not only hated Sky Shield, but had also run an aggressive public relations campaign claiming that the Sky Shield was actually an offensive weapons system masquerading as being defensive.

There had been a ton of saber-rattling coming out of the Kremlin and it had only increased as the D.C. summit had gotten closer. Moscow was now publicly stating that Sky Shield, if fully adopted by NATO, would bring the world to the threshold of nuclear war.

The isolationist wing of Mitchell's base seemed to hate Sky Shield as much, if not more, than the Russians. They wanted the United States fully out of NATO and didn't want any further American weaponry or technology being shared with the Europeans. Unbowed by what had happened in front of the Vice President's Residence, they had a massive "Don't Poke the Bear" protest planned for the opening day of the summit. Thousands of people had already RSVP'd online and were headed to D.C. It was going to be a security nightmare for D.C. Police and the Secret Service.

The protest, however, wasn't Blackwood's main concern. Two Missouri technology companies, who also happened to be substantial political donors of his, had interests in seeing Sky Shield move forward. Their CEOs had asked the senator to introduce them to some of the European delegations at the cocktail party being held at the White House tomorrow night. Even though these companies would have big splashy booths in the exhibition hall next to where the summit was being held and would likely end up chatting with the very same delegates, they wanted any "pregame" leg up they could get over their competition.

Blackwood couldn't give a damn about Sky Shield or the Europeans, but he needed to keep up the appearance that he cared about the President's initiatives. He also wanted to keep money flowing from his donors.

For those reasons, he had asked his staff to prepare a briefing book for him, which he was now studying.

He was only on the second page when the encrypted messaging app on his personal phone pinged with a text.

Taking out his phone, he read the message. Vice President Chris Cates's chief of staff was letting him know that everything was set. At the appointed time, the VP would be exactly where he needed to be and prepared to say exactly what he needed to say.

Senator Blackwood smiled and, after returning the phone to his jacket pocket, tore the executive summary out of the binder in front of him and threw the rest of the Sky Shield briefing book into the garbage. If he had to, he could wing it.

In reality, he knew that after today, Sky Shield was the last thing anyone was going to be talking about.

CHAPTER 33

With nothing but her passport and cell phone, Sølvi had shown up at the Embassy of Norway, ready to begin her stint as an adjunct protection agent for Norwegian Prime Minister Anita Stang.

Prime Minister Stang and the Norwegian delegation would be arriving at Dulles International Airport. Sølvi, and the U.S. Secret Service agents augmenting Stang's existing detail from the Norwegian Police Security Service, also known by the acronym PST, would meet them at their plane and escort them to waiting vehicles on the tarmac.

One of the PST agents, an old friend of Sølvi's named Bente Bergstrøm, would be transporting her body armor, CZ Nighthawk Custom pistol, her Norwegian Intelligence Service credentials, and a handful of other items she had left behind in Oslo.

The Secret Service would be providing all the Norwegian protective agents, including Sølvi, with special, temporary credentials, as well as a unique lapel pin that readily identified them as precleared security professionals.

Arriving at the embassy, Sølvi parked her car and sought out the chief of embassy security. They did a full walk-through of both the embassy and the Ambassador's residence. Since it was technically still an "active" crime scene, portions of the residence, including the kitchen, had been closed off with heavy sheets of plastic and yellow crime tape. Nevertheless, because she was a detail person, Sølvi wanted to have eyes on any and every area that the PM might elect to see or pass through.

Because of all the stress and upheaval caused by the attacks, President Mitchell had graciously offered Ambassador Hansen rooms at Blair House, the state guesthouse just across Pennsylvania Avenue from the White House. While the Ambassador and her husband had politely declined, they had accepted on behalf of Prime Minister Stang, who under normal circumstances would have stayed at the Ambassador's residence. Blair House was where Sølvi had scheduled to go next.

The Secret Service team augmenting Prime Minister Stang's Norwegian detail was composed of two male and two female agents. Sølvi had been given their information the day before during her meeting at Secret Service headquarters, but had yet to meet them.

The team arrived at the embassy a few minutes early and double-parked their black Chevy Suburban outside. When Sølvi stepped out, they exited the vehicle and introduced themselves.

They all shook hands and traded cell phone information, then the agent in charge, Jonathan Miller, gave her a quick tour of the vehicle, pointing out where the medical kit was, along with some other equipment. Once that was complete, they mounted up and headed for Blair House.

As they made the short, two-and-a-half-mile drive, Miller broke down how the rest of the day would unfold.

The Secret Service had arranged for a large private suite at one of the fixed base operator buildings at Dulles Airport.

Once Prime Minister Stang's Scandinavian Airlines flight had arrived at the gate, the Norwegian delegation would be deplaned first and taken down the jet-bridge stairs to three waiting Secret Service vehicles and driven to the FBO. There the Prime Minister and her team could relax, have something to eat, and even shower if they wanted, while their luggage was collected and their passports were processed. Then, once everything was in order, they would head to Blair House.

It was all pretty straightforward. Removing a special NATO Summit lapel pin from his pocket, the agent in charge handed it to her and indicated which side it should be pinned to.

When they rolled up to the police checkpoint just before Blair House, the young, broad-shouldered FBI agent driving their Suburban, Eric Sorola, bantered with one of the cops. As the barrier arm was raised, the cop saw him off with the Marine Corps motto, "Semper Fi," which Eric proudly repeated.

"A United States Marine," Sølvi said approvingly from the second row of seats.

"Yes, ma'am," Sorola replied.

"How long were you in?"

"Eight years. Then college. Now the Bureau."

"Did you see any combat?" she asked.

"Yes, ma'am."

"Afghanistan?" she asked.

"And Iraq," the young man responded.

"What was your MOS?"

"Started out infantry, drifted into Marine Security Guard duty, and ended up doing a lot of dignitary protection."

"Makes you perfect for this assignment," said Sølvi.

Sorola chuckled as he pulled up in front of Blair House and parked. "When I was in Iraq, I drove Route Irish so many times my buddies said I should start my own version of Uber and call it Suber."

Sølvi smiled. It was a funny line.

Route Irish, however, was no laughing matter. It was an extremely dangerous, seven-and-a-half-mile stretch of the Baghdad Airport Road that connected the International Green Zone, where the U.S. Embassy was, with Baghdad International Airport.

Getting out of the Suburban, the team was greeted by the director of Blair House, who welcomed them and explained that the complex was made up of four separate nineteenth-century homes, boasted fourteen guest bedrooms, and spanned over 70,000 feet, making it bigger than the Executive Residence across the street at the White House. Guests have included Queen Elizabeth II, Nikita Khrushchev, Charles de Gaulle, Margaret Thatcher, and even Afghan leader Hamid Karzai.

Normally reserved for heads of state, it was considered quite an honor to have it extended to the Norwegian NATO delegation. President Mitchell had been deeply saddened by the loss of Norwegian lives at Ambassador Hansen's residence and wanted the entire delegation to feel safe and at home.

The director took them on an overall tour and answered all of Sølvi's questions along the way. Any door Sølvi wanted opened or space she wanted to look into, the director happily obliged.

Maintaining her thorough attention to detail, and knowing her fellow Norwegians as well as she did, Sølvi asked where the closest watering hole was. She was interested in something upscale, with good security, that also served food.

Miller and Blair House's director both agreed—the Off the Record bar in the basement of the Hay-Adams hotel, just across Lafayette Square.

Sølvi asked if they might trace the walk right now and even get a bite to eat before heading out to Dulles. The director offered to call over and see if she could reserve a table on their behalf.

Sixty seconds later, they were on their way.

Strolling across the park, they were met in the lobby by the hotel's gracious concierge, who took them downstairs and got them all set up.

As they ate, Sølvi got to know more about the team, including the two female agents, Longwell and Del Vecchio.

Sorola also discussed more about his time in Iraq, a country Sølvi had been to a couple of times, and the myriad vehicles he had used for his airport runs, including the M1117 armored security vehicle that had been nicknamed the "Guardian."

When the bill came, Sølvi insisted on paying. The elegant Hay-Adams had been her idea. She didn't want to put the Secret Service agents in a difficult position if their per diems wouldn't cover their lunches.

On the way back to Blair House, they continued to chat. Sølvi had filled them in on her military history and now it was mostly just personal stuff—families, relationships, that kind of thing.

Hopping back in the Suburban, they headed west on I-66, crossed the Potomac River via the Theodore Roosevelt Bridge, and kept going till they merged with the Dulles Access Road and eventually arrived at the airport about forty-five minutes later.

All in all, it wasn't a terrible trip, though the Dulles Access Road had to be one of the ugliest stretches of highway Sølvi had ever experienced. Stain-covered sound-attenuation barriers, anonymous, unattractive low-rise office buildings, orange traffic barrels, and patchy, overgrown highway grass.

It was nothing like the ride in from Oslo's international airport, where the road was lined with majestic pines. She was just sorry Scot wasn't with her so she could point out the difference and see if she could get a rise out of him.

Pulling up to the FBO, she could see a fleet of pristine black SUVs with U.S. government plates. Two of them—a Chevy Suburban and a Chevy Tahoe—were armored.

As she had been told that the Dutch delegation was landing at the same time and that they would all be caravaning back to D.C. together, she wondered which armored vehicle was for Prime Minister Stang.

Getting out of the Suburban, she stretched her legs as Miller chatted with a couple of agents who were standing nearby.

When he was done, he came back over and explained that because the Suburban was bigger and considered more prestigious, it was the one that had been reserved for the Norwegians.

While Miller headed inside, Sølvi walked over to look at it. Sorola joined her.

"You get the big one," he said. "First class."

She didn't know about that. "Do you have a penny on you?" she asked as she continued to examine the vehicle.

Reaching into his pocket, he pulled out some change and handed her one.

Circling the vehicle, Sølvi used the penny—head down—to gauge the level of treads on the run-flat tires. It was a trick Scot had taught her.

After she had done a full 360, she got up on the driver's-side running board and motioned for Sorola to join her.

Once he was standing next to her, she grabbed hold of the roof rack and said, "Let's see how much play there is in the suspension."

Using their combined body weight, the young FBI agent helped her rock the vehicle up and down.

"Now let's try the Tahoe," she said.

They put it through the same test and then she walked around the vehicle with the penny, checking out all the treads.

"What are you thinking?" Sorola asked as she took a step back and gazed at both SUVs.

"Culturally, I think Americans believe bigger is always better. We don't see things that way in Norway."

"You don't want the Suburban?"

"I think *everybody* wants the Suburban. That's the problem."

He looked at her. "What's wrong with it?"

"At a glance, nothing. But judging by the difference in the treads and the stiffness of the suspensions, the Suburban has seen more use."

"We can totally switch you over to the Tahoe. That's not a problem. They're both the same model year, same engine, and have the same level of armor."

Sølvi smiled. "Thank you. Yes. Let's take the Tahoe. And there's one other thing I need."

"What's that?"

"I want you to drive it," she replied.

CHAPTER 34

As the Secret Service agent in charge, Miller wasn't crazy about Sølvi changing up his roster, but he had been given specific instructions to cooperate with her and the Norwegians. As long as they didn't present any unreasonable requests, his job was to comply.

The armored vehicles came with dedicated drivers, but if Sølvi wanted to take the Tahoe over the Suburban and swap Sorola in as the driver, he wasn't going to lose any sleep over it. Sorola had been fully certified at the Rowley Training Center on both SUVs. What's more, the M1117 Guardian he had piloted in Iraq weighed in at 30,000 pounds. An armored Tahoe would be a walk in the park for him.

An hour before the PM's flight was due to land, Ambassador Hansen and a handful of key embassy staff arrived at the FBO. Sølvi introduced them to the Secret Service detail and then led them into the private suite that had been set up for Stang and the Norwegian delegation.

In addition to coffee, tea, bottled water, and soft drinks, there was a full bar and catered food. A protocol officer from the State Department had definitely been hovering somewhere over the Secret Service's shoulder.

"This all looks very good," said Hansen. "So take me through what will happen when the Prime Minister arrives."

"I will be on the jet bridge," said Sølvi, "along with Special Agent Miller when the door to the aircraft opens. Prime Minister Stang and her PST detail will deplane first, followed by the rest of her team.

"We will then take the exterior jet-bridge stairs down to the tarmac, where three Secret Service vehicles will be waiting. Once we have every-one loaded, we will head back here where you can officially greet the Prime Minister. The FBO has a red carpet they will be putting outside the main entrance. That's where you and your staff will receive Prime Minister Stang."

"And you will text me to let me know when you have the Prime Min-ister and are on your way back here?"

Sølvi nodded. "Yes, ma'am. Absolutely."

"Okay then," Hansen replied, eyeing the catering. "I think I may grab a cookie, a cup of tea, and return some emails while we wait for the Prime Minister's plane to land."

With the Ambassador and her staff taken care of, Sølvi exited the suite and found Agent Miller standing in the FBO's lobby with the rest of his team.

"Everything good?" he asked.

She nodded. "How's traffic going to be on the way back?"

"We're going to have a police escort, plus we'll be traveling in the opposite direction of all the rush-hour commuters, so it shouldn't be too bad. But you never know. It could still take a while."

"I'll make sure the Ambassador encourages them to eat something. Just in case."

"Good thinking," said Miller. "By the way, you still want to do a walk-through of the convention center tomorrow, right?"

"Yes," Sølvi replied. "Ideally, while the Prime Minister is in her meet-ings at the embassy."

"Just let me know. Whenever you're ready to go, we can head down there."

"Great. I should have a better handle on her schedule in the morning."

Miller nodded and the team dispersed in search of seats—a last chance to rest before the PM's flight landed.

Sølvi located a chair and repositioned it so that she had a clear view of the door to the private suite. If the Ambassador needed her and stuck her head out, it was the professional thing to do to be positioned close by.

All the agents either flipped through magazines or scrolled their phones to kill time, but soon enough the flights from Oslo and Amsterdam were on the ground and it was time to move.

An airport police car led one phalanx of Secret Service vehicles to the KLM gate to meet the Dutch Prime Minister and another to meet the Norwegian PM.

Agents were posted at the top of the jet bridge as well as on the tarmac at the bottom of the stairs to make sure that there were no unwanted surprises.

When the gate agent opened the large blue and white forward door, Sølvi saw a flight attendant, followed by two muscular PST agents, and immediately behind them Anita Stang herself.

As the Prime Minister stepped onto the jet bridge, followed by three more protection agents, she walked right up to Sølvi and extended her hand. "Thank you for agreeing to do this."

"It is my honor, Madame Prime Minister," Sølvi responded, shaking hands with her. Then, stepping aside, she said, "This is Special Agent Jonathan Miller of the Secret Service. We have cars waiting for you down on the tarmac."

Miller led the way and Sølvi mentally checked off each member of the PM's team as they deplaned. Bringing up the rear was her redheaded, freckled ass-kicker of a friend, Bente.

They indulged in a smile and a very quick hug, after which Bente handed over to Sølvi a large, hard-sided plastic case.

"I brought everything you asked for," she said. "Including that last-minute item."

"You put it in there with my body armor?"

"It's vacuum-sealed and I wrapped it in three trash bags. Don't worry."

"Thank you. I love you. And Scot's going to hate us for this. But we'll have a good laugh."

Pointing toward the door, Sølvi showed Bente to the jet-bridge stairs and they descended to the tarmac together as Sølvi texted Ambassador Hansen.

After Sølvi climbed into the lead vehicle with Bente, the two of them waited for everyone to be loaded into their respective SUVs and then they all rolled to the FBO.

Upon arrival, Ambassador Hansen was standing at the red carpet with her staff, waiting to greet the PM. Stang climbed out of the SUV, shook hands with Hansen, and then wrapped her arms around her, commending her for how brave she had been and consoling her over the loss of her two security agents.

They stood there like that for a moment before separating. Hansen led Prime Minister Stang inside to the private suite, where the PST and Secret Service agents were switched on, their heads on swivels.

While they got settled in and awaited the customs official who would take care of their passports and organize the retrieval of their luggage, Sølvi took her hard-sided case into one of the private shower rooms and locked the door behind her.

Taking off her jacket, she hung it on a peg and opened the case. In addition to everything she had asked for, Bente had included an encrypted PST radio with a fully charged battery, backup batteries, a charger, an earpiece, and a microphone.

Fishing out the last-minute item she had requested, she raised it to her nose and took a deep breath in. Thankfully, Bente had been right. She couldn't smell a thing.

Taking off her shirt, she strapped the soft armor, which had been cut for her body, over her jog bra and then put her shirt back on, tucking it into her pants.

After stripping and reassembling her 9mm CZ tactical pistol, which one of her armorers had cleaned and lubricated for her, she seated a round in the weapon's chamber and set it aside. Threading her gun belt through her holster and belt loops, she clipped on two additional magazine holders with two nineteen-round mags in each, and returned the CZ to the holster. All told, she was now carrying ninety-six rounds of ammunition.

The last thing she did was set up her radio and turn it on. After a quick comms check with the team, she closed her case and exited the shower room.

On her way to the private suite, Miller caught up with her and let her know that the Dutch had touched down. Sølvi thanked him and went to brief the Ambassador and the Prime Minister.

Forty-five minutes later, once the passports for both delegations had been processed, their luggage brought to the FBO and loaded into their respective Secret Service vehicles, and the police escort was in place, it was time to head for D.C.

The combined Norwegian–Dutch motorcade consisted of eight SUVs. The Dutch Prime Minister rode in the armored Suburban with the Dutch Ambassador to the U.S., the PM's chief of staff, as well as a mixture of Secret Service agents and the PM's Dutch bodyguards.

The Norwegians were distributed similarly in the armored Tahoe. Sorola was behind the wheel, and as the Secret Service agent in charge, Miller rode shotgun. In the two captain's chairs behind them sat the Ambassador and the Prime Minister. In the third row sat the head of the PM's PST detail, Svend Haugen; the PM's chief of staff, Henrik Oppen; and finally, Sølvi.

Bente and the remaining PST agents, as well as the rest of the Norwegian delegation, rode in the other Secret Service vehicles, while the embassy personnel returned in their own vehicle, separate from the motorcade.

It was wonderful for Sølvi to hear her mother tongue being spoken— especially with how boring and unattractive the drive was.

As they drove, she listened to the Ambassador and the Prime Minister discussing the events that had happened at the residence, as well as what they were expecting at the summit, not the least of which was the reluctance of the French and the Italians to sign on to the Sky Shield initiative. The representatives of those two countries, as well as those of Spain and Poland—who were also holdouts—would be a major focus of the PM while she was in D.C. Not only did Stang consider it a serious cornerstone of European security and a significant deterrent against Russian aggression, but it was also a matter of national pride for Norway to shepherd the remaining NATO members into the Sky Shield fold.

Sølvi appreciated that the two women were circumspect in their discussions, knowing full well they were in an American government vehicle and that their conversation, while in Norwegian, might be recorded—even by an ally.

Glancing out the passenger-side window, she watched as another section of dingy sound-attenuation wall, choked with vines, flashed by. It was followed by a stretch of overgrown woods.

The motorcade had just drawn even with it when she saw a flash and she shouted to Sorola and Miller, before repeating the same over her radio, "Contact right! Contact right! RPG!"

CHAPTER 35

Sorola took immediate and evasive action. As he jerked the wheel hard to the left, one of the RPGs passed so close that it left burn marks across their windshield.

In front of and behind them, other RPGs found their targets, slamming into Secret Service vehicles and exploding.

Careening into the median, Sorola struggled to keep the armored Tahoe from flipping over. He swerved left and right to avoid the pieces of flaming wreckage that were raining down around them. There was smoke everywhere.

Seeing a hole up ahead, Sorola gunned the engine. There was only one course of action in this scenario and that was for the Secret Service to get away from the attack and get their protectees to safety.

But no sooner had Sorola thought he found a way out than he was forced to slam on the brakes. Ahead of them was a massive pileup, and there was no way they could cut across the Metro lines and access the lanes of oncoming traffic. They were trapped and there was no telling if their attackers had more punishment in store.

While Miller and Haugen frantically worked their radios, Sølvi assessed Ambassador Hansen, Prime Minister Stang, and her chief of staff, Oppen. None of them, thankfully, was injured.

Now she had a very dangerous decision to make. The three diplomats would be safe inside the vehicle, as long as it didn't sustain a hit from a high-explosive antitank RPG "HEAT" round or come under a prolonged attack. Eventually the armor or bulletproof glass or both would fail.

The security team needed to get out and set up a defensive perimeter. One agent, though, needed to remain inside the Tahoe as a last line of defense and to drive away if an escape route made itself available. It had to be Sorola. Miller agreed.

After formulating a plan of action, Miller made sure Haugen and Sølvi were ready to move and then gave the "Go" command.

Bailing out of the Tahoe, Sølvi stayed low and ran forward as Haugen and Miller ran to the rear of the SUV.

The acrid smoke was thick and black. Burning cars were everywhere. She couldn't begin to imagine how many members of each delegation had been killed. The armored Suburban carrying the Dutch Prime Minister had been destroyed and none of the Norwegian PST agents, including Bente, had responded to radio calls. It was a nightmare and not yet over.

Somewhere behind them, members of the Dutch delegation in a different vehicle were trapped and at risk of being burned alive. Desperate calls were going out over the Secret Service radios for help.

Miller relayed the situation and told Sølvi and Haugen to stay with the Tahoe. He would be back as soon as he could. Then, holstering his weapon, he prepared to heroically run back into the thick of the fire and the chaos.

But the moment he stepped out from behind the armored Tahoe, a shot was fired from a very high-powered, large-caliber rifle that went right through his head like it was an overripe watermelon, killing him instantly.

"Sniper!" Haugen yelled. "In the tree line!"

Sølvi knew better than to poke her head up above the hood to try to catch a glimpse of the shooter. That was undoubtedly what he wanted—to pick off survivors. And judging by the distance to the trees, whoever he was, he was very good at his job.

It was shades of Monday's attack all over again. If they stayed where they were, it was only a matter of time before he got them too, as well as the Prime Minister and everyone else inside the vehicle. She had to figure out a way to get to him first.

With their high fences covered in razor wire, using the Metro tracks to get a safe distance away before crossing into the woods and doubling back was out of the question. So was the path that Miller had attempted.

That left moving in the opposite direction and heading toward the pileup of cars in front of the Tahoe. In an ideal situation, Sorola would have put the SUV in gear and rolled slowly forward, providing a big, armored shield for her until she could get there. Unfortunately, this was anything but an ideal situation.

The instant the Tahoe started moving, it would attract the attention of the sniper, who would start putting rounds on it. Sølvi was going to have to make a run for it. Haugen, however, could help provide cover.

The PST agent didn't like her plan. He felt it was too dangerous. Surely the Secret Service and local police had reinforcements on the way. Their job was to stay put and protect the Prime Minister.

Sølvi had neither the time nor the inclination to explain herself to Haugen. Her agreement with Stang was to make sure that the Secret Service didn't screw up and, if they did anyway, to fix it.

While an RPG attack on their motorcade, followed by a secondary attack via sniper, wasn't technically a "screwup" by the Secret Service, Sølvi intended to fix it. Sorola and Haugen would have to hold down the fort. She was going to take the fight directly to the Indians.

Leaving no further room for argument, she got into a crouch at the front of the Tahoe and prepared to run. Over the radio, she counted down from five in Norwegian.

When she got to "one" she began sprinting as Haugen unleashed a barrage of pistol fire into the tree line.

She ran like she had never run before, sliding through a pile of broken glass and plastic as she arrived at the multicar pileup and grabbed the first piece of cover she could find.

From the woods, the sniper fired multiple rounds at Haugen, her, and the Tahoe itself.

Unwilling to sacrifice even a few seconds to catch her breath, Sølvi radioed the PST agent to lay down more cover fire. The moment he started shooting, she was off and running again.

She zigzagged through the sea of cars, leaping over hoods and bumpers where necessary, eventually making her way to the other side of the highway.

This time when Sølvi stopped, she was at a sufficient enough angle that the smoke and flames from the crippled motorcade helped conceal her.

Nevertheless, she took nothing for granted and quickly abandoned the position for something safer.

Her lungs burning and heaving for air, she finally allowed herself a few moments to catch her breath. She radioed Haugen that she had made it and told him to sit tight and wait for her signal. She was headed into the woods and would need him to help flush the sniper out for her.

After a few more deep breaths, Sølvi got herself together and headed into the trees. Taking out her phone, she pulled up her geolocating app and got a fix on her position.

What she was hoping to find was some sort of access road or parking area that the attackers had used to leave their vehicles. They would want to be able to make a quick exit and that required having transport nearby. If she could figure out where their cars were, she could better narrow the search area for the sniper.

Beyond the woods, however, there was nothing but apartment complexes, home associations, and office parks. Their vehicles could be anywhere.

Sølvi tried to remember exactly where she had seen the RPGs being fired from and, drawing her pistol, headed toward that spot.

The dense underbrush clawed at her feet and legs. It was like trying to march through miles of heavy steel cable. She had been at it for several hundred feet when suddenly the underbrush gave way to some sort of jogging or hiking trail that hadn't appeared on her app.

If the motorcade's attackers had found the tangled vines and bushes of the forest floor as disagreeable as she had, the chances were pretty good that they were using this same path to get as close as possible to where they had launched their ambush from. Stepping onto the path, Sølvi began following it back toward where the attack had been launched.

The heavy tree cover made it difficult to get her exact position on her phone. She also didn't like having her attention divided. Where there was a sniper, there very well could be someone watching the sniper's back. Any local suburbanite out for a run or walking their dog could have stumbled upon the attackers. They would have needed a way to deal with that possibility.

Sølvi switched over to a mapping feature that relied on cell towers—along the Dulles Access Road there were undoubtedly many—got an approximate fix on her current position, and slid the phone back into her pocket. She was much closer than she had thought. As slowly and as soundlessly as possible, just as she had been trained, she moved forward.

The heat and humidity were beyond oppressive. Instead of the bug-infested woods providing a little bit of shade and a lessening of the temperature, it seemed hotter, closer, and more difficult to breathe. Sølvi's body armor, not to mention her shirt and jacket, were stifling. She could feel the sweat running straight down the middle of her back. She was a long way from her days as a pampered fashion model.

This, however, was exactly what her army training had prepared her for. The Norwegian government had agreed to the formation of an all-female special forces unit, but only if the selection standards were impossibly high and presented some of the most difficult training any military had ever imposed—even on its male recruits.

The newly formed "Hunter" unit, or *Jegertropen*, had been looking for women who wouldn't quit. Then, once a highly select few had applied and been accepted, the Norwegian Army had done everything in their power to get them to drop out.

Many did quit, but Sølvi wasn't one of them. She had taken everything the instructors had thrown at her and had doubled down on her commitment to see it through. In that crucible, she had been reborn a stronger, fiercer, more determined warrior. A hot day and some rough terrain weren't going to get in the way of her eliminating this threat.

Feeling she had to be almost on top of the sniper, she found a tree big enough to provide cover, stepped off the path, and quietly radioed Haugen to begin firing.

As soon as he did, she heard two shots fired from just up the path. Staying in the trees, she worked her way toward the sound, maintaining her situational awareness and keeping her eyes and ears open for the possibility of a spotter or some sort of security element.

When she had traveled as far as she dared, Sølvi took cover behind another tree and scanned the area around her, searching for the gunman, but to no avail.

In addition to being an exceptional shot, the sniper also appeared to be quite skilled when it came to camouflage—two traits that spoke to a high level of training, likely achieved in the military.

Where are you? she wondered, her pistol up and ready to engage.

Sølvi continued to slowly scan the wooded hillside looking for places she would have chosen had the task been given to her to establish a hide site from which to snipe the survivors of the motorcade. Yet no matter how hard she focused, she couldn't see a damn thing beyond leaves, branches, bushes, and vines. It was like the guy was invisible, until all of a sudden she noticed something.

There was what looked like a dried-up pile of forest rot, which was interesting considering how verdant and overgrown everything else was. The pile was just long enough for a man to be lying prone underneath. But that wasn't what convinced her that she'd found the sniper.

Protruding from the pile was what looked like a piece of MultiCam green nylon that had been wrapped around a Pringles can and secured with black elastic cordage. And while it may have looked like nylon, it was more than likely constructed of Kevlar or Nomex.

It was called a suppressor heat wrap and one of its key uses was to prevent heat waves from rising off a hot suppressor and creating a mirage effect that could disrupt a sniper's magnified optics. With her target identified, Sølvi opened fire.

She riddled the pile with bullets, pumping round after round into it. Then, retreating behind the tree, she inserted a fresh magazine and paused.

There was no response, no fusillade of bullets sent her way. Taking a deep breath and applying pressure to her trigger, she stepped from behind the tree and moved in on the pile.

The closer she got, the more certain she became. Pumping six more rounds into it, she advanced the rest of the way. Checking her surroundings to make sure she was alone, she then reached down and pulled back what turned out to be a ghillie blanket.

Underneath was one dead sniper and an Accuracy International AXSR long-range rifle—complete with a heat wrap over its suppressor. There was no second person with him, no spotter.

Sølvi had just begun to pat him down when she heard a noise from the woods behind her.

Rasing her left elbow, she thrust her pistol under her arm and turned her head to look over her shoulder—the entire time applying more and more pressure to her trigger. It was muscle memory, instinct, and training all wrapped up in one.

At the moment she processed that there was indeed a threat, the first bullet was already leaving her gun. It was followed by two more in rapid succession.

Her would-be attacker fell to the ground dead, but before she could sweep the area for additional threats, there was another gunshot; a second attacker had come from the other direction.

But as Sølvi swung her pistol and was about to fire, the attacker dropped his weapon and collapsed.

Standing behind him, the smoke still rising from her Glock, was a bloodied and bruised Bente Bergstrøm.

CHAPTER 36

Harvath had managed to get several hours of sleep and felt somewhat refreshed. After taking a shower and shaving, he put on a navy suit with a light blue shirt and, once again, no tie.

Downstairs in the kitchen, he turned on the TV while he started making a late lunch before heading into D.C. for his meeting with Russ Gaines. The story of a shoot-out and a stack of dead bodies being found at the home of the former National Security Advisor was playing on every local channel, as well as the cable news outlets.

He decided to give McGee a call and check in on how Rogers was doing.

"He's fine," the ex–CIA director stated. "A little concerned about what all the media coverage may do to his resale value, but other than that, no complaints."

"I just turned on my TV," said Harvath. "When did it break?"

"A couple hours ago."

"Anything I need to be worried about?"

"Not at the moment," McGee replied. "They're asking the public to contact Fairfax County PD if they have information related to the events. I'm sure their phones are jammed with crackpots from coast to coast offering up all sorts of conspiracy theories. By tonight those nuts will be all over the internet linking Rogers with MLK, JFK Jr., and the Hamburglar in a covert plot to use *Terminator*-style robots to overthrow Cuba."

Harvath smiled. "Sounds like the Ambassador might have bigger problems than just his home's resale value."

"We should have a serious talk about his home and his problems. When will you be back?"

"My meeting with Gaines is at three thirty. As soon as it's over, I'm going to hit the road. Hopefully, I'll get a jump on the traffic. But with that said, I'll need to run a few SDRs to make sure he's not having me followed."

"Understood. We'll see you when we see you."

Disconnecting the call, Harvath finished making his lunch, and ate. Then, after packing clothes and additional gear in Haney's Bronco, he headed to D.C.

The headquarters of the Secret Service were half a mile due east of the White House. But what Harvath had always found more interesting was that the headquarters was also only three blocks from Ford's Theatre, where Abraham Lincoln was assassinated. More interesting still was that, allegedly, on the day that Lincoln was shot, he had signed the approval for the Secret Service's creation.

Just as it had been odd for Harvath to return to the Carlton Group offices, it also felt odd to return to the Secret Service. His recruitment from the SEALs to help bolster counterterrorism protections at the White House felt like ages ago. It had also taken him down a career path he had never seen coming.

That was part of why it felt odd being back. The Secret Service had marked a major shift in his life.

The bigger reason it felt strange being back was that he had come to lay a very serious allegation at the feet of an old friend. Until this morning, *disloyal* and *dishonorable* were not terms he could have ever imagined using to describe Russ Gaines. But all of that was about to change.

Entering the building, with its soaring glass atrium, he proceeded through security screening before checking in at the main desk and being issued a pass, which he hung around his neck via a lanyard. He was then told to take a seat in the marble-clad lobby and that someone would be down to retrieve him shortly.

That someone turned out to be Russ's assistant, Kyle Marshall, a short man in his late twenties with an overeager manner.

Showing Harvath to one of the elevators, he said, "I can't tell you what an honor it is to meet you."

"It's nice to meet you as well."

"Me? I'm nobody, honestly. But you're a legend. Do you know how many agents dream of saving a president's life? Basically all of them. Even the ones who don't do protective work. And you not only saved a president, but you also saved his daughter."

"Two different days," Harvath replied with a polite smile.

"Still," said Marshall, as the elevator arrived and he motioned for Harvath to go ahead of him. Scanning his key card, he continued his praise as they rode upstairs. "And then everything that happened two days ago at the Naval Observatory and the Norwegian ambassador's residence? Come on. Amazing."

Harvath had never been comfortable with such fulsome praise, but Marshall seemed like a decent person and so he continued to remain polite. "I think any other Secret Service agent would have done the same thing. That's what they train us for, right?"

It took Marshall a minute to realize that Harvath was including him in the "us." When it clicked, he stood up a bit taller and nodded in agreement. "That *is* what they train us for."

Finally, the elevator opened and Marshall walked him over to a set of ballistic glass doors, laser-engraved with the Secret Service logo. Swiping his card again, he led Harvath down a long, carpeted hallway to a cluster of executive offices.

Gesturing to a seating area, Marshall told him to make himself comfortable. Gaines was on a call but would be out shortly.

He was in the middle of asking Harvath if he wanted coffee when his phone chimed. Looking down at the text, Marshall quickly excused himself and disappeared through a secure door, which Harvath assumed led to Russ's office. Why he had departed so hastily, however, was anyone's guess.

Harvath had only been there for about two minutes when the same door was thrown forcefully open. He looked up to see Gaines, a powerfully built man in his mid-fifties, his reddish-blond hair more gray than blond now, and his complexion ruddier than he remembered, step out. Something was happening. And whatever it was, it wasn't good.

"Come with me," he ordered.

Standing up, Harvath asked, "What's going on?"

Gaines shook his head. "Not here," he replied. "In the TOC."

They walked down another hallway and quickly arrived at a wall of small, secure lockers. Harvath didn't need to be told what to do. Removing his cell phone, he put it inside one of them, locked it, and put the key in his pocket. Gaines then swiped his card at another secure door and led him into a large tactical operations center.

Flat-panel monitors lined the walls. Digital clocks with bright red numbers broadcast the time across the United States and cities around the world. The overhead lighting was dimmed to make it easier to watch the images on the monitors. It was a hive of activity as agents clicked furiously away at keyboards, worked communication equipment, and shuttled between workstations.

As they entered, Gaines shouted, "Let's get video up! Now!"

Harvath still had no idea what was going on. But as soon as traffic camera footage started coming online, he recognized the Dulles Access Road and what looked like a horrible multicar accident.

But *accident* didn't seem to be the right word. Too many of the cars were on fire and spaced too far apart to have all collided with each other.

"What the hell is this?"

"One of our motorcades has come under attack."

Instantly, Harvath's mind went to Sølvi. "Which motorcade? Who was in it?"

Gaines didn't pull any punches. "The Norwegian and Dutch prime ministers."

Harvath couldn't believe what he was hearing. It felt like the oxygen had been sucked out of the room. "When?"

"It just happened. Multiple RPGs."

RPGs? In the D.C. suburbs? The nation's capital had spun completely out of control.

"What's their status?"

"Multiple dead and wounded. We have CAT teams en route," said Gaines, referring to the Secret Service's Counter Assault Teams. "Local law enforcement, fire, and EMS are also on their way."

Harvath beat back the urge to go get his phone and text Sølvi. It looked like an absolute shitstorm. The last thing she would need at this moment was him blowing up her phone.

One of the agents monitoring the encrypted radio traffic from the site of the attack piped up and said, "Agent down. Repeat, agent down. Active sniper on scene."

"Where, precisely?" Gaines demanded. "Do we have a fix on the shooter's location?"

"Somewhere in the trees on the south side of the Dulles Access Road."

A secondary attack. Harvath's heart all but stopped in his chest.

It was chilling to stand there, less than twenty miles away, not knowing if Sølvi was alive or dead and not being able to impact the outcome either way. He felt helpless, and *helplessness* was not a word in his personal vocabulary.

Making it even more difficult, there were no air assets yet on scene. The only eyes they had were the traffic cams along the access road and the live feeds streaming from the Secret Service dashcams. It was impossible to have a full, 360-degree view of the battlespace as it were. He would have given anything just to have Nicholas's two Dragonflies overhead.

As reports of sniper fire continued to be radioed in, Harvath began to formulate a plan. He couldn't sit here in the TOC, not while Sølvi was somewhere in the middle of that fight and might need him. It would take forever to get there via car, but he had to try.

He was about to tell Gaines he was leaving when Marshall entered the TOC, got his boss's attention, and said, "HMX-1. Ten minutes out. South Lawn."

Flashing his assistant the thumbs-up, Gaines looked at Harvath, who understood what had just been said. "HMX-1" was Marine Helicopter Squadron One, the Marine Corps unit responsible for transporting the President and other dignitaries by helicopter.

With assets five miles away at Joint Base Anacostia-Bolling, all it would have taken was one call to the White House's Military Office to arrange for a speedy pickup on the South Lawn. The fact that the Secret Service didn't have its own helicopters was yet another failing by Congress, yet also a fight for another day.

Nodding toward the door, Gaines said, "We've got an extra seat. Want it?"

Harvath didn't need to be asked twice.

He followed Gaines out of the TOC, to the elevators, and down to the lobby, where a fully geared-up, six-man Quick Reaction Force was waiting. They handed both Gaines and Harvath chest rigs with hard plates and large patches front and back, which read POLICE–SECRET SERVICE.

Outside at the curb, two black Secret Service SUVs, their lightbars flashing, were ready to go. After loading up, they took off.

By the time the VH-60N White Hawk helicopter flared and touched down on the South Lawn, Harvath, Gaines, and the QRF team were in position.

Though it hardly could have been part of the fast-moving calculus, having a presidential helicopter—with its distinct green paint job and white top—rush to the location of where Americans and European allies had come under attack was a smart move. It showed a White House managing the situation, committing any and all resources necessary, as rapidly as possible.

Everyone climbed aboard and strapped in. As the heavy door slid closed, the pilots powered up the twin turboshaft engines and the long black rotors chopped at the hot, humid air, lifting the helo quickly off the ground.

Banking hard to the west, Harvath watched the White House disappear beneath them.

And as it did, he prayed to God, asking for just one thing—that when they arrived, he would find Sølvi alive.

CHAPTER 37

The HMX-1 pilots got them out to the attack site in minutes, landing the helicopter on the Dulles Access Road, which had been closed to traffic.

By the time they arrived, word was already spreading that the sniper, along with two additional attackers, had been neutralized. Whether or not there were any more attackers, no one knew.

Along with Gaines and the QRF team, Harvath located the armored Tahoe containing Ambassador Hansen, Prime Minister Stang, and her chief of staff. The lead Norwegian PST agent, a man named Haugen, filled him in on what Sølvi had done.

Harvath felt relieved at hearing she was alive and unharmed. Looking around him at the death and destruction, it was an absolute miracle.

Haugen raised her on the radio and let her know that her husband was on scene. She asked that he bring her a med kit.

Gaines had one of the QRF guys grab the kit out of the Tahoe for him. He then pulled out his backup gun, a Glock 43X, and handed it to Harvath.

"Just in case," he said.

"Thank you," Harvath replied, setting his suit jacket aside.

He conducted a press check to make sure a round was chambered and tucked the weapon in the center pocket of his plate carrier. Shouldering the med kit, he then headed for the woods.

It took him a moment to find the path Sølvi had described, but once he was on it, he found her in no time.

Despite all the carnage, she didn't have a scratch on her. He wrapped his arms around her and hugged her like he had never hugged her before. She hugged him right back but cut it off after several seconds. There was still work to be done.

Taking the med kit from him, she introduced him to Bente as she searched for the items she needed.

"Nice to meet you," he said, crouching down and carefully giving her right hand a soft fist bump.

The female PST agent looked like she had been dragged down eight miles of unpaved highway. She was covered with abrasions and what appeared to be second-degree burns. Something also appeared to be wrong with her left arm, which lay limp in her lap.

Bente had caught a bunch of broken glass in her face and upper torso. Thankfully, none of it had gotten in her eyes. Sølvi did what she could to remove the most uncomfortable pieces. The smaller bits, the ones that had embedded themselves beneath her skin, would have to be addressed at a hospital.

Next, she used the kit's triangular bandage to fashion a sling and gently positioned it around Bente's neck and left arm.

The last injury she had to deal with was Bente's right leg, near her knee. She was in a lot of pain and couldn't put much weight on it. Cracking a cold pack, Sølvi let Bente place it where it hurt the most and then wrapped it with an Israeli bandage.

As Sølvi tended her injuries, Bente explained to Harvath everything that had happened and how she had been the only person in her SUV to have survived.

Her radio had been damaged, so she couldn't transmit, but she could receive. That was how she knew Sølvi was coming into the woods to locate and take out the sniper. Bente had decided to provide backup.

"Saving my life in the process," Sølvi admitted.

Harvath looked at the three corpses. "Have you been able to search them?"

She shook her head.

Standing up, Harvath walked over and went through all their pockets.

"Anything?" Sølvi asked as she finished tending to Bente and zipped back up the medical kit.

"Nothing," he replied, taking photos of each of them. "No phones. No ID. No pocket litter even."

"More professionals."

Harvath nodded. "There seems to be an outbreak of them."

Sølvi motioned him over and they helped get Bente to her feet.

"Can you make it back to the road?" she asked.

"I think so," the PST agent responded.

"Put all your weight on Scot," Sølvi instructed. "He can take it."

Bente nodded and Harvath let her lean on him as hard as she wanted, grateful that she didn't need to be carried.

As they neared the edge of the woods, Haugen radioed that the Prime Minister and the Ambassador were being evacuated back to the White House via helicopter and that he was going with them. Sølvi responded that she would link up with them as soon as possible.

Moments later, they heard the presidential helicopter powering up and then, stepping out of the trees, they saw it take off and head for D.C. In the distance, more helos were inbound.

A triage area, with plastic tarps stretched between two large trucks to help provide shade, had been established. They placed Bente there for the time being, sitting her on the ground, and returned to the armored Tahoe.

It was empty. Everyone was gone, except for Sorola, who had removed his suit jacket and used it to cover Miller's body.

"I'm so sorry," said Sølvi.

"Thank you," the FBI agent replied. "He was a good man."

"My condolences," replied Harvath.

"Agent Sorola, this is my husband, Scot Harvath."

The two men shook hands as Sorola asked, "Did you teach her that thing with the penny?"

"What thing?"

"Measuring the treads," she replied. "Yes, he did."

"It saved our lives," the man continued. "That and having the tighter of the two suspensions. I'm sure of it."

"What *I'm* sure of is that we had the best driver. It was Suber that saved us. So, thank you."

"You're welcome," Sorola said, the weight of losing Miller evident in his voice.

Sølvi didn't want to trouble the man any further, but needed to ask, "Did the PM's chief of staff go with her too?"

"No. He's here somewhere. He stayed behind to help. I told him I wouldn't leave without either of you."

Thanking him, Sølvi retained the med kit and she and Harvath went off in search of others who needed medical attention.

The dead and wounded seemed to be everywhere. Multiple Secret Service vehicles were still on fire.

The sounds of helicopters, ambulances, and fire trucks only got louder as more first responders arrived on scene.

It was a different kind of chaos, but chaos nonetheless.

Eventually they located Henrik—the Prime Minister's chief of staff. He was holding a water bottle up to the lips of a member from the Dutch delegation, helping her drink.

When the woman had had enough to drink, he sat the bottle next to her and held her hand for a moment, before stepping away to speak with Sølvi.

He pulled a small pad from his pocket and gave her a rundown of everything he had been able to establish regarding the Norwegian delegation's status. Seven were dead—four of those being PST agents—and eleven were injured, five of them seriously enough to have been transported out on the presidential helicopter.

The Dutch, according to Henrik, had suffered even greater losses, but other than losing their Prime Minister and their Ambassador to the United States, he couldn't account for exactly who had been killed in their group.

And, of course, the Secret Service had lost multiple agents, including Miller and the two female agents attached to the Norwegian delegation—Longwell and Del Vecchio.

Sølvi appreciated the man's levelheadedness, even in the midst of such a horrific attack. She told him, in Norwegian, that he should be as circumspect as possible, but that the Prime Minister would need to brief Oslo, and any video and still footage he covertly captured would be valuable, especially of the vehicles themselves.

Seeing Gaines nearby, Harvath excused himself and went to give him his gun back. The man had set up a makeshift command center and was trying to make sure that anyone who was injured had been triaged and all available evidence was being preserved. In the distance, Harvath could see some of the QRF guys trying to keep people back from a couple of the vehicles that had been struck by RPGs. Undoubtedly, the BATF was already on their way and would be combing through everything, including the woods where the rocket-propelled grenades and sniper rounds had been fired from.

"Thanks for this," Harvath said, returning the Glock to Gaines and setting the plate carrier down next to him on the ground.

"I didn't hear any gunshots, so I'll take that as good news," the Secret Service man replied.

"Sølvi and one of the PST agents mopped up the woods."

"That's what we heard. Took out the sniper and two other attackers."

Harvath nodded. "This was a really bad day, Russ."

"Been a bad week. Speaking of which, the shooting at Ambassador Rogers's house was all over the news this morning, but it didn't break until *after* you called me and asked to meet. Did you have something to do with that?"

This wasn't how Harvath had planned to have this conversation, but it looked like they were about to have it, so he came right out with it. "An eight-man team hit Rogers's house. They knew his alarm code, how to access his security cameras, and what the weakest point of his safe room was. The only people who knew all of that, besides Rogers, was the Secret Service."

Gaines was stunned, obvious both from the look on his face and the tenor of his response. "You think *we* had something to do with it?"

"Monday they sent two guys after him. Then right after you and I chat, eight guys show up."

"Jesus Christ, Harvath. You think *I* was behind that?"

"I think somebody figured out that Rogers had gotten himself protection. And they showed up armed to the teeth, complete with information only you guys have."

"Well I will tell you right now, it wasn't me."

Harvath was a pro at detecting microexpressions—little telltale signs that a subject was lying. But nothing he was getting from Gaines suggested the man was telling him anything but the truth.

The problem, however, was that detecting microexpressions was a skill taught by the Secret Service. He and Gaines had both had the same training, which meant Gaines had had years to perfect covering his up.

Yet he didn't think Gaines was lying. He believed the man was telling him the truth. But if Gaines hadn't leaked the information, who had? It was now another question added to Harvath's very long list.

"Listen," he said, trying to put out the fire before the bridge between them was completely burned. "It's a terrible question. I apologize, but I had to ask."

Gaines took a breath and exhaled. "I get it. And yeah, it sucks, but I would have asked it too."

"Do you have any idea how the information could have gotten out?"

"Zero," the Secret Service man replied. "The security of our protectees and their personal information is sacrosanct. That doesn't end just because we're no longer actively protecting them."

Harvath didn't waste time feeling guilty about asking the question. It had to be asked. It had been asked. And he now had his answer. But the topic couldn't be closed. Not without a follow-up.

"And the attackers who hit the motorcade? Where do you think they got their information?"

It was a gut punch, but the question didn't come as a surprise to Gaines. "I've been asking myself the same thing."

"I'm not trying to rub salt in the wound," said Harvath. "Not after what the Secret Service has been through today."

"It's a fair question and you're not going to be the only one asking it. We're in for a lot of scrutiny. And rightfully so."

"While we're on the subject, there's something else from Monday night that you might want to be thinking about."

Gaines looked at him. "What's that?"

"Secret Service has a CAT team behind the gates at the Naval Observatory, but they have to stay put and defend the residence. They can't get baited out onto the street, especially when it could be a ruse by bad actors wanting to get inside. So how did the attackers know that? How did they know that the D.C. Metro police would be the only guns in that fight?"

"Shit," the man said, shaking his head. "You're right."

"I don't want to be right," Harvath replied. "I want to be wrong. Because, if I'm right, then there's a source inside the Secret Service who's working for some very bad people."

The weight of it all was growing on Gaines by the second. Harvath could see it in the man's posture. There was no need to keep pressing the point.

Instead he pivoted to how he and Sølvi were getting back to D.C. His hope was that once authorities began clearing the pileup, Sorola could take them.

Unfortunately, Gaines explained, because the Tahoe had been grazed by one of the RPGs, it was part of the investigation and needed to stay exactly where it was. This entire section of the Dulles Access Road was going to remain shut down for the rest of the night.

Buses were being sent to pick up surviving members of the delegations and transport them to their respective embassies, where they were likely to be debriefed by their people and then taken to their accommodations.

Harvath asked when the buses would arrive, but Gaines had no idea. With rush-hour traffic building, plus a chunk of the access road being out of commission, it could take hours.

He explained that Sølvi didn't have hours. She needed to get back to the Prime Minister ASAP. Not only was waiting for buses to arrive not an option, but neither was spending all evening walking the investigative team through everything that had happened in the woods. Sølvi would be happy to give the Secret Service a full, detailed debrief, just not right now.

Before Gaines could push back, Harvath let him know that they would get themselves back to D.C. and that if anyone needed to reach Sølvi, they could do so through the Norwegian Embassy.

Gaines knew he couldn't force them to stay—at least not without things getting very ugly. Shaking hands, they said their goodbyes and the Secret Service man promised that if he heard anything regarding Rogers, he'd let Harvath know right away.

Scot thanked him, and after rejoining Sølvi they walked back over to Sorola to hand over what was left of the Tahoe's medical kit and to let him know that they were going to arrange their own transport back to D.C.

They extended their condolences again over the loss of his colleagues and then, after Harvath had collected his suit jacket, went to check in one last time with Bente.

She was right where they had left her, although now she was being treated by a pair of paramedics.

While they checked her blood pressure and examined her injuries, Sølvi shared with her everything she had learned from Henrik, minus the deaths of Bente's fellow PST agents and the others in her SUV, which she already knew about.

Harvath asked if there was anything they could do for her, and Bente shook her head. She understood that they had to leave, and she encouraged them to get moving. You could get paid doing a lot of things in Norway, but standing around wasn't one of them.

Sølvi found the one place on her friend's face that hadn't been injured, gave her a kiss, and promised to call her as soon as she knew that Stang was safe and what everyone was planning to do next.

Bente nodded and said goodbye.

"So how are we getting out of here?" Sølvi asked as they began walking toward the nearest exit ramp. "Uber?"

Harvath shook his head. "I already checked. They're backed up for hours. The Carlton Group, though, is less than eight miles away."

This time it was Sølvi who shook her head. "I've had a bad day. I'm sorry, but we're not walking eight miles."

"Of course not," he replied as he finished composing a text and hit send. "I'm having Nicholas come pick us up."

"And take us back to D.C.?"

"Sure. Why not?"

"Because it's the exact opposite direction he needs to go to get home."

"That's okay. What are friends for?"

"He and Nina are exhausted. The baby has colic and they lost their night nurse. They haven't slept in a week. Give the guy a break."

"You know who else hasn't slept much and is on the verge of developing colic?" he asked, pointing at himself.

Sølvi wasn't in the mood. "Find a Plan B."

Taking his phone back out, he texted Nicholas again. A few moments later, he received a response.

"We good?" she asked.

Harvath nodded. "Yep, but you're not going to like it."

CHAPTER 38

Vice President Chris Cates, who had been on the Hill for an impromptu push of the President's priorities for the National Defense Authorization Act, stepped in front of a gaggle of reporters.

"Ladies and gentlemen, thank you for gathering here on such a tragic afternoon. Just two days ago, on Monday, we witnessed the horrific loss of life as citizens, peacefully assembled, and law enforcement officers, there to safeguard that peace, were attacked in the streets outside the Vice President's Residence. Their deaths are a bracing reminder that this nation, our democracy, is under threat from all sides. As we mourn those lost, we stand firm in our commitment to protect the values that make this country great—freedom, peace, and the safety of every American citizen."

Taking a moment to look into the cameras, Cates paused, and then hardening his tone, continued. "Today, we find ourselves reeling from another violent and senseless attack—this time on a United States Secret Service motorcade transporting the Dutch and Norwegian delegations. Let me be clear: This was an attack not just on foreign diplomats, but on American security itself. These foreign delegations may have been here for a NATO Summit, but make no mistake—this attack was aimed directly at us, the American people.

"While we mourn the loss of life, we cannot ignore the reality that these attacks—both the barbarity we saw Monday and today's act of violence—are a direct result of our government's own failures. For far too long, we have sent our men and women overseas to fight wars that do not concern us, pouring our resources into international commitments while neglecting the security of our own borders, our own citizens."

Cates paused again, visibly frustrated, his voice sharper. "President Mitchell and I will not stand by while the entrenched powers in Washington continue to put the interests of foreign nations ahead of the safety and well-being of the American people. We cannot continue to expend our blood and treasure to be the world's police force. This attack today is just another wake-up call—a stark reminder that the globalist establishment's agenda is a direct threat to everything We the People hold dear.

"I want to make one thing perfectly clear: America *must* come first. We must take control of our own destiny. We must secure our borders and ensure that any enemy who seeks to harm us, foreign or domestic, will pay the price for their actions.

"To those who would think that America is weak, or divided, or vulnerable: You're wrong. To the enemies of this nation, whether they are terror groups, foreign governments, or the global elite: We will not back down.

"We are going to hunt down those responsible for both today's attack and Monday's. We will absolutely make sure they face justice. And we will leave no doubt that our number one priority is the safety of the American people."

Looking once more directly into the cameras, Cates spoke firmly and closed with "This is America's time. This is the moment where we choose to defend what is ours. No more apologies. No more distractions. This ends now. Thank you and God bless you."

Sitting in his Senate office watching on TV, Bill Blackwood marveled at the Vice President's remarks. They were strong and intelligent and struck exactly the right chord for the moment. On top of that, Cates appeared to have done it all off the cuff. With no notes and no teleprompter.

Talk about some impressive shit, Blackwood thought to himself. *But will it play in Peoria?*

Muting the TV, he opened a tab on his browser and surfed over to Chuck Coughlin's site, where the podcaster was already dissecting the VP's remarks for his millions of followers.

"All right folks," Coughlin began, his neon American flag blazing behind him, "you just heard it—live, direct from Capitol Hill—Vice President Chris Cates addressing the nation in the wake of today's tragic attack on a Secret Service motorcade transporting the Dutch and Norwegian delegations in town for the big NATO Summit on Friday. And let me tell you, Cates didn't mince words. He didn't hide behind political rhetoric or empty promises. What we heard today was the kind of leadership America needs, and frankly, the kind we've been *begging* for.

"You could feel the weight in his words, couldn't you? The Vice President didn't just speak about the attack in vague terms. He didn't give us the same tired speeches about 'thoughts and prayers' and 'strengthening alliances' like we're used to hearing from the establishment. No. Cates made it clear that this wasn't just an attack on foreign diplomats, this was an attack on *America*. This was an attack on our borders, on our sovereignty, on our security. And you know what? I'm glad he said it. Because someone had to."

Leaning in as if talking to a trusted friend, Coughlin said, "And let's not forget, Cates didn't stop there. He laid it out for everyone to hear: These attacks, the loss of innocent lives—they are a wake-up call. The chaos in our streets, the bloodshed, it's all a symptom of a much bigger problem. A broken system that has ignored the needs of the American people for far too long. Cates has *finally* said what we've all known, what I've been telling you for years: America is under attack—from within and from abroad—and if we're going to survive, it's time to stop being the world's police, to stop giving our hard-earned dollars away to other countries, and to stop apologizing for putting *America* first.

"I'll tell you this—that speech? That wasn't just a Vice President doing his job. That was a leader stepping up and *showing* us the way forward. You could see it in his eyes, hear it in his voice—Cates is ready to make the hard calls. He's ready to put the globalists in their place and put the safety of the American people above all else. And folks, let's be honest, that's the kind of leader this country *desperately* needs right now.

"And here's the bottom line—President Mitchell? He had his chance.

He campaigned on the same platform, promising to put We the People first. Yet what has he done? More of the same—empty speeches, global appeasement, and zero action. He's *soft*, folks. He's soft on America's security, soft on defeating the establishment, and soft on defending our interests. And that's why, as much as it hurts me to say it, President Mitchell must step aside. He's not the leader this country needs."

Coughlin paused to let that sink in and then, with his voice more resolute, stated, "But Cates? He's the real deal. Cates is the man who's *not afraid* to take the tough steps to put America first. He's the one who's going to stand up to the global elites and take our country back. And let me tell you, folks, I'm not the only one who sees it. People across this country are waking up to the fact that Vice President Cates is the leader we have been waiting for.

"Now, I want you to think about this—Cates just said it himself: No more apologies. No more distractions. This ends *now*. We can't afford to wait any longer. It's time for America to take charge of its future again. And I have to say, after hearing Cates today . . . I believe we're on the verge of something big. Something *great*."

As his stirring and patriotic outro music faded in, Coughlin brought it all home. "My friends, we are entering a new chapter. And it looks like Chris Cates is going to be the one to lead us there. All I can say is buckle up, because this is just the beginning.

"And with that, it's another three hours of Bunker Radio in the can. I'll see you right back here tomorrow. Until then, remember—when you're under attack, Chuck Coughlin has your back. And we are all, *definitely*, under attack. Stay safe, America."

Closing the tab on his computer, Senator Blackwood smiled. *That* was more like it. That was what he had wanted from Coughlin—a resounding denunciation of President Mitchell and a rousing vote of confidence for Vice President Cates.

Combined with Cates's fantastic remarks, that was going to help get people leaning even more in the right direction.

Then all America would need was one good push.

CHAPTER 39

The crappy, dark blue 2010 Chevy Malibu with no air-conditioning, dented rims, and a scratch down the right rear quarter panel was waiting for them, about two miles later, when they finally made their way off the Dulles Access Road.

When Harvath had informed Nicholas that morning that he didn't need it anymore, Nicholas had sent a team to the parking garage in McLean to retrieve it. Sliding the keys from behind the rear license plate, he sent Nicholas a quick thank-you text. He was grateful that it was so close and easy to drop off. Somewhere inside the Carlton Group, there was probably an angry employee who, tired of being a glorified valet, was putting together a Scot Harvath voodoo doll.

"Pretty nice, huh?" he asked as Sølvi tossed her jacket next to his on the back seat and fastened her seat belt.

She grunted in response.

"You should probably take your body armor off too."

"Can we just get going please?"

"Fine," he replied, firing up the car and putting it in gear.

As soon as they started moving, Sølvi reached for the air-conditioning controls, switching the temperature to *max cold* and turning the fan up as high as it would go. He knew it was useless, but he kept his mouth shut. She'd figure it out soon enough.

"Damn it," she eventually said and rolled her window down.

Removing her sweat-drenched shirt, she peeled off her body armor, tossed both in back, and sat in the passenger seat in her jog bra, hands behind her head, trying to cool off.

"Sorry about the AC," he said, rolling his own window down now.

Closing her eyes, she stated, "If you've got any more bad news for me, now would be the time to get it out of your system."

He toyed with the idea of admitting that the car was only a four-banger, but even people with exquisite senses of humor had their limits. She'd been through hell. She deserved a break.

"Other than the fact that we're not the only people trying to get back into D.C. using surface streets? No more bad news," he replied.

"Good," she said, lowering her arms, her eyes still closed. "I'm going to try to get a little sleep."

Leaving the radio off, he let her get some rest and focused on the drive. It didn't take long, though, for his mind to wander.

He thought about the sniper Sølvi had killed, as well as the man's two accomplices. All three of them looked as American as the shooters at Rogers's house early this morning, and the men outside the Vice President's Residence two nights ago. Yet the targets themselves couldn't have been more diverse—a group of protesters, a former National Security Advisor, and a motorcade made up of Norwegian and Dutch delegations for a NATO Summit centered on missile defense. And while there had to be something that all these victims had in common, he still wasn't seeing it.

The idea that McGee had posited, that this was all about weakening the new president, still seemed to be the only theory that could knit all the attacks together.

That, and the fact that someone seemed to have a mole inside the Secret Service. Which, after what just happened, was making the Norwegian Prime Minister look incredibly prescient.

Ambassador Rogers had also been prescient, though not when it came to the identity and, likely, the motivation of his attackers.

All of which reminded Harvath that there was still so much that he had to figure out. Hopefully, once he got back to Kent Island, he and McGee, along with Haney, could start putting more of the pieces together.

As he neared the Chain Bridge and prepared to cross over from Virginia into the District of Columbia, he checked the traffic on his GPS and realized there were two different routes he could take. One of them went right past the Norwegian Embassy.

Gently stroking Sølvi's arm, he woke her up and offered her the option.

She looked around, trying to get her bearings, and then, studying his phone, said, "Let's go the embassy route. My car is there with my go-bag. I can grab a sixty-second shower and put on fresh clothes. Thank you."

He was glad to have given her the choice.

After crossing the Potomac, he made his way toward the traffic circle at American University, then followed Massachusetts Avenue south until he reached the Norwegian ambassador's residence at Thirty-Fourth Street. The Norwegian flag had already been lowered to half-staff.

He turned left onto Thirty-Fourth, drove half a block down, and pulled into the driveway leading to the embassy's parking garage.

As he pressed the call button, he reclined slightly in his seat, allowing Sølvi—who had already put her shirt back on—to do the talking. But instead of the usual cheerful voice of the embassy's receptionist, a deep, serious voice responded—likely one of the security personnel. Given the circumstances, Harvath thought, it made sense that the Norwegians had ramped up their protective measures. Moments later, the gate slid open, and he drove through.

He found a spot in the visitors' area, not far from Sølvi's Mustang, and parked. While she got her go-bag from her trunk, he donned his suit jacket and worked on smoothing out the wrinkles in his trousers and sweat-stained shirt. He wasn't going to win any style competition, but it was important for him that he show respect.

Upon being buzzed into the embassy lobby, the solemnity was massive. Employees were consoling each other and the security presence was highly visible. Harvath noticed Christoffe, or "Just Chris," whom he'd been told had been driving separate from the official motorcade when the attack had happened, and gave him a subtle nod.

What didn't make sense to him, however, was why they were all gathered in the lobby. It seemed a rather cold and empty space in which to grieve. Certainly, there were more intimate spaces farther inside.

He soon had an answer, as Sølvi saw the chief of security and stepped away to have a word.

"Prime Minister Stang and Ambassador Hansen are ten minutes out," she said as she walked back over.

"From where?" asked Harvath.

"Originally, the plan was to fly the presidential helicopter back to the White House, where they had ambulances standing by, but one of the Dutch victims started getting worse in flight. They were worried that he might have internal bleeding, so they flew directly to GW Hospital and offloaded the wounded there. Stang and Hansen wanted to stay with the Norwegian patients, but Haugen and the Secret Service talked them into returning to the White House for their safety."

"Probably a good idea."

Sølvi nodded. "And while a new protective detail was being assembled for them, President Mitchell invited them into the Oval Office. He wanted to console them and discuss some decisions that needed to be made. Starting with tomorrow night's cocktail reception."

"Which they've canceled, right?"

Again, Sølvi nodded. "It would have been inappropriate for people to get dressed up and stand around with glasses of champagne after today's events."

"Agreed. What about the summit itself?"

"That's going to be a NATO decision, which is why the Prime Minister is on her way here. She'll need to talk with Oslo first, then NATO has a member-wide video call scheduled for a few hours from now."

"So until further notice," Harvath replied, "it sounds like you'll be here."

"Yes. It's going to be a long night."

With the Prime Minister en route to the embassy, Sølvi no longer needed Scot to wait around to drive her to Blair House. He could get back on the road and head for Kent Island.

It was for the best. The Norwegians would want to share their grief together and he would just be an outsider.

After a quick kiss, they said their goodbyes and he quietly exited the embassy via the parking area.

With traffic, it was going to take him at least twenty minutes to get to the parking garage where he'd left Haney's Bronco and then another hour and a half to get to the safe house at the Cove Creek Club. Removing his jacket, he tossed it on the back seat of the Malibu and was about to put the key in the ignition when his phone rang.

Picking it up, he saw it was McGee calling and answered.

"That's a good start," said the ex–CIA director. "At least you're still alive."

"Been a long day," Harvath replied. "I'll explain when I get there. Leaving D.C. now. ETA about two hours."

"Negative. You're going to want to see what I've got ASAP. I'm already on my way to your place."

"What about our guest?"

"He'll be fine. Mike's going to keep an eye on him."

Harvath was intrigued. "Can you give me a hint as to what you've got?"

"Remember those photos I took this morning?" McGee said. "We got a hit on one of them—a *big* hit. And you're going to want to act on it tonight."

CHAPTER 40

J esus," said Fields as she walked into the office and looked at the TV screen. "RPGs? On a Secret Service motorcade?"

"The agents on scene say it's absolutely horrific," Carolan replied. "Blood, bodies, burned-out vehicles—it sounds like a war zone."

"The whole damn city is under siege. Did you hear about the shoot-out at Ambassador Rogers's house this morning?"

Carolan nodded.

"Do we know any more about it?"

"No," he replied. "Not yet."

"Do we think these are connected?"

"Until we have evidence to the contrary, we probably should assume that."

Fields didn't seem convinced. "As far as Operation Black Line and the Russians are concerned," she said, pointing at the TV, "this makes sense. They get to take a swipe at NATO and create chaos. But Rogers? The average person has no idea who he is. What do the Russians get out of going after him?"

"I don't know yet. But we're going to find out," he replied. Then, pointing to the document in her hand, he asked. "Is that it?"

Fields nodded and read from it: "In light of exigent circumstances, and having been screened by appropriate FBI psychological personnel, Special Agent Jennifer Elizabeth Fields is hereby provisionally returned to duty, pending the next full meeting of the FBI's Shooting Incident Review Group. Signed, Special Agent Alan Gallo, Assistant Director, FBI Counterintelligence Division."

"That only took all day."

"I had to wait for the shrink to sign off and then Gallo was out of the building at the National Counterterrorism Center, so once his assistant typed up the letter, I had to drive it up there for his signature. But at least it's done. And I'm back. How'd that lead you were working on pan out?"

"Remember when I sent the underground fight-club video for facial recognition?"

Fields nodded as she pulled up a chair and sat down.

"While I was waiting for it to come back," he continued, "I ran the sword-and-tree tattoo through all the federal databases—the Bureau of Prisons, our own National Gang Intelligence Center, you name it— especially as one of the things that gang intelligence units track is tattoos. But I didn't get any hits. Which at the time, I just took in stride. You hit a brick wall, you go around it, over it, whatever."

"Okay," she replied, not fully understanding where he was going.

"But the fact that we couldn't identify a single attacker from the Naval Observatory was driving me crazy. These were young men, eighteen to thirty-four with not only no criminal backgrounds, but also no discernable social media presence. I kept asking myself, how is that possible?"

"It isn't," said Fields. "Not in today's world. One guy, maybe. All of them? No way."

"Precisely. Somebody very skilled would have had to help them do that."

She looked at him. "Do you have any idea how difficult that would be? Breaking into government databases would require next-level hacking ability. I don't think the Russians could even do it."

"Put a pin in the 'who' for a moment," said Carolan. "Let's talk about the 'what.' What would you get by erasing these people?"

"Easy question. Anonymity. If we don't know who any of them are, we can't map their networks and link them together. We wouldn't know who their associates are, nor how many of them there may be out there."

Carolan smiled. "Bingo. They'd have an invisible army."

"An army that's piling up a lot of casualties," Fields responded. "Six bodies from the attack outside the VP's Residence, eight at Rogers's house, and it sounds like at least three more at the motorcade attack."

"True, they're taking serious losses, but let's get back to the databases. What if the 'who' wasn't some hacker on the outside? What if it was somebody on the inside doing the erasing?"

Her eyes widened. "A mole?"

"Think about it. Someone with the right access, someone who knew what they were doing . . . Why not? It wouldn't be the first time the government had a bad actor on its payroll. Snowden, Manning, Winner, Teixeira—we've been particularly awash in these antigovernment types over the last decade."

"Where would you even start looking?"

"That's the problem," Carolan admitted. "A needle in a haystack is one thing, but a needle somewhere in a sea of haystacks is something you and I aren't equipped to go after. Which brought me back to the National Gang Intelligence Center.

"Even though it acts as a national clearinghouse for gang-related information, its intel comes through FBI field offices via their local and state law enforcement partners. So, if anything got erased from the NGIC federal database, like data about our sword-and-tree tattoo, maybe there's copy of it on a computer, in a file drawer, or an iPhone of some local cop or state trooper somewhere.

"All I had to do was send an email, with the picture of the tattoo, to all the FBI field offices and ask them to reach out to their contacts. Then hope they'd kick back someone like Weber, who had a pressure point we could leverage, and we'd be off to the races."

"And did we get anything?" Fields asked.

"So far, just one," Carolan replied, pulling up the man's information on his computer. "Richard 'Ricky' Thomas Russell."

"And does this Ricky Russell have something we can leverage?"

Her boss nodded. "Big-time."

"Well done. You did it."

Carolan, however, didn't share her enthusiasm. Shaking his head, he said, "I don't think Gallo is going to okay my plan."

"Why not?"

"Because the leverage is Russell's six-year-old child."

CHAPTER 41

Harvath drove to the public parking garage he had used near Secret Service headquarters and swapped the Malibu for Haney's Bronco. Even running multiple SDRs on the way out of D.C., he still made it back to his place with forty-five minutes to spare before McGee got there.

After a shower and a change of clothes, Harvath turned on the TV in his office and got caught up on the news.

With few to no facts, speculation was rampant. *The United States was under attack from a foreign power. Domestic terrorists were running wild. The attack outside the Vice President's Residence was a "false flag" meant to weaken President Mitchell, while the attack on the Dulles Access Road was meant to drive a wedge between America and its NATO allies, weakening the transatlantic organization.*

Harvath didn't know much, but at this point he knew enough to know that any and all of those options were possible. He hoped that whatever McGee had uncovered, it would help make sense out of some of this.

When the former CIA director arrived, he set up his laptop at Harvath's kitchen table and walked him through what he had learned from his contact back at the Agency.

He began with the photo of the attacker he had recognized at Ambassador Rogers's house. "Alex Cobb," he said. "He was ex–Ground Branch."

First, some sort of Secret Service leak and now CIA assassins? Harvath wondered what agency would be uncovered next.

Ground Branch was particularly hard-core. It was the CIA's paramilitary detachment and was operated under the auspices of the Special Activities Center. It recruited from some of the military's most elite units. Harvath had known a lot of Ground Branch members, including Mike Haney, who had crossed over when he left the Marine Corps.

"He was 'ex' Ground Branch?" Harvath asked, seeking clarification.

"Correct. He was fired six months ago when the new director took over."

"Fired for what?"

"For not having been there longer," McGee explained. "He was a 'probationary' employee. Hadn't hit the two-year mark. They're easier to fire because they don't have all the civil service protections yet. President Mitchell wanted deep cuts at CIA. You know how he feels about the intelligence community."

"He's not a fan," Harvath replied. "I know that much."

"The president believes the IC was behind the whole October Surprise thing exposing his college romance when he studied abroad in Russia."

"Were you?"

"I don't know where it came from, but it wasn't CIA."

"You're sure?" Harvath asked.

McGee nodded before continuing, "Anyway, Mitchell campaigned on paring the size of government way back. And that went double, if not triple for the CIA. The new director began swinging the ax the moment he rolled into the parking lot. It was an absolute bloodbath. The probationary people like Cobb took it right in the neck."

"So, Cobb gets cut loose and then what? Hangs a murder-for-hire shingle across the street at Immanuel Presbyterian?"

"I'm not sure what he did, but by the following month, his home was listed on the MLS. The month after that, he was in default on his mortgage, and behind on both his car payment and his wife's."

"Sounds like the wolf was at the door."

"Then everything changes the next month," said McGee. "The for-sale sign comes down, the house is taken off the market, and Cobb magically writes a series of checks, which all clear, catching him up on his mortgage and car payments."

"Apparently someone suddenly came into some money."

"Exactly."

"But did a rich old aunt step in to save him?" asked Harvath. "Or could he have quietly put himself out there and actually been hired by the Iranians?"

"I was wondering the same thing, but according to my source, after he got his finances back in order, the money trail goes cold."

"What about the other shooters?"

McGee pulled up their photos and stated, "All probationary employees. All Ground Branch. All fired."

Harvath studied the pictures. They looked like photographs taken of hard copy, paper files. "Who's your source at Langley? The archivist?"

"Everything inside the Special Activities Center, especially personnel files, is locked down tighter than tight. If you access any of the computerized databases, you leave a trail of digital breadcrumbs a mile long. Sometimes the old ways still are the best ways. Believe me."

Harvath had seen that proven enough times to know that it was true. "What about the financial information? Where's that coming from?"

"Someone I trust at Treasury."

"And do we know anything about the rest of the attackers' finances?"

"More or less, they all drop off the banking grid about the same time."

"Interesting," said Harvath. "So unless they had the same benevolent old aunt, it would suggest a more unsavory source of income."

The former CIA chief nodded. "It looks like somebody may have bought themselves their own wet-work team."

"Do we have any idea who?"

"That's what I wanted to figure out. I recognized Cobb because he was featured in a mission briefing I signed off on about a year and a half ago. However, I hadn't interacted with any of the others, so I pushed my source to find a link. And it looks like we hit the jackpot.

"Every one of the attackers at Ambassador Rogers's house was recruited to Ground Branch by the same CIA officer—a former Green Beret by the name of Dennis Hale. Him, I remember. He was an exceptional strategist and played an important role in a lot of the more difficult missions that Ground Branch was asked to undertake."

"Is this guy Hale still at CIA?" Harvath asked.

McGee shook his head. "When President Mitchell's people offered buyouts for anyone looking to take early retirement, he jumped at the chance. Scored a job as head of security for a very wealthy Virginia family."

"So he leaves, goes into the private sector, and when a bunch of people he recruited to CIA get let go, he launches a small, private military corporation as a side hustle?"

"Maybe. Or perhaps he hires people for legit security positions and they do a bunch of other things using their day jobs as cover."

It was intriguing, Harvath had to give McGee that, but it was still thin. "Your guy at Treasury couldn't find a way to connect all of them?"

"He was already doing me a favor giving me what he did. You either need a warrant, or someone who doesn't mind stepping outside the bounds of the law."

There was an arch to McGee's left eyebrow as he finished his sentence and Harvath knew exactly who he was referring to. *Nicholas.*

"I can ask him. Did your archivist provide you with the attackers' dates of birth and Social Security numbers?"

"Yes. It's all in their files."

"That should be enough to get our mutual friend started. In the meantime, you said I was going to want to act on this tonight. Why?"

McGee took a breath before responding. "One of the reasons Dennis Hale took the early retirement package was because he was being investigated inside the Agency."

"For what?"

"Special Activities Center, as you know, has multiple branches."

"Ground, Maritime, and Air," said Harvath, very familiar with all of them.

"There's another branch most people outside the Agency don't know much about—the Armor and Special Programs Branch. They provide anything the other branches need to conduct high-risk operations in sensitive or hostile environments. And I mean anything—any kind of vehicle you can imagine, right down to any type of weapon. Their specialty is plausible deniability, meaning none of their gear can be tied back to the United States."

"So where does it come from?"

"Some of it is bought from foreign arms dealers via third-party cut-outs, but a lot of it they steal, often from dead bad guys. Hale was spear-heading a program with that express purpose down in Mexico. One of the cartels had gotten its hands on a batch of shoulder-fired weapons. Hale's job was to track down their stockpile and if possible liberate it. If not, he was to blow it in place.

"His op, allegedly, went sideways and he was forced to blow up the warehouse with everything in it. Shit happens. You move on. Nobody thought anything more about it. But a couple of months later, a source claimed that the warehouse had been emptied out before Hale blew it up. The source stated that Hale had made a deal with the cartel and in return he was given a portion of the weapons—weapons that were never handed over to Armor and Special Programs, nor anyone else at CIA.

"An investigation was launched, but before it could get fully up and running, Hale took the early-retirement package and the investigation was put to bed. I had heard the rumors, but they were just that. There were no witnesses to contradict Hale. His teammates all told the same story. They came under heavy fire and blew the building before their ex-filtration. There was a big explosion, consistent with what they all be-lieved to have been inside. It was Hale's word against the source's down in Mexico. The new director wanted no part of it and so they just closed the book."

"Jesus," said Harvath, starting to understand the picture McGee was painting. "What kind of shoulder-fired weapons did they think the cartel had?"

"Stinger surface-to-air missiles, AT-4 antitank weapons, and RPG-7 rocket-propelled grenades."

And there it is. Harvath now had the picture in full. "RPGs. The same weapon Sølvi and the Secret Service say was used against their motorcade today."

"Which is why I thought you'd be very interested in confronting Hale tonight. That and the fact that the family he works for is leaving tomor-row for their ranch in Wyoming and he's expected to travel with them."

Taking out his phone, Harvath pulled up the photos of the three men

Sølvi and Bente had killed in the woods off the Dulles Access Road and showed them to McGee.

"Recognize any of them?" he asked.

The ex–CIA chief studied them for several seconds before admitting, "No, I don't."

"How quickly can you get these to your source at Langley?"

"As soon as we get them from your phone to my laptop."

Transferring them over, Harvath said, "If it turns out that they also worked at CIA, we'll need everything in their files."

"Understood," McGee replied as he began preparing everything for his contact back at Langley.

"So," Harvath mused aloud, trying to connect the dots, "if Hale's behind the attack on the motorcade and the attack on Rogers, what's the connection?"

"I keep trying to make it make sense, but I think that's something you're going to have to ask him yourself."

"Where can I find him?"

"The family he works for has a pretty substantial estate. He lives on the property most of the time. There's just one problem."

"What's that?"

"Before hiring Hale, the family did a top-to-bottom security review and enacted a bunch of enhancements. Allegedly, it's all cutting-edge, top-of-the-line stuff. Spared no expense. Even put in buoys along the shorefront to detect people coming in by boat."

Harvath looked at him. "What's this family's name?"

"Willis. The husband made his fortune in—"

"Chemicals."

McGee was surprised. "You know him?"

"The Carlton Group did the security review. I was the team leader."

CHAPTER 42

The review at the Willis estate had been done last fall, soon after Scot had returned from spending most of the summer in Norway with Sølvi. It had been sandwiched between a quick but very dangerous assignment in China and a string of brutal, back-to-back operations that had taken him to Tajikistan, Afghanistan, India, and the war-torn front lines of Ukraine.

Nicholas and Gary Lawlor, who had been running day-to-day operations at the Carlton Group, had been punishing him. They had wanted him in the office full-time, so they had handed him the lucrative, low-stress Willis security review as an example of the easy life he could be enjoying if he would simply hang up his cleats and weld himself to a desk. The plan backfired.

After getting caught up in one of Sølvi's operations and the subsequent blackmail attempt by the CIA, he had made up his mind to walk away from the Carlton Group. Although truly walking away was proving to be quite difficult.

While he and McGee waited to hear back from McGee's CIA source and to see what Nicholas could do with the files on the first batch of attackers, they discussed the best way to confront Hale.

Because the Willis family had been a client, they debated bringing Mr. Willis into their confidence. But as easy at that might seem, it was loaded with pitfalls, not the least of which being that it was unprofessional and could seriously damage the Carlton Group's reputation.

There was no way Lawlor—who was currently on vacation in Europe—would ever allow it, especially not without concrete evidence that Hale was dirty.

There was also the risk that Willis himself couldn't be trusted; that he might tip their hand to Hale and that the ex-operative might have a very nasty surprise waiting for Harvath when he showed up. That possibility alone was enough to disqualify Willis. The element of surprise was too valuable. Trading it for easier access to Hale wasn't worth it. Harvath would have to devise a plan without him.

In addition to not roping in Willis, there was a discussion of whether Nicholas might break their way in and, if so, how much he should be told. Regardless of Harvath's current state of "non" employment with the Carlton Group, if any of this went wrong and he was caught on the Willis estate, it wouldn't look good. It would look like he was using proprietary knowledge gained as a contractor to the Willis family for his own ends, which was exactly what he was planning to do. And even if Nicholas was tempted to go along with it, his involvement, if exposed, would make things exponentially worse for the company. A man like Willis could sue the Carlton Group out of existence.

Out of loyalty to the firm's founder, a man who had been like a father to Harvath, he owed it to Reed Carlton not to be reckless with the company. Many good, patriotic people counted on it for their livelihood. Harvath needed to take every precaution to make sure that those people were protected. Bottom line: Any plan they developed to get to Hale could only include him and McGee.

Harvath still remembered the Willis estate. It was impossible to forget. The sale of the eighteen-acre estate, listed at $60 million, marked the most expensive residential real estate transaction ever in the greater Washington area.

Named "River Edge," the gated waterfront home along the Potomac was only five and a half miles north of Harvath's.

Built in the American Federalist style, the house had eight bedrooms and something crazy like fifteen bathrooms. Wherever possible, the rooms were built to capitalize on their stunning views of the Potomac.

The home had a massive game room, a twenty-seat movie theater, a spa with an indoor pool, a luxury family kitchen, plus a commercial chef's kitchen for big events. There was a three-bedroom, three-bath guesthouse on the property, as well as a carriage house with a four-car garage and a studio apartment above, where Hale was likely staying.

When Harvath had conducted his security review, he had done so with the mindset of someone wanting to either steal from or physically do the Willis family harm. Sophisticated thieves looking to target the family's priceless art collection. Environmentalists angry at the global pollution they believed Willis Chemicals had caused. Extremist factions unhappy with the political stances and donations of the family. Kidnappers hoping to snatch Mrs. Willis or one of their children to hold for ransom.

The list of possible intruders had been extensive and Harvath had worked hard to see the estate through all of their eyes as each would have had a different approach. He and the Carlton Group had been hired to literally think of everything.

Having done red-teaming as a SEAL, testing the security of American military bases and other governmental installations around the world, it was something Harvath had become quite good at. He had applied that same knowledge and expertise to the security review for the Willis family.

The question, however, was how much had Mr. and Mrs. Willis taken to heart? How many of the recommended upgrades had they made?

According to McGee, they had spared no expense. But did that mean they had gone with best-in-class commercial products, or did they actually buy military-grade equipment? It was impossible to know because the technical improvements weren't Harvath's area of expertise and by the time they had ordered everything and were updating their property, he was already halfway around the world on his next mission.

This was where having Nicholas on board really could have made a difference. Not only would he have been aware of what the Willis family had opted to purchase, but he would have also known how to turn it all off. Had he wanted, with a handful of keystrokes, Nicholas could have opened up a hole in the Willis security net big enough for Harvath to drive Haney's Bronco through.

At the same time, such a request might have run the chance of offending him. Nicholas was not the same thieving, mercenary man he had once been twenty years ago. Finding a purpose greater than himself had changed him and it was Harvath who had led him to that greater purpose.

The Carlton Group had become Nicholas's family—the most precious thing in the world for a person abandoned by his own parents. The stability and purpose it provided had, in turn, led to a real, true family of Nicholas's own via Nina and their new baby. It was a life he had never allowed himself to dare dream of.

But as happy as Harvath had been for his friend, there were days when he missed the old Nicholas—a man willing to do the most expedient thing regardless of the costs.

Nevertheless, he had to come up with something and pushed a series of arguments around in his head.

Could he create an appeal to family that would sway Nicholas? Scot and Sølvi, the godparents of Nicholas's daughter, had both come under attack. Hale was looking like he could have been behind the siege on the Secret Service motorcade, as well as Ambassador Rogers's house. He might have even orchestrated the attack on the protesters and police outside the Naval Observatory that had spilled into Ambassador Hansen's residence, killing two of her security agents and critically injuring the chef. Shouldn't Nicholas want to help Harvath ascertain if Hale was involved?

What about the Willis family? If Hale was guilty of all the things Harvath suspected him of, what responsibility did the Carlton Group have to the Willises, even if the company hadn't consulted on his being hired as their chief of security? If any other sort of threat ever came to Nicholas's attention, would he bury it? Or would he find a way to get to the bottom of it?

It was a thorny issue, one that Harvath didn't enjoy wrestling with. The older he got, the more he both understood and disliked the ambiguity of his former profession. It required a certain moral flexibility that took a lot of energy to justify.

Ultimately, however, if he wanted Nicholas's help, which he did, he was going to have to shoot him straight and let the chips fall where they may.

Excusing himself, he got up from the table and told McGee he needed to make a call.

As he walked back to his office, he texted Nicholas and asked if he was free for a quick chat. He needed a favor. A serious one.

CHAPTER 43

S o much for *The X Files*," Fields quipped as she and Carolan sat outside the FBI director's office, waiting to see if they'd be called in.

"The whole *X Files* thing and putting us down in the basement was Gallo's idea. He's not going to burn us with any mentions of Russia. He understands what's at stake," replied Carolan.

"The reason we moved down to the basement was to stay off his radar. Now look at us. We've got a dead neo-Nazi in Baltimore, whom I shot, and a request to rope one of the largest bureaucracies in the United States government into a massive sting operation."

"Listen, I don't like this any more than you do, but it's not like we have a choice. Besides, Gallo wouldn't have kicked this upstairs if he didn't think it had merit. And for the last time, this isn't a sting operation. I don't want to lie to Russell. He may be a scumbag, but that's not his kid's fault. I want him to walk in, of his own accord, and for us to be able to talk with him without worrying he's going to go psycho like Weber did."

Fields shook her head. "There's no telling if he'll go psycho or not. All we're doing is making sure he doesn't have a gun in his waistband if he does."

"As long as he doesn't have a gun, we'll be safe."

"Do you have any idea how many other weapons can make it through a magnetometer?"

"A few," Carolan replied.

"Tons, actually. So, unless you're planning on conducting full pat-downs, which I know you're not because it would be too suspicious, stop saying 'we'll be safe,' okay?"

"There's going to be an FBI SWAT team in the next room."

"I could kill half the Bureau's senior leadership, without a pistol, be-fore the first SWAT team member made it through that door. You want to give this asshole the same opportunity?"

"Of course not."

"Then don't give him the benefit of the doubt. Expect the unexpected. He's a piece of shit, just like Weber. Having a sick kid doesn't change that. Don't feel sorry for him. Don't you dare."

"For fuck's sake, Jenny, I get it. Okay?" he replied.

Fields chuckled. It wasn't often that she got a rise out of him, even with his renowned temper. It was less often still that she caused him to utter a grade-A curse word.

"What's so funny?"

"Apparently, shit's finally getting real. Sugar Bear just dropped the f-bomb."

"Don't start with me," he warned. "Not now. And good Lord, defi-nitely not here."

Before anything further could be said between them, the door to the conference room opened and FBI Director Stephen Price, along with Assistant Director Gallo, stepped out.

"Is this her?" Price asked.

"Yes, sir," Gallo replied.

Walking over to Fields, the FBI director extended his hand and said, "I saw the video from Baltimore. You were incredible. Do we teach all our FBI agents to shoot like that?"

"Thank you, sir," she responded, shaking the man's hand, not sur-prised that Gallo might have used the video to impress him. "We're all taught to be prepared."

"And we encourage them to practice as if their lives depend on it," stated Gallo, "because someday, as you saw, it just might."

"Let's get a picture," Price said, pulling out his phone.

Fields looked at Gallo, who shot her a look back that encouraged her to humor the new director.

After taking a picture with Fields, Price waved Carolan over and got one with him as well.

"Director Price is very pleased with the progress your investigation has made," Gallo declared. "He knows that getting to the bottom of the attacks at the Vice President's Residence, as soon as possible, will not only look good for the FBI, but will also look good for the President. To that end, the director has given his full blessing to Operation Switchback."

Both Carolan and Fields were about to ask what the hell Operation Switchback was, but there was something in the new look Gallo shot them that told them not to ask.

"You have the green light," said Price, smiling almost a little too broadly, as if he was giddy with the idea of approving his first covert FBI mission.

Going along with it, Carolan and Fields both replied, "Thank you, sir. We won't let you down."

"We're going to get challenge coins made for this, right?" Price asked, referring to the commemorative coins popular in the military and law enforcement communities. "I want to give coin number one to President Mitchell."

"Of course," Gallo replied, signaling to Carolan and Fields with a tilt of his head that they had achieved their objective, the dog-and-pony show was over, and they were free to leave.

After thanking the new director for green-lighting Operation Switchback, which Price confessed he had named himself, they disappeared into the hall and headed for the elevators.

A long-standing rumor since the J. Edgar Hoover days was that every elevator at headquarters was bugged and monitored by the Bureau director. Though it was highly unlikely, Carolan and Fields wouldn't be fully comfortable talking until they had returned to their office.

As an elevator arrived and its doors opened, they were surprised when Agent Kennedy stepped out. He seemed equally surprised to see them.

"Carolan. Fields," he stated. "What are you two doing up here?"

"Shoot a Nazi," Fields replied, "and you get to meet the new director."

Sometimes Fields could be a little too flippant for her own good. Even though it was her way of dealing with having gone through a stressful, life-or-death situation, that kind of attitude could come back to bite her in the ass.

"The director wanted an in-person briefing on the shooting," said Carolan. "What about you? What are you doing up here?"

"Same, except I'm here for the Naval Observatory shooting. He wants regular briefings, all in person."

"Any updates?"

Kennedy shook his head. "Still collecting evidence, trying to catch a break."

The elevator doors, which Carolan had been holding open, began to buzz. The trio said goodbye and Carolan and Fields headed down to the basement.

"Operation Switchback?" Fields asked as she dropped into a chair and her boss closed the door to their office.

"Gallo was smart to let him name it. Now the director has skin in the game. If he wants to show off for Mitchell, this is his chance."

"Wouldn't it have been more fun to call it Operation 'Punch a Nazi' or 'Hang 'em Heil'?"

Carolan laughed. "We just got everything we asked for, so don't be a pain in the ass. As soon as Director Price gets confirmation from the HHS secretary, we'll be able to put everything in motion. In the meantime, we need to prep a script. When we reach out to Russell, the pitch has to be absolutely perfect. Zero room for error."

While Fields took a certain pleasure in pulling her boss's chain, she knew he was right. Weber's shooting had probably already been reported far and wide across the sword-and-tree community of lost boys. They needed to expect that word had made it to Russell and that he would have his guard up.

That was why exploiting his son was so critical. It was the only weak spot Carolan had been able to identify. If they could use the little boy's infirmity as a way to open the door, Russell might crack it enough to let them all the way inside.

A half hour after returning to the basement, Fields and Carolan had an update from Gallo. FBI Director Price had reached out to the secretary of health and human services. Their request had been approved. The computer systems were in the process of being updated with the new information and the paperwork would be forwarded to the FBI as soon as it was complete.

In the meantime, Price asked that Carolan and Fields set aside the number two challenge coin for him and that number three be reserved for the HHS secretary.

The two FBI agents couldn't help but shake their heads. After all the death and injury and destruction over the last couple of days, it was mind-boggling to see U.S. government agency heads preoccupied with challenge coins.

At the same time, if that was all it took to keep Price in their corner, but out of their hair, it was a bargain. When this was all over, they would design the coolest challenge coin the man had ever seen. In the meantime, they had work to do.

Now that they had the bait, they needed to place it on the hook, dangle it in front of Russell, and get him to bite.

However, years of experience had taught them both that getting a fish on the hook was one thing. Reeling it into the boat without your line breaking could be something else entirely.

CHAPTER 44

Harvath's concerns about where Nicholas would fall on the Willis estate issue were well-founded. Their discussion had not gone well.

His friend's bad mood had likely been compounded by his lack of sleep. When Harvath connected with him, he could hear the baby crying in the background until Nicholas stepped into his home office and shut the door.

The weariness in the man's voice told Harvath many things—chief among them that Scot had been a crappy godfather and an even crappier friend. It was inexcusable that he hadn't even thought to offer to come over with Sølvi to babysit. Nicholas and Nina were drowning and he could have easily tossed them a lifeline—especially after returning home rested and recharged from a six-month honeymoon.

He apologized to his friend and let him know that no matter what Nicholas decided to do regarding the Willis issue, he was going to pitch in and lend him a hand. It wasn't a bribe. It was simply a matter of doing the right thing. Harvath didn't usually drop the ball, especially not when it came to those closest to him, but he had and he needed to fix it.

Simply hearing those words had caused a shift in Nicholas. Harvath could see it in the man's face via their encrypted video chat. His friend had taken a true interest in not only his well-being, but also his family's. The cavalry was coming. Even if Scot and Sølvi couldn't be there immediately, the offer of the lifeline had been extended.

It didn't wipe out Nicholas's reservations about the Willises having been Carlton Group clients, but it did make him a little more receptive to Harvath's arguments.

Wanting to use that shift to his advantage, Harvath believed he could win Nicholas fully over to his side by slowing everything down. He suggested they start with the personnel files McGee had already secured and see if Nicholas could uncover direct payments by Hale to the dead attackers from Ambassador Rogers's house. Nicholas agreed to see what he could find. He made no promises beyond that.

Nicholas also made clear that he was drawing a bright line around the Willis estate. It was a line that Harvath was absolutely not allowed to cross. Nicholas not only had asked if Harvath had understood him, but had also made him repeat it back. Over the entire course of their friendship, Nicholas had never so firmly put Harvath on the spot like that.

After disconnecting the call, he returned to the kitchen to give McGee an update and to see if he had come up with any new developments.

"It's going to take my source back at Langley a little bit of time," he replied.

Harvath looked at his watch. A plan was forming in his mind and, regardless of what Nicholas ultimately decided, there were some very specific supplies he was going to need. There was a shop nearby where he could get them, but it would be closing soon. He invited McGee to join him.

USA Dive was a veteran-owned SCUBA shop about twenty minutes south of Harvath's house. Calling ahead to make sure they had what he needed and wouldn't close before he got there, he hunted down his own bag of dive gear, tossed it in the back of Haney's Bronco, and they hit the road.

While Virginia was an extremely patriotic state year-round, all the additional red, white, and blue coming out in advance of this Fourth of July was especially noticeable.

It had always been Harvath's favorite holiday. The story of the nation's birth and, most importantly, its hard-won independence from Britain filled him with a deep sense of awe and pride.

He had especially been looking forward to this year's celebration and to showing Sølvi what it truly meant to be American.

But with three attacks over as many days, with the Secret Service and the Central Intelligence Agency implicated, he was beginning to question what America stood for and how so much could have changed in such a short amount of time.

Even if there was some malign, foreign threat at work, how had it been able to find so many willing American conspirators? By almost every single metric, America remained the envy of the world. In a nation defined by its freedom, its prosperity and its abundance of opportunity, how do you find citizens willing to attack and kill their fellow countrymen and women?

None of it made any sense to him.

None of it made any sense to McGee either. "We're living in the greatest nation in history," he said. "I've heard it said that if you were a soul in heaven, and could choose any time and any place to be born—not knowing anything else about what your circumstances would be—you would choose right here, right now. Our ancestors would marvel at how incredibly good we have it. Yet people seem angrier and more pissed-off than ever before."

Holding up his phone, Harvath replied, "I blame this. Keeping up with the Joneses used to mean keeping up with the people in your neighborhood. The Joneses got a new car, you strove to get a new car. They went on vacation to Florida, you shot for the same thing. These were not only people you economically had things in common with, but they were living real, authentic lives. You knew when Mr. and Mrs. Jones had a fight or that Mrs. Jones had a health scare.

"Today, people try to keep up with what they see on social media, but none of it is real. It's all fake. Thirty influencers rent a mansion or lease a Bentley together and shoot all their content on the one day of each month they get to pretend that stuff is theirs. It's crazy. And worse than that, it's just unrealistic. Yet people convince themselves their life sucks because they don't enjoy the lifestyles they believe those influencers are living. If I found a lamp with a genie and only got one wish, it would be for the internet to disappear. It's like a vampire—it just takes and takes and takes from you, never reciprocating. Time is our most precious commodity, but we willingly sink it into that black hole. The internet is where human potential goes to die."

McGee nodded. "I think one day, maybe not too long from now, we're going to get definitive science that proves how bad it is, not just for kids, but for adults too. It'll have to come with a health warning, the way cigarettes do."

Harvath laughed. "I admire your optimism. The idea that internet and tech-related companies would ever allow that research to see the light of day is kind of funny. If they couldn't bury the information, I'm sure they'd find a way to push enough money to the politicians to look the other way."

"You don't think, if the research was indisputable, that there wouldn't be a massive cultural backlash?"

"I think we already have the information and nobody cares. The Boston Marathon Bombing is a perfect example. Studies show that people with prolonged exposure to media coverage of the event experienced more acute stress than people who were actually there. That's crazy—and it was over a decade ago. Today the average person spends over six hours a day on screens. I think the internet in general, and phones in particular, have rewired people's brains to such a degree that they've convinced themselves that they can't live without them."

"Garbage in, garbage out," said McGee.

"And there's a lot of garbage on the internet," Harvath agreed, bringing them back around to the original point. "Large portions of which is being used to turn Americans against each other and their country."

Entering the historic town of Occoquan, Virginia, Harvath found a spot in front of the dive shop and pulled in.

While he went inside, McGee walked to a café up the street and ordered dinner for the two of them to go.

In addition to picking up a fresh tank, Harvath had the USA Dive team look over his gear and bench-test his regulator. It had been a while since he'd had any of it in the water. If something wasn't working, or was nearing failure, now was the time to fix it.

By the time McGee returned with the food, Harvath was wrapping up. The bill for all the work the guys had done was ridiculously reasonable. Not only that, but they had insisted on doing everything by the book, which meant that they had stayed past closing for him.

That kind of pride and commitment to the customer was something Harvath truly valued. He tried to give them a tip, but the men politely refused.

Sitting atop the counter next to the register was a large watercooler-style jug. Taped to the outside was a photo of a group of disabled veterans on a previous dive trip, and a call for donations to help pay for this year's dive. Reaching into his pocket, Harvath peeled three hundred bucks off his wedge of cash and dropped it into the jug.

He thanked the men and, with McGee's help, carried everything out of the shop and loaded it into the back of the Bronco.

Nodding at the to-go bags as he backed out of the space, he asked McGee, "What'd you get us?"

"You wanted healthy," the ex–CIA boss replied, "so I got you the Greek chicken. And, because today's my cheat day, I got an extra-large cheesesteak."

"You know cheat days pretty much don't work and are no longer a thing, right?"

"Mind your own business," the man said, smiling, "or I'm going to put a hole in your fucking wetsuit."

The last thing Harvath needed was a beef with the likes of McGee and so he quietly let it drop. Besides, whatever the man was doing to stay in shape, it was working. He was as lean as the first day Harvath had met him.

"When did Nicholas say he'd be getting back to you?" he asked, pulling a fry from one of the bags and popping it into his mouth.

"He didn't," Harvath replied as he headed toward US-1. "What about your source at Langley?"

Sliding the phone from his pocket, McGee opened one of his many encrypted apps and checked his messages. "Looks like something came in," he said, opening an email and reading it. "Not good. Three more attackers ID'd as ex–Ground Branch members. All with ties to Hale."

The man was right. It wasn't good. The fact that Americans had attacked a motorcade filled with U.S. allies was bad enough, but the fact that they were ex–U.S. military and ex–CIA employees was going to push this into crisis territory. It could be seen as an act of war.

Harvath had some decisions to make. His biggest concern, though, was that no matter which way he decided to go, he ran a very high likelihood of making things worse.

CHAPTER 45

Harvath and McGee, back at Harvath's kitchen table, sat and ate their dinner as they tried to figure out what to do. As Harvath had done previously with Sølvi, both his phone and McGee's were sealed in the faraday bag, in a desk drawer, in his office.

"Worst-case to best-case, we should rank what we're looking at here," the former CIA director suggested.

"It's all worst-case," Harvath replied. "There is no upside."

"Agreed, but if we can't grade this, we're not going to be able to come up with the best possible plan."

The man was right. Without getting a handle on what they were most likely dealing with, there was no way to formulate the most foolproof response.

"Starting from what we know," said Harvath, "ex–probationary Ground Branch members crossed paths in some shape or form at CIA with Hale, who took the retirement buyout and left under a cloud involving shoulder-fired weapons. The attacks on the residence of Ambassador Rogers Tuesday morning and on a Secret Service motorcade this afternoon carrying delegations to Friday's NATO Summit appear to be connected, orchestrated by Hale, and committed by these Ground Branch guys.

"Authorities have not yet publicly identified the attackers. We don't know if these two groups of attackers are connected to the attack outside the Vice President's Residence, though at this point it is not something we can, or should, rule out. Also, the finances of the attackers seem to be connected."

"A depressing, but succinct, summation," said McGee.

"So, who's the next rung up from Hale?" Harvath asked. "Somebody has got to be pulling his strings."

"And what is that person or persons' end goal? Are they just getting warmed up? Is there something bigger coming? A coup? A decapitation strike? That's what I mean when I say we need to rank this stuff."

"Why does it need to be us ranking it? We've ID'd two sets of attackers. Why not hand it over?"

"To whom? Secret Service? FBI?" McGee asked. "We have no idea how high up any of this goes."

"That's my point. We don't have the resources to chase this through every single agency in D.C. What's more, Hale may have another attack in the pipeline, ready to go. If we don't do anything and more people die, that'll be on us for sitting on it."

"Then we don't sit on it. Whether Nicholas is in or out, we need to get to Hale, tonight. We need to get him to talk so we can get our arms around whatever this is and begin to understand what we're dealing with. Only then can we start thinking of who to take this to."

Harvath didn't like hitting the pause button, but McGee's position made sense. If they tipped off the wrong person, all of the key conspirators could vanish, or worse—they could accelerate the conspirators' timetable and launch some horrific, endgame attack and even more lives could be lost. From a tactical perspective, he really couldn't see a better option. They had to go after Hale, and it had to be tonight.

The biggest issue now was whether Nicholas was going to play ball. Harvath needed to let him know that McGee's source had identified the attackers who had hit the motorcade. Hopefully that would be enough to sway him.

Excusing himself once again, Harvath walked back to his office and retrieved his phone. Opening the app they used for encrypted conversations, he sent him a quick update. Seconds later, Nicholas called via the video feature.

"You're positive?" Nicholas asked.

"McGee is," Harvath replied. "His source at Langley ran it down."

"I'd be very careful how much intel you share with that source."

"Why is that?"

"Because the deeper I dig, the more CIA dirt ends up on my shovel."

"What kind of dirt?" Harvath asked.

"You and McGee were correct about the dead attackers being on Hale's payroll. He makes it hard to trace the money, lots of shell companies and the like, but he was paying them all like regular employees."

"What does it say on their 1099s? That he was paying them to be domestic terrorists?"

Nicholas shook his head. "The stuff for Hale, while convoluted, appears to be legit security work—or at least enough of it that if the ex–Ground Branch people needed to apply for a loan or have proof of employment, they could point to their work for him. But that didn't appear to be their only source of income."

"There was more?"

"A lot more, but it's going to take some time to unpack. It looks like the CIA has a bunch of Dark Web, cryptocurrency accounts that have been paying out monthly. If I had to guess, Hale was paying his ex–Ground Branch people equivalent salaries for jobs in the private security industry, and then someone was making up the difference to them via crypto. My guess is that the new people McGee's source has identified will show the same pattern."

Harvath had to get him to back up. "A CIA crypto account? Meaning someone at Langley is actively involved?"

"I have to keep digging, but right now, that's the direction all of this is pointing to."

"Shit."

"Not the word I used, but close," said Nicholas. "Do you still want to go after Hale? Tonight?"

"According to McGee, he leaves in the morning, so it's our best shot. I know the property. I also don't want to let any more time pass only to see another attack. If that happens, we'll all have blood on our hands."

Nicholas was silent for several moments before finally saying, "You remember that the water is the best way in, right? You can't get a boat close enough without tipping them off, but you could swim it."

"I remember," said Harvath, glad to have him on board. He decided to keep it to himself that he had already begun making plans on how to infiltrate the estate.

"What do you need from me?"

"I can get myself to the shore, but I'll need a clear path up to the carriage house. Ground sensors, IR cameras, anything like that is going to have to be disabled."

After taking a deep breath, Nicholas exhaled. "Everything on the Willis property is state-of-the-art. At least everything we recommended to them in our review. It's all self-contained and supplemented by AI. I can't hack my way into their systems and shut things off. Even if we attempted to cut the power, they still have a backup for that."

Harvath didn't like where this was going. "In a perfect world, if you could pull any tool from your toolbox, what would it be?"

Nicholas smiled. "I'd detonate an EMP right above the estate. Fry everything."

"Something tells me it's going to be pretty hard to get our hands on one of those between now and tomorrow morning. I think we should narrow our focus and think a little bit smaller."

"That's it," Nicholas said, a spark igniting in his brain.

"What is?" asked Harvath.

"Something *smaller*. I know how we can do this."

"I'm all ears."

Nicholas smiled once again, running the plan through his head. "It's an old trick of mine. In fact, the first time you saw it, was the very first night we met."

CHAPTER 46

T he biggest issue Harvath had yet to sort out was a boat that could drop him in the water near the Willis estate. The Chris-Craft back at the safe house on Kent Island would have been perfect, but it was too far away. He needed something closer. He also needed someone he could trust to pilot it—someone who wouldn't ask a lot of questions. There was only one person he could think of who ticked all those boxes.

When Harvath had moved into the old church property known as Bishop's Gate, his first unannounced visitor had been a retired U.S. Navy officer who lived down the road. Out walking his dog one morning, he had noticed an uptick in activity at the house and so decided to investigate.

Admiral David Tyson was in his early seventies but had the energy and stamina of a man half his age. He was a good neighbor and always kept an eye on the house when Harvath was away.

The Admiral was also a good salesman and had talked Harvath into becoming a member of the Mount Vernon Yacht Club, a volunteer-based, neighborhood social organization two miles down from the house. The MVYC had a small marina, a twenty-five-meter pool, and a three-story, year-round clubhouse complete with a gym and a small bar.

By nature, Harvath wasn't much of a "joiner," but it was nice to have a local spot where he could drop by for a drink or jog down to in the mornings for a swim.

As far as the members were concerned, Harvath was a global security consultant who consulted for businesses around the world. The Admiral, however, had seen enough over the course of his career to know that there was a lot more to Harvath than met the eye.

To his credit, he never pushed for more information. Not when they sat and swapped Navy stories at the bar, or on the handful of times he had taken Harvath out on his boat—a forty-foot Sea Ray cabin cruiser he had christened *Pier Pressure*.

As laid-back as the yacht club was, they had two rules that were sacrosanct inside the clubhouse: no smoking and absolutely no cell phones.

As his call had gone to voicemail and he hadn't received an answer to the text he'd sent, Harvath figured the Admiral had either left his phone in the car or had turned the ringer off. Either way, the man was probably holding court at the club bar. Telling McGee that he would be right back, he hopped in the Bronco and drove down to look for him.

Harvath knew a handful of other club members with boats, but none he trusted like Tyson. If the Admiral wasn't around, he was going to have to come up with another plan.

Pulling up to the club, he was relieved to see Tyson's car parked outside. He parked in the row behind it and headed in.

The snowy-haired, barrel-chested Admiral was at his usual spot. Upon seeing Harvath, he called out his name and waved him over.

There was a big crowd for a Wednesday night and as Harvath made his way to the bar, he saw many faces he recognized.

Because he'd only been in for early-morning workouts, there were lots of folks who hadn't seen him for six months and wanted to say hello. Eventually, he made it over to Tyson.

"Not even married a year and already sneaking out to the pub," the man said as he greeted him.

"Sølvi sends her regards," Harvath replied.

"Tough business up at the Norwegian Embassy the other night. I hope you all didn't know anyone who was mixed up in all that."

"Yeah, it wasn't good. Listen, Admiral, can I have a moment of your time outside?"

"Sure, let's have a drink first. Then I can show you the boat. Just got her detailed. She looks fantastic."

When Harvath had seen what a primo parking space the Admiral had snagged, he should have realized that the man had gotten to the club early. Seeing the glassiness in his eyes, and picking up a hint of a slur in his speech, it appeared that he was already a couple of rounds in.

"I'd love to see her," Harvath replied. "In fact, let's go now before it gets too dark."

Thinking for a moment, the Admiral realized that was probably a good idea. Setting his almost-empty drink on the bar, he stated, "We'll be right back." Then, turning to Harvath, he motioned to the glass doors facing the water and said, "After you."

Sitting on Dogue Creek, just past Ferry Point, the Mount Vernon Yacht Club's narrow marina boasted over one hundred slips. *Pier Pressure* was about halfway down.

As they walked—and once they were out of earshot of anyone else—Harvath explained the favor he needed.

"That's it?" the Admiral asked. "I shove you off the stern and head home?"

"That's it," Harvath replied.

"Do I get to carry a gun?"

Harvath laughed. "I bet you already do."

"True, but not when I am drinking. Which, I need to be honest with you about. I've already had a couple."

"How about this? We can move *Pier Pressure* from here up to my dock. I'll drive and we can tie up there. You come up to the house, have some coffee, and watch *SportsCenter* for a bit. By the time we need to set sail, you'll be shipshape. Sound good?"

Harvath preferred this option since it would allow him to privately load all his gear via his own dock, rather than driving it down to the club and running the risk of witnesses. The fewer people who knew even the smallest of details, the better.

The Admiral gave him the thumbs-up. "Okay. I'm in."

CHAPTER 47

By the time Senator Blackwood had left his office, he had already received multiple messages from Vice President Cates's chief of staff.

The VP's remarks had been exceedingly well received by the public and were going viral. President Mitchell and his team were beyond pissed that Cates had undercut them. They were planning a presidential address to the nation and now had to figure out how to match the VP's tone and tenor. The last thing Mitchell's team wanted getting out was that the White House wasn't in full unison. Via his remarks, Cates had backed them into a corner.

Blackwood loved it. He didn't feel sorry for Mitchell and his team at all. In fact, he knew exactly what was going to happen next. The President was going to try to revert to the fiery nationalist he had been on the campaign trail. He would trot out his stump speech about how America needed to put Americans first, but there was just one problem. He wasn't the outsider running against the establishment anymore. He was the President of the United States. *He* was the establishment. He was the one who had gone soft and wasn't protecting the people.

And no matter what he said, no matter how soaring his rhetoric, Chuck Coughlin was going to tear him apart. Anything Mitchell promised, it would be too little, too late. Americans were dead. Mitchell was to blame. It was time for him to resign. America wouldn't be safe until it had a *real* leader in the Oval Office.

All of which was correct. Mitchell had been a complete and unmitigated disaster. He'd been so clear-eyed, so tuned in to what the country needed when he'd been running for office. But the abrupt 180 once he got in, the almost total abandonment of what he had promised his voters he would do, was proof positive that he had been captured by the swamp.

The NATO Summit was a prime example. Mitchell had promised to pull out of the alliance, to stop footing their bills, and to force Europe to stand on their own two feet.

But ultimately that wasn't what happened at all. He signed on to the Sky Shield initiative, touting the benefits for the defense industrial complex, and pushed the U.S. ever closer to war with Russia.

Initially, Blackwood hadn't been able to understand the policy shifts, but the more he and Claire spoke, the clearer everything had become.

He had been ready to go after Mitchell hammer and tongs, but she'd been the one to talk him down, to take the long view. Publicly challenging the President would turn his supporters against Blackwood. The senator needed to be a loyal soldier. He needed to stand firmly by Mitchell's side until it was no longer tenable to do so. Then, at that moment, he would explain to the President that, for the good of the country, it was time to resign.

Every wrong he suffered, every slight at Mitchell's hand, was another chip in his political stack. His time was coming. All he had to do was play his cards patiently, wisely.

Claire Bennet was nothing short of brilliant. She was the best thing to have ever happened to him. The more he thought of her, the more he wanted her—and he had been thinking about her all day.

She had promised to top her performance on the terrace last night and he couldn't wait to see what she had planned.

He had an exquisite bottle of Ruinart Blanc de Blancs on ice, two dozen oysters, and a large tin of Beluga caviar.

As Friday loomed and the crisis was set to explode, he didn't know what his schedule was going to look like. He wanted every moment he could get with Claire before then.

With the canceling of the NATO cocktail reception tomorrow night, he had thought he could get an extra evening with her, but his donors had called, tasking him with a series of meetings they wanted set up in its stead. He was going to be occupied very late. Whether he could convince her to come by once he was finally done was yet to be seen. At least they had tonight.

They would watch the presidential address and have a few laughs, all while enjoying some fabulous champagne, caviar, and oysters. Then their real fun would begin.

But no sooner had Blackwood begun thinking again of what Claire might have planned for him than he received a text from her, which read: Got pulled into a meeting. Going to be late. Start without me.

He texted back, asking how late, but she didn't reply.

Disappointed, he opened the Ruinart, poured himself a glass, and turned on the TV. At least he could hate-watch the President's address.

The old, rent-controlled apartment was in a neighborhood in Northwest D.C. called Woodley Park. From Claire's office near the Treasury Annex, it was a fifteen-minute ride via taxi or twenty-five minutes by public transportation. When the weather was especially nice and she wanted to get her steps in, the walk was at least an hour.

None of the aforementioned times included the surveillance-detection routes her handler had drilled into her to take.

One of the benefits of the Woodley Park neighborhood was that it was sandwiched between two popular D.C. attractions—the National Cathedral and the National Zoo. Weather and time of day notwithstanding, they were both normally packed with tourists and provided excellent opportunities for her to ascertain whether she had a tail. And if someone was following her, she could easily use the crowds to her advantage and disappear.

Nighttime meetings, like this one, were of a different kind and provided their own challenges, as well as opportunities.

There were darkened alleys and backyards and gangways. There were also motion-activated lights, excitable dogs, and police cruisers that weren't obvious until they were practically on top of you. She had to be exceedingly careful and always thinking three steps ahead.

Past faded blue and green garbage cans, narrow garages, and cracked concrete parking pads, she made her way along until finally arriving at her destination.

It was an ugly, three-story brick building pockmarked with window air-conditioning units decades old. The key for the service door was taped behind a large dumpster. Removing it, she opened the rear entrance and slipped inside.

There was no reason for Claire Bennet to disguise herself or avert her face. The barely maintained property had no cameras to worry about. Nonetheless, she followed her training and kept her head down, profiting where she could by staying in the shadows.

As the building's ancient elevator was never in service, she headed for the stairs, which smelled like urine and weeks-old garbage.

The apartment she wanted was on the third floor at the end of the hall. When she reached the top of the stairs, she pulled out her phone, opened her messaging app, and sent a text. Seconds later, she received a response.

Stepping out into the hall, she walked quietly to the apartment and opened the door, which had been unlocked for her.

On a table, just inside, was a small, metallic box. She knew the drill. Closing and locking the door behind her, she removed her phone and placed it inside the box.

Her handler was waiting for her in the living room.

Despite the AC unit grinding away, the apartment smelled as it always did—like stale cigarettes and even staler air. She wondered if it was used for anything other than their meetings.

The blinds were drawn and only one cheap lamp was on. He was sitting in the same chair he always sat in. Looking at the plastic ashtray on the table in front of him, she saw that it was empty. He must have only just arrived.

"Did you bring it?" he asked as he motioned for her to take a seat.

She nodded and removed one of the cufflinks from her French cuff shirt as she sat down across from him. Popping it open, she withdrew the tiny memory card and handed it over.

Holding it up in the semidarkness, he examined it in the way a jeweler might look at a diamond. The difference, however, was that what he held between his thumb and forefinger was more valuable than any precious stone.

Satisfied, he pulled out his keys, secreted the memory card in a specially made door fob, and returned the keys to his pocket.

"You've done a good job," he stated. "We are pleased with your work."

She was glad to hear that and couldn't help but feel a sense of pride.

"Thank you," she replied. "As to the next phase, I think that—"

Raising his hand, her handler cut her off. "There has been a change of plans."

"A change of plans? I don't understand."

"We're pulling you."

She was confused. "From Blackwood?"

"From everything," the man replied.

"Define *everything*."

"We're sending you home."

"*Home*, home?" she asked.

He looked at her. "Isn't that what you want? To be reunited with your family? To be among your people again?"

"Yes," she answered, knowing it was the only acceptable response. "Of course. But what about Blackwood?"

"That's not for you. We will handle the senator."

She wasn't sure what he meant by "handle" and didn't dare ask. All she could say was "When?"

"You leave tomorrow."

"*Tomorrow?*"

He nodded. "We have already made your arrangements."

"If I up and vanish, aren't you worried that Blackwood will be suspicious?"

"You're not going to vanish. You're going to tell him exactly what you're doing."

"Which is?"

"That you are headed to Istanbul on business."

Now she was even more confused. "Turkey? I thought you said you were sending me home?"

"We are. But you'll go to Istanbul first for your debriefing."

She didn't know if she liked the sound of that.

Seeing the concern in her face, the handler stated, "Relax. You are one of the SSD's first success stories. Without you, *Chernaya Liniya* would have never have gotten off the ground. The GRU is talking about giving you a medal."

She brushed that aside. "There is no success story. Operation Black Line isn't complete yet."

He stood, indicating that their meeting was over. "It will be," he replied. "In the meantime, I hear the weather is lovely in Istanbul. We've arranged an apartment for you with a beautiful view of the Bosphorus. Pack light. Just for a week. Leave everything else behind in your condo."

It was all so sudden. So seismic. After all the training and preparation, it was now over. Just like that. She was speechless.

"Vy ponimayete?" he asked.

When she didn't reply, he repeated himself.

Pulling herself together, she answered. "Yes, I understand."

"No. I want to hear you say it in Russian."

"We don't need to do that now. There'll be plenty of time for me to speak Russian once I'm back."

Her handler insisted. "In Russian, please. Now."

"Fine," she relented. "Ya panimayu. *Okay?* Ya panimayu."

The man smiled and gestured her toward the door. "Enjoy your last evening with Senator Blackwood."

CHAPTER 48

Harvath had texted ahead to let McGee know he was on his way back, but via the water, and along with Admiral Tyson. He wanted to give McGee the opportunity to make himself scarce. It was bad enough that he had roped a civilian into his plan. He didn't need Tyson to know that the ex–CIA director was a part of it too.

After tying up the boat at the end of the dock, he led the Admiral up to the house, got some coffee going, and then sat him down in front of the TV in the living room. Once he was sure Tyson had everything he needed, he walked to the bottom of the driveway, where McGee was in his car just finishing up a call.

"Any updates?" Harvath asked as the man rolled down his window.

"Nicholas and I just set a time to meet. I'm on my way to see him now. How's Admiral Cocktail?"

Harvath smiled. "Admiral *Tyson* will be fine. I offered to put on the Golf Channel for him, but he wanted to watch the President's address instead."

McGee looked at his watch. "I forgot all about that."

"At this point, we probably know more than he does, so you're not missing anything."

"True," the man replied. "Listen, before I go, do you want a ride down to the club to pick up the Bronco?"

Harvath nodded. "That was going to be my next question for you."

"Hop in."

Climbing in the passenger side, Harvath closed his door, and McGee rolled out of the darkened driveway.

"We should probably talk about ROEs for tonight," the ex–CIA director said as he made a left on the road and headed for the MVYC.

Establishing rules of engagement had been on Harvath's mind as well.

"Hale's people at the estate are operating in their capacity as private security. They're there to defend the Willis family. We can't use lethal force."

"Those were my thoughts too."

"In this scenario, as far as they're concerned, we're the bad guys. They can engage us with lethal force. I've got no idea how many, if any, of these guys moonlight on the dark side for Hale. I'm not taking a father or a husband away from some family just because they may have answered the wrong want ad."

"So tonight, you're Casper, the *friendly* ghost."

"I'll be a ghost all right," said Harvath. "But I won't be so friendly once I get my hands on Hale."

"Understood. Which brings me to my next question. Are you sure you don't want backup once you're on the estate?"

Harvath shook his head. "Just knowing I have the cavalry on the other side of the hill is all the backup I need," he stated, adding, "That, and you having my beacon in place on time."

"It'll be in place. Don't worry."

"If not, I hope you've got a ton of trash bags with you because there's going to be pieces of me all over the place."

"It'll be there," McGee once again promised. "In the meantime, is there anything else you need me and Nicholas to pick up?"

Harvath smiled. "Undoubtedly, I'll think of a million other things once my feet hit the water, but right now, we're good."

Up ahead was the club and he pointed to the area where he had parked Haney's Bronco.

As McGee pulled up behind, Scot reached over and shook the man's hand.

"I know it's not as much fun as fishing or house-sitting, but I appreciate all your help."

The ex–CIA director chuckled. "True, but hopefully it'll make for a good story someday."

Getting out of the car, Harvath had just closed the door when McGee rolled down the passenger-side window and said, "Word of advice. I read Hale's file all the way through. You've been through a lot of scrapes but so has he. Be careful."

"Copy that," Harvath replied. "Keep an eye on Nicholas for me. He hasn't been sleeping lately and could turn out to be an even bigger threat than Hale."

Smiling, McGee pulled away as Harvath got into the Bronco and headed back to the house.

After parking in the driveway, he headed inside to check on Tyson. He found the Admiral right where he had left him. The President's address was complete, and a cable news panel was discussing what little information there was to parse.

Harvath refilled the man's mug full of coffee, checked to see if he needed anything else, and let him know he'd be back and forth getting things ready for their boat trip.

Grabbing a headlamp, he made multiple trips, carrying all his dive equipment down to the dock and loading everything aboard *Pier Pressure*.

Once that task was complete, he walked over to the church, unlocked the door, and headed down into his gun room.

Wanting to make sure that Haney and McGee had every possible advantage should they come under attack again, he had left all of his weapons and equipment with them and was now starting from scratch.

As far as Harvath was concerned, gearing up for a water insertion was a completely different animal. What could get wet, would get wet. Anything else needed to be placed in a dry bag. And even then there was only so much he could physically swim with to shore. He began laying equipment on the center table piece by piece.

Removing a waterproof night-vision monocular from its case, he inserted fresh batteries and put it through the same testing process he had recently run his night-vision goggles through. Confident that it was in good working order, he found the flip-up head-mount assembly that went with it, which would allow him to wear it like a headlamp, and set both items on the table.

Next up was a little something the techs at Taser had been working on. Called the *Neptune*, it was a fully submersible, six-shot energy weapon. Grabbing a holster, an extended power magazine, and an additional six-shot cartridge, he added those to the table as well.

Along with it went one of his favorite fixed-blade knives—a Gerber LMF II Infantry with a rubberized handle, and a fully waterproof tactical light with multiple beams.

Everything else, including a suppressed Glock 19 and four spare magazines, a battle belt, a small blowout trauma kit, boots and BDUs, and an additional tourniquet went into his dry bag.

The Glock was coming along as a very last resort. As discussed with McGee, he wasn't headed to the estate to harm anyone. It was the same reason he wasn't bringing a rifle. His job was to be a ghost—get in and get out without any of the personnel knowing he had been there.

There was also the issue of getting off the estate if his primary means of exfiltrating failed. While he could get back in the water and swim downriver, he would need a way to transport Hale. His answer was an extremely small, inflatable dinghy. It came tightly rolled in its own compact dry sack and, via an adaptor, could be inflated from the air left in his SCUBA tank. It wasn't exactly a process he'd want to attempt under fire, but if guns were blazing and he was rushing toward the Potomac, chances were pretty good that he would have already ditched Hale.

It wasn't the worst backup plan he'd ever come up with. It also wasn't the best. But it was a plan nonetheless, and considering how little they had to work with, it was better than nothing.

Going through all the gear two more times, he bagged everything and carried it upstairs.

Next on his list was to prep the small storage room off his gun room. As the room was all stone, he had to get clever with how he attached the heavy plastic sheeting. For the work lamps, he ran extension cords from the nearest outlet. And though it would have been nice to be able to fully adjust the temperature in the space, that simply wasn't an option. The church basement had never been intended to serve as a black site.

When all of his work was complete, he carried everything else down to the boat and then returned to the house to check on Admiral Tyson. He was still in the living room, watching TV and drinking coffee.

Retreating to his office, he hopped online and checked the latest data from the Chesapeake Bay Interpretive Buoy System. On a small pad, he noted the water temperature, the speed and direction of the current and the wind, the wave heights, and the time of the tides. Then, pulling out a nautical chart and laying it on his desk, he located the shoreline in front of the Willis estate and worked upriver to the point where he wanted Tyson to drop him.

Switching back to his computer, he pinpointed both sets of GPS coordinates and wrote them down. It was time to give the Admiral his pre-mission briefing.

He brought it all into the kitchen, laid it out on the table, and had the man come join him.

Coffee, and time away from the yacht club bar, seemed to have served Tyson well. The man was much improved—his eyes no longer glassy, his speech no longer slurred. He paid attention and asked a handful of good questions.

Once the briefing was over, Harvath went upstairs to get into his bathing suit and load the GPS data into his Garmin tactix watch, which was charging next to his bed.

After texting McGee to make sure he was en route, he grabbed a pair of flip-flops from his closet and returned to the kitchen, where he found the Admiral ready to go.

Together they made sure the house was all locked up, Harvath set his alarm, and they walked down to the dock.

Once *Pier Pressure* was fired up and Tyson gave him the command, Harvath cast off the lines. Helping ease the boat off his dock, he then hopped aboard and they began cruising up the Potomac.

The Admiral punched the coordinates for the drop-off point into his GPS while Harvath got into his wetsuit and readied all his gear.

Looking out over the water, he realized there was something else he should have asked McGee to pick up for him—the biggest shot of penicillin he could lay his hands on. The Potomac, although better than it had been a decade ago, was filthy.

It was even worse after a heavy rain when sewage and other polluted runoff ended up in the river. Harvath figured he should be grateful that he was doing his swim tonight. Storms were in the forecast Friday—right in time for the NATO Summit.

Wrapping up his gear prep, he joined Tyson at the helm.

"Five minutes out," the man said, his tone flat, eyes fixed on the dark ribbon of the Potomac stretching ahead.

Harvath flashed him the thumbs-up and turned his focus back to the river, helping scan for logs and debris.

The men didn't say much. Harvath appreciated the quiet. He needed to get his head in the game. Something easier said than done.

So many things still didn't make sense. Not the attack at the Naval Observatory. Not the attack at Ambassador Rogers's house. And not the attack on Sølvi's motorcade. They were all mysteries to him; serious questions in search of equally serious answers—answers he hoped he was closing in on.

Soon enough, the boat slowed to a crawl, its engines' hum quieting to a low murmur.

They were about five hundred yards from shore and something in the stillness of the water made the moment feel suspended, as if time itself had paused, waiting for something to happen.

As Tyson killed the engines, Harvath texted McGee, who confirmed that he and Nicholas were in place. The operation was a go.

Walking to the stern, Harvath donned his SCUBA equipment and checked the readout on his Garmin. It was time to get wet.

Thanking the Admiral one final time for his help, he placed the regulator into his mouth and did a backward roll off the port side.

Once he was in the water, Tyson handed him his dry bag with the rest of his equipment, as well as the sack containing the dinghy.

With a few powerful kicks of his fins, Harvath separated from the boat and allowed the current to start carrying him toward the Willis estate. As it did, he focused on all the things that needed to go right over the next hour.

If a single one of them went wrong, the entire operation would be shot. And if the operation ended up shot, there was a very good chance that he would be too.

CHAPTER 49

The murky water of the Potomac was clouded with silt and he had to surface several times to verify his bearing. Eventually he could see the lights of the estate and he started to refine his course.

His target was the family's long pier, which jutted far out into the river. But before he got to the pier, he had to make sure he didn't bang into any of the acoustic security buoys they used to detect approaching watercraft.

Pulling out his night-vision monocular, he powered it up and scanned the waterline. It took a few moments, but he finally saw the first buoy and was able to give it a wide berth.

Once he made it past the second and the third, he was safe to head for the dock and take temporary refuge underneath.

Dropping back beneath the water, he kicked his fins until he got there, and then used a piling for support against the current.

Breaking the surface, he raised his diving mask and took his time peering through his night-vision device. As he scanned the shoreline and what he could see of the estate, he paid close attention to the positions he knew contained the lights and security cameras. So far, nothing looked out of the ordinary.

Confident that it was safe to move closer, he stowed the monocular and, fighting against the sideways current, proceeded under the dock toward shore.

As soon as it was shallow enough, he shrugged off his tank, turned off the air, and, using his weight belt and some ratchet tie-down straps, secreted a chunk of his gear under the dock.

When that was complete, he pulled his phone out of its waterproof pouch and texted McGee. The next phase of the operation was up to them. Harvath would wait under the pier until he received word that it was safe to make his way to the narrow strip of beach at the water's edge.

Seeing the text from Harvath pop up on his phone, McGee turned to Nicholas and said, "Scot's in place. Are you ready?"

He gave the harness around Draco's chest a tug to make sure that it was secure. The last thing he needed was for it to slip. If that happened, he could be severely injured, if not killed.

Of his two dogs, Draco had always been better with the harness. What's more, the last time he had done this, Argos had been shot. It was the night he and Scot had first crossed paths. They had come to the same villa to kill the same man. Nicholas had barely escaped with his life. Harvath had saved Argos's. It was the beginning of an intense and deeply felt friendship for all of them.

In addition to being better with the harness, Draco was younger than Argos and in better shape; more physically capable of the job Nicholas was about to ask him to perform. Caressing his dog along its powerful lower jaw, he quietly apologized that it wasn't cooler outside. The heat and humidity were going to make the animal's task that much more difficult.

McGee had his work cut out for him as well. Turning to him, Nicholas nodded and then asked, "You're all good on the drones? No last-minute questions?"

"I'm good on the drones."

"And the beacon?"

"Also good on the beacon," the ex–CIA director replied. He could tell Nicholas was nervous about his role. "You're going to be fine. Just be careful."

Nicholas flashed him an uncomfortable smile. "Okay, let's do it."

Smiling back, McGee stepped out of the van onto the darkened grounds of River Farm, a popular tourist attraction and home to the American Horticultural Association. It was also the immediate next-door neighbor to the Willis estate.

With a limited system of outdoor security cameras, which had been easy for Nicholas to loop the feeds on, it made for the perfect staging ground.

As he came around to the side of the van, McGee saw that Nicholas had already opened the large sliding door.

"Anything I can do to help?" he asked as he watched the man put on a small, child's-sized backpack.

Nicholas was proud and didn't like taking help from anyone. It had been drilled into him from an early age that if he were to survive in this world, he had to be able to fully fend for himself.

With that said, he knew how brittle his bones were. Falling from the van to the pavement could result in multiple fractures, possibly even an open fracture, not to mention a punctured lung or worse.

"If you could just give me a spot," he replied.

McGee was happy to do it and positioned himself accordingly.

Nicholas gave Argos the command to wait in the van and then ordered Draco to climb out.

Once the dog was standing on the asphalt, he had the animal sidle up to the vehicle so that Nicholas could mount him like a jockey. It was one of the most unusual things McGee had ever seen.

Arms out, ready to catch him if the dog suddenly moved or the harness failed, the ex–CIA director asked, "Everything good? You okay?"

"I'm good," Nicholas replied. "Thank you. Let's get the drones out. I want number one in the air the minute I hit the tree line."

McGee removed both drones from the van, along with their payloads, and setting them on the pavement said, "There you go. We're good. You need to get moving. Scot's waiting on us."

Nodding, Nicholas flipped down his custom night-vision goggles. "No matter what happens," he told McGee, "if Nina ever asks, you and I were in my office talking about a Carlton Group board position."

The ex–CIA director laughed. "Until this week, I didn't realize how much I miss this stuff. Don't tempt me with a seat on the board. I just might take it."

Nicholas knew when to let good enough alone and, giving Draco his cue, gripped the harness and spurred the beast into action.

Racing away from the van, the dog headed for the trees.

Nicholas tried to relax into the rhythm, to allow his body to be fluid and meld with the movements of the animal beneath him, but it had been a long time.

He knew that gripping the harness too tightly and stiffening up could be just as destructive as falling off, but he couldn't help himself. Falling off was certain death. Anything short of that, no matter how destructive to his body, was unquestionably preferable.

"Approaching the tree line," he announced over the earbone microphone attached to his radio.

"Roger that," McGee replied, powering up the first drone and pushing the launch button. "Drone one away."

Nicholas and Draco pushed into the trees. The woods between River Farm and the Willis estate were not terribly dense, nor were they particularly wide. But what they did have were lots of ground sensors and more than a few cameras. This was where Nicholas's contribution would be absolutely critical to the mission.

Because of the rampant deer population, motion sensors were set at a level that allowed deer and other four-legged creatures to pass undetected. What's more, the advanced AI cameras being used at the Willis estate were trained to identify human beings and to ignore everything else.

Passing through the woods, Nicholas continued to guide Draco and encouraged him onward. There was no knowing what Hale's people were seeing in their command center, nor if the security system had been tripped at all.

Nicholas decided that it was time to test their luck.

Directing Draco toward the Willis estate, he pushed into a zone he knew was tightly covered by cameras.

Lowering his head, he clung tightly to the dog's neck and urged the beast forward. Five yards became ten. Ten became twenty. Nothing happened.

There was no activation of floodlights, no launch of security personnel in 4x4s. It was like they were exactly what Nicholas had intended them to be—simple forest creatures. The AI couldn't spot the threat they posed because the AI had never seen such a threat.

"Drone one status," Nicholas said over his radio as he steered Draco back on a more direct course to their objective.

"Drone one is directly overhead," McGee replied. "You're all clear."

The degree to which developers had been able to dampen drone-rotor noise astounded Nicholas. It was, in his opinion, one of the most remarkable achievements of physics and tech. Someday very soon, he believed, we would be in an age of practically silent helicopters. The science was moving that fast.

Focusing on their objective, yet mindful of the temperature, he encouraged Draco to move a little faster. They were almost there.

As the dog moved, Nicholas used his night-vision goggles to scan from side to side, making sure that there were no threats approaching.

When he redirected his attention forward, he could see their target. It was a small, tastefully designed structure, meant to blend in with all the other buildings on the estate. Even the landscaping was in keeping with the main house.

Surrounded by mature trees and a stone walk, and fronted by a pair of wrought-iron benches, the main security building could have easily been mistaken for a tasteful guesthouse.

Keeping Draco in the trees, he approached the building from the back. In addition to twin AC condensers, there was a generator and a large, locked cage containing the terminus of all the security cabling and wiring from across the property. This was the estate's nerve center, its brain. If you wanted to interrupt its ability to hear, see, or sense any intrusion, this is where you had to do it from.

When he got there, he coaxed the dog to the edge of the tree line and paused. It was make-or-break time.

"How do we look?" Nicholas quietly asked over the radio.

"Still clear," McGee responded.

"Roger that. Going in."

Urging Draco forward, he headed directly for the large metal cage.

The moment he got there, he had the dog stop. Removing the pack from one of his shoulders, he swung it in front of his chest and pulled out what looked like a hockey puck made from brushed aluminum.

Activating a power button, he watched as an LED light went from red to green and then stuck the magnetized device to the side of the cage.

"Goblin one in place," he said. "Setting Goblin two."

Directing Draco to the back of the cage, he repeated the process, and alerted McGee. "Goblin two in place."

Looking over his shoulder at one of the screens in Nicholas's van, the ex–CIA director could see multiple CCTV feeds from the Willis estate security cameras.

"We're in," said McGee.

"Roger that," said Nicholas. "Prep drone two and tell Norseman to stand by. I'm on my way back."

CHAPTER 50

Having kept one eye on his phone, he knew the moment the text from McGee had come in telling him that Nicholas had completed the first phase of the plan.

The Goblins, placed on the metal cage behind the security building, would allow Nicholas to access the estate's security system, with the drone overhead functioning like a satellite. It would relay signals to and from Nicholas in his van, which was serving as a mobile command center. So far, so good.

When the next text came, informing him that it was safe to head to the beach, Harvath was ready to move. Taking one last look through his night-vision device, he made his way to shore.

There was a copse of trees at the north end of the narrow strip of sand that acted as a beach. That was where it had been decided Harvath would gear up and change out of his wetsuit.

He moved quietly through the water, cautious not to give himself away in case any security personnel were near. He knew Nicholas was monitoring everything, spoofing cameras and sensors for him, but in his book, you could never be too careful.

It felt good to feel the bottom under his feet and then to be standing on dry land. Reaching the trees, he texted McGee FD—their code for "Feet Dry."

Drone two inbound. Ninety seconds out, the man texted back.

Scot barely had time to unpack his weapons and peel off his wetsuit, before a drone dropped out of the night sky and hovered, several yards away, above the beach.

Suspended underneath it was a small case. Harvath detached it, stood back, and flashed the drone's camera the thumbs-up.

He watched as it rose back into the air and disappeared, at which point he returned to the trees, and opened it up.

Among the items inside was a radio, complete with a bone microphone. Powering it up, he inserted the earpiece and conducted a comms check with McGee.

"Reading you five by five," the man replied.

"Any sign of Hale?" Harvath asked as he continued to get dressed.

"Negative. Probably already turned in."

"Roger that. Stand by. Almost ready to move."

Harvath finished tying his boots, gave all of his equipment a final check, and, once he'd attached the monocular to his head mount assembly, let the team know he was good to go.

With Nicholas manipulating the security system, McGee guided Harvath through each step, letting him know where and when it was safe to move.

The trek from the beach up to the main compound was tedious and slow going, but it was working. And as hot, humid, and buggy as it was, Harvath reminded himself that it could have been much worse. The security team could have had dogs.

Picking his way through the trees at the edge of the property, he chose his steps with great care, making sure not to snap any twigs or branches underfoot, as if he were traversing hostile enemy territory. Though he, as the intruder, wouldn't have been justified in shooting any of Hale's people, this was Virginia and they would absolutely be justified in shooting him. He had no intention of letting that happen.

Up ahead, he could start to pick out the landscape lighting leading to the main house. Beyond that would be the garage and the apartment used by Hale. Even though he knew he had to be wary, he found himself eager to increase his pace. Taking a deep breath, he willed himself to relax. Nothing good ever came from being in a hurry.

As he drew closer to the house, he could see that most of its lights were out. What illumination was visible was simply interior accent lighting in case anyone had to move around in the middle of the night. By all appearances, the Willis family was asleep.

That was good. The fewer people up, around, and able to raise the alarm if they heard or saw something, the better. Harvath had no idea what was going to happen once he finally reached Hale; he just knew he didn't want an audience for it.

Arriving at the motor court, he scanned the area. The apartment above the garage was dark.

"You're all clear," McGee said over the radio. "Keep it tight and stay sharp. Remember what I told you."

"Good copy," Harvath replied. He hadn't forgotten the man's ominous warning and wasn't planning on letting his guard down.

The carriage house had five bays—four were for vehicles and the fifth had a regular pedestrian door cut into it. He didn't linger. Cutting across the motor court, he made a beeline straight for it.

Silently wrapping his hand around the brass handle, he pressed down. The door gave with a soft click and he slipped inside.

The interior was dark, but his night-vision device gave him a clear view. A narrow hallway led straight to the stairs. Up to Hale's apartment. There was no one in sight.

Drawing his Taser, he moved through the quiet darkness and opened the door leading into the garage. Inside was a Range Rover, a Land Rover, a Porsche 911, and a Mercedes AMG sedan. All of their fobs hung on a rack.

There was no sign of Hale.

Returning to the hall, he crept up the stairs, slowly applying pressure to each step. The last thing he wanted to do was to announce his presence through a creaky board.

At the top of the landing was the door to the man's apartment. Harvath gave the knob a try. It was locked. *Fuck*.

He had a small set of lockpick tools with him, but the job would require both of his hands, meaning he'd have to reholster the Taser.

The alternatives, he supposed, were to either kick the door in and risk giving the man a head start, or to knock softly and whisper Hale's name—

à la the bin Laden raid—and hope the man was dumb enough to pop his head out so Harvath could zap him in the face.

All things considered, preserving the element of surprise offered him the best odds, and so, after securing the Taser, he pulled out his lockpick tools and went to work. In less than minute, he had the door open.

Pulling his Taser back out and setting his tactical light to strobe, he crept into the apartment.

The suitcase in the living room told him McGee's intel had been right on the money. Moving past it, Harvath headed for the bedroom.

Pausing outside the partially open door, he listened for any sound of Hale. There was no snoring, no rustling of bedclothes, only the droning of a large box fan.

Like many vets who had experienced hearing damage from being exposed to explosions and weapons fire, the man probably suffered from tinnitus, which could be more debilitating at night.

Harvath would have to keep that in mind. If he ended up deciding to kill Hale, he'd make sure he had a suppressor on his weapon, just out of kindness.

Easing into the bedroom, he could see Hale in sweats lying on the bed, the sheets and blankets having been kicked to the floor. The guy was a monster; much bigger than Harvath had expected. Based on sheer size alone, before ever getting to his resume, it was obvious why the man might make a compelling head of security.

But to those in the know, security wasn't about size, it was about smarts. And by not sufficiently scrubbing his trail, Hale had screwed up and led Harvath right to him. Definitely not smart.

Activating the laser sight on his Taser, Harvath took a step forward and found the one board in the entire carriage house that groaned.

CHAPTER 51

D espite the thrum of the box fan, the sound of Harvath's weight atop the warped floorboard was like an air horn going off.

Hale shot straight up in bed, with his eyes blinking and his head swinging back and forth as he tried to pinpoint the threat.

His element of surprise obliterated, Harvath did the only thing he could do. Aiming the Taser at center mass on Hale, he pressed the trigger and fired.

The nitrogen-propelled probes sizzled across the bedroom and embedded themselves right in the security chief's chest.

The metal barbs went straight through his sweatshirt and dug into his flesh, then pulses of electricity began racing down the attached copper wires, intent on inducing neuromuscular incapacitation.

Hale let out a howl and stiffened up, but then he did something Harvath had only heard about before. Reaching down, he grabbed hold of the insulated wires and ripped the probes out.

Harvath didn't hesitate. Pressing his trigger, he deployed a new set of probes and let the man ride the lightning again.

There was another howl from Hale, but this time as he stiffened, he rolled toward his right side.

It took Harvath a moment to realize that the movement wasn't caused by the Taser. Hale was going for his nightstand. Which could only mean one thing. He had a gun.

Lighting him up with the strobe from his flashlight, Harvath tried to disorient him as he rapidly closed the distance between them. And, knowing that clothing could sometimes disrupt the efficacy of a Taser, he also changed his point of aim, trying to hit Hale somewhere in the neck, or the side of the face.

Pressing the trigger, he let a third pair of probes fly, but only one found its mark, just below the man's left ear. The other probe kept going, hitting the wall behind the nightstand.

There wasn't time for Harvath to take aim and fire again. Hale had already opened the drawer and had his hand inside the nightstand.

Launching himself forward, Harvath delivered a blistering kick to the front of the drawer, breaking the man's forearm.

Hale roared in pain.

Pulling his arm back, he brought the entire drawer with it, which he swung at Harvath.

As the drawer flew at Harvath's face and he put up his hands to parry it away, Hale spun out of bed. Planting his right foot on the floor, he used his left leg to kick Harvath in his exposed rib cage. The force of the blow sent Harvath into the wall next to the bed.

Before Harvath could regain his balance, Hale delivered an incredibly painful peroneal strike to his right leg and took him to the ground.

In an instant, Hale was on top of him and had him in a crushing pin. He was not only half a foot taller, but also weighed a good seventy pounds more and was using that weight to make it difficult for Harvath to breathe and keep him locked in place so he could rain down punches with his uninjured left hand.

Isolating the man's injured arm, Harvath applied as much pressure as he could, causing Hale intense pain as he pulled it in close, trapping it to his side. He then blocked the man's right foot with his own to keep him off-balance, and then, locking his hands behind the giant's back, he lifted his hips as high as possible in a bridge, leaned to the man's right, and rolled over.

Instantly, the fight had changed. Now Harvath was on top, and the first thing he did was deliver a blistering headbutt, shattering the man's nose and sending a spray of blood everywhere.

He followed it with two more, further bludgeoning the man's cinder block of a head before freeing up his left hand and fumbling for something in his left cargo pocket.

As he did, he felt Hale's good arm move, as if reaching for something off to the side. Instantly, Harvath knew what it had to be—*the gun.*

Delivering a forearm choke, he applied downward pressure across Hale's throat as he used his right hand to try to wrestle the pistol away from him. Even after all the punishment he had dished out, the man was insanely strong.

Leaning even further into the choke, Harvath tried to finish off his oxygen supply. Despite having a broken right arm, Hale used it to push back, forcing Harvath to ease off. It was a contest of wills.

The only way Harvath could end this was to slip his other hand behind Hale's head and make it a full choke. But if he did that, it would leave the man's gun-grasping hand free, which was an absolute nonstarter.

Abandoning the choke, Harvath added his left hand to the fight for the gun.

But as he did, it changed his weight distribution, allowing Hale to bridge his hips and begin attempting to throw Harvath off.

Again and again, Harvath slammed the giant's meaty left hand against the floor, trying to get him to release the pistol. Finally, it worked.

With a sweep of his hand, Harvath sent the weapon scudding across the bedroom floor and went to reestablish the choke, but Hale was already scrambling to get out from under him.

Using his right hand, Harvath pummeled the man with blows to his jaw and the left side of his head, including his ear.

As he did, he used his other hand to locate the hypodermic needle in his outer left cargo pocket.

Once his fingers closed around it, he pulled it out, flicked off the hinged safety cap, and drove the needle through Hale's sweatpants into his thigh.

Depressing the plunger, he gave him the full injection of ketamine and stayed on top of him for several minutes until the man went limp.

Harvath knew he didn't have much time. The effects of the drug could wear off in as little as five minutes. Considering how big Hale was, he worried the man might metabolize it even faster. He needed to get moving.

Standing up, he gave McGee a SITREP as he folded Hale's blanket in half and rolled the monster onto it.

After gathering up his tactical light, Taser, and the hypodermic needle, he grabbed the top two corners of the blanket and dragged Hale out of the apartment.

Getting the man down the stairs was a pain in the ass, but Harvath managed. The real challenge was getting him up and into the cargo area of the nearest vehicle in the garage, which was the Range Rover.

Try as he might, however, Harvath couldn't do it. Lifting that much dead weight up that high was a two-man job at least. He was wasting precious time.

Laying Hale back on the blanket, Harvath dragged the man to the other side of the garage.

Like an automotive version of Goldilocks, he walked past the also impossibly high Land Rover, past the 911 with its tiny front trunk or "frunk" as it was known, until he arrived at the Mercedes, which was just right.

With his muscles burning from hefting Hale into the trunk, he zip-tied the man's feet and hands, put a piece of duct tape over his mouth, rolled a down over his head, and shut the lid.

Grabbing the fob from where it was hanging, he climbed behind the wheel and let McGee know he was ready to move.

"Roger that," McGee replied over the radio. "I'm in place."

They were at the final and, quite possibly, the most difficult phase of the plan. Opening the armrest, Harvath found the vehicle's lone remote. It was capable of opening and closing the garage door, but that was it. There wasn't a clicker for the front gate. That had to be activated by security personnel in a guard shack at the end of the driveway.

Separate from the rest of the estate's security system, it wasn't something that Nicholas had control over. McGee's timing was going to need to be absolutely perfect.

Firing up the almost 800-horsepower V-8, he hit the button, raised the garage door, and pulled slowly into the motor court. Ahead of him the driveway loomed, dark and oppressive.

Trying to make as little noise as possible, he rolled forward, driving past the main house, the guesthouse, and then the security building where Nicholas had placed the Goblins. Nothing stirred and no one came out to flag him down. So far, so good.

As he neared the end of the driveway, he could see the guard booth and the silhouette of the lone security agent inside, illuminated by his monitor.

Harvath flashed his hi-beams, as he hoped members of the Willis family had done on countless occasions when leaving the property at night, signaling to the guard to begin retracting the gate so that he could drive right out and wouldn't have to slow down when he got there.

The guard turned to look out the window behind him, but the gate remained closed, blocking Harvath's path to the main road beyond.

"Come on . . ." he muttered under his breath, as he gripped the leather steering wheel tighter.

The guard turned back around, but instead of pushing the button, the armed man got up out of his chair and exited the booth.

Harvath could feel his heart rate increasing and forced himself to take a couple of deep breaths.

Radioing McGee, he said, "That's it. He's not opening the gate."

"Five seconds," the ex–CIA director replied.

His voice was calm, a stark contrast to the anxiety that was building in the center of Harvath's chest. Of course that was easy for McGee; he was on the right side of the heavy gate and not facing down an armed security agent.

Suddenly there was an eruption of flashing lights—strobes of bright blue and red that cut through the darkness and cast shadows across the wrought iron of the gate.

"Now!" McGee ordered over the radio.

Harvath slammed his foot down on the accelerator and the Mercedes lurched forward. The strobe light suspended beneath Nicholas's drone mimicked the rhythm of a police cruiser's lightbar, fooling the gate's strobe-light sensor into believing it was an emergency vehicle and opening wide.

The gate began to retract as the guard radioed his colleagues, wondering what was going on. But by then it was too late.

The gap in the gate was wide enough and the exit was clear.

"Hit it!" McGee insisted. "Go!"

Scot punched the accelerator and the big sedan rocketed through. Behind him there was no sudden burst of gunfire. The guard had no idea who was in the vehicle and would not have risked killing a member of the Willis family.

The car's headlights sliced through the darkness and the tires squealed as they bit into the pavement of the main road. In less than three and a half seconds, Harvath was already doing sixty miles an hour.

But even with the gate falling farther behind him, he knew better than to think they were in the clear. He wasn't safe yet. Not by a long shot.

CHAPTER 52

Joe Carolan looked at his watch and stood up from the conference table. "That's it. I'm calling it. He's not coming."

In the next room, monitoring everything via an array of hidden cameras and microphones, the FBI SWAT commander relayed the order over the radio that they were shutting down.

"Are you sure you don't want to give him a little more time?" Fields asked.

Carolan looked at her. "If your child had a terminal illness and you were trying to get him into a clinical trial, when a slot opened would you be late to sign all the paperwork? No. Of course not. You'd be so damn grateful you'd be in the hospital lobby the minute you got the call."

"He did sound grateful when we spoke with him last night."

"That was last night. This is today, and he's over two hours late. He's not even answering his phone."

"Maybe he got in a car accident," said Fields.

"Or maybe he got abducted by aliens. I don't care. The fact is he isn't here. Let's pack it in."

Gathering up the paperwork, Carolan placed everything in his briefcase, thanked the SWAT team, and headed downstairs to thank the agents who were at the magnetometer posing as uniformed security.

He thanked the hospital administrators who had agreed to work with the Bureau on such short notice and then thanked the agents in the parking garage who would have tagged and wired Russell's vehicle for sound.

With his obligations as the operation's lead agent complete, he and Fields got into his car and, without another word, exited the hospital grounds. But instead of heading back to headquarters, he drove them in a different direction.

"Where are we going?" she asked.

"Fredericksburg," he replied.

"We're going after Russell, aren't we?"

Carolan nodded. "Somebody got to him. I want to know who and I want to know why."

The tool-and-die shop was south of the city, near a truck and trailer repair company along the Rappahannock River. The entire business was humming and every piece of equipment, from the punch presses and vertical mills to the surface grinders and arm saws, was in use.

Entering the shop, Carolan asked a heavyset man with glasses hanging around his neck if he could speak with the manager.

"I'll do you one better," the man replied. "I'm the owner."

Carolan showed the owner his credentials and stated, "We're looking for Ricky Russell."

"Is he in some sort of trouble?"

"We just want to talk with him. Is he around?"

The owner shook his head. "Took the day off. His boy, Jacob, is sick and they've been trying to get him into some clinical trial. A slot opened and Ricky and his wife were going up to D.C. this morning to do all the paperwork."

"When did he let you know he wouldn't be coming in?" Fields asked. Her head had been on a swivel since entering, alert to any possible danger.

"Called me last night and told me the good news."

Carolan scrolled to an image on his phone from Russell's parole file. "Can you confirm his home address for me?"

"They live about twenty minutes from here on Roxbury Mill Road. Not far from the River of Life church in Spotsylvania Courthouse. I can get the exact address from my office if you want. You're sure he's not in trouble?"

The FBI man shook his head. "Again, we just want to speak with him. Did he have any other plans that you know of today?"

"Not that I know of," the machine shop owner responded.

"If you hear from him," said Carolan, removing a business card and handing it to the man, "ask him to call me, please."

"Yes, sir. Will do."

As they left the business and walked back to Carolan's car, Fields asked, "Next stop the house?"

Her boss nodded.

After doing a long, slow pass, they pulled into the Russell's driveway and parked behind a purple Toyota missing its rear bumper cover. A small soccer net and an empty kiddie pool sat in the front yard. The roof of the house needed to be reshingled, and in several spots, the vinyl siding was warped.

Fishing the folder with the paperwork out of his briefcase, Carolan asked, "Ready?"

"Are you kidding me?" said Fields. "This place is so depressing, I'm going to need a Zoloft just to get out of the car."

Her boss didn't disagree. The Russells had it rough. Their son having a rare disease certainly didn't help their situation. But there were plenty of other people who had it just as bad, or worse, and didn't end up turning to crime and going to prison.

As they approached the front door, Carolan noticed a Confederate flag sticker in the window. Nodding toward it, he asked, "Do you want to ring the bell, or should I?"

"Very funny," Fields replied.

From inside, a television could be heard playing.

Holding the white folder emblazoned with its blue Children's National Hospital logo so it could be easily seen, Carolan pressed the doorbell.

Someone muted the TV, but no one came to the door. Carolan rang the bell again. Nothing.

Knocking, Carolan said loud enough to be heard inside, "Mr. and

Mrs. Russell. It's Joe Carolan. I don't know what happened this morning, but we've got Jacob's paperwork."

As he waited for a reply, Fields scanned the windows and sides of the house, making sure they weren't about to get ambushed. That said, if Richard Thomas Russell was sitting on the other side of the door with a shotgun, all he'd have to do was pull the trigger. The effects would be devastating.

Abandoning the bell, Carolan knocked solidly, "Mr. and Mrs. Russell. If we can't get you to sign the paperwork, Jacob will lose his slot. This space will have to be given to another child."

He was about to knock again when a young woman in her early twenties, with a nose ring and stringy blond hair, opened the door and peeked out.

"Mrs. Russell?" Carolan asked.

The woman nodded.

He tried to look past her, into the house. "Is Mr. Russell home?"

She shook her head. "He's not here."

"Mrs. Russell, I'm—"

"I know who you are," she said, cutting him off. "You're FBI. Both of you."

Carolan didn't need to look at Fields to know that she was just as shocked as he was. Someone had tipped Russell off. Someone *inside* the Bureau.

"Mrs. Russell, may we come in and speak with you?"

"Haven't you done enough?" the woman asked.

"Excuse me?"

"You gave us hope. And then you took it away. I can't think of anything more terrible. We may not matter to people like you, but we care about our child's life."

He looked at her. "Mrs. Russell, we are indeed from the FBI, but I want you to understand that this opportunity is one hundred percent real. There is a space available for Jacob in the trial at Children's National Hospital." Emphasizing the point, he held up the folder. "It's conditional, however, on your husband cooperating with us."

She studied him and then Fields, wanting to believe them, but unsure of whether she should.

"Other lives are at stake, Mrs. Russell. Not just Jacob's," said Carolan. "We need to speak with Ricky. It's urgent."

"And if he speaks with you, Jacob gets into the trial?"

"Yes, ma'am. You have our word. As long as your husband is honest with us, Jacob is in."

She stood at the door for several moments, weighing her options. Finally, she stated, "Wait here. I'm going to get my keys. I'll take you to him."

As they drove, Tammy Russell answered every single question they asked. She was polite and to the point.

She was on full disability for a medical condition of her own—a back injury she had suffered at her previous job. When asked where Jacob was, Tammy explained that they had dropped him with her mother last night. She wasn't due to pick him up until later.

Though Carolan and Fields had both seen people who gamed the disability system, Tammy's situation wasn't germane to their investigation. They were here for her husband. And as to him, his tattoos, and his associations, she was extremely forthright.

Ricky had been a member of a White nationalist organization known as the Iron Tree. But they had grown more extreme and violent, *too* extreme, even for Ricky, who was worried about violating his parole. About six months ago, he had left the organization.

They had been very angry with him for leaving and there had been many threats. It got so bad at one point that Ricky thought they might kill him. Eventually, though, they left him alone. In fact, both Tammy and Ricky thought they had all but forgotten him. Then, late last night, his phone had rung. One of the members of Iron Tree was calling.

The man knew all about Children's National Hospital and the invitation that had been extended to Jacob. It was a con, he explained—a sting operation set up by the FBI as part of a crackdown on so-called extremist groups.

Not only was the offer not real, but if the Russells showed up for the appointment, they would all be targets of Iron Tree—all three of them, *including* Jacob.

She had never seen Ricky afraid before. That call, however, had scared him. Not wanting to admit to his boss or her mother that the trial invitation had been fake, they decided to keep it to themselves. Tammy had stayed home watching TV while Ricky had gone to hang out at his cousin's place.

When asked how the man from Iron Tree had known that the FBI was involved in the offer for Jacob, she had no idea. For that, they were going to have to ask Ricky.

When they arrived at the home of Ricky's cousin, they agreed to let Tammy go up to the front door and bring Ricky out. And, just to make sure he didn't do something stupid and try to make a run for it, Fields went around to the rear of the dwelling and kept an eye on the back door. Ricky Russell was their one and only lead at this point and they had no intention of losing him.

To say Ricky was not happy to see his wife would have been an understatement. He was furious that she had not only spoken with the FBI, but had also brought them right to him.

Tammy Russell, however, didn't care. Her instincts as a mother had fully kicked in. She had listened to Carolan's pitch and believed that the offer was indeed legitimate. She made it crystal clear that, for Jacob's sake, she expected Ricky to fully cooperate with them.

When Ricky asked what the hell they were supposed to do about the Iron Tree threats, Tammy waved Carolan over.

After introducing himself, he explained that in addition to getting Jacob into the clinical trial at Children's National, if there were threats against their family, the FBI would put them in protective custody.

With his arguments stripped away, his wife leaning on him, and most important of all—his son and a potential lifesaving cure hanging in the balance, Ricky Russell did the only thing he could. He agreed to fully cooperate.

Carolan and Fields didn't waste any time. Accompanying the Russells back to their home, they began debriefing Ricky right there.

Within fifteen minutes, Carolan had to step outside to call Gallo. Ricky Russell had dropped a major bombshell. The FBI needed to move. *Fast*.

CHAPTER 53

Harvath had met McGee and Nicholas at the rendezvous point, transferred Hale into the trunk of McGee's car, and then abandoned the Mercedes.

After thanking Nicholas for his help, Harvath and McGee had driven back to Harvath's, where they secured Hale to a chair in the storage room off Harvath's gun room and Harvath had gone to work interrogating him.

Hale, however, had proven to be a tough nut to crack, and now Harvath had no choice but to double down.

Leaving Hale with headphones duct-taped to his head and German heavy metal music blasting in his ears, he had reached out to Nicholas for another favor.

An hour and a half later, a team from the Carlton Group arrived with an Igloo cooler and a brown paper bag. Stapled to the bag was an envelope.

Opening the envelope, Harvath found a one-year employment contract along with a Post-it note that read *Any further requests need to be submitted with the attached, fully executed agreement.*

Smiling, he tossed it in the garbage.

About that time, Sølvi came down, showered, and headed off to work. The NATO Summit was still on for tomorrow and she had a meeting with the Secret Service to walk the venue and go over transport to and from Blair House.

They had barely chatted last night. Sølvi had returned home exhausted and had collapsed into bed. Hours later, Harvath had joined her while McGee kept an eye on Hale.

After a brief chat, they had both fallen asleep only to have the alarm on Scot's phone wake them both up when it was time for him to relieve McGee. Kissing her, he had gotten out of bed and told her to go back to sleep.

Now she was on her way out the door.

Handing her a coffee, they kissed once more and she disappeared out the front door.

Soon enough, he heard the rev of the Mustang's engine and the spinning of its tires as Sølvi headed back to D.C.

Two ships passing in the night was no way to run a marriage and he was looking forward to all of this being over.

Gathering up some rubber gloves and a couple of N95 masks, he grabbed the Igloo cooler, the paper bag, and the bonus item Admiral Tyson had dropped off for him and headed back over to the basement storeroom.

McGee was sitting in a chair at the bottom of the stairs reading a Ken Follett novel.

"How's our guest?" asked Harvath as he set everything down on a small table they had set up off to the side.

"I don't think he likes your taste in music."

"Then he should probably choose his kidnappers a little more wisely."

McGee chuckled and, nodding at the cooler, asked, "Is that it?"

"Yup," said Harvath, handing him a mask. "You should put this on."

"You want to explain to me what that all is?"

Opening the paper bag, Harvath pulled out a black hood with a special pocket sewn in the front and several strips of cloth.

Laying them all on the table, he put his own mask on and donned the rubber gloves, before opening the cooler and removing its contents.

"The Carlton Group has a special relationship with a facility over in Malta," said Harvath as he began soaking the strips of cloth. "The doctor who runs it came up with an interesting chemical compound that can be very helpful with difficult interrogation subjects."

"Is it some kind of truth serum?"

He nodded. "Once the strips of cloth are saturated, they go into this pocket at the front of the hood. When the hood is placed over Hale's head, he'll be inhaling the fumes. As they enter the nasal passages, they head straight for a precise part of the brain—the amygdala; specifically the fear center. No matter how big and badass you are, this breaks you. And it does it in a matter of hours, not days."

"So why didn't you just start with it?"

"Because it's pretty dangerous," Harvath replied. "And there's a lot about it we still don't understand."

"But you've used this before."

"Normally, the doctor from Malta administers it. I've only done it solo once."

McGee looked at him. "And?"

"The guy had a heart attack," said Harvath, nodding at the device Tyson had dropped off. "That's why I had the Admiral borrow one of the AED defibrillators from the yacht club for me. The chemical-to-cloth ratio can be a bit tricky to dial in."

"What if the guy has a grabber and we can't revive him?"

"We'll jump off that bridge when we come to it."

Finishing his prep work, Harvath returned the chemicals to the cooler and put his balaclava back on.

"Ready?"

"Ready," McGee replied as he rolled down his own balaclava.

Together they entered the storage room and fired up the intense floodlights, which were pointed directly at Hale's face.

Snatching off the hood that Hale had been wearing, Harvath took out his knife and cut away enough of the duct tape to remove the headphones from the man's head. There was no point in asking him any questions, as his ears would have been ringing too loudly from the music to have heard them.

Placing the new hood, with its chemical-infused strips, over Hale's head, he pressed his fingers against the man's carotid and took his pulse.

Now it was simply a waiting game.

———

Because of his size, Hale had been difficult to dose. Instead of a couple of hours, it had taken nearly five to get the result that Harvath had been aiming for.

But when the compound finally kicked all the way in, the man was reduced to a state of almost abject terror. His heart rate climbed so high that Harvath was concerned that he had overdone it and that the man's heart was going to explode right there in his chest. It was like trying to catch a falling knife.

Harvath watched Hale heaving for breath and struggling against his restraints. Looking at McGee, he said, "Get the AED ready."

If he had to drive the man into cardiac arrest to get what he wanted, then that was what he was going to do.

Leaning in, he began to aggressively interrogate Hale, physically assaulting him with open-handed strikes when the man even so much as hesitated to answer a question.

When he had him right where he wanted him, he posed his two biggest questions: what was the next attack and who was he working for.

The answers were incredible. Harvath couldn't believe what he was hearing.

CHAPTER 54

Removing the hood, Harvath put the headphones back on, duct-taped them in place, and covered Hale's head with his original blackout hood.

Instead of German death-metal music, Harvath now piped in white noise and allowed the man's nervous system to stabilize.

Stepping out of the storage room, he joined McGee at the staircase.

"Do you believe him?" the ex–CIA director asked.

"I've never known the process not to be solid."

"Except for the only other time you've administered it solo and you gave someone a heart attack."

"Yeah," Harvath admitted. "Except for that."

"First somebody somewhere inside the Secret Service and now Andy Conroy? The fucking deputy director of operations at CIA? This has got all the hallmarks of a straight-up coup. They're just not using the military to carry it out."

"Seeing as how Conroy is the one who froze my money and tried to blackmail me into spying against Sølvi, you'll forgive me for believing he's capable of anything."

"That was dirty pool," McGee replied. "I told you, had I known, I never would have allowed it. But you need to understand, Conroy has been at Langley forever. We're talking something like forty years. This doesn't make any sense."

"Nothing that's happened this week has made any sense."

"So what do we do now?"

Harvath looked at him. "With Hale?"

"With everything."

He thought about it for a minute. "If Conroy is dirty, if he really is the one pulling Hale's strings, we'd have to be able to prove that. What we got out of Hale, that's not going to be admissible anywhere. And then we'd have to figure out who we can trust with the proof. Which brings us back to where we started—we don't know how high this thing goes, nor how widespread."

"What if there was someone I trusted at the Bureau?"

"Who?"

"An agent named Alan Gallo," said McGee. "He's an assistant director and head of the FBI's Counterintelligence Division. We've done a lot of counter-Russia stuff together over the years. If I had to trust anyone there, it'd be him."

"So we'd go to Gallo and tell him what? You got someone at Langley to send you classified personnel files and we kidnapped some ex-employee and I used enhanced interrogation methods on him to elicit further evidence? What's to stop your FBI buddy from putting us in cuffs and throwing us in a cell?"

"If he's corrupt? Nothing at all. In fact, jail would probably be the least of our worries. But if he's still the man I knew, he might be the only one who can help us."

"How do we figure out if he is?" Harvath asked.

"We'd have to meet with Gallo. Feel him out."

"And then what?"

"If we're convinced he's clean and he wants to take this, we let him take it. If we have any reservations, we keep going without him."

It was a possibility, but it had one snag. "We can't leave Hale here alone," Harvath said. "Somebody needs to keep an eye on him."

"What about Haney? If he and Rogers get an Uber, they can be here in an hour and a half. That gives us plenty of time to figure out what we want to share with Gallo and what we should keep in reserve."

Harvath looked at his watch. "All doable. And, like it or not, we're going to have to tell him what Hale revealed about the next attack."

McGee nodded. "That just leaves us with where to set up the meeting. Ideally, it'd be someplace where we could have a secure conversation. No eavesdropping. No recordings."

"Which cancels out FBI headquarters. In fact, considering all the intel we've amassed, I think Gallo should come to us."

"Here?" the ex–CIA director remarked. "To your house?"

Harvath shook his head. "Fort Belvoir is just down the road. The Army Intelligence and Security Command has a SCIF. No phones. No recording devices. Just the three of us having a very private and very frank discussion."

"I like it. And Gallo definitely has enough pull to make that happen."

"Why don't you take a break and see if you can get it all set up. I'll stay down here with Hale."

Grabbing his water bottle, McGee headed upstairs to put everything together.

When they were getting close in their Uber, Haney texted Harvath, who met them at Mount Vernon.

Doing a 360-degree inspection of his Bronco, Haney commented, "No bullet holes. Good job."

After returning to the house, getting Ambassador Rogers set up in the den, and familiarizing Haney with all things Hale, Harvath and McGee got on the road for the fifteen-minute drive to Fort Belvoir.

After showing their IDs at the gate, they were issued a vehicle pass and told how to find the Army Intelligence and Security Command, also known as INSCOM, which was adjacent to U.S. Army Cyber Command.

Finding a spot in the lot, they entered the lobby and did another ID and security check. Once they had been issued badges, a soldier escorted them to INSCOM, where they were handed off to a different soldier, who walked them the rest of the way to Alan Gallo, who was waiting for them outside the secure area that contained the SCIF they would be using.

He was an extremely fit, middle-aged man, with a perfectly parted haircut and a dark blue suit. After he greeted the two visitors with a firm handshake, they all deposited their electronic devices in the nearby cubby and then Gallo waved them into the SCIF.

They chatted for a moment as Gallo caught up quickly with McGee, and informed Harvath that he was aware of how everything had unfolded Monday evening and that he was proud to be meeting him in person.

Then, sitting down at one of the chairs around the short conference table, he looked at McGee and said, "You called this meeting, Bob. I'll let you helm it."

After thanking him again for coming down to Fort Belvoir, the ex–CIA director launched into everything he and Harvath had agreed would be in his speech.

Gallo looked as if someone had not just walked across his grave but had driven over it with an F-150 too.

"Anything else?" asked the FBI agent.

McGee looked at Harvath and nodded, signaling that he was okay with dropping the other shoe as long as he was.

"Hale says there's another attack coming," Harvath replied. "It's not his people, however. And he doesn't know anything about the target. Apparently, whoever is behind all this, they've got another roster of hitters they're drawing from."

"I think we're getting close to uncovering that other roster."

Upon hearing that, both Harvath's and McGee's eyebrows went up. Though neither man said anything, it was obvious that they were waiting for Gallo to elaborate. When he did, it was substantial.

First, however, he reaffirmed the ground rules. "Both of you have maintained your top-secret clearances. I expect you to abide by all the rules and regulations therein. Nothing I am about to share with you gets repeated. Is that clear?"

Harvath and McGee both agreed.

"Seven months ago, the FBI apprehended a Russian intelligence officer. In debriefing him, we learned that about a year ago, Russia had stood up a new covert spy unit, the Department of Special Tasks, or SSD. Their goal is to destabilize the West and one of their first operations is called *Chernaya Liniya*, or Operation Black Line. The object is to tip America into chaos and collapse the country from within."

"And you think that's what we're experiencing now?" Harvath asked.

Gallo nodded. "According to our Russian intelligence officer, everything we're seeing is in keeping with that plan. You start with terrorism to make Americans feel unsafe, and then you apply downward pressure on our political and cultural fault lines, sow distrust not only in the government, but in each other as well."

"What did I tell you?" McGee said, looking at Harvath.

"But how did the Russians get a bunch of Americans on board with their plan, much less current and former CIA people, as well as someone at Secret Service?" Harvath asked.

"My best guess would be that these people don't know that they're doing Russia's bidding. I think there's probably something else between them and the Russians. What that is, though, we haven't figured out yet."

"What about this other roster of hitters?" Harvath asked. "Who are they?"

"They're a White nationalist group called Iron Tree. Real blood-and-soil, neo-Nazi types. The Russians have covertly been using combat sports as a recruiting ground. They teach these guys how to fight, in an expectation that eventually they'll be called out onto American streets to commit violence against those they see as their political opponents. Based on intelligence we just received, we believe they've taken things to the next level with training in weapons and small unit tactics."

"And you think that's what my wife and I encountered outside the Vice President's Residence?"

"There, as well as with the final shooter inside the Norwegian ambassador's residence," Gallop replied.

"So shooting at the D.C. cops and the protesters was handled by this Iron Tree group," said McGee. "And the attack on the Secret Service motorcade was Hale's ex–Ground Branch people. All of which causes chaos, a feeling that no one is safe, et cetera. But what's the rationale for going after Brendan Rogers?"

"Did you ask Hale?"

"I tried," said Harvath. "But by that point, it looked like he was headed for a rapid unscheduled disassembly."

Gallo tilted his head, confused.

"He was redlining. His pulse had spiked so high that I thought he was going to go into cardiac arrest. So I stopped the interrogation."

"Rendition. Chemical interrogation. You realize that I can't use any of this, right?" the FBI agent stated. "None of it's admissible in court."

"With all due respect, we're under attack and we're losing. They've killed and injured a lot more of us than we have of them. I'm more concerned with stopping the threat than making sure they get their day in court."

"You guys are hammers. I get that. My job and my oath, however, are different. I'm bound by a more complicated set of rules."

"I understand. Believe me," said McGee, who'd had to straddle both worlds—the lawful and the lawless—when heading the CIA. "We're here as a courtesy. We're not looking to get in your way. We just want to help."

"I've got to be honest," Gallo admitted. "I'm not sure where to even start. If the Russians are ultimately behind this, they've effectively weaponized pieces of our national security apparatus against us. There's no telling how long it could take to unwind this and clean out all the infection. Anyone we turn to for help, in any organization, could be part of the plot."

"Which is exactly where we are in looking at all of this," said Harvath.

"That's why we came to you," McGee added.

The FBI agent shook his head. "I don't know whether to thank you, or to tell you to lose my number and never call me again."

The men shared an uncomfortable laugh.

"As far as I see it," McGee continued, "we've got to stop the bleeding. Stop the attacks."

"I agree," said Gallo. "But I don't want any of the perpetrators walking free because we couldn't build cases against them."

Harvath looked at him. "I guarantee you: Not a single one of them is going to walk. Not one."

Based on his ominous tone, Gallo didn't doubt it. "There's a lot of things I'm hearing in here that, for the record, I'm going to pretend I didn't."

"So, what do you want to do?" asked McGee, cutting to the chase. "Do you want us to go home, set Hale loose, and encourage Ambassador Rogers to make his peace with God?"

"Or," interjected Harvath, "do you want to find a way to put us to work?"

CHAPTER 55

I t's official, folks," said Chuck Coughlin, his neon American flag burning brightly behind him. "We are living in a time where leadership has failed us. Where the very promises that brought tens of millions to the polls—promises of strength, of honor, of reclaiming this country from the forces that seek to destroy it—have been abandoned in the name of . . . what? Political expediency? Corruption? I don't know. But I'll tell you this: It's not what we voted for. It's not what *America* voted for."

Staring into the camera, Coughlin gripped the edge of his desk, the passion increasing in his voice, and continued, "James Mitchell, the man We the People put into office, is not the man we thought he was. This isn't about policy decisions or a few hiccups. This is about betrayal. We saw it in his speech last night—his so-called calm address after the attack on the NATO motorcade. Calm? You call that calm? That was weakness, ladies and gentlemen.

"The President couldn't even bring himself to say what we all know: *This was an act of war.* You think he's going to stand up to the radicals, the globalists, the ones who've been pulling the strings for decades? Of course he isn't. He's too busy worrying about his approval ratings, too busy playing nice with the very people who've sold us out. The man's a puppet—and he's no longer in control of his own strings.

"Vice President Cates, on the other hand, is the real deal. He has been with us from the beginning. He speaks the language of the people—real

Americans—while Mitchell is only interested in cozying up to the elites. I'm telling you this country needs leadership. *Desperately*. We need someone in that Oval Office who will do what has to be done—no matter how hard and no matter what the consequences."

Chuckling bitterly, Coughlin said, "The media is calling this a 'moment of crisis.' Well, let me tell you something: This is not a moment of crisis. This is the moment when We the People decide *who* is in charge. And it's not Mitchell anymore. I don't care if he's been elected. I don't care if he's got the sharp suits and all the advisors. We *deserve* better. We *demand* better. And we will not sit idly by while this so-called leader squanders the future of our country.

"I, Charles Armstrong Coughlin, am calling for Mitchell to step down. Not just for the good of the country—though I believe that's reason enough. But because it's the only way we can truly honor the promises that were made on the campaign trail, not to mention all the sacrifices since then. Mitchell's weakness isn't just hurting us politically—it's costing lives. Lives lost in that senseless terrorist attack on his own supporters, people who trusted him, who believed in his leadership, as well as those killed in the NATO motorcade attack—people attacked for the sake of global diplomacy while our own people are left to fend for themselves. These are the consequences of failed leadership.

"Mitchell can't do it. He's lost his spine. We need someone who hasn't been corrupted, who still believes in the fight—someone who will put the people first and not apologize for doing what's right for us, for America. And that someone, my friends, is Vice President Christopher Cates.

"It's time for change. It's time for James Mitchell to resign and for Chris Cates to take the reins. We can no longer sit back and watch as our country slides into chaos and is torn apart by a leader too scared to make the tough calls. We need Cates to lead. And if Mitchell won't step aside, then we need to *force him out*.

"This is about the survival of this nation—about preserving the future of America. For ourselves, our children, and our grandchildren."

Glancing up at the digital clock upon the wall, he then announced, "And that's going to do it for us today, folks. Another three hours of

Bunker Radio in the can. I'll see you right back here tomorrow. Until then, remember—when you're under attack, Chuck Coughlin has your back. And we are all, God help us, *definitely* under attack. Stay safe, America."

Senator Blackwood closed the tab on his computer and couldn't help but smile. Coughlin's quick social media take last night had been good, but today's extensive takedown of the President's national address had been absolutely perfect.

The only thing more perfect, and for which he had smiled even more broadly, had been Claire Bennet last night. It was like makeup sex, but without ever having broken up.

The woman was beyond incredible—not only in the physical realm, but also in the personal, or more to the point, the professional. He truly wondered if he would have been able to accomplish what he had, if he would have ever reached this far, without her encouragement and her incredible gift for strategy.

Quietly in the background, without desire for credit or recognition, she had helped him put his entire plan together. Her dislike for Mitchell, his abandonment of his principles, and for what Mitchell had done to him, had caused her to be his biggest champion.

She had seen angles he had never considered, had helped avoid pitfalls he didn't realize could be coming, and had shored up his confidence when he had wondered if the plot was ultimately achievable. Claire Bennet had been his rock.

Which made her not being in D.C. for the next, most exciting phase of all extremely disappointing.

No doubt she would be watching it all unfold on a TV somewhere in Istanbul, but that wouldn't be the same as having her here. There was nothing as erotic, no aphrodisiac as all-consuming, as power—and they were about to bring down an American presidency.

This week had already been one for the history books. Of course, history would never know, not for sure, who had been behind the events, but he and Claire would know, as would their coconspirators. By this time tomorrow, Mitchell's administration would be on life support, if not completely over.

The fact that he wouldn't have Claire to celebrate with was unfortunate, but perhaps it was for the best. With her irresistible pull out of his immediate vicinity, he could focus on being the stoic elder statesman others would expect him to be.

There was no telling who might call on him for advice and counsel—from advisors and Cabinet members, right up to James Mitchell himself.

And if the President should reach out to him, Senator Bill Blackwood knew exactly what he would say. He had rehearsed and refined it a thousand times with Claire. "Mr. President," he would begin, after taking a long pause, ostensibly reflecting on the seriousness of the matter he was being asked to consult on, "America elected you because you're a fighter. But sometimes, a leader has to know when to step aside. He has to recognize that the fight is no longer his to win."

He would tell Mitchell that resigning wouldn't be a defeat and that no one would fault him. He would be doing the right thing, and in stepping aside, rather than clinging to power, he could shape the future from the outside, from a place of wisdom and respect, with the true appreciation of the American people for having put them and the country first.

While the delivery might have a certain *Blackwoodian* flare, the words were completely Claire's. From start to finish, she had crafted every one of them.

But to walk out of the Oval Office and not be able to immediately share with her the excitement of helping convince Mitchell to step down felt anticlimactic.

Such a long and dangerous road, especially one so meticulously traveled, deserved a very special, mutual celebration upon its completion.

He had relayed this sentiment to Claire last night and she had agreed, promising they would celebrate when she got back next week.

Just the thought of it brought joy to his heart—celebrating the nation's birthday, at the White House, with a brand-new president.

Even better, there was a very good chance that *President* Chris Cates would have a plum Cabinet position waiting for him.

All he and his coconspirators had to do was to successfully get through tomorrow.

If they could do that, the American government would get a much-needed reset—and once that happened, the sky was the limit for what Bill Blackwood could achieve.

Friday couldn't get here soon enough.

CHAPTER 56

State police had established DUI "checkpoints" at both ends of the narrow dirt road along the South Fork of the Shenandoah River.

Plainclothes detectives, in unmarked vehicles, were positioned farther back in case anyone tried to turn around and avoid being stopped. The last thing they wanted was for word to leak.

In the meantime, agents from the FBI's Richmond Field Office had assembled for the serving of a search warrant on the five-hundred-acre farm of a Paul Taylor Jordan—titular head of the Iron Tree movement. Based upon the chilling testimony of Ricky Russell, it was one of the fastest warrants to have ever been approved in the history of the state of Virginia.

The farm had been under surveillance for several hours. The plan was to launch the raid before dawn. The weather, however, wasn't cooperating.

A front of thunderstorms had moved in and parked themselves over the foothills of the Blue Ridge Mountains. It was pissing down rain.

Even worse, the claps of thunder were so loud that it had to be near impossible for anyone on the property to be sleeping.

Worst of all, however, were the intense flashes of lightning. Any hope the FBI had of using the cover of darkness to hide their approach was all but dashed. The odds were stacked in the bad guys' favor that they'd not only be awake when the raid happened, but that they'd see it coming too.

The Virginia State Police had provided three six-man tactical teams, along with three Bearcat armored vehicles, a critical addition considering how quickly the rain had turned the road to mud.

With the forecast showing no letup in the storms anytime soon, Carolan and Fields, in conjunction with their FBI colleagues and the leader of the tactical teams, made a decision. Lightning, thunder, and rain be damned, they were going in.

Word was passed over the radios, weapons were checked, and body armor was adjusted. It was time to roll.

Because of the size of the Bearcats, four FBI agents could ride with each tactical team. Carolan and Fields rode in the lead vehicle. The pucker factor was off the charts.

According to Ricky Russell, the Jordan farm had been a training ground for Iron Tree members in hand-to-hand combat, fully automatic weapons, fire-and-maneuver techniques, improvised explosives, and a host of other military operations, especially those on urban terrain. In Russell's words, the farm was like a "Hillbilly al-Qaeda" camp.

Riding in the first Bearcat, Carolan and Fields had no idea what they might face. Had the road been laid with mines? Were there antipersonnel devices, such as claymores, hidden around the buildings? Had these guys gotten their hands on standoff weapons like grenade launchers? Russell had only been able to comment on what he had seen while he had been a member of Iron Tree. What steps they were taking now and what additional weapons they had availed themselves of was anyone's guess. That was one of the purposes of the surveillance.

In the time that they'd been watching the compound, several vehicles had arrived. By their count, there were at least seventeen different trucks and cars parked at the farm. Due to the weather, it had been impossible to get a drone in the air. Intelligence had to be gathered the old-fashioned way—through binoculars and long-range rifle scopes. They didn't dare send anyone in on foot and risk blowing the operation.

To that end, agents from the Richmond Field Office had been kept in the dark about the high-risk warrant service for as long as possible. Whoever the Bureau's leaker was, Carolan, Fields, and Gallo wanted to make sure that this person was cut off from any information that might have let the bad guys know that they were coming.

The cluster of buildings, including the main farmhouse, a barn, a bunkhouse, and a large garage-style structure, was a half mile in from the main road. Thankfully, it wasn't a straight shot. The long, windy drive ducked in and out of the trees, which, along with the storm, helped deaden some of the sound from the Bearcats' turbo-diesel engines.

"Thirty seconds!" the tac-team leader announced.

All around them, the men in their helmets and night-vision goggles adjusted their slings, tightened their grips on their weapons, and made sure their magazines were firmly seated in the mag wells of their rifles. Fields said a quiet prayer that they would be kept safe and no one would be injured.

"Five seconds!" came the booming voice of the tac-team leader.

It had already been planned how everyone inside the armored vehicles would debus. The first and second tac teams would exit and take up defensive firing positions, while the third team would hit the farmhouse and make a swift, overwhelming, no-knock entry.

The idea, storm notwithstanding, was to catch Paul Taylor Jordan in his bed, take physical custody of him, and get him to convince his followers to stand down. No one wanted a Ruby Ridge or Branch Davidian–style bloodbath.

Nearing the farmhouse, the Bearcats split off out of their column and came to a halt. As soon as they did, the back doors flew open and the tac-team members leapt out into the storm.

Team three ran up to the front door of the darkened farmhouse and called their breacher forward. Stepping up to the threshold with his thirty-five-pound battering ram, he drew it back and then sent it crashing into the door.

The moment it connected, splintering the door and ripping it from its hinges, a high-pitched whine could be heard from inside.

Before the breacher could step back from the frame and warn his teammates, the entire house exploded.

The shock wave knocked the members of teams one and two to the ground, showering them with flaming debris, and could even be felt by the FBI agents inside the armored vehicles.

No sooner had the farmhouse detonated than two different shooters, armed with heavy, belt-fed machine guns, opened up on them—one from the barn's hayloft and the other from a window at the corner of the bunkhouse.

The remaining tac teams scrambled to their feet and immediately began returning fire. Pouring out of the back of all three Bearcats, the FBI agents—shotguns and M4 rifles in hand—joined them.

The bloodbath they all hoped they would avoid was well underway.

Soon enough, the tac-team leader was radioing for team one to get back in their Bearcat. They were going to make a run for the barn.

Moving quickly, Fields and Carolan got in first, followed by the rest of the team. As soon as they closed the rear hatch, the Bearcat driver had the vehicle in gear and was speeding toward the barn.

As he drove, the heavy rounds of the machine guns slammed into the heavy armor plating and thick bulletproof glass of his vehicle. He didn't let any of it slow him down. In fact, he had been ordered by the tac-team leader to increase his speed.

The man wanted him to rip through the barn, taking out as many structural supports as possible. If they could cause a full or even partial collapse of the structure, it would hopefully dislodge the shooter in the hayloft.

Crashing through the old, empty barn in a shower of splintered wood, the Bearcat driver aimed for every structural support beam as well as the stairs leading to the hayloft.

At the far end, as the machine gunner tried to readjust his weapon, he slammed on the brakes and allowed two tac-team members to bail out to the back. As soon as the hatch had been reclosed, he returned to Berserker mode and sent the twenty-thousand-pound Bearcat on one final rampage before blasting through the wall on the other side, back into the storm.

Looking through the window on the rear hatch, they could see multiple flashes of gunfire as the structure began to tilt precariously to the right, before completely collapsing.

Over the roar of the Bearcat's engine, the storm, and the continuing heavy gunfire from the bunkhouse, you could sense the tac-team operators in the vehicle holding their collective breath until their colleagues radioed that they had taken out the shooter in the barn and had safely escaped its collapse.

The sense of relief they felt, however, was short-lived as the driver warned them all to brace for immediate impact.

Jerking the wheel at the last moment, he ran the Bearcat down the length of the bunkhouse, sheering off its entire façade, exposing the full interior and all of the Iron Tree members gathered inside.

As soon as the armored vehicle had cleared the line of fire, the members of team two began to light it up—putting round after round on the now fully exposed enemy.

Positioning themselves to flank, the Bearcat sloshed to a muddy stop, the tac-team members jumped out of the back, and, joined by Carolan and Fields, they all started firing.

The gunfight was punctuated by slashes of lightning that tore through the sky and even more thunder, which shook the ground beneath their feet.

Together, the FBI and Virginia State Police tactical teams felled the Iron Tree attackers one by one, starting with the heavy machine gunner and working their way through their ranks.

When the gunfight ended, the ground was a sea of spent shell casings and empty magazines. The Iron Tree members had been ready for combat, but not for an armored vehicle to upend their dug-in, defensive advantage.

With their FBI partners, the tac-team members spread out, searching for survivors. But what they found were only a handful of dead bodies.

"Over here!" Fields shouted from the kitchen area of the bunkhouse.

As soon as Carolan saw what she was looking at, he ordered, "Do not touch that! Step away. Right now."

Fields did exactly as her boss instructed.

The tac-team leader brought over one of his demolition experts, who studied what Fields had uncovered. Peeling back a rug, she exposed a trapdoor. Where it led—and who or what was down there—wasn't apparent. What they all did know was that, like the front door of the farmhouse, it was very likely booby-trapped.

Ordering everyone to exit the bunkhouse, he went out to the Bearcat and returned with a spool of galvanized steel cable and a handful of other items he needed.

He ran the cable over one of the wooden beams above the kitchen, attached it to the door's ring pull, and unspooled enough cable to get him outside to the safety of the armored vehicle. There, using a hand winch, he began reeling in the cable and lifting open the trapdoor.

When the door got to a certain point, there was an enormous explosion. Shrapnel, which would have killed anyone standing nearby, erupted in all directions. Like the booby trap on the farmhouse, this one had also been designed to be incredibly devastating.

Waiting for the smoke to clear, the tac team reassembled and descended into the dark, underground space beneath the bunkhouse.

It was a small basement area with workbenches covered in tools and electronic components.

At the far end was a set of metal lockers. Examining them, one of the tac-team guys figured out that they had been hung on a cleverly hidden track.

Once he found the release, he slid the lockers to the side, revealing a long, rough-hewn tunnel lit by industrial string lights.

The tac team flooded into the tunnel and soon found that it wasn't just one tunnel, but a whole, interconnected series of them beneath the compound. They also discovered lots of blood on the ground. Apparently, this was the escape route for all the Iron Tree members who had been able to make it out of the bunkhouse.

Soon enough, however, they came upon their first body. The man had either been carried this far and subsequently abandoned or had made it to this point via his own power and had expired from his gunshot wounds. Either way, he was dead.

Fifty feet later, they came across another corpse.

When they stumbled upon a third man, motionless on the ground, they assumed they had another lifeless body. Then the man moved.

"We've got a survivor," the lead tac-team member radioed as his colleagues stripped the injured attacker of his weapons.

———

Paul Taylor Jordan wasn't much of a talker. After receiving medical attention and being deemed fit for interrogation, both Carolan and Fields—
in multiple rounds of bad cop, worse cop—had gone to work on him
while the tac teams had searched the rest of the tunnels and the woods
beyond for the remaining Iron Tree members involved in the shoot-out.

Not only did they not get anywhere with Jordan, he soon began com-
plaining of the pain he was in and saying he wanted an attorney. They had
hit the proverbial brick wall.

And it was at that point, when they were absolutely certain that Jordan
wasn't going to give them anything, that Gallo had said he wanted to be
notified.

Up on the road, he had been present for the entire operation and had
brought something with him just in case.

Handcuffed to a chair in the basement, Jordan—a paunchy man in his
early sixties with rheumy eyes and severe psoriasis—watched as Carolan
and Fields left him alone and returned upstairs.

Minutes ticked by. And with each one that did, he was left to wonder
what they planned to do with him.

Eventually there was the sound of heavy footsteps descending the
stairs into the basement. Because of a set of shelving, he couldn't see who
it was—not right away—but the person moved with a quiet, almost dark
purpose and confidence that was instantly unnerving.

When the man was finally revealed, Jordan could see he was wearing rubber gloves and an N95 mask. In one hand he carried a small Igloo
cooler. In the other was an AED defibrillator.

"Mr. Jordan," said Harvath as he set his equipment down on the nearest workbench, "I'm going to give you one chance to cooperate. If you do,
this will be over quickly and we can get you the further medical treatment
you need. If you don't cooperate, I can make this quite painful."

The man looked at him and spat, "Fuck you."

"Option B," Harvath replied, smiling behind his mask. "I was hoping
that would be your choice."

CHAPTER 57

Much like Hale, Jordan had also been an extremely difficult interrogation subject. Worried about his age, health, and injuries from the gunfight, Harvath had been careful with how he had dosed him—starting low and gradually ratcheting it up. Before the interrogation had even begun, the man had looked like a heart attack waiting to happen. Thankfully, Harvath was able to eventually get what he needed out of him without Jordan flatlining. Had the guy been younger or in better shape, Harvath was certain he could have moved much faster.

The length of the interrogation was strike one. Strike two was the fact that the storm prevented an FBI or Virginia State Police helicopter from picking them up and getting them rapidly back to D.C. Instead, Harvath, Gallo, Carolan, and Fields had been forced to drive.

As soon as Jordan had coughed up his information, they had hopped in Gallo's Suburban and, with lights and sirens going full tilt, hightailed it all the way back to Washington.

Strike three was that the intelligence he had extracted from Jordan was incomplete. There was an attack planned. The target was the NATO Summit. Where at the summit and when, he didn't know. Everything had been compartmentalized and he'd only been given information on a need-to-know basis. When asked who had given him his orders, he'd dropped a massive bombshell. It was a member of the FBI.

Harvath wasn't familiar with the man, but the moment Agent Joe Carolan had heard the name, he knew exactly who it was. So did Fields.

Agent Matthew Kennedy had been with the Bureau for decades. But like turncoats inside the Secret Service and CIA, he had decided to betray his country.

Harvath didn't need to know why. He just needed to stop him. Gallo had already assembled a small team of trusted agents from his division to find and detain Kennedy.

In the meantime, Harvath had reached out to Sølvi to warn her. Because she was on duty, she wasn't answering her phone, but she was able to check her texts. The threat itself sounded like it could be explosives, but no explosive devices had been assembled at Jordan's compound—only an odd kind of detonator, which somewhat explained all the wiring and electronic junk found in the basement of the bunkhouse.

His next communication was to Russ Gaines. It was important that he know that there was a credible threat to the summit. Harvath also needed to ask for a pretty serious favor. He heard Russ put the phone down and issue a series of rapid orders to his assistant Kyle before getting back on the line and saying, "I'll have everything waiting by the time you arrive."

Gallo and Carolan were also working their phones as Fields rocketed up the rain-slicked highway to Washington like a professional Formula 1 driver.

By the time they reached the Walter E. Washington Convention Center, the NATO Summit was in full swing. They had no idea what they were looking for, but they did know who.

Gallo was headed to the security command post to be their eye in the sky, while Carolan and Fields would comb the 2.3-million-square-foot convention center looking for Kennedy, whose photo had already been texted to every police officer, Secret Service agent, and security guard in the vicinity of the summit.

Harvath's job was equally broad. Whatever this Kennedy guy had planned, he had been reliant on a handful of Iron Tree men who happened to be labor union members approved to work at the convention center. Like Kennedy, if they were on-site, they could be anywhere.

As they pulled up to the loading dock, Harvath saw Russ Gaines already waiting for him. He introduced Gallo, Carolan, and Fields before agreeing to how often they would check in via text and watching them disappear inside.

Standing next to Russ were two of the Quick Reaction Force agents he had flown out to the scene of the motorcade attack with yesterday—an older operative named Fuller and a very switched-on man named Wallace.

They handed Harvath a radio with an earpiece, a Secret Service plate carrier like he had worn yesterday, and asked him if he needed a weapon. Harvath had his Glock, so he shook his head and thanked them.

Gaines then handed over a set of Secret Service credentials, including an all-access badge on a lanyard.

Harvath put on the plate carrier and hung the badge around his neck. Then, after setting up his radio and doing a quick comms check, they all headed into the convention center.

Like Gallo, Gaines made a beeline for the command center, which left Harvath with the QRF duo.

"Where do you want to go first?" Fuller asked.

In addition to Kennedy, Jordan had provided the names of the three men the rogue FBI agent was using to infiltrate the convention center. Gallo had had their photos pulled from their ID badges and blasted out to all the security people, the same way he had done with Kennedy's. They were confident they had found their haystack; the only question was whether the needles were still there.

What worried Harvath was that it had taken two days to set up the NATO Summit. Not only were there conferences, but there was also the exhibit hall where all the defense contractors had their booths. If Kennedy's ultimate goal was to plant bombs, it could have happened at any point over the last couple of days. Looking for these guys here, this morning, could be a wild-goose chase.

Also, the Secret Service had one of the best bomb-detection divisions in the world. They would have been sweeping their sniffer dogs throughout the convention center over the last forty-eight hours. Those animals were amazing. If there was so much as a firecracker inside a garbage can, they would have found it.

Now that the summit had started, security screening had only gotten more difficult. It would be nearly impossible to sneak anything in at this point, which made Harvath think that whatever they planned to use for the attack had to already be here—the dogs just hadn't gotten near it.

"Lower level," he said to Fuller.

"What are we looking for?" asked Wallace.

"The companies that hire the union guys to install and dismantle their trade show booths have cages they keep their supplies and equipment in. It's one of the only places you can leave things for extended periods and not draw attention."

The two men nodded and followed Harvath to the service elevators.

As they rode down, he received a video call from Nicholas.

Activating it, he said, "Tell me you've got something good."

"I don't know how good it is," the man replied, "but I may have something. The pictures you sent from Jordan's compound, all those pieces of electronics."

"That were being used to build the alleged detonators? What about them?"

"I think we ID'd one of the components. It's like a very sclerotic AirTag."

Harvath held his phone higher, as if that might help him better understand what his friend was saying. "I don't get it."

Nicholas pulled up a picture of it. "Secret Service is going to be sweeping for all sorts of electronic devices—both for eavesdropping on the summit, but also for bomb triggers. This device works on a frequency well below anything they'd pay attention to. The only problem is, it's so weak, you'd practically have to be standing right next to it to trigger it."

"That doesn't make much sense. Unless you're a suicide bomber, close proximity to your device is usually considered a negative."

"Agreed," his friend said. "Which brings me to those sharps you found."

At the end of one of the workbenches, Harvath had discovered an empty chewing tobacco tin filled with the tips of large gauge hypodermic needles.

"What about them?"

"You're the one that said it. Only a suicide bomber would want to be standing next to his bomb when he hit the detonator. Unless . . ."

"There was a lag before the bomb actually went off."

"Exactly."

"What are we talking about?" Harvath asked. "Are the sharps meant to puncture something? Is there some sort of a slow bleed that gives the bomber time to get away?"

Nicholas looked at him through the screen. "DHS and Secret Service have dogs that can sniff out chemical weapons, but if those weapons are small, well contained, and coated with an outer layer of paint thinner or even jalapeño jelly, the dogs don't hit on them. They walk right by. Compared to the volume of explosive material you'd need for a substantial attack, chemical weapons require a lot less. In essence, you can take a much smaller risk of being uncovered and, if successful, get a much bigger bang for your buck."

"How sure are you that we're dealing with a chemical weapon?"

"I've got photos of a bunch of shredded wire, some needle tips, and a weak Bluetooth receiver. How sure would you be?"

Sure enough to know that this was above his pay grade. He needed to kick this up to Gaines and let him make the call.

If they kept going and succeeded in tracking Kennedy or any of the Iron Tree members down, they might be able to get to any potential devices before they were detonated.

On the other hand, if they attempted to evacuate the convention center, Kennedy and his men might clack off their devices, killing untold numbers as they fled.

Harvath was about to say something to Nicholas when the service elevator they were riding in slowed and then stopped at the mezzanine level.

As the doors opened, he saw four uniformed Secret Service officers looking back at him. There was something about them, however, that didn't seem right.

CHAPTER 58

As the men entered the elevator and the doors closed, Harvath noticed a nervousness about them. One was tapping his foot, while another was tapping his left index finger against his thigh.

Without saying goodbye, he disconnected his call with Nicholas, slipped his phone into his back pocket, and placed both hands, as casually as he could, on his hips.

He watched the men who kept looking at their sergeant, as if waiting for some kind of command. Then he noticed their hands inching toward their sidearms.

As the sergeant pulled his pistol, he yelled, "Now!"

Harvath came out with his dagger, which he used to stab the officer next to him in the neck. At the same time, he drew his Glock with his right hand and shot the officer standing directly in front of him.

The sergeant got off three rounds, all of which appeared to have bounced off Fuller's plate carrier.

Wallace put a bullet into the sergeant's head and then two rounds into the remaining officer, who had been standing just next to him. The entire altercation had gone down in less than four seconds.

As the elevator chimed and they arrived at the lower level, they had their weapons up and at the ready—not knowing what would be waiting for them.

When the doors opened, there was a smattering of bystanders, who had likely heard the shots and gathered to see what was going on, but nothing immediately threatening. Pulling the elevator's stop button and triggering the alarm, Harvath stepped out, followed by Wallace. Fuller, however, didn't move.

Turning around to see what the holdup was, Harvath could see blood running from under Fuller's arm and down the side of his plate carrier.

"I think I've been shot," the big man admitted, shallow of breath.

Together Harvath and Wallace helped him from the elevator and sat him down in a nearby chair. As Harvath radioed Gaines to tell him what had happened, one of the bystanders ran to get a medical kit.

"Uniformed Secret Service?" Gaines asked. "Are you positive?"

"Come down here and check for yourself," he replied angrily. "You've still got a fucking leak, Russ. If you don't find it and plug it, I will."

"I'm working on it."

"How far out are the paramedics for Fuller?"

"They're already on their way to you."

"Good," said Harvath. "Now all I need are those three Iron Tree assholes I'm looking for."

"We just got a report that one of them was spotted on your level. I'm texting a schematic with a pin to your phone now."

When the text came through, Harvath checked it and replied, "Got it. On my way."

The bystander had returned with the medical kit, and Wallace, who had helped remove Fuller's plate carrier, was already applying a pressure bandage.

"You going to be okay?" Harvath asked.

"He'll be fine," Wallace responded. "Go."

That was all Harvath needed to hear. Getting his bearings, he charged off toward where a security guard believed he had seen a man who matched the photo of one of their suspects.

As he moved, he dictated texts to both Sølvi and Carolan. He wanted them to know what was happening down below and to be cautious around any Secret Service personnel they saw.

When he got close to the portion of the lower level where the "cages" were kept, he took one last look at the schematic and then slid his phone back into his pocket.

He thought about relaying an update to Gaines over the radio but decided against it. If the man wanted to track him via the CCTV system, that was fine. Other than that, he didn't want to directly contribute any information to the Secret Service pipeline. Someone had already tried to have him killed. He didn't intend to give them another opportunity.

Up ahead he saw one of the convention center's private security guards. She was a short, middle-aged Asian woman with glasses who looked like she took her job very seriously.

Walking up to her, Harvath held up his phone with the three pictures on it. She pointed to the man in the middle.

"Where'd you see him?" he asked.

"Four aisles down," she replied. "Third cage on the left."

"Is he alone?"

The woman shrugged. "I didn't want to get too close."

Thanking her, Harvath asked that she not let anyone else pass until he got back. She gave him a nod, crossed her arms, and stepped into the middle of the hall to physically block the way of anyone who might come along.

Judging by the size of most of the union workers he'd already seen, she wasn't going to scare any of them. But by the same token, she had a pretty good don't-fuck-with-me-fellas attitude that might actually prevail.

Leaving her to "guard" his six, Harvath took out his Glock and headed toward the cages.

The unending rows of metal storage units reminded him of the Indiana Jones movie where the Ark of the Covenant is hidden away in a massive government facility.

When he neared the fourth aisle, he came to a stop and listened for several moments. He didn't hear anything.

Even though the cages were made from heavy-gauge wire mesh and therefore technically see-through, the one he was standing next to was so crammed with rolls of carpets and construction materials, he couldn't use it to steal a glimpse down the aisle. To do that, he was going to have to expose himself and pop his head out around the corner of the cage.

As soon as he did, he saw not just one but two of the men he was looking for. He figured the third one was inside the open cage.

"Hands up!" he yelled, drawing down on them. "Don't even fucking twitch."

Both of the heavily tattooed men spun to face him, with the result that the man in the cage was completely hidden from view.

"Hands!" Harvath shouted again.

Man number one complied but man number two didn't, which was the only green light Harvath needed.

He shot man number one in his left thigh, dropping him to the ground. It revealed that man number two, standing slightly behind him, had just pulled a pistol.

Harvath shot man number two—twice in the chest and once in the head, dropping him to the floor next to his neo-Nazi buddy.

The only question was, had the third man gone for coffee, or was he actually in the cage? Harvath figured he was close.

"Step out of the cage!" Harvath ordered. "Do it now!"

His instructions were answered with a series of shotgun blasts.

In response, he crouched down, carefully peeked around the corner, and unloaded his pistol in the shooter's direction. He then ejected his spent mag, inserted a fresh one, and repeated the process.

There was a loud thud from inside the cage he was targeting. It could have easily been something inanimate, but it also could have been human. He decided to take a beat and wait it out. There were no other sounds.

"You, inside the cage, come out now!" he ordered.

Nothing happened.

"Inside the cage! Hands above your head. Come out now!"

Still nothing.

Addressing the man he had shot in the thigh, Harvath stated, "You, on the ground. Face down, hands behind your head. Do it now!"

As the man complied, Harvath added, "Interlace your fingers. Do it now!"

The man did what he had been told to do and, with one eye on him and another on the cage that had contained the man with the shotgun,

Harvath stepped out of his position of concealment and moved cautiously down the aisle.

At the open cage, he saw the body of the man with the shotgun, perforated with multiple rounds from Harvath's Glock. Taking his shotgun away, he also put an additional round through the side of his head, just to be sure. Jackass number two was lying, clearly dead, in the aisle from the shots to the chest and head.

Sliding the shotgun out of reach, he removed a pair of plastic restraints and secured the hands of number one behind his back.

Then, sitting him upright, he said, "Now you and I are going to have a talk."

"Fuck you," the man replied.

Harvath smiled. "You sound a lot like my friend Paul Jordan. I am going to make you a similar offer to the one I made him. If you cooperate, I won't hurt you any further. If you make this difficult, though, I'm going to make this the most painful experience you've ever had."

The man spat right at him, making his decision crystal clear.

"Option B," Harvath replied, smiling even wider. "Just like Paul."

Standing up, he walked into the cage and stepped over the body of the man who had been wielding the shotgun. It only took him a moment to find what he was looking for.

Exiting the cage with his Glock having been returned to its holster and a new set of tools in hand, he asked, "What are you planning and how do I stop it?"

"Fuck you," the man repeated.

Taking the screwdriver from one of the toolboxes he'd found inside the cage, Harvath jammed it into the open wound in the man's left thigh.

As he screamed in pain, Harvath repeated his question. And each time the man refused to answer, Harvath used the hammer he had found to drive the screwdriver even farther into the man's leg. Soon enough, Harvath had his answer.

———————

Racing toward the nearest stairwell, he ran up the stairs to the main level. According to the guy he had just interrogated, Kennedy was in the exhibition hall. And according to the last text he'd received from Sølvi, so was she, along with the Norwegian Prime Minister and all the other delegations. This was where the attack was to happen.

Bursting into the crowded public area, he found Carolan and Fields already heading toward him, alerted by his text.

He gave them a description of what Kennedy was allegedly wearing and they all split up. They needed to find Kennedy and neutralize him before he could trigger the devices. Any attempt to pull the fire alarm or otherwise cause a migration toward the exits would only accelerate Kennedy's plan.

With the help of the Iron Tree union members, multiple sarin gas dispersal devices had been hidden in the displays of various defense contractors at the NATO Summit. All Kennedy had to do was walk by the specific booths, near enough to establish a low-level Bluetooth connection, and hit a button on his phone. The needle would puncture the container and the sarin vapor would slowly begin to drift outward.

Taking out his phone, he called Sølvi. Set to "Do Not Disturb," it instantly went to voicemail. Hanging up, he called right back, knowing that she had preapproved his calls to break through if he called a second time within three minutes.

"What's going on?" she asked, getting right to business when she saw it was him and accepted the call.

"Where are you?"

Sølvi glanced overhead and read the aisle indicator aloud.

"The east exit is your closest way out. Start calmly moving the PM and the rest of the delegation that way now."

"What should I tell Secret Service?"

"Don't tell them anything," Harvath replied. "We can't trust them. Go. Now. I'll meet you at the exit."

Sølvi hung up the phone and then quietly informed her PST colleagues that there was a possible threat, but that they had to evacuate slowly so as not to create a panic and potentially trigger the attacker.

The Norwegian security team closed ranks around Prime Minister

Stang, and once Sølvi had whispered in her ear, the woman nodded and was completely compliant.

As they prepared to move her to the exit, the Secret Service agents augmenting their team asked what was happening. A skilled intelligence operative, Sølvi knew that the bigger the lie the better, and told them that the Russians had just invaded Norway.

Before the Secret Service team could even process what they had heard, Sølvi and her colleagues were moving Stang toward the exit.

They had almost made it to the doors when an enormous plainclothes law enforcement officer stepped out of nowhere and yelled, "Kennedy! Get on the ground! It's over!"

Another man, tall and slim, with a wispy beard and wearing a janitor's uniform, pulled an FN P90 submachine gun from the supply cart he was pushing and began firing into the crowd.

With people screaming and running in all directions, Sølvi covered the Prime Minister's body with her own and, unable to move her toward the exit, guided her backward, toward the nearest exhibition booth.

As she retreated, she saw Scot come racing past her, his Glock exploding in his hand. Every round he fired into the janitor was joined by the rounds of two other shooters: the tall plainclothes law enforcement officer who had yelled "Kennedy! Get on the ground!" and another plainclothes officer, a Black woman who, despite running directly into the shooter's line of fire, was absolutely fearless and an incredible markswoman as she pounded headshot after headshot into the man's face.

CHAPTER 59

A ndrew Conroy, the CIA's deputy director of operations, returned home to his three-bedroom, three-bath house on Tournay Road in Westmoreland Hills. It had been an absolute shit day.

He had yet to hear anything from Hale. Despite accompanying the Willis family out to their ranch in Wyoming, the man was still expected to check in via their secure channel. There had been nothing so far but radio silence.

Compounding Conroy's frustration, the attack on the NATO Summit at the Washington Convention Center had been an absolute flop. Kennedy was dead, as were several of the neo-Nazis he was using, and the summit had been reconvened at the White House with the principals and their chiefs of staff.

Instead of a mass-casualty event, dominating every television and cable news station as the attack on the motorcade had, it was being reported as an evacuation based on unspecified security concerns.

Worse still, NATO seemed more determined than ever to ratify Sky Shield, and its reluctant members were now leaning toward yes votes.

Undoubtedly, that prick in the Oval Office was going to find a way to spin all of this into good news for himself. Conroy needed a drink. A big one. And then he needed to figure out what he was going to do.

Walking into his study, he had a tall gin and tonic in mind. What he received, however, was a literal and figurative shock to his entire system.

Gagged and duct-taped to a chair in the middle of the room was

Dennis Hale. Conroy had only a fraction of a second to process what he was seeing before a man with a Taser materialized and pressed the device's trigger.

Every muscle in Conroy's body seized and he lost control of his bladder as he fell to the floor and wet himself.

No sooner had he fallen than another chair was dragged into the center of the room and he was roughly hauled up, shoved into it, and duct-taped securely in place. Unlike Hale, however, he hadn't been gagged.

His attacker set the Taser on the desk and turned to face him. "Do you know who I am?" the man asked.

"Fuck," Conroy blurted out, recognizing him.

"I'll take that as a yes," Harvath replied.

"What do you want?" he demanded.

"All of it. Every single piece of information you have. I want to know about the entire plot, front to back, and I want the names of everyone involved."

"I'm not telling you anything," said Conrad.

"Option B then," Harvath responded, walking around the desk and picking up a small Igloo cooler and an AED defibrillator. "Popular choice today."

CHAPTER 60

On Sunday afternoon, after Prime Minister Stang and the Norwegian delegation had boarded their SAS flight back to Oslo, Scot and Sølvi felt like they could finally breathe again. Finally relax.

After saying goodbye to the Secret Service agents who had accompanied them, they walked outside to where Harvath had parked Sølvi's Mustang.

Saying farewell to everyone, wishing the Norwegians who'd been injured, including Bente, speedy recoveries, and seeing to the dignified transfer of the coffins filled with the Norwegian dead into the cargo hold had been a lot.

"Do you want to drive?" he asked her.

She shook her head. "I'm exhausted. You drive."

Stripping off their gear, they threw everything in the trunk and got on the road. But instead of heading for the Dulles Access Road and home, they struck off in a completely different direction—toward their god-daughter and their friends Nicholas and Nina.

While the new parents enjoyed a well-deserved evening out, Scot and Sølvi enjoyed a well-deserved evening in, playing with the baby and quietly being together.

As a bonus gift, they had spent the night, with Harvath getting up with the baby so Nicholas, Nina, and even Sølvi didn't have to.

The next morning over coffee, it was obvious how much a solid eight hours of sleep had done for all of them.

With reserves yet to be tapped, Scot and Sølvi had offered to stay another night, but their friends had insisted they return home and promised that they'd take them up on their babysitting offer again very soon.

They had lingered in the kitchen, waiting for Monday morning traffic to die down, and then had headed home.

That afternoon, as Harvath had been busy turning his interrogation room back into a storage room, cleaning and restowing his gear, Alan Gallo had shown up at the house, along with Russ Gaines, who was carrying a large, gift-wrapped box.

Inviting them inside, he showed them into the kitchen.

"Can I get you guys anything?" he asked.

"Do you have any soft drinks?" Gallo replied.

"Sure. Sam Adams or Heineken?"

Both men chuckled.

"I guess, since it's Fourth of July week," said Gaines, "I'll take a Sam Adams."

"Me too," Gallo agreed.

Pulling three beers from the fridge, Harvath opened them and handed them to his guests, reserving the third one for himself.

After a long slug, he asked, "Who's the present for?"

Gaines pushed it across the table. "Open it."

Harvath set his beer down. "If there's a human head in here, Sølvi's going to be pissed. I'm supposed to do that kind of stuff in the garage."

Once again, his guests chuckled.

Lifting the lid, Harvath looked inside and saw that Gaines had brought his guns back from the attack outside the Naval Observatory.

"Are you granting me full custody? Or is this just a supervised visit?"

"The investigation is closed," said Gaines. "At least that part of it. I also have this for you." Pulling out an envelope, he handed it to him.

"What's this?"

"Two tickets to the White House Fourth of July celebration."

"Thank you," said Harvath as he handed the envelope back. "Unfortunately, we have other plans."

"Are you sure?"

Harvath nodded and Gaines put the envelope back in his pocket.

Looking at Gallo, Harvath smiled and said, "Those were two pretty good gifts. How are you going to beat that?"

Gallo shook his head. "I don't know if I can, but I'll try. How would you like an update on the investigation?"

For the next twenty minutes, Gallo laid out everything they had—much of which Harvath had already learned from his interrogation of Conroy.

Harvath knew, for instance, that the mole inside the FBI had been Kennedy and, shockingly enough, that the mole inside the Secret Service had turned out to be Gaines's own unctuous assistant, Kyle Marshall. And of course, Conroy had been behind everything at the CIA.

The cabal of Washington insiders looking to unseat President Mitchell from power included the Vice President's chief of staff, Missouri Senator Bill Blackwood, and even some podcaster whom Harvath had never paid any attention to named Coughlin.

The one thing all the men had in common was a deep sense of anger at Mitchell. They used this anger, cloaked in a warped, nationalistic patriotism, to recruit others to their cause.

Behind everything, however, Gallo still believed there lurked the unseen hand of the Russians and their new chaos group the SSD.

"And Operation Black Line," said Harvath.

The FBI man nodded. "We're still looking for a connection, but haven't been able to find anything yet."

"Sounds like you'll be busy for a while."

Again, Gallo nodded. "It's about to get even busier. Blackwood was using a penthouse apartment belonging to one of his donors for his coup meetings. Somebody, my guess is the Russians, bugged it. Videos of the meetings were given to *60 Minutes*. They're doing a special prime-time exposé tonight."

Harvath was stunned. "More chaos."

"Lots more. It's going to shatter America's already shaky faith in its institutions."

"And give birth to oceans of conspiracy theories. They'll be saying 'If high-ranking people in the government can do this, what can't they do?'"

"There's no reason for your name to come up in any of this; we still haven't released your name or Sølvi's from the Naval Observatory attacks, but I thought you'd want to know."

"Thank you," said Harvath.

"One other thing," said Gallo, rather matter-of-fact. "As you know, Hale and Conroy were both found dead at Conroy's house."

"You don't say."

"Mm-hmm. Investigators believe they were arguing, pulled pistols at the same time, and shot each other."

"That sounds extremely violent," Harvath, who had spent more time getting rid of the traces of duct tape afterward and staging the scene than he had interrogating Conroy, replied.

"According to Hale's employer, he disappeared under very strange circumstances, along with their very expensive Mercedes, which only recently was found abandoned."

"Sounds like he was a bit unstable."

"That's the line investigators are taking. Of course, once this *60 Minutes* piece drops and Conroy gets exposed, all attention will be on the coup. This'll probably look like anger or payback for the failed attack at the Convention Center. Bottom line: As long as there's no evidence tying you to Conroy's house or the Willis estate, you should be fine. There isn't, is there?"

Harvath shook his head. "Nope." He had already returned to reclaim his wetsuit, the inflatable dingy, and all the other dive gear he had left behind. The Goblins Nicholas had placed near the security building came complete with a tiny tungsten charge that had fried their insides soon after Harvath had fled the property. He was completely clean.

The most personal piece of information for Harvath had to do with Ambassador Rogers, and it was one of the last items he had extracted from Conroy.

Though Rogers had been critical of the Mitchell administration on TV, it was his connections to their national security team that had earned him the ire of Blackwood and his cabal.

Along with the secretaries of state and defense, Rogers was seen to be exhibiting too much influence inside the White House. They were seen as holdovers from the last administration who wouldn't leave—"swamp creatures," as the cabal called them—responsible for Mitchell softening his stances, particularly on things like NATO and not involving American defense contractors in the Sky Shield missile system.

The sheer magnitude of the plot, as well as the depth of the anger toward Mitchell, was still stunning to Harvath. While he abhorred the injuries and the tragic loss of life, if the Russians had pulled this off without a single fingerprint, it would have marked an incredible leap forward for one of America's most dangerous enemies.

It was *almost* enough to make him want to stay in the game, at least long enough to get even. But by the same token, he had fifty-million-and-one reasons, including Sølvi, not to.

After finishing their beers, Harvath had walked the men out to their cars, wished them a Happy Fourth, and, after asking Gallo to relay his regards to Carolan and Fields, watched them drive away.

Returning to the house, he found Sølvi in the kitchen. She had just come up from the dock and was putting a plan together for dinner.

Holding up her phone, she showed Scot a news story.

"What's that about?" he asked.

"Some D.C. lobbyist named Claire Bennet went to Istanbul to meet with potential clients," Sølvi replied. "Police found her in an alley this morning with her throat cut."

"Did I ever tell you about my first trip to Istanbul?"

"Were there also dead people involved?"

He nodded. "Lots of them."

"I don't think I want to hear this story," she said, opening the fridge. "We've experienced enough death for a while."

"Speaking of which," said Harvath, "I think something died in our fridge. It smells terrible."

Sølvi smiled. "Nothing died. It's just a little present Bente brought us from Oslo."

"What is it?"

"You'll see."

———

The remainder of the week had passed quickly. They went back out to babysit on Wednesday, but other than that, had played things close to home—mostly spending time on their dock, working on their tans, and enjoying the ultimate luxury of just sitting still.

When Friday and the Fourth of July finally arrived, Scot was in pretty good spirits. The *60 Minutes* special had indeed been devastating, but in a strange sort of way, it had given President Mitchell an opportunity— especially in the run-up to America's birthday—to promote the importance of Americans coming together, of working to build an even stronger union. It was a difficult moment for the country, but Mitchell was proving himself the right man for it.

Running a brand-new American flag up the Bishop's Gate flagpole, Scot stood there for several minutes, admiring it as it blew in the breeze. If the people who had once lived on this property could see where the nation was now, they would be amazed. The American experiment had not only endured, it had prospered. As he always said, there was no other place he would rather be than in the United States and in no other time in history.

From the open kitchen window, Sølvi watched her husband staring up at the flag. Pulling out her phone, she snapped a picture. She wanted to capture the moment. It was the essence of the man she had married— strong, proud, and patriotic—quintessential Scot Harvath.

When Ambassador Rogers arrived, they already had cocktails prepared. Sølvi had wanted to do something to represent the colors of the flag and they had settled on highly alcoholic red, white, and blue daiquiris.

Haney and his wife, Jenna, were next to show up, and after Mike had carried in the food they had prepared, they both gladly accepted insulated tumblers with Sølvi's special Fourth of July concoction.

They had invited Nicholas and Nina, but they had politely declined, thinking it might be too much for the baby.

Eventually, McGee texted to let them know that he was getting close. As soon as he did, they gathered everything up and took it all down to the dock.

The ex–CIA director had graciously offered, and everyone had accepted, to pilot the Chris-Craft over from Kent Island, so they could all watch the D.C. fireworks from the water.

It was a long trip, but McGee enjoyed being out on the boat. Harvath had also offered to let him tie up at his dock and spend the night, so he didn't have to go all the way back in the dark.

"Do you have the coordinates for me?" McGee asked once they had cast off and started heading up the Potomac.

Harvath helped entered them in the GPS unit and then, after offering his friend something to drink, joined Sølvi at the stern.

Putting his arm around her, he didn't say anything. He just took in the moment, savoring the breeze and the slowly setting sun.

When they got to the rendezvous point, they found Admiral Tyson and *Pier Pressure* right where he had promised to be. His boat was loaded down with friends, many of them female, and they were having a terrific time drinking and passing around plates of food.

"Hungry?" Sølvi asked, getting up and pulling out paper plates and plastic utensils.

"I am," Harvath said, knowing that she'd been out shopping. "Ravenous actually. What do we have?"

"Sushi."

"Perfect. What kind?"

An impish grin spread across her face as she handed him his own special container to open. "Viking sushi."

That didn't sound very good, and the moment he peeled away the lid he knew why. Entering his nostrils, the smell was like getting punched in the face. Even being in the fresh air, on a boat, out on the open water couldn't blunt its impact.

It was a smell Harvath had only encountered once before. One he would never forget. His body had an instant aversion to it and there was no question what it was—*lutefisk*.

As he looked up at his wife, the disgust written across his face, she snapped his photo—another quintessential Harvath moment she wanted to capture.

"When we get back to shore, I'm calling the police," he stated.

"What for?"

"Spousal abuse."

Sølvi rolled her eyes. "Weak. Just like my brothers said."

He smiled and she leaned into him as he put his arm around her again. Unseen was his dumping the lutefisk over the side of the boat into the Potomac. With all the lye it contained, it could only help but improve the quality of the water.

Thankfully, Sølvi, as well as the Haneys, had brought plenty of other, palatable things to eat.

As they ate and enjoyed each other's company, Harvath reflected on how fortunate he was—not only to have such wonderful friends and such a fantastic wife, but also to have been able to serve his country and to have done so with honor.

Kissing Sølvi, he sat back and watched as the fireworks began with an enormous bloom of red, white, and blue.

ACKNOWLEDGMENTS

My goal with *Edge of Honor* was to bring Harvath home. I wanted to create a patriotic thriller, set in the nation's capital, right around the Fourth of July.

Like Harvath, the Fourth is one of my favorite holidays. Sitting on the dock with a good book in my hands is how I like to spend it. And every year, no one gave me a better adventure than Nelson DeMille. When I published my first novel, *The Lions of Lucerne*, Nelson was gracious enough to give me one of my very first blurbs. I have been forever grateful.

Sadly, during the writing of *Edge of Honor*, Nelson passed away. I wanted to pay homage to him and so, when Harvath offers Gallo his choice of "soft" drinks in the form of Sam Adams or Heineken, that's me spinning an old John Corey joke he wrote.

Nelson was an amazing author and an even more amazing person. If you haven't read him, do yourself a favor, start.

Now . . . on to the part where I get to thank everyone who made this book possible.

As always, I want to begin by offering my deepest gratitude to you, my terrific **readers**. Each year, I'm grateful for the opportunity to invite you into the world of Scot Harvath. With *Edge of Honor*, it's been a thrilling writing experience, and I sincerely hope that has been your experience reading it.

To the incredible **booksellers**, who remain the lifeblood of the literary world—thank you. Your unwavering dedication is what makes it possible for readers to find books, like this one, and for those stories to continue to live and breathe. You do a service that is beyond words.

I'm fortunate to have great friends like **Sean Fontaine**, **Knut Grini**, **Fred Burton**, and **David Vennett**, who have all been invaluable resources once again. To this list, I need to add **Danielle Frank**, whose expertise and kindness were most appreciated. Thank you all.

Jon Karp, president and CEO of Simon & Schuster, has been an exceptional leader and a true supporter of my books throughout this journey. Your dedication to the publishing world and to me personally is something I am deeply grateful for. Thank you for everything you do to bring my books to readers year after year.

My phenomenal editor and publisher, **Emily Bestler**, has once again helped shape every word of this novel. Emily, I cannot thank you enough for the wisdom, patience, and clarity you bring to my work. Your support means the world to me. Thank you.

The outstanding team at **Emily Bestler Books**, particularly **Lara Jones** and **Hydia Scott-Riley**, have once again gone above and beyond in helping bring *Edge of Honor* to the finish line. You all make sure nothing falls through the cracks and for that, I'm eternally grateful.

My powerhouse Atria publisher, **Libby McGuire**, and amazing associate publisher, **Dana Trocker**, have taken our game to a whole new level this year. Your dedication to getting my work out into the world never ceases to amaze me. Thank you both for your unflagging commitment.

David Brown, my publicist extraordinaire, continues to be my guiding light in the media world. Every year, you make sure that my books reach the readers who matter most and for that, I am so thankful.

It's always a privilege to work alongside the fantastic people at **Simon & Schuster**. In particular, I want to thank **Kim Shannon**, senior VP of sales, and her brilliant **sales team**, who ensure that my work has the reach it deserves.

Jen Long and the magnificent team at **Pocket Books**, thank you for the awesome presence my books continue to have in paperback. Every time I see one of my titles on a shelf, I'm reminded of your tireless work behind the scenes. I can't thank you enough.

A big thank-you to the astounding **Jason Chappell**, **Tom Pitoniak**, and **Paige Lytle** along with the entire **Atria/Emily Bestler Books production department**. Your perfection and attention to detail that go into every book's production is remarkable, and I'm beyond thankful for your efforts.

I also want to extend my heartfelt thanks to the sensational **Suzanne Donahue** and **Karlyn Hixon**. Your hard work and dedication allow me to focus on writing, and I am so thankful for you.

To the glorious **Atria/Emily Bestler Books** and **Pocket Books sales teams**—you are the engine that drives this book to the world, and I am so appreciative of your tireless efforts. Thank you for CRUSHING it day in and day out!

The five-star **Atria/Emily Bestler Books** and **Pocket Books art departments**, led by the visionary **Jimmy Iacobelli**, have once again delivered a fantastic cover. Every year, I'm amazed at the creativity and professionalism you all bring. Thank you for making my books look so good.

A big thank you to the exceptional **Simon & Schuster audio team**—**Chris Lynch**, **Tom Spain**, **Sarah Lieberman**, **Desiree Vecchio**, and my longtime narrator, **Armand Schultz**. Your continued excellence in bringing my work to life in audio form is something I deeply cherish. Thank you for everything on the audio edition of *Edge of Honor*. It's fantastic.

Heide Lange, my brilliant agent and dear friend at **Sanford J. Greenburger Associates**, has been my rock once again. Heide, your support has been unwavering, and I'm so grateful for everything you do. Thank you for always being there for me.

I also want to extend my gratitude to **Iwalani Kim**, **Madeline Wallace**, and **Charles Loffredo** at SJGA. Your outstanding professionalism and skill make all the difference, and I'm lucky to have you on my team.

A special thanks to the incredibly talented **Yvonne Ralsky**, who has made yet another year of my life much easier by plowing the road so I can stay focused on writing. I couldn't do it without you. Thank you for everything.

Scott Schwimer, my dear friend, trusted advisor, and my entertainment attorney par excellence. We did it! I can't wait for the world to see Scot Harvath in living color. Thank you for getting us there.

Finally, I want to express my love and heartfelt gratitude to my amazing **family**, especially my spectacular wife, **Trish**. You all continue to support and inspire me every single day. I am truly blessed to have you in my life. Your love and patience make all of this possible and worth it. Thank you. Let's celebrate!